THE€ JOURNAL 1919

A Thriller / Suspense

Written by Dwayne A. Cannon

(Inspired By Films)

Publisher: **Emerge Productions Group LLC.**

Cover Illustration by: **Emerge Productions Group**

Direct Distribution: **Ingram Spark**

D€dication

I would like to dedicate this book, to all the inspired writers who have a story to tell, the writers who believe that writing, is truly an inspirational and imaginative sport. And when they write, they embrace the mental athleticism of freedom, to express themselves outspokenly without holding anything back, by any words necessary…

THE€ JOURNAL 1919

A PAPER A DAY KEEPS THE GOOD NEWS AWAY

Contents

THE€ JOURNAL 1919

The year is 2015 and in New Jersey, there is a disturbing fidelity throughout the city, that has a lot of people rerouting their lives. From a newspaper that paints terrible pictures, not on the walls but in the lives of families and friends! Causing a frightening epidemic to those who cannot seem to figure out, where this newspaper that's dated back to 1919 is coming from. So, instead of ignoring its presence, this one family decides to get involved and when they do, they become victims to the mirror mimicking articles printed inside. Set aside from most newspapers, this was not your average publishing and only some chosen few, would receive the opportunity to experience this newspaper welcoming parody. And whoever was fortunate enough to read the articles inside, became prey. to this un-aging newspaper that left a bitter and unfavorable taste, to everyone who connected with its stories of the past, present, and future. Many incidents were shocking to the world, causing devastating, destruction and erupting chaos in and out of the city. But what was hidden from the world, the media and the people living in the city, was a contagious orbit, of what only some chosen few knew as

THE€ JOURNAL 1919

NEXT OF KIN

"When Honest Sympathy, Tends To Mask All Relationships"

TH€ NEXT OF KIN

Born and raised in the city and now at the age of thirty-seven. Stacie Largen considers these years to be her productive years, she's independent and works very hard to obtain what she has. Stacie loves patting herself on the back. Just to remind herself that everything she have; she's accomplished all by herself on her own. Stacie's job description, a principle for a reputable school that helps blind kids. The school has a great reputation for its achievements in education and has received several outstanding awards in excellence. Stacie's, never been the one who listens to other people's unconfirmed opinions or accepts constructive criticism, very well from strangers. But she is known and will accept words of advice and sometimes that even depends on who is giving her the advice. Stacie hopes she never gives anybody a reason to say anything negative about her, before they get to know her. And with both parents still alive, two brothers and one sister, her abuse to herself is basically not being able to be more open, with her immediate family about some of the strange, mysterious and abnormal things that has been happening in her life.

Things that she's been questioning for some time now, things that are affecting the way she now interacts with the world. Sunday is when Stacie's Parents Mr. and Mrs. Largen attends church and for the last couple of weeks Stacie's little sister Tara, has been feeling like her Parents has been trying to force religion down her throat. So instead of attending church on Sundays with her parents like she used too on Sunday Mornings Tara, could be found trying to follow in her big sister footsteps and dodge every Sunday all together. Stacie was still and absolutely a God-fearing person altogether, but when she suddenly had this dreamlike experience. That was far from any dream she could have ever imagined; Stacie's faith started to fall apart and unravel. Because this dream was true and the things that were happening not only woke Stacie right on up, it also opened her eyes. As for Stacie's younger sister Tara, she was just getting tired of letting her parents insinuate, what she should believe in and why she should believe in it. As for Mr. and Mrs. Largen, they just ignored the adolescence behavior of Tara and continued living their life day to day. While trying to keep their family together, apart from a few secrets that could define the significance of the Largens past. Mr. and Mrs. Largen worry too much about their four children and if anything was to ever happen to them Mr. and Mrs. Largen would hope and pray that the skeletons in the closet would stay buried within the skin and bones of their children.

Mrs. Largen thinks Stacie her oldest daughter should take more responsibility when it comes down to family planning. But Mr. Largen feels the opposite, he feels Stacie should continue living her life the way she decides to live it especially if what she is doing is making her happy. But Tara, disagrees with her Mother and just like any other daughter, she loves her Father to death unconditional. Tara, always take sides with her Father because he always listens to her and agrees with just about everything she says. And when Mrs. Largen is not around Mr. Largen patronizes Tara. Mark, and Edward are Mr. and Mrs. Largen two other children. The, brothers. Edward, who is the oldest and Mark the youngest. Mark is the poet in the family, still in school like his younger sister Tara. And Edward, the family man who is a decorated soldier who was just discharged honorably with highly ranked medals and souvenirs from serving his country overseas. Mark has no children unlike his big brother Edward who is happily married with kids. Mark, consider himself the ladies' man whose way of living revolves around reading and quoting verses from poetry books and seeing how many female's numbers he can get in a day. And when Marks around, you can practically bet on it that he has a book of poems with him. The youngest of the Largen family is Tara. Who doesn't look nearly her age with an old soul, still in school and suffering from asthma.

Tara is an A student who loves music and wants to follow in her big sister Stacie footsteps. Tara wants to be a singer. Whose favorite artist consist of soulful R&B greats such as Florence Ballard, Arlene Smith, Donnie Pointer and Etta James. These artists can be heard on the regular playing from Tara's bedroom at high volume and when people would ask how Tara, even know about these artists. Being that they all are from a time way before Tara was even born. Tara, explains that it's all in the genes, being that her Father Mr. Largen used to be in a singing group back in his day. Who sung soulful oldies but goodies and out of all Tara's siblings, Tara was the one who choose to follow in her Fathers tradition and continue singing. Ever since Tara, was in grammar school she adored and fell in love with her Fathers style of music, and since then she's been singing it, imitating it, while trying to become the artist he was. Tara loves her big sister Stacie to death and without a doubt, her big sister Stacie feelings is mutual. But lately Tara, hasn't been getting the chance to hang out with Stacie, as much as she would like. And when Tara, gets the chance. She takes advantage of the opportunity to plead with Stacie about taking some time off from work to relax. Stacie was Drowning in her own unhappiness due to her confidential, uncontrolled, cloak and dagger lifestyle. And Tara, had to remind herself every day not to forget, to remind Stacie, that maybe what her Mother Mrs. Largen kept telling her was right. Maybe Stacie did need a family planned relationship outside of work.

Tara, was hoping that her visits to Stacie's house more often, might just be the remedy and answer they both needed to reconnect. Tara, was hoping that being around Stacie some more, would bring back those good old times she and Stacie used to have. Before Stacie became so miserable and hollow. Stacie was now burying her feelings and emotions knee deep, in something so extraordinary and confidential to her. It made the rest of the family start masking their relations with one another. And even though their parents Mr. and Mrs. Largen were showing little to some concern. Mr. and Mrs. Largen were also holding back a great deal of honest sympathy. But just like any other tight lipped, secret, anybody has had. Mr. and Mrs. Largen not only masked their relationship with their children, they also upheld their innocence about what they had already known and experienced.

WHY SO CURIOUS

"When The Cats Out The Bag, And The Skeletons Are Still In The Closet"

THE CURIOUSITY

(Radio) Good Morning New Jersey, It's Friday May 4th the end of the week and I am Evan Riles your number one DJ, I play nothing but the best and whether your home still in bed, or in line at your nearest Star Bucks, or outside stuck in traffic. I got something to start your Morning off the right way. Here's "Wake Up" by you know, the one and only Teddy Pendergrass! (Song Playing) … Stacie reaches for the radio and turns the volume up while tapping her fingers to the beat of the song with her fingers on the steering wheel. Stacie closes her eyes and enjoys the sound of Teddy Pendergrass's distinctive voice, through the car's speakers. Stacie starts singing along with the song, she pulls the sun visor down and looks at herself in the sun visor's mirror. And as the song comes to an end, Stacie closes the sun visor, reaches forward and turns the volume on the radio back down… *Ok Mr. Riles, I hear you! Keep playing songs like that in the Morning and I might not never make it to work! (Radio) Ok! Guys and Girls, I hope you listeners out there enjoyed that, because I know I did! But we must pay some bills! (Commercial)… And now to keep you Morning listeners, up with the Views on News, here's Debra Jenkins, but first let's hear from Charles Peterson with the weather this Morning!...*

Thank you, Evan, great song by the way! I love that song! Joking around the weatherman continues singing the song in the background in a low voice for few seconds after the song goes off.... *(Singing)* The weatherman starts laughing...*(Radio) I can't sing! Not like teddy anyway! (Laughing) Anyway, here's the Views on Weather! Looks like some sun today, so you won't be needing that umbrella you got for Christmas. And with a promising 75 degrees high, the clouds will be pushing fine winds at a low 52 tonight! I'm Charles Peterson, with the Views on Weather! And here's Debra with the News!... Thankyou Charles! And that is one of my favorite songs too! But for all the gamblers out there, someone again has hit the Three hundred and seventy-five dollars, Power-Ball lottery. Yes, that's the third one in two years. So, there you have it! More proof that anything's possible, here in the wonderful Garden State! Congratulation Mr. and Mrs. Elmwood! Debra!... Debra!... Are you still there? Well, it looks like Debra has some technical issues so, back to you Evan!... That figures! Did you all here Charles voice? Wow! I wish I could sing like that! (Laughing) Nice voice Charles! Didn't know you had it in you! And did she say, Three hundred and seventy-five million? Stacie looks to her left, to her right and then in the rear-view mirror at the congested traffic behind her that's been backed up for about fifteen to twenty minutes. Stacie looks at the newspaper lying there in the passenger seat...*

(Radio) Lucky couple, good for them! Again, I'm Evan Riles and if you enjoyed that last song, here's something I know you're going to enjoy! Here's one for the workers driving to work, or maybe just leaving work! This is Stevie Wonder "Superstition" …

Oh my God, I love this song! Full of excitement and anxious to hear the song that's playing on the radio. Stacie sits there in traffic behind the steering wheel tolerant with absolute patients. As she continues waiting for the traffic to start moving and the traffic light ahead to turn green, Stacie continues tapping her fingers on the steering wheel and her foot on the floor. She then grabs her cup of mocha late from the cup holder and takes a sip, a vehicle bumps her car from behind, the bump causes Stacie's body to jerk forward, she spills some coffee in her lap… *Dam It! Now look at this mess! My pants are ruined! Who's this fool behind me!* Stacie, puts the cup of coffee back in the cup holder, turns the volume down on the radio, opens the glove compartment and takes out a wet wipe.

Stacie looks into the rear-view mirror and sees a female in the driver's seat in the car behind her, with her hand up to her ear talking on a cellphone. The female in the car behind Stacie looks at her and shrugs both of her shoulders up in the air. signaling that she doesn't know how that just happened. Trying to avoid road rage Stacie stays in her car and pats the coffee that just spilled on her pants with the wet wipe from the glove compartment.

Only because the bump was light and no major damage to her car was done, Stacie ignored and overlooked the minor incident that just happened. The female in the car behind Stacie puts the cellphone down she has up to her ear and looks at Stacie through the windshield. The female has one hand up in the air shrugging her shoulders... *I'm Sorry!* Stacie could see the female's lips moving like she was whispering through the windshield; Stacie couldn't hear what the female was saying but she knew it had something to do with the bump… *(Yelling) I'm Sorry!*

Stacie interpreted the females lip movement and eventually understood that the female was basically apologizing for bumping into the back of her car. After accepting the female's apology Stacie, reaches back into the glove compartment and takes out another wet wipe. Stacie pats her lap again trying to remove as much of the spilled coffee on her pants as she could. Stacie rolls the driver's side window down and tosses both the cup of coffee and the wet wipes out into the street.

She, then reaches over onto the passenger seat and grabs the daily newspaper that's lying there, Stacie opens the newspaper and looks at the pictures, before reading some of the articles on the front page…

Same old boring news! Why do I even waste my time buying these unimportant, worthless newspapers! The Times, The World, The Daily! The daily what? Everything in these newspapers, has nothing to do with anything important these days! Extinct animals, figit spinners and weight loss pills!

Are you serious? And who cares who running for president, I'm so not political today!

Out of frustration Stacie, smacks the newspaper with the back of her hand. She closes the newspaper and tosses it back onto the passenger's seat, while impatiently sitting behind the steering wheel waiting for traffic to start moving. Stacie hears loud music playing from a car a few feet behind her. So, she rolls the driver's side window up and turns the volume back up on the radio. Stacie, changes radio stations until she hears the song *"I can feel it"* on the radio by Phil Collins *(Song Playing)* … While enjoying the song playing Stacie, grabs the cup of coffee that's in the cup holder, she takes a sip and immediately spits the cold coffee back into the cup... *Oh no, I can't drink this! This coffee is disgusting, It's cold! Who does that? Yuk!* Stacie opens the driver's side door just a little, she leans down to her left with the coffee cup in her hand and removes the lid. Stacie, pours the cold coffee out onto the ground, drops the empty cup, leans back up and closes the driver's side door. She looks to her right and sees a tall man dressed in an all-black suit, Stepping off the sidewalk into the street. The expression on the tall man's face is priceless. He's looking like he's either unhappy with his job or whoever he's working for must be a very, unpleasant boss. Or somebody just pissed him off early this Morning, something awful. The tall man walks in between the front of Stacie's car and the car in front of her.

Stacie, then notices that the tall man has something cuffed in his hand down by his side. Not able to make out what the man is holding. Stacie rolls down the passenger side window and leans over the passenger's seat to get a better look at what the tall man has in his hand. The tall man turns his head to the right as he's crossing the street and with a medieval smile on his face. He stares into Stacie's eyes with promising conviction, the look on his face quickly changes Stacie's opinion about what she thought the tall man's career might have been, before considering looking into her eyes.

Stacie cautiously looks back at the tall man, but the look he's giving Stacie is much worse, it was dangerous. The look pierced her soul like a knife, his eyes were nocturnal, and his smile was slaying Stacie's confidence with conviction. The tall man was looking and acting like he had no respect for the way Stacie was feeling.

As the tall man walked by something strange started to happen. And Stacie knew something wasn't right. The volume on the radio in Stacie's car increased all by itself, the hairs on the back of her neck stood up like a porcupine's coat, Stacie starts feeling goosebumps all over her body as the temperature drops in her car. It's gets cold. And the sight of the tall man dressed in the all black suit, had Stacie feeling uncomfortable and abnormal. The look the tall man was giving Stacie was horrifying and unexplainable.

But Stacie couldn't stop looking at him, the energy he was releasing out towards her, was demanding Stacie's full undivided attention. The tall man seemed thrilled and a little overexcited as he walked on by, like as if he was possessed with vengeance or was born with a license to scare the heck out of people. Stacie takes a deep breath and forces herself to close her eyes, she inhales and exhales out a long breath of cold air that could be seen lingering inside the car from the drop-in temperature. A knot forms in Stacie's throat, and out of fear she tightens her grip with both of her hands on the steering wheel. All the vehicles in traffic around her starts honking their horns, their head and taillights start blinking out of control. The sounds of the car horns annoy Stacie so much, it forces her to immediately roll up the passenger side window. And after a few minutes what felt like twenty-four hours of torment. The volume on the radio lowers, the temperature in the car goes back to normal, the blinking head and taillights and honking horns from all the cars waiting in traffic stops. Stacie loosens the tightened grip she has on the steering wheel. Everything is silent. Now, sitting back behind the driver's seat Stacie notices that the tall man dressed in the all black suit is holding something in his hand down by his side.

Stacie leans forward towards the windshield and places one hand on the dashboard, she squinches her eyes and sees that the creepy, hair raising tall man dressed in the all black suit has a newspaper in his hand.

Turning her head slightly to her left, Stacie looks at the daily newspaper she has in her car lying on the passenger seat. She, then rolls down the passenger side window, leans over onto the passenger side and sticks her head out the window. Out of pure and genuine curiosity Stacie tries to get the tall man's attention...

Excuse me sir! Hello! Sir! Excuse me mister!

The tall man ignores Stacie as he continues to walk across the street towards the black tinted limousine, that's double parked a few cars ahead to the left of Stacie's car. The tall man walks up to the driver's side door of the limousine, stands there, raises his right arm and lays the newspaper he has in his hand on the roof of the limousine. Opening the driver's side door to the limousine, the tall man gets in and closes the limousine door shut. Leaving the newspaper on the roof behind. Stacie leans back inside the car and sits there quietly not saying a word. She turns the volume back down on the radio and leans back up. That's when she notices the back-seat window to the limousine is slowly rolling down. Stacie leans her head forward closer to the windshield, she squinches her eyes and notices that the old lady is looking back at her from the back seat of the limousine. The look on the old lady's face is a poltergeist pale. Her eyes the color of the sky before the storm and her hair was disguised by a black hat that shadowed her face from the large round rim that circled around the whole hat like an umbrella.

The feeling Stacie was now experiencing was unexplainable, something she could described and imagine as fearful and frightening. Stacie was basically scared to death sitting in her own car and she didn't know why or how all this was happening. So, out of fear Stacie, was forced to roll up all her windows and lock all the doors. Slouched down in the driver's seat Stacie watches as the tinted limousine slowly drive's off. The back-seat window to the limousine where the old lady was sitting was rolling up. Everything seemed to be back to normal. Stacie looks and watches as the newspaper drops to the ground, from the roof of the limousine. Traffic starts moving. The woman in traffic behind Stacie starts beeping her horn trying to get Stacie's attention, so she can move her car along with the traffic ahead of her. Stacie puts the car in drive, sits back up in the seat and slowly pulls up. Stacie looks to her left out the passenger window as she slowly rides pass where the limousine was parked.

Wrapped in a black rubber band lying there on the ground in the street, Stacie sees the newspaper. So, she puts her right blinker on and crosses over in front of a car, that is now slowing up on Stacie's right side. Stacie pulls her car over to the curb, a few feet ahead from where the newspaper is lying on the ground. Stacie sits there for a few minutes and waits as the moving cars in traffic drive on pass. And when the coast is clear Stacie unlocks the driver's side door, opens the door, gets out leaving the door wide open.

Stacie walks over to where the newspaper is and quickly bends down and picks the newspaper up from off the ground. Then out of nowhere she hears a car horn, honking repeatedly...

Get out of the street lady! You, want to get hit?

Stacie hears yelling from a man's voice she looks and sees a yellow taxi speeding directly towards her, the speeding taxi serves around Stacie's body. It comes so close that if the taxi would have hit Stacie, it would have killed her. The taxi's horn is so loud it startles Stacie, she jumps back milliseconds as the taxi speeds on pass… *You idiot! Who gave you a license mister?* Stacie screams at the taxi with the newspaper in her hand... *Oh my God! That car almost hit me! That maniac could have killed me!* Stacie takes another step back onto the sidewalk grasping the newspaper tightly around her chest with both arms. While looking at the reckless driver, drive on down the street out of control. Stacie looks around before rushing back to her car and opening the driver's side door, she gets in, tosses the newspaper wrapped in the black rubber band she has in her hand on the passenger seat. Stacie closes the driver's side door shut… *I can't believe I just did that! All for this stupid newspaper! What's wrong with me? I almost got killed for some stupid newspaper! Tara's not going to believe this. I don't even believe this. Where's my cell phone?* Stacie takes in a deep breath and exhales while looking around the car for her cellphone. She puts the cellphone to her ear the phone on the other end rings…

(Phone Ringing) Stacie lets the phone ring a couple times before seeing a police car at the red light ahead of her. Stacie drops the cellphone in her lap. She can hear her sister Tara's voice in the background on the cellphone… *(On The Phone) Hello! Hello! Stacie, is that you? Hello! Now why on earth would she call me and don't say anything? Stacie!*

Now looking in her rear-view mirror Stacie, looks back at the newspaper she just picked up off the ground. She puts the car in drive, pulls out of the parking space and slowly drives off through the green traffic lightheaded to work. Relaxed and laidback Stacie sees a police patrol car ahead of her, that's about to pass by her on the opposite side of traffic.

Once the patrol car is directly in front of Stacie, the police officer who's driving the patrol car slightly turns his head to the left and looks at her, through his driver side window. Not trying to make eye contact with the police officer Stacie, could feel the police officer looking at her it was rubbing her the wrong way. The feeling was making Stacie, nervous she was feeling paralyzed from the neck up. And she wasn't trying to let the cat out of the bag or find out if there were any skeletons in the closet. Having done nothing wrong Stacie, wasn't afraid, she was just curious. She just knew the police officer was still looking at her for some apparent reason. Stacie didn't want to give the police officer any reason under probable cause to have a lawful excuse, to turn his siren on, make a u turn and pull her over.

And with the thought of that Stacie, consciously kept both hands in sight where the police officer could see them, on the steering wheel. So, instead of becoming alarmed and ignoring the police officer's attentive observation of her. Stacie turns her head slightly to the left and smiles, respectfully at the police officer who's still looking at her. The police officer smiles back, he then raises his right hand up by the window and waves back at Stacie, who's jaw is tightening from the prolonged smile. Back at Stacie the police officer nods his head up and down, signaling a civil gesture to Stacie at that appropriate time meaning for her to have a good day. As Stacie, drives on by she realizes that it's unlikely that she'll be getting pulled over by that police officer today. So, when the police officer and his patrol car were clearly out of sight. Stacie, relaxes and turns the volume back up on the radio a notch while reaching for her cellphone. Remembering her sister Tara and how she immediately but unintentionally left her hanging and unannounced on the cellphone a few minutes ago. Before she thought she was going to have a Morning confrontation with the law.

Stacie puts her right blinker on and pulls the car over to double park. She finds the cellphone that's in her lap, picks it up and calls her younger sister Tara back. The cellphone rings several times before Stacie hears Tara's voice…

(Cellphone) Hello! This is Tara, who is this? Tara, it's me Stacie I'm sorry sis but I… Aha! Thought you was talking to me? Sorry! But I can't get to the phone right now please leave a message and I will get back to as soon as possible! Stacie starts laughing at the particle joke her younger sister Tara just pulled over the cellphone. The thought alone and just hearing Tara's voice made Stacie feel good about how the rest of her day might go. So, Stacie hangs up and calls her job to let them know she'll be late coming in today.

Because she has something important to do with family. Stacie tosses her cellphone over in the passenger seat. The cellphone lands on top of the other two newspapers Stacie has in the car and one of them being TH€ JOURNAL!

EARLY SUNDAY MORNING

"When Secrets Destroys Your Mind, Body And Soul"

THE MORNING

The night has fallen and there's an eerie breeze sweeping through the air. The stars in the sky glistens while the nights creepy silence wraps itself into the arms of the city. And for the last couple of days the city's appearance in attendance has been limited. Due to all the news camera vans, the press and the city's police department. Who all have been focusing their attention solely on the havoc and mayhem that has been hugging the city. At home and at work Stacie tries her best not to draw any unusual attention to herself, which is starting to become impossible. Her commute back and forth from work lately has been ridiculous and the issue right now that Stacie, has. Is not with the news or the press or even the police department. Stacie's issue is purely and solely with this strange, mysterious looking newspaper that continues showing up at her doorstep every Sunday Morning. Stacie had no idea why this newspaper kept popping up, or where the mysterious newspaper was coming from. But after days maybe even weeks showing up on her doorstep. Stacie was starting to realize that this all might have started the Morning she was sitting in traffic on her way to work and she saw the spooky looking tall man dressed in the all black suit. The tall man she made frightening eye contact with, the tall man she first seen with THE JOURNAL!

The newspaper that Stacie was skeptical about reading, the newspaper she almost got her hit by a speeding car over, the newspaper that almost ended her life, the newspaper Stacie eventually brought into her home. Ever since then Stacie has noticed that there has been a flood of unexplained and unsolved events surrounded her life. Stacie was seeing a lot of bizarre things and a lot of and abnormal things happening to and around her, that she simply could not explain. Things that would be unpleasing to any human eye. Things that was making Stacie's life so uncomfortable and distressing that Stacie decided to distance herself from family and friends. Stacie was finding herself behind the steering wheel of her car, driving recklessly out on the road more often than she normally would do. Her job was now a second priority the job she so loved and cared for. Her work schedule was increased with shorter hours and fewer days. Stacie could remember when Sunday's use to be a time when she would reach out to family and maybe attend church with her Parents and her younger sister Tara her better other half.

Especially Tara, but ever since Stacie had become a victim who was secretly being wounded by this newspaper! And the scars Stacie was suffering with, were not healing fast enough. Stacie was now a target who would soon become a casualty to some dreadful, malicious, unexplainable force of nature. That was making Stacie faithfully dedicate herself to reading THE JOURNAL! every Sunday Morning.

Whenever Stacie was in the presence of THЄ JOURNAL!

It easily and certainly made the hairs on the back of her neck stand up, it caused chills down her spine and goose bumps all over her body. It made Stacie feel some kind of way. THЄ JOURNAL, was playing tricks on Stacie's mind, this newspaper was becoming a part of her DNA. The dangerous articles inside that Stacie was reading was starting to repeat themselves and Stacie had no idea when or what was going to happen next. Besides the reality of what was already happening throughout the city. Stacie's life had changed, ever since she got introduced to this mysterious newspaper called THЄ JOURNAL! Nothing mattered to Stacie anymore and none of what was happening throughout the city because of this newspaper, was putting a dent in how Stacie felt. To Stacie her life was exploding in uncomfortable excitement now more than ever before and she wanted it to stop. But she couldn't seem to figure out how to make it stop. Stacie was finding herself reading THЄ JOURNAL! everyday. The anticipation of whether the newspaper was going to be there, had Stacie feeling some kind of way. Stacie kept thinking about the creepy old lady sitting in the backseat of the limousine, the spooky tall man dressed in the all black suit and the reckless speeding driver that almost killed her over this newspaper. All that was a part of Stacie's illness now. Her concern now was all about how to conceal THЄ JOURNAL and make it disappear.

Stacie now was even afraid to get out of bed on Sunday Mornings, knowing when she opened her front door THE JOURNAL! Was going to be there waiting for her. The excitement in her life was gone, the motivation Stacie had for impendent improvement was gone. There was no more motivation, just get up, open her front door, look down on her porch and pick up THE JOURNAL! Lying there like a welcome home mat in front of someone's door. Stacie's life was now all about THE JOURNAL and the life changing articles that was printed inside. And she knew it and felt that one day the tables might turn on her and the possibilities of her picture on the front page of the newspaper had Stacie in awe. The thought of somebody else reading about her while being victimized. Like her sister Tara or her Mother this was becoming all too real.

But even with the frightening vision all of that was just a little bit too farfetched for Stacie right now. Stacie knew that her life wasn't going to be the same again. She just prayed that she or anyone in her family get harmed in the process. Acting off instinct Stacie continued her daily rituals. Her emotions were leading her down a road that eventually she wasn't going to be able to get off. A road that was going to be so destructive and detrimental to her wellbeing. That it was showing in her behavior, it was corrupting Stacie's mind, body and her soul in the process, with no clue of what THE JOURNAL!

Was getting her into so, she just ignored all the past occurrences and made it her responsibility to face whatever battle she was fighting with this newspaper. Back home Stacie had no idea that both of her parents Mr. and Mrs. Largen was aware of the situation Stacie was facing. They could smell the danger a mile away that was lurking around the corner. Tara also knew something was wrong with her big sister Stacie, but Tara had a different perspective on the situation. Tara was on the outside of what was going on with her sister looking in. While Mr. and Mrs. Largen were on the inside and knew exactly what was happening with their daughter Stacie looking out. Mr. and Mrs. Largen were paying close attention to the change in Stacie's behavior. They both knew that one day this was going to happen, they just didn't know which one of their kids it was going to happen to first. Mr. and Mrs. Largen knew the change in Stacie was all so too familiar. Mr. and Mrs. Largen had already known about all the buried skeletons in the families closet ever since Mr. Largen was singing alto in his teenage group named …*The Reasonable's* And Mrs. Largen, was his biggest fan and sweetheart in high school. Mr. and Mrs. Largen had long waited for this day to come and it's been a long time coming. They both knew the past was coming back to haunt their family, they just didn't know when and if lightening was going to strike twice. Mr. and Mrs. Largen had witnessed this type of behavior in the past before from somebody dear and close to them, way before any of their children was ever born.

Mr. Largen knew Stacie's conduct was becoming a problem and if it wasn't a bigger enough problem now then sooner or later all their children were going to get caught up in this wicked and malicious contagious orbit of what Mr. and Mrs. Largen had always knew and always feared as THE JOURNAL!

NEWSPAPERS AND RUBBERBANDS

"When A Plague Of Bad News, Becomes Haunting"

TH€ NEWSPAPER

Eight o'clock a.m. Sunday Morning and Stacie is standing on her porch dressed in a bath robe and slippers with a towel wrapped around her head. She takes in a deep breath before raising both of her arms in the air and stretching. She looks down on her porch at the mysterious newspaper that's just lying there wrapped in a black rubber band. Stacie starts reflecting about what's she's been seeing on the news and what's been happening throughout the city for the last couple of days. Then it dawns on her, the thought strikes her memory like some really bad news. Stacie was thinking that maybe, just maybe that everything that's been happening in the city, just might have something to do with this mysterious and malicious newspaper people were referring to as TH€ JOURNAL!

Holding the top of her robe close by her neck with her left hand. Stacie looks up and down the street, hoping to see someone else that might be up and about early this Morning. But there was no one in sight, the streets were clear of any vehicles and pedestrians, apart from some before noon birds chirping. Stacie was alone. So, she starts thinking that maybe all of this was just part of her imagination, or maybe she's sleep walking and has yet to wake up, or maybe, just maybe it was all a dream. Stacie really had no idea what was going on. She had no idea whose newspaper this was, or why the newspaper kept showing up on her porch every Sunday Morning for the last couple of weeks.

So, Stacie just stood there on her porch like she did every Sunday Morning, contemplating different scenarios. Because to Stacie, there was absolutely no sensible explanation that could explain this mysterious newspaper. And if there were any explanations out there, who had them and where were they? Stacie just kept asking herself who had the answers. She even prayed, hoping that one day someone would eventually come out of hiding and explain the unexplainable. But despite everything she was thinking about, her intentions remained respectable. And at the end of the day there still was THE JOURNAL! That strange and mysterious newspaper. That seemed like it wasn't going anywhere, and Stacie knew from this moment on THE JOURNAL! was here for a real reason.

And the reason was to cause as much mayhem and havoc it possibly could. And today wasn't different, so instead of ignoring the newspaper and just going back inside of her house and closing the door. Stacie made up her mind and decided to bend down and pick up the THE JOURNAL!

While getting up off the ground Stacie, looks at the houses across the street while holding the THE JOURNAL! in the palms of both of her hands. Like a newborn baby, she was seeing and touching for the first time. Stacie stuffs the THE JOURNAL! up underneath her left arm pit, turns around and goes back inside the house, leaving the door halfway open behind her. Stacie starts getting cold the temperature drops to freezing. It was starting to feel like the middle of December in June.

When Stacie, opened her mouth to breathe she watched the heat from her breath rise into the air, evaporating like steam from a boiling pot of hot water on the stove. A spine-chilling feeling blankets Stacie's entire body, the stormy looking sky starts turning the color of burnt smoke. The limbs and leaves on the trees start blowing out of control, from the thrusting force of wind pushing outside. While rubbing her shoulders and arms Stacie, turns around to close the front door after realizing she had left it open. The thrusting force of wind from outside pushes the door wide open, slamming the door into the wall, leaving a hole in the wall from the doorknobs hard impact. The wind moves Stacie, two steps back for everyone step she tries to take forward. Now leaning on the back of the door with her right shoulder and her hand tightly gripped on the doorknob. Stacie uses her legs and upper body strength to try and close the front door shut. She hears a car door opening and slamming shut. The sound gets Stacie's attention so by force she slowly turns around while shivering and shaking from the freezing temperature drop, still clutching tightly to the newspaper that's underneath her arm pit. The thrusting force of wind calms down, the freezing temperature is dropping, and the sun starts shining through the stormy looking sky that has the clouds and sky the color of burnt smoke. Stacie, squinches her eyes and looks outside across the street from where she's standing in the doorway. She sees a tinted limousine and a tall man dressed in all black suit.

The man is standing there with his right hand on the limousine's backseat door handle, holding the door open. Stacie takes a step back and leans on her front door. The tall man dressed in the all black suit turns his head to the left, reaches out his hand and helps the old lady who is now stepping out of the backseat of the limousine. The old lady who is also dressed in all black looks at the tall man, the tall man looks back at the old lady, then simultaneously they both turn their heads and start looking at Stacie who is now trying to get back inside the house, but the front door is locked. Stacie turns the door knob several times, she pushes the door and kicks it but after several attempts Stacie realizes that it's no use the door is locked, and she's now locked out of her own house.

The old lady and the tall man stand there looking at Stacie as she nervously freaks out. Stacie gradually turns back around with THE JOURNAL! cuffed underneath her arms. Her eyes start watering up from deep emotion, her face and hands are freezing, and her heart worried in fear. The old lady has a look on her face that's unworldly. The long black dress she has on is covering her whole body from her neck down to the top of her shoes, both of her hands are interlocked in front of her. The look on the old lady's face is a poltergeist pale. Her eyes the color of the sky before the storm and her hair was disguised by a black hat that shadowed her face, from the large round rim that circled around the whole hat like an umbrella.

The old lady looks up and down the street, then at the limousine driver who looks back at her while standing there holding the limousines back seat door open. Stacie holds her head down and looks at the newspaper in her hand again and when she lifts her head back up. She sees the back door to the limousine slowly closes and the old lady securing herself inside. The limousine driver walks around the back of the limousine and stands by the driver's side door. The old lady rolls the backseat limousines window down and looks at Stacie one more time before rolling the window up. The limousines driver gets in the driver side of the limousine, closes the door and the limousine pulls off. The limousines back tire makes a loud screeching noise so intensifying it causes Stacie, to drop the newspaper on the ground. Terrified Stacie raises both of her arms in the air and places her hands on her head covering up both of her ears with each hand. Stacie's right ear drum bust from the sound the limousines back tires are making.

Out of pain, she bends down to the ground and applies pressure against both ears, trying to block out the intensifying, loud, irritating sound. The limousine drives off down the street leaving a dark cloud of black smoke lingering in the air, leaving the smell of burnt rubber and flaming tire tracks in the street. With both eyes closed and her hands still covering both of her ears Stacie stands up, opens her eyes and tries to get a good look at the limousines license plate. But with all the heavy smoke still lingering in the air Stacie was unable to see a thing.

Now the old lady, the driver and the limousine are gone. Stacie puts her arms down and looks at her hand and see's blood on her right hand, Stacie realizes that her ear drum has bust. Stacie wipes the right side of her face with her hand she then bends down and picks up the newspaper and holds it down by her side in with her left hand. Stacie turns around, pushes the front door open, rushes back inside the house and quickly locks the door.

Now Standing by the door, with her back up against the door and down by her side in her hand she's holding THE JOURNAL! She throws the newspaper on the couch Stacie, runs towards the bathroom, grabs a piece of tissue, wipes her ear and then washes her face and hands. Stacie goes to the window near the front door and peeks out the blinds in the window to see if the limousine has circled the block and returned. But it hasn't. So, Stacie walks over to the couch picks up the newspaper and the doorbell rings… *(Doorbell Ringing)* Stacie stands still and panics while looking back and forth at the newspaper, that's she's holding in her hand by the front door. The doorbell rings again… (Doorbell Ringing) Stacie raises her right hand and adds pressure up against her ear with the tissue she has in her hand trying to stop the bleeding. The doorbell rings again… *(Doorbell Ringing)* Then a voice from behind the door yells out. The voice startles Stacie but at her same time she recognizes the voice and it catches Stacie's undivided attention! A voice that was all too familiar to Stacie! …

"Stacie! It's me open the Door"! Stacie starts taking a few steps towards the door. The doorbell rings *(Doorbell Ringing)* again followed by a few hard knocks on the door. Stacie coming to her senses and now realizing that the voice behind the door is her baby sister Tara. Who is now yelling and screaming out Stacie's name standing outside waiting for her big sister Stacie to open the door...

"It's me Tara! Your sister! Stacie open the door"! Stacie, feeling some relief now that she is quite aware who's at the door. So, Stacie drops the newspaper on the floor and walks over to the front door. Stacie takes a deep breath and exhales before looking through the peek hole and with her left-hand Stacie slowly unlocks the door... *Stacie! What took you so long, where and what were you doing, are you by yourself, do you have company?* Tara immediately notices the bloody tissue Stacie is holding up to her right ear… *No! But come on in, and what brings you by here on this beautiful Sunday Morning? Sunday Morning yes! But beautiful I don't think so!* Tara frowns her face up and jerks her head back at the remark. Tara then leans her head to the side and tries to get a better look at Stacie's ear and the bloody tissue Stacie's holding up too it... *You really don't remember, do you sis? You asked me to stop by today to help you clean the attic. Oh! That's right how can I forget, it's a mess too. Did you bring the music I asked you to bring? Sure, did how can I forget! You have been bugging me since last week. Yea! But did I bug you to show up early this Morning? Whatever!* Tara pushes Stacie to the side and makes her way inside the house.

Once Tara's inside Stacie walks in behind her and before Stacie closes the door, she sticks her head back out and looks up and down the street again out of curiosity and fear. With the door closed Stacie, locks it, turns around and looks at Tara who is now bending down by the door... *Sis! Is this your newspaper?* Tara picks the newspaper up from off the floor and holds the newspaper up eye level... *Oh, that newspaper! You can leave it there or trash it, it really doesn't matter. I've been meaning to throw it out, but I keep forgetting!* Stacie's feeling nervous, a trickle of sweat starts running down the side of her face. Stacie slowly lowers her right arm and places the bloody tissue; she has in her hand down by her side. Stacie now afraid that her sister Tara might think she's crazy if she knew the truth about what she really thought about this newspaper. And how it keeps popping up on her doorstep every Sunday, with her having no knowledge of where this newspaper is coming from... *Sis! I never saw this newspaper before where'd you get it? Oh! I think I picked it up at the supermarket or the corner store! You know these places Tara! They have just about anything lying around. Supermarket! Corner store you don't say!* With one eyebrow turned up in the air Tara looks at the newspaper and then back at Stacie with curiosity and concern. Tara just feels like something isn't right, but she never knew her big sister Stacie to be one who tell lies… *And for the love of God Stacie! Could, you please tell me why you still have that bloody tissue in your hand? Wait! Don't tell me, an ear infection am I right?*

Here let me see sis! You know if you put honey in your ear it supposed to stop the pain, well I don't know about the bleeding but that's what I heard anyway! Tara walks over closer to Stacie. Tara reaches out her arm and touches Stacie's right ear. Stacie pulls her head back away from Tara. Stacie looks at the tissue she has in her hand and then back at Tara... *I was just cleaning out the wax, you know how sensitive these ears can be. Wax! Stacie are for real? You're kidding me, right?* Tara shakes her head side to side after what Stacie just said… *OK Stacie! So, your cleaning out your ears for wax! Then tell me, why is there blood on the tissue Stacie? What were you cleaning out your ears with a knife? What are you talking about Tara! Come on now don't be silly, I Um!* Stacie stutters while trying not to tell Tara about what really happened to her ear... *I must of have punctured it with a q-tip.* Stacie puts her head down and starts walking towards the bathroom leaving Tara standing there speechless... *Now this right here is a weird looking newspaper I must say, what did you say the name of this newspaper was again Stacie?* Tara unravels the black rubber band from off the newspaper, she unfolds it and stares at the front page... *Oh! I see what the name of this mysterious looking newspaper is, it's called THE€ JOURNAL!*

Once Stacie is in the bathroom, she tosses the bloody tissue in the trash and looks in the bathroom mirror. Now yelling out the name of the newspaper from the other room Stacie, can hear her sister Tara and the expression on Stacie's face was terrifying.

Stacie puts one hand over her mouth that's wide open out of surprise and with the other hand she grabs the bathroom doorknob. Stacie pushes the door shut, and then stands there starring at herself in the bathroom mirror. After a few seconds Stacie drops her hand from her mouth, turns around moves closer to the bathroom door leans her head in and places her left ear on the door. Stacie stands there for a second and listens before she opens the door and walks out the bathroom and back over to Tara who is now reading the front page of THE JOURNAL!...

Stacie, you didn't mention that you knew the publishers! Frowning her face up after the remark Tara watches as her big sister Stacie, eyes widen... *The Publishers Tara? What Publishers? And please tell me what gave you that crazy idea? That's just ridiculous!* Stacie looks at her sister like she's senseless, hoping the look she was giving her sister would help to avoid any more direct question from Tara about THE JOURNAL!... *What are you talking about Tara! Listen, I don't know any publishers and I truly don't know where that newspaper came from, honestly!* Stacie walks over to the window and peeks out the blinds while Tara stands there looking confused again. *Stacie, I thought you said you... Oh never mind!* Tara walks over to Stacie and holds the newspaper up in front of her face... *Well Stacie for somebody who don't know the publishers or where this newspaper came from, all jokes aside it's kind of funny Stacie that I happen to have found this newspaper here in your house on your floor! But the newspaper isn't yours!* Stacie shrugs both of her shoulders up while taking in a deep breath.

Stacie walks away from Tara over to the window... *Don't ignore me Stacie! Ok, then explain this to me Sherlock?* Stacie turns around and faces Tara... *What Tara? Well Sis, do they always put your picture on the front page of newspapers, you don't know about, standing next to old ladies dressed in all black. In between open backseat doors of tinted black limousines?*

STUCK IN TRAFFIC

"When Objects In Mirrors,

Aren't What they Perceive To Be"

TH€ TRAFFIC

Sitting in traffic with both hands clutched to the steering wheel, on her way home from work. Stacie, turns the radio on, adjust the volume and finds the news station. Stacie listens as the weatherman reports todays weather…*Traffic backed on route 280. so, if you are thinking about taking the highway home be patient. There's been a bad accident and there probably won't be any movement for about an hour or two! So, drive carefully and please folks avoid the road rage! Coming to you live from the station that brings you "Views on news Kl2 news for you" I knew I should have taken the expressway way home!* Stacie turns the radio off. She then randomly off impulse turns around and looks through her back window at a man who's tail gating behind her bumper to bumper. Out of aggravation Stacie throws her right hand up in the air and brushes the driver off, she then turns back around and watches as another reckless driver tries to cut in front of her... *Watch it, you moron! I don't believe it, they a give license to anybody these days. Look at these fools driving like they got their eyes closed, Now what? I'm going to be stuck, here in traffic for another forty-five minutes! I'm going to be late for work! Where's my pocketbook?*

Stacie reaches in the back seat for her pocketbook. She lifts up her pocketbook and there lying underneath her pocketbook in plain sight, wrapped in a black rubber band is TH€ JOURNAL! In shock Stacie, tries not to get excited or emotional about the newspaper so, she stays calm and picks the newspaper up.

Attentively Stacie holds the newspaper with both hands while controlling the steering wheel and watching the cars in traffic... *Now how did this newspaper get in here? I know I left this in the living room, or did Tara put it in here? She couldn't have, I didn't give Tara a ride. Tara, drove her own car*! An impatient driver immediately passes Stacie on her right side. The driver forcefully cuts in front of Stacie's car without using their blinkers, causing Stacie to turn her steering wheel to the left. Stacie's car swerves slightly out of control, the newspaper drops in her lap... *Where did you get your license Mister? Some people! I don't believe them; they have some freaking nerve!* While slowly passing the man in the car that just bullied her in traffic Stacie, shakes her head side to side at the man disgusted and outraged. The man in the car looks at Stacie through his passenger side window. The man driving the car raises his hand and gives Stacie the finger, he then rolls his driver side window down....

Hey! The hell with you lady! Can't you see I was trying to get over in that lane? You drive like an old lady! Without being able to hear what the man was saying due to her passenger side window being rolled up. Instead Stacie, tries her hand at reading the man's lips and the expression on his face. And right there she pretty much knew that any words followed by an expletive hand gesture was not good. In rage, the man honks his horn at Stacie, she honks her horn back on spike while checking to make sure all of the doors in her car were locked.

Now out of genuine feelings and pure emotion caused by the insult the man just exposed. Stacie sticks her tongue out at the man who is now driving pass her carelessly in and out of traffic... *Look at this idiot! That right there is how accidents happen! From irresponsible, uncontrolled drivers, who should never, ever had been granted permission to drive.* Stacie moves her car up slowly ahead with the jammed bumper to bumper traffic still in route... *Finally! Thank God, Traffic is moving, and I can't believe its seven o'clock already. I should have been home by now! Where's my cellphone? I need to call Tara!* The radio in Stacie's car comes on by itself and starts blasting music through the speakers. The radio plays a song by The Doors…*(Radio) Riders of the storm / There's a killer on the road! Now what is wrong with this radio? And why is the volume up so loud?* Yelling, at herself from inside the car over the loud music Stacie, is having a hard time hearing herself think. So, with the cellphone still in her hand she tries to turn the volume on the radio down. But it's no use the volume gets louder. She tries again, the volume becomes even louder. Stacie now aggravated and annoyed by what's happening right now, the loud volume from the radio is wrecking her nerves, she's becoming unstable. She starts panicking which is now clearly the reason Stacie is unable to drive. So, out of fear and concern for her own safety and others, Stacie immediately steps on the breaks. The car stops unexpectedly in the middle of the street, causing the traffic behind her to come to a halt.

Once the driver behind her becomes aware of what was happening in front of them, the driver puts on their left blinker and switch lanes effortlessly. Without hesitation, the driver passes Stacie's car while looking at her inhumanly through their passenger side window in the process. Not too excited or even a little concerned as to why Stacie's car had just stopped. The driver slowly drives on pass. Stacie looks back at the not too excited driver as they slowly drive by. And with her cellphone in her right hand and her left hand firmly gripped on the steering wheel, she stares out of her driver's side window and watches all the cars that are now passing by her in traffic. Some drivers are paying attention, while others just drive pass with no importance to whether Stacie is in danger or even showing little to no concern of her wellbeing. Even with all the dodging and weaving that's taking place, due to the detouring caused by Stacie's car that's obstructing traffic. Without any accidents happening the cars in traffic continue moving along, aside from several annoyed drivers that constantly keep honking their horns at Stacie's car, as they all drive pass her. Out of frustration Stacie pounds her fist on the steering wheel, she tries turning the volume down on the radio but it's no use, she then tries turning the radio off all together but that's a disappointment. So, Stacie takes her foot of the breaks, steps on the gas, grabs the steering wheel and with both hands she slowly but cautiously drives off. Looking through her rear-view mirror Stacie can see the backed-up cars that she has initiated by her simply not moving.

Then suddenly, out of nowhere she hears a loud screeching noise from tires brushing over the pavement, the sound is so loud it causes Stacie to close her eyes. She lets go of the steering wheel, raises her hands and cover both ears once again. The sound pulsates into Stacie's ear like a thousand newborn babies crying all at once, like a teacher scrapping her fingernails over a chalk board, like a dentist drilling into a sensitive tooth. The torture causes Stacie to lose control of the steering wheel. Stacie drops the cellphone while trying her best to gain back control of her car. But the noise gets louder and louder her vision starts to dim, her ear starts to bleed again. She's losing focus and the loud irritating noise is becoming louder and louder, now the smoke from the tires is making the oncoming traffic unbelievably hard to see. Stacie closes her eyes and when she opens them, she can't believe what she is now seeing. The thought alone had Stacie in awe, she was in disbelief to open her eyes and find herself driving in the wrong direction. Not only was she driving in the wrong direction, but Stacie was now driving on the other side of traffic into oncoming traffic. A minute ago, Stacie, was like any other normal driver on the road but now she was destroyed by what was happening to her. Her life was in danger and her conscious was being manipulated by the severe and critical actions she was now facing ahead. Stacie was fearing for her life. She had no other choice; she was just trying to understand the speechless situation she was now in. Stacie was now driving her car into oncoming traffic.

The radio shuts off and then immediately comes back on again. The music continues playing at a loud volume. But this time instead of turning the radio off or trying to turn the volume down Stacie, ignores the loud music and surrenders devotedly to the song playing…
(Radio) "Riders of the storm / There's a killer on the road "

Weaving in and out of lanes recklessly while dodging the oncoming traffic uncontrollably Stacie is unable to control her car. She's now unstable and frantic and with all the car horns honking aggressively it's making matters worse. All the cars in front of her head lights are blinding off and on which is also making Stacie's situation even more unhealthy. Again, she is losing control of the vehicle and this time the back wheels on her car are spinning out of control. Stacie lifts her head up and looks in the rear-view mirror. She sees blood easing out of her right ear, her headlights are blinking off and on she's slipping in and out of consciousness while sliding down in the driver's seat. Stacie can't see a thing through her windshield, it's getting cold. The loud volume coming from the radio is adding discomfort to the several others disturbing things that is causing Stacie to lose her mind. The song is still playing on the radio...

(Radio) "Riders of the storm / There's a killer on the road"

The oncoming drivers are now fully aware that there is a reckless driver on the road and the driver is driving in the opposite direction, headed straight towards them.

The responsiveness of the life-threatening situation causes a chain reaction of drivers weaving in and out of lanes recklessly, while trying to dodge Stacie's car uncontrollably. Stacie hears a deep horn the sound is so loud and deep It causes her to lift her head up and open her eyes. Stacie tries looking through the windshield but all the windows in Stacie's car are fogged out due to the temperature drop inside the car and the heavy tire burning rubber caused by the sixteen wheelers truck tires. The closer the sixteen-wheeler gets, the louder the sound from the tires becomes. The bright headlights from the sixteen-wheeler shining through Stacie's windshield is blinding Stacie's vision, the headlights cut through the windshield like a razor, forcing Stacie to close her eyes. She tightens her grip on the steering wheel, trying to gain back control of the car but she can't. She's lost control. Stacie is unstable, and her behavior is erratic; her performance is uncoordinated; her mood is awkward and her attitude sucks. Now all the vehicles headlights ahead of her are flashing off and on. Stacie is totally blinded; she starts shouting hysterically inside the car.... *Please! Somebody help me! God! Help me! I don't want to die like this! God! Please don't let me die like this!* Stacie lowers her head and places her forehead on the steering wheel. With both of her eyes closed she gently eases her foot off the gas pedal and places her arms over her head with her fingers interlocked. Stacie starts breathing strongly through her nose and mouth. Her breath lingers in the air like steam inside the car from the temperature drop.

It's not unpredictable now to Stacie what might happen next. The only thing Stacie could think about was dying. Seeing herself lying in a casket dressed in all black, with flowers all around her in a church. People singing, the preacher doing the eulogy. The thought of her family mourning and crying at her funeral, her picture on the front of an obituary, the meeting and social gatherings at her parents' home, her face on the front page of THE JOURNAL! None of this was at all familiar too Stacie, but it was what she was being faced with now, so it was crucial and extremely uncomfortable due to the position she was now in. Which made it more than a life-threatening arrangement. And Stacie, knew it. She couldn't do anything else but accept it. What was she going to do? Who was going to help her? It was about to happen, the buck had stopped here, her last call for drinks, the bar was closing, this was her expiration, her termination, her departure from the rest of the world. So, she reaches down between her legs and picks up her cellphone, she dials her younger sister Tara, the phone rings on the other end… (Phone Ringing) Tara, answers… *Hello! Hello! Stacie is that you? Hello!* Then suddenly, the deep loud horn can be heard no more, the headlights cutting through the windshield ends. The irritating noise from the sixteen-wheeler truck tires stops, the black smoke outside fogging up Stacie's car windows from the sixteen-wheeler trucks burning rubber tires clears, all the vehicles in traffic driving towards her including the sixteen-wheeler truck is gone.

The temperature is back to normal, the music shuts off Stacie loosens the tight grip she has on the steering wheel before slowly lifting her head up with her eyes still closed. Stacie, then opens her eyes and the sight of what she's seeing right now is mind blowing, it's a miracle that incredibly overwhelming. The sun is shining and Stacie, is now standing outside of her house on her front porch dressed in a full bath robe and slippers, with a towel wrapped around her head. Stacie can't believe what is happening right now. With her arms folded, she closes her eyes and opens them back up while inhaling and exhaling a deep breath, Absorbing the miraculous miracle that's has just unfolded before her very eyes. While unfolding her arms Stacie, passionately looks down and beside her feet lying there on the porch she sees THE JOURNAL! Shocked by what she's seeing Stacie, decides to pick up the newspaper and as she's bending over and reaching her arm out to grab the newspaper Stacie, hears a man's voice. A voice that wasn't quite recognizable to her but distinguishing enough for her to acknowledge. So, she quickly leans back up and with her right hand she holds the top of her robe together by the neck. She puts her left hand in her bath robes front pocket, she looks across the street and sees a man standing on his porch dressed in a silk two piece buttoned up pajama set with a silk house coat on and leather house shoes, holding an unlit wooden pipe in his hand. After the man realizes that he has Stacie's attention, he waves at her from is porch Stacie, waves back and smiles.

The man across the street starts walking down the stairs, once he is off his porch, he steps onto the sidewalk and walks towards the street. He then raises his right arm and puts the unlit pipe in his mouth, the pipe hangs from the side of his mouth like a cigarette waiting to get lit. So, with his left hand he takes out the lighter that's in his house coat front pocket and lights the pipe, he takes a few light pulls, before blowing smoke out into the air from the corner of his mouth. He places the lighter back inside his pocket and with the pipe in his mouth the man crosses the street and walks down Stacie's driveway. He looks at Stacie, and notices that she has an unpleasant facial expression on her face. So, he removes the lit pipe from his mouth and holds it in his left hand, while extending his right arm out to Stacie, she takes her right hand out of her bath robes pocket and then Stacie and the man greet one another by shaking hands...

First let me say hello! Why, hello to you too sir! I don't mean to be rude and please miss you don't have to call me sir! I appreciate the gracious respect, but I'm just your neighbor who lives across the street! Well it is out of respect that I said hello! And how can I help you neighbor? I'm glad you asked!

The man lifts the pipe he has in his right hand up to his mouth he then digs in his silk house coat with his left hand a takes the lighter back out. He lights the pipe, pulls on it and blows the smoke out the corner of his mouth before putting the lighter back in his pocket... *Is That Your Car?*

The man turns his head to his left and with the hand he is holding the pipe with, he points in the direction where there's a car blocking his driveway. Stacie looks in the direction where the man is pointing and sees her car double parked with the driver's side door wide open...

Oh my God! That sure is my car! How I... I don't...Sir! I'm so sorry! Don't be sorry miss! But please! I would appreciate it if you would move It, you seem to be blocking my driveway! Oh! I'm so sorry sir I mean neighbor, I'll be just a moment! Just let me get my keys! Mam Um! But your keys are in the car already, I know because you left the driver side door to your car wide open! Is everything alright?

Embarrassed at what she just heard and what she is seeing Stacie, grabs her forehead and rubs her face with her head down. She looks up and shakes her head side to side signaling that she is ashamed at her actions and humiliated by the thought of not being able to remember what had happened. So, instead of giving him the opportunity to embarrass her even more Stacie, decides to end the interrogation before it even begins. The man turns back around looks at the car and then back at Stacie, while kindly pulling on the pipe he has in his hand. The man leisurely takes a few lighter pulls, before blowing the smoke out of the corner of his mouth. The man from across the street removes the pipe from his mouth, lowers the pipe and holds it a few inches away from his chest up in the air. Again, the man looks in the direction where Stacie's car is double parked blocking his driveway...

Mister! I'm truly Sorry! I don't know what I was thinking, I must have run inside to get something and have gotten sidetracked by something else I must have been doing! How did I forget to park my car and I left the driver's side door wide open? Wow! Excuse me sir? But would you happen to know what time it is?

The man standing there in front of Stacie, puts the pipe back in his mouth, raises his left arm and pushes the house coat sleeve back that's covering the watch that he has on his right wrist. He looks down at the watch he has on his arm... *Why yes! It's fifteen minutes after eight!* Stacie looks up at the sky before stepping off her porch. She gently walks pass the man who is just standing there leisurely taking pulls off the pipe and blowing out smoke. Stacie, now thinking to herself how in the world could she have left her driver side door wide open and her car double parked and for how long was the significant question. Stacie, hops in the driver's seat, closes the driver's side door, backs the car up and pulls the car up into her own driveway. The man steps back away from the car and smoothly starts walking towards the street. Stacie sits there for a minute looking at the man through the rearview mirror wondering if he had seen the newspaper that was left on her doorstep. Or if him or his wife had been receiving the same newspaper as well. The man keeps looking at his watch like he has a court date or late for a wedding.

Stacie turns the car's ignition off and gets out and before she closes the car door she reaches back in and grabs her cellphone from off the passenger's front seat. Stacie turns the cellphone on, but the cellphone battery is dead. So, she leans up out the driver's side and slams the driver's side door shut. She walks around the car and heads towards her front porch. She stops in her tracks and acts like she is calling somebody with her cellphone, trying not to make eye contact with her neighbor or give the man any reason to return.

Out of curiosity Stacie, turns around and looks up at her neighbor who's standing near the curb of the sidewalk, smoking his pipe about to step into the street. The man turns around holds the pipe down and shouts out to Stacie... *Why thank you so much! You just saved me a headache from the wife! If you know what I mean?* The man mumbles under his breath. *Crazy Lady! Who leaves their car keys in the ignition with the driver's side door wide open anyway? What is she a Psych Ward patient?* Stacie lifts her arm up in the air and waves at the man with an imaginary smile on her face. Stacie shouts back at her neighbor while holding the cellphone in her hand... *Nice meeting you too neighbor! And don't forget to tell the wife I apologize? It really was nice meeting you! I really mean that!* Stacie mumbles under her breath. *Idiot! Like he's never blocked anyone's driveway before, who does he think he is anyway, with his silk pajamas and pipe. Looking like Thurston Howell, the third from Gilligan's Island.* Stacie, and her neighbor both look at each other one more time from a distant.

They smile at each other while pretending they both were pleased by the introduction of meeting one another. Stacie steps up onto her porch, she extends out her arm and grabs the front door handle and just as she's about to open the door she gets startled by a tap on the back of her shoulder... *Excuse me, miss!* Stacie, jumps surprised by the distinguished voice and the unannounced approach. Stacie lets the door handle go and quickly turns around while holding the top of her bath robe together around her neck... *My goodness you scared me! I thought you were in the house already with the misses! Well almost, until I realized I still had this!* The man from across the street stands directly in front of Stacie with his left arm behind his back. They stare into each other's eyes; the look is so transparent that it misleads them both into thinking dishonest things about one another. The man moves his arm from behind his back and the expression he's seeing on Stacie's face is priceless... *I just wanted to give this back to you! I totally forgot I had it! I just so happened to pick it up, while you were moving your car! I hope you're not upset.* Stacie looks at what the man has in his hand, her eyes widen by what she's seeing, her heart skips a beat, she takes a swallow of dry air, while a trickle of sweat starts running down the side of her face. Stacie becomes nervous... *And I am truly sorry if I startled you! My God you almost gave me a heart attack! I have been frightened, much worse than that believe me. But that my friend, was very sneaky neighbor. Well again miss, I apologize! And here is your newspaper!*

The butterflies in her stomach takes flight, her hand start trembling, as she extends her arm out and reaches for the newspaper, the man is holding. Stacie thoughts are so loud inside her head, she actually thinks that the man standing in front of her can hear them. Silently praying to God, that her neighbor doesn't ask her anything else. Stacie is also asking God to forgive her for wanting this man to choke on his words and swallow his tongue, if he even thinks about asking her anything pertaining to or concerning THE JOURNAL! Stacie kindly grabs the newspaper and quickly turns around to go back inside her house... *Miss! If you don't mind me asking!* Stacie turns back around. *Yes! Did I leave something else? No! Nothing like that! But believe me, I'm not trying to be nosy or anything! But now that we've met, I still don't think I know your name! If you don't mind me asking? Oh! That's certainly all right! By the way my name is Mr. Elmwood! Well! Mr. Elmwood, it is nice to meet you my name is Stacie, Stacie Largen! Well Stacie it sure was nice talking to you! No Mr. Elmwood the pleasure was all mines Oh! And by the way Stacie before you go! Yes Mr. Elmwood! I was just looking at your newspaper and l said to myself. Self! I have never seen an issue like that before are you a writer for the company.* Not surprised by the question because this is the second time Stacie, can recall that someone has asked her that same question. Mr. Elmwood eyes now shifting to the newspaper Stacie has in her hand... *That newspaper! It looks like it has a lot of good stories and articles in it, so are you?* Stacie looks back at Mr. Elmwood...

Am I What Mr. Elmwood? A writer for the newspaper's publishing! I wanted to know if you were a writer or editor for the newspaper? Mr. Elmwood patiently waits for Stacie to answer... *The name of that newspaper is it called The Journal! Am I right? Why Yes! Mr. Elmwood, that is the name of the newspaper! Well Actually! The reason I asked is because they have a picture of you on the front-page siting inside this black tinted limousine next to an old lady dressed in all black*! Mr. Elmwood takes a few more pulls from the pipe he has in his mouth, he blows the smoke out of the corner of his mouth before turning around and walking back across the street towards his house. Stacie stands there on her porch baffled by what just happened, while holding THE JOURNAL! in her hand down by her side. She watches as Mr. Elmwood crosses the street, he then raises his right arm in the air with the smoking lit pipe still in his hand and waves goodbye. Stacie, turns around, opens her front door, goes inside the house, closes and locks the door behind her. With her back leaned up against the door, she opens THE JOURNAL! Stacie stands there and looks at the picture on the front page of the newspaper. The picture of her siting inside a black tinted limousine next to an old lady who's dressed in all black!

PICTURES AND WORDS

"When Everybody Hears You, But Nobodies Listening"

THE PICTURE

In the kitchen getting the last preparations ready for dinner, Mrs. Largen yells throughout the house from the kitchen... *Edward! Tell Tara to turn that radio down! And Edward, where are my beautiful grandchildren? They are out with the wife, she said she is going to try and make it but if not, she'll see you tomorrow! Ma, she's always asking about you and the kids*! Mrs. Largen smiles while cleaning off the kitchen table... *I know they wonder why you are always out and about? Ma! They know, I have a lot of work on my hands right now! Well! Ae you staying for dinner? Because it's almost ready!* Edward walks over by the stove and start removing tops off of the pots, he leans in and starts smelling the aroma from the steam rising from the simmering meal that's preparing... *I can't lie, it sure does smell good! But the wife would kill me if she cooked and I didn't come home and eat something! So, I'll just have a portion! Do whatever you want! Just go in there and tell your Father that dinner is almost ready! And Edward, ask your Father what he would like to drink!* Edward puts the lids back on the pots that's on the stove, before walking out from the kitchen into the room where Mr. Largen is sitting down. Edward peeks at his Father, before walking back into the kitchen... *He has a soda already, Ma! Ok! How about you Edward No! I'm Good! Only if you have beer*! Standing by the kitchen table Mrs. Largen starts shaking her head side to side signaling that she doesn't agree at all with what Edward just said.

Edward, walks over to the refrigerator and stands there with the refrigerator door wide open, staring in. Mrs. Largen walks over by Edward and slams the refrigerator door close. Mrs. Largen smacks Edward on the shoulder... *Boy, get out of my kitchen. And stop letting the cold out of my refrigerator! And where's your brother Mark? He should have been home from school by now! That boy! I tell you; he's going to give me a heart attack one of these days! Edward, go and tell Tara I need some help in this kitchen!* The front door to the Largens house slams shuts... *Pops! What's going on? Son! Your Mother was just asking about you!*

Mark drops his bookbag on the floor, turns around and locks the front door... Mark, bends down, unzips his bookbag and takes out a book. Mark zips the bookbag back up and then walks over to his Father. He shakes his Fathers hand before promptly walking pass him, straight into the kitchen... *Speaking of the devil? Here's the Poet now!* Mark puts the book into his jacket pocket, as he walks pass his Brother Edward in the kitchen who is now walking out the kitchen headed into the living room.

Ma! What's for dinner? Mrs. Largen looks at her son Mark. She then walks over to the kitchen cabinet. Mark opens the cabinet door. Mrs. Largen reaches up and takes out some plates. Mark tries to help Mrs. Largen with the plates, but she brushes him away and turns around. Mrs. Largen walks back over to the kitchen table and sits the plates down on the table herself...

Dinner! I think you better go and wash them hands, before you start worrying about what's for dinner! I see you over there eyeballing those biscuits too! And where have you been? You were supposed to come straight home after school today! Boy, don't start that hanging out all day after school! I know exactly what boy's your age are up to these days! With the corner of her eye Mrs. Largen looks at Mark. While she stands there and places each plate by each chair at the kitchen table... *Sis! Want to hear this verse from Sam Elmwood? Wait A Minute! Did you just say Sam Elmwood?* Stacie looks at her brother like something terrible just happened or that the name Sam Elmwood had ringed a bell and the bell she was hearing was not associated with anything good. Stacie had heard that name before but could not quite remember where she had heard it. The thought of not remembering was clouding her judgement, it also was striking some bad vibes. Some vibes that was making Stacie look suspicious... *Sam Elmwood! Sam Elmwood!* Stacie just kept repeating the name over and over in her head, her facial expression revealed that she was not only getting nervous but Stacie, was absolutely and extremely worried. Mark, looking at his sister with deep concern on his face... *Sam Elmwood!* Sis, your acting like you and him had met before! Mark opens his book of poems... *That name just sounds so familiar!* Mark looks at the book he has in his hands, he then focuses his attention on his older Sister, Stacie. Mark starts turning pages in the book...

No! it's nothing like that Mark, it's just that name and for the life of me, I don't know why but... Anyway! let me hear the poem! Edward looks at Stacie... *Stacie are you losing your mind? You were always the first one to tell him to shut up, Edward Be Quiet! If the boy wants to go around quoting verses of poems, let him! Because there's much worse things he could be doing besides quoting poetry! ...Amen, to that!!* Mrs. Largen walks out from the kitchen wiping her hands with a dish towel, after checking the pots on the stove... *At least the boy is not going around addressing these girls with every letter in the alphabet, with his pants hanging down to his ankles!* Everybody in the room starts laughing... *And imitating that tongue twisting music! What is it called Lip Bop? No Ma! It's Hip Hop Well! Anyway, go on boy get to quoting I 'm still getting dinner prepared! You heard Mother! Get to quoting already!*

Stacie hops onto the couch while Mark walks over and stands in front of the room, with the book of poems in his hand. Mark holds the book with one hand right below his face and starts reading... *Ok! Listen it's called "Pictures" ...*

PICTURES

Only gifted words will paint brilliant pictures, of well-hidden emotions that be,
And only a hideous imagination, can turn all noble thoughts weary.

Framing creativity from the inspiration that you see,
Will hang drawings on the walls, placed alongside your productive energy.

Leaving a selected few, to become victims of their own situations,
And not even time can heal those wounds, caused by a self-destructive imagination.

Tearing apart and destroying, the truth in one's evidence,
Leaving true hearts to depart rooms, that support houses filled with false confidence.

Look into your own soul, there you'll see what really beholds,
And if you find out what's being concealed, never reveal what you've been told.

Because only some things you should shelter, throughout the days, months and years,
And if you live to see that day, it will eventually leak out, in your strongest Fears…

CLASS IS IN SESSION

"When You Remember to Go To Work,

But Forget Your 9 To 5"

Good morning Mr. Butler! Good morning Principle Largen! And how was your weekend Principle? Fine! Just fine Mr. Butler! And the family Principle? Oh! They are all doing just great! Well, that's good to know! You know Principle, you had a phone call this Morning! Just before you walked in, an older woman, she did not say much, but she specifically asked for you! Sounded like she was in her late 70's! Well, Mr. Butler, did she say what it was in reference to? No! But she did say she would be calling back later today! Well, that's good Mr. Butler! Principle, and I know this is none of my business but as I was picking up some files off your desk for the council meeting this afternoon, I happen to see... Oh! Never mind it was nothing! Are you sure it was nothing Mr. butler? Yes! I'm sure, it's just, well!... Principle, I better get going I have a lot of work to do! Mr. Butler turns around and starts walking out of the office...

You enjoy your day Principle! And if you need me, I'll be in my office! By the way Mr. Butler! Before you go, where is the 2nd floor students? Stacie stands by the open office door with one hand on the doorknob and the other hand on her hip. Mr. Butler lifts a folder up, opens it and reads what's inside...*They went on a field trip today Principle, to hear a live band play in New York City! Oh, that's right with Mr. Gean and the new girl what's her name again Mr. Butler?* Standing there in the hallway outside Stacie's office.

Mr. Butler, stares at the folder he has in hand, not trying to make eye contact with Stacie, being that the question she just asked him is clouding his judgement. So, Mr. Butler scratches his head, closes the open folder and holds it down by his side. Mr. Butler then looks up at Stacie... *Carlen? Yes! that's her name Principle! The girls name is Carlen!* Mr. Butler now worried with an uneasy smile all over his face. He's standing there hoping that his boss Stacie doesn't start feeling like he's getting too old to be working here. Because if she does that can only mean one thing, Stacie will definitely think it's Alzheimer's!...

Principle, that's because Mr. Gean called out sick this Morning! And did I mention the 2nd floor students went with a substitute teacher from a school downtown. I think the information is on your desk Principle! A Substitute, Mr. Butler! Now don't you think that is something you should have told me sooner. Mr. butler holds his head down and looks at the folder he has in his hand trying to avoid eye contact again with Stacie. Just in case Stacie, looks for a response. Stacie, let's go of the office doorknob, walks over to her desk, brushes over all the paperwork on top of her desk with a while infuriated frown on her face.

Ok Mr. Butler! I'll look for the paperwork concerning the substitute teacher like you said! Mr. Butler turns around, and heads for the office door. He then turns back around and looks at Stacie, who is standing over her office desk, looking for the folder with the paperwork concerning the substitute teacher...

You know Principle! The strangest thing occurred this Morning also! Go on! Mr. Butler, I'm listening! And please don't tell me the 3rd Floor students are out on a field trip as well! Well, are they? Mr. Butler starts laughing, he immediately stops laughing, when he notices the impression on Stacie's face is showing that she sees nothing funny. And what Mr. butler has found hysterical. Stacie believes is pure disturbing. Stacie stands there behind her desk with a folder in one hand and the other hand rested on top of the office chair... *Mr. Butler! Please, proceed, if you don't mind!* Why yes! Principle, I apologize! Principle, the strangest thing was that the woman that called for you this Morning, had the same last name as the substitute teacher. Wait a minute! Let me guess, was the last name Elmwood? Yes, Principle! But how did you know? That's a long story Mr. Butler! Oh! And by the way Mr. Butler! Yes, Principle! Was there a newspaper involved? Mr. Butler now smiling why shaking his head side to side. Your good Principle Largen, I mean really good and yes! There was a newspaper! One that I didn't quite recognize either if must say! I know, I know, I was standing in front of an all-black tinted limousine, right? Well not exactly Principle! What I mean to say is, it wasn't you who was standing in the front on the limousine! Stacie's, facial expressions changes again. She turns around by her desk and with her back towards Mr. Butler she looks out the enormous three glass window that's behind her desk in her office...

NO! Then who was it Mr. butler? Tell me! Who was standing there? Stacie's voice raises in turmoil, with her back still towards Mr. Butler, as she continues looking out the enormous window. Stacie, then folds both of her arms, turns around and looks Mr. Butler right in his eyes. The fear Mr. Butler has on his face gets Stacie's attention. So, before picking up the newspaper, Stacie, stands there and waits for Mr. butler to answer the question. Mr. Butler sluggishly takes a step back. He, looks at the newspaper Stacie, is now holding in her hand. Mr. Butler extends his arm out behind him and reaches for the office doorknob. Mr. Butler takes in a deep breath and with caution he gets ready to answer the question... *Well, are you going to tell me who was standing there or not? Forget it, Mr. Butler I have the newspaper in front of me. I can find out myself! Because, to be honest with you Mr. Butler. You look like you should, use the bathroom right now? And with all due respect Mr. Butler, please don't piss on yourself in my office, dear God not in front of me!*

Principle Largen, I'm afraid to say that It was the substitute teacher! Stacie's, eyebrows turn up, a slight frown appears on her face as she looks down at the newspaper that's lying there on top of her desk. Stacie walks around her desk. She rushes over to Mr. Butler with one arm extended out. She lightly pushes Mr. Butler out into the hallway... *Thank you, Mr. Butler, and I mean that sincerely but if there isn't anything else you need to inform me about this Morning! Concerning my school and my kids!*

Then I guess your services here are no longer needed! Am I making myself clear Mr. Butler? Shaking his head up and down Mr. Butler signals that he fully understands what Stacie is saying... *Ok Then, Mr. Butler, I guess that will be all! And again, thank you for sharing that!* Stacie, removes her hand from off Mr. Butlers shoulder, takes a step back inside her office and locks the office door in Mr. Butlers face. Outside in the hallway, standing on the other side of the office door. Mr. Butler pretends to stab himself in the chest with a knife made from air. He holds his arm up by his chest, balls his fist up and hits himself lightly in the chest several times. Referring to how he feels about how Stacie is killing him softly. Mr. Butler was thinking that at the age he is right now and how Stacie was treating him was only going to speed up the process of his death sooner or later. Mr. Butler takes a few steps away from the door. He turns around and shakes his head side to side again this time referring that Stacie should feel sorry for treating him, and old man at his age like that. Mr. Butler starts talking low to himself... *She got some nerve! And to think I'm not even her secretary! I'm just helping! Some people don't appreciate nothing!...* A teacher catches Mr. Butler by surprise as she peacefully walks by him, as he stands there a few feet away. Outside of Stacie's office bitter, talking to himself under his breath... *Good Morning, Mr. Butler!* Mr. Butler is startled, he then turns his head slightly to his right, as the teacher walks up peacefully behind him. *Good Morning!*

The teacher passes Mr. Butler in the hallway, she raises her voice informally as she starts walking down the school's hallway stairs... *Mr. Butler, you should smile it's a beautiful day to be alive!* Back in the office Stacie, walks back over to her desk, sits down in her office chair and picks up the newspaper. Stacie opens the newspaper and as she's looking at the front page, she clearly doesn't recognize the gentleman standing there, next to the limousine. Stacie now felt kind of pleased because she was thinking that throughout everything she had seen and known. Looking at the gentleman on the front page didn't give her that feeling of embarrassment and humiliation that she usually would get from THE€ JOURNAL! Still the sight of THE€ JOURNAL! made Stacie's skin crawl. And whenever it was in her presence Stacie, felt some kind of way and that was more than a concern to her. Stacie was involved, and she knew it. She had become prey to whatever force of nature this newspaper had derived from. While staring at the mysterious newspaper she has in her hand. Stacie's, eyes are glued to the gentleman standing next to the limousine. Stacie also noticed the gentleman had his arm extended out and he was pointing at a house. Now taking a closer look Stacie, was sure the limousine the gentleman was standing next to, was without a doubt parked on the street she lived on. And the house the gentleman was pointing at was hers. Just to make sure Stacie, opens her desk draw and takes out a magnifying glass, she places the magnifying glass over the picture and that's when she noticed something even more dramatic and thrilling.

Something else in the picture on the front page that really caught Stacie's undivided attention. Leaning her head down closer towards the desk, with one eye open Stacie, saw another person in the picture sitting inside the limousine next to an old lady dressed in all black. Without hesitation and out of strong disbelief Stacie, drops the magnifying glass on the desk and quickly pushes herself back away from the desk in the office chair. The phone on her desk starts blinking an incoming call Stacie, ignores the blinking. With her head leaned back Stacie, just knew and was ready to bet her life on it, that the other person in the picture was none other than her older brother Edward! Stacie places her hand over her mouth traumatized by the photo. Not wanting to believe what she is seeing or even have her mind cross that thought of why her brother was in the picture. Let alone why right now. To Stacie, it seemed like one by one her immediate family was now being targeted by this newspaper, a selected few was referring to as TH€ JOURNAL! This was not a prank and everything that was happening was authentic and extremely true and Stacie knew it. She knew, this newspaper was not going anywhere, and the situation was going to get worse, before it was going to get any better. Stacie was starting to feel like she was being haunted by this newspaper called TH€ JOURNAL! The sight of it and thought of knowing it was there, had Stacie's heart beating faster than a sexual encounter by two rabbits. Nothing else seemed to be more Important. Stacie just couldn't believe her oldest brother was sitting in that limousine.

This is what most normal people would have considered creepy and THE JOURNAL! is what Stacie was considering wicked. Her main concern now was genuinely and nothing less than serious about where this newspaper called THE JOURNAL! Was coming from! Hoping to stop this madness Stacie tried narrowing down some reliable options concerning this mysterious newspaper. Options that could impact her concern of where the THE JOURNAL! was exactly coming from and at the same time save someone's life in the process, including her own. Startled by the knock on her office door. She quickly opens the desk draw and shoves the newspaper inside. She closes the desk drawer so hard, the desk chair that she's sitting in almost tips over caused by the dramatic force she just used. Stacie shoves the newspaper inside the desk drawer and slams the drawer shut. Stacie hears someone calling out her name from outside of her office in the hallway the persons voice is loud and clear… *Principle, you have a phone call on line three! I tried calling you myself, but you wouldn't answer the phone. Would you like me to take a message*? Stacie looks at the phone on her desk blinking an incoming call... *No! I will take it in here. Thank you, Mr. Butler!* After a few minutes and when Stacie, thinks Mr. Butler is finally gone she gets up, walks over to the door and makes sure the office door is still locked. She sits back down at her desk while rubbing both of her eyes. She opens the desk drawer and takes out THE JOURNAL! She picks up the magnifying glass and places it back in front of the image on the front page of the newspaper.

And like earth is considered a planet and water is considered wet, sure enough it was true the person sitting inside the limousine was her brother Edward. Who had his head slightly turned to his right. And lying on his lap, what looked like a newspaper definitely was. The sight of her Brother caused Stacie, to start questioning everything that was happening to her since TH€ JOURNAL! started appearing at her doorstep. Not only was she questioning the newspaper but she, also was questioning the old lady and the tall man, the tinted limousine, the dreams, the accident, the ear bleeds, the phone calls and now her Brother Edward. What could all this be leading to Stacie, asked herself and she didn't have a single clue. Nothing was making sense. Mr. Butler knocks on the office door again... *Principle Largen!* *Give me just a minute Mr. Butler!* Stacie, gets up to open the door *It's the elderly woman on line three, would you like me to take a message?* Now standing up by her desk Stacie, looks at the door... *No thanks, I'll take the call in here Mr. Butler. Thank you!* She picks up the phones hand receiver on her desk and presses line three. *Hello! Hello!* Stacie, then presses line one and line two. And after realizing that there is no one on the line Stacie, hangs the phone receiver up and sits back down. Looking at the clock on her wall Stacie, realizes that the Morning went by so fast she didn't even get a chance to take lunch... *Oh my God! Look at the time! It's already after four. The kids should be on their way back from the field trip!* She picks up the phone and calls Mr. Butler who should be in Stacie's secretary office right now.

The phone on the other end rings Stacie, lets the phone ring three times. Mr. Butler doesn't answer the phone so Stacie, decides to leave him a message…

(Phone Ringing) Hello! Mr. Butler, this is Principle Largen, I will be leaving my office headed on my way to the cafeteria to have lunch! If you need me, you can reach me there or if you're out of the building, call me on my cell phone Goodbye! After Stacie, cleans off her desk and turns off all the lights in her office she unlocks the door, steps out into the hallway, closes the office door behind her and then locks the door. Stacie walks down the hall towards the stairs, at the top of the stairs she runs into Mr. Butler, who is surprised to see the Principle. But deep down inside he's disappointed. With a phony smile on his face Mr. Butler walks up to Stacie... *Principle Largen, are you leaving? If so, would you like me to do anything for you while you're gone? Make some calls or file some papers? No Mr. Butler! You have done enough but thank you for asking! Wait a minute! There is something you can do Mr. Butler, if it's not too much trouble! Sure Principle, what is it? Would you mind checking to see if Mr. Gean, will be coming back to work tomorrow and if so, could you tell him that Principle Largen said I hope he feels better! I certainly will do so, enjoy your lunch Principle! Oh, I intend to Mr. Butler!* Standing there disappointed Mr. Butler, watches as Stacie takes her time and walks down the stairs. After a few steps Mr. Butler, turns around and walks in the opposite direction. While holding on to the staircase railing Stacie, notices that the lights in the school's hallway are starting to dim.

Stacie stops takes out her cellphone and leaves Mr. Butler a text message. She, the looks up at the ceiling and notices the lights are flickering off and on. The hallway becomes darker, the temperature in the school drops then suddenly, Stacie hears footsteps throughout the hallway. The footsteps echo bounces off the walls the sound travels up and down through the school's hallway. Frightened Stacie slowly walks down the stairs and just before she gets to the bottom, she starts hearing ghostlike whispers. The whispering becomes louder the closer Stacie gets to the bottom of the stairs. The atmosphere in the hallway now has a paranormal feel. Stacie's now nervous and afraid so, she stops on the stairs tightly holding the rail. She then looks back up to see if there's anybody around but there's no one in sight. The hallway starts looking eerie her imagination was running wild and what was happening was unreal…

Hello! Is anybody there? Hello! Who else is in this hallway? Somebody say something! This is Principle Largen and I don't allow playing in these hallways! So, I demand to know who is out there! The ghostlike whispering automatically stops. The paranormal atmosphere Stacie felt ended. The temperature balances back to normal. So, she continues walking down the stairs holding the rail. Once at the bottom of the stairs she turns around and looks back up. Stacie sees a shadow... *Who Is That? I said Who is that?*

The shadow she was seeing starts moving closer, towards her not being able to make out if the shadow was real or just a figment of her extraordinary imagination, due to the flickering and very dim lights in the hallway not being as bright as they supposed to be. Stacie starts taking steps backwards as she grabs hold of the banister. She looks around the hallway left and right hoping someone would show up and save her from whatever was happening. The shadow gets closer and closer. Stacie takes a reckless step backwards she lets go of the rail which causes her to trip over herself and fall to the ground in the process. Stacie is now lying on the ground in the school's hallway. Her eyes are closed, she hears a man's voice… *Principle! Are you alright? Here let me help you up! You must be more careful Principle! You could have really hurt yourself!* Stacie feels a hand grabbing on to her arm. The man standing over Stacie pulls forward and helps her up off the ground. Stacie's eyes open and there standing right in front of her. The shadow she was seeing has now turned into an image of a human being and that human being was none other than Stacie's' neighbor from across the street Mr. Elmwood. The reaction on Stacie's face was more than priceless, it had her speechless for about a minute or two. Then Stacie, returned to her senses and that's when she realized that this was the second time today that her neighbor Mr. Elmwood who lived across the street from her had scared the lived mess out of her…

Mr. Elmwood! Is that you? Why I don't believe this, Ms. Largen I had now idea you worked here and who would have known we live on the same block and just met this Morning! Well, isn't that the God honest truth! Well, first of all let me apologize again for sneaking up on you! We must stop meeting like this, Stacie! Who you telling?

Wiping her clothes off from being on the ground Stacie, looks down at her outfit before leaning up and looking Mr. Elmwood directly in between the eyes... *I must ask Mr. Elmwood; do you have a thing for scaring woman? Or are you just the sneaking up on woman type?* Mr. Elmwood starts laughing while Stacie. Stands there with a sober look upon her face...

Not at all Ms. Largen, I don't have a thing for sneaking up on woman especially beautiful woman! Stacie starts smiling. *Flattery will get you know where Mr. Elmwood! Well, maybe lunch! And please call me Stacie! Ok Stacie, I really appreciate the offer but I'm here on business! Well are you looking to teach here at the school, Mr. Elmwood? Well no, not exactly! You see Ms. Largen, I am here looking to buy the school! Did you just say buy the school? Yes!* The expression now on Stacie's face was again beyond priceless. She was looking at Mr. Elmwood like he just hit lottery and the school was his first investment... *Well you don't say, Wow! I guess anything is possible these days and hey you never know! Right Mr. Elmwood? Your one hundred percent correct! I couldn't agree with you more Stacie!*

And just think about it, the last time I saw you Mr. Elmwood, you were blocking my driveway and now look at you, blocking my stairs, trying to the buy the school! What a day! So, Mr. Elmwood you got my attention at buy! But besides that, who are you here to see? Glad you asked Ms. Largen, I mean Stacie! I was looking for the Principles office! Because that is someone I need to talk to also and then the superintendents, teachers, staff and so on! You understand! Stacie stands there in shock but amazed. Stacie, enough about me! Please, tell me what business do you have here? Are you a teacher as well? Mr. Elmwood looks around the school's hallway. And then the voices of teachers can be heard throughout the school's hallways. Stacie looks up and there's two teachers and a classroom of kids standing at the top of the stairs. The children are holding hands while both teachers help escort the children down the stairs. Stacie and Mr. Elmwood move to the side and watch as the two teachers and the children all walk down the stairs together. The two teaches stop by Stacie and Mr. Elmwood. One of the teachers turns, looks at the children and addresses them in sign language... *Ok children, on the count of three let's all say good afternoon to Principle Largen!*

Mr. Elmwood looks at Stacie and smiles at her by what he is witnessing. Stacie smiles back at Mr. Elmwood before focusing her attention back on the children... *Ok ready one, two, three good afternoon Principle Largen*!

The children all simultaneously raise their hands and in volume they speak in sign language in the school's hallway, looking like a rehearsed children's drama class. Stacie walks up towards the two teachers and the children. She starts hugging the children one by one before raising both her hands and addresses them back in sign language while speaking out loud... *And good afternoon to you all as well children! Now behave yourselves and remember, as long as you have breath in your body, anything and everything is possible! And remember the sky's the limit!*

The children, the two teachers and Stacie, all simultaneously silently shout out the sky's the limit in sign language. The two teachers then escort all the children back to their classroom. Mr. Elmwood, smiles turns and faces Stacie shaking his head side to side signaling that he truly and honestly loved what he just witnessed... *Principle Largen! I'm speechless. Anyway, with all respect due I'm delighted and pleased right now, I must say! Now back to business, Principle! I think I'll take you up on your offer, I've rounded up quite an appetite just talking about your offer!* Stacie frowns at the gesture...! *My Offer Mr. Elmwood? Yes, Lunch! Oh, Lunch sure thing, well let's not waste any more time. Follow me Mr. Elmwood, the cafeteria is this way and believe me you must try the burgers they're the best! You do look like a cheeseburger, fries and milkshake kind of guy! You're absolutely right! But I prefer turkey burgers, fries and a Pepsi! Just don't tell the wife, she'll kill me if she knew!*

Laughing at what Mr. Elmwood just said Stacie raises her arm and points in the direction where they are headed... *I understand Mr. Elmwood! Don't worry I can keep a secret! Oh, and please Principle Largen, call me Sam!*

After ordering their lunch Principle Largen and Mr. Elmwood find a seat in the cafeteria. They sit down across from one another and wait on their lunch to finish getting prepared... *Mr. Elmwood, I mean Sam! Can I ask you something? Sure, what's bothering you? You remember earlier by the hallway stairs? Yes! Well, just minutes before you showed up, I was…*

Oh, never mind it probably was nothing! Sam picks up a napkin and wipes his mouth. He starts talking with food in his mouth... *No, I insist! What is it Principle?* Stacie turns her head to the left and looks at the cashier who is ringer up a few orders. She then looks back at Sam! *Listen Stacie, if something is on your mind. Please by all means le it out! And if it concerns me, I will not leave this cafeteria, until you have said what you needed to say! Well, since you put it that way and heaven know, I don't want you spending the night here in the cafeteria!* Stacie grabs her glass takes a sip of her lemonade iced tea. She then pushes the glass to the side... *Sam! What I'm trying to say is, just minutes before you showed up at the stairs, I heard someone talking. Well that's what I thought anyway! And the strangest thing was that, the voice didn't sound human! You must think I'm crazy, don't you? Not at all go on! I mean it all seemed so unreal but real. If you know what I mean?*

The voices sounded like some ghost whisper, like some supernatural unrehearsed, not on key humming! And I thought somebody was playing a prank on m. Until I saw you and even the shadow of you was creeping me out! Sam picks up his glass and takes a sip of his soda. He puts the glass down and looks at Stacie...

Well Stacie, do you want the truth? Of course! It sounds to me like the building! The building, what do you mean the building? What I mean is this school is very, very old! You see Stacie, when very old buildings like this start aging in the walls, sometimes you hear the walls settling. And if you are in a quiet place like the hallway where sound travels. Then you Stacie, are going to hear some strange sounds, just like the ones you were hearing earlier! And just to clear the air. I guarantee you Principle, I was not whispering or making any kind of strange sounds before we met! That would just be downright foolish! I'll tell you what Sam! I truly appreciate the concern and that explains what I was hearing! Thank you so much Mr. Elmwood, I mean Sam! Mr. Elmwood looks at the watch he has on his arm... *Wow, would you look at the time! Principle, thank you for lunch. I hate to eat and run but I have another appointment. So, I must be leaving now!* Stacie tries to get up from her seat... *No! Don't, please stay seated and finish your lunch. I found myself in, I can surely find myself out! Oh, and I have your number, I ran into a Mr. Butler on my way in and he gave it to me! And don't forget we are also neighbors!*

Sam and Stacie shakes hands before Sam, walks off headed out the cafeteria to the exit of the school. With Stacie, still sitting at the cafeteria table finishing her lunch, with her back-facing Sam. Mr. Elmwood, quietly walks back up behind Stacie and shakes her on her shoulders... *Boo!* Stacie jumps from the silent, alarming scare. Stacie gets ready to turn her head slightly to the side until she hears the creepy, spooky sound coming from the persons laugh. The laughter is ghostlike It reminded her of the paranormal whispers she was hearing, when she was in the hallway by herself earlier. The laughter is so spine chilling it becomes frightening. Stacie doesn't even want to turn around in her seat at the table and see who's behind her. She, then grabs her seat from the bottom and pushes the chair she's sitting in, up closer to the table. Stacie, lays her head down on the table, closes her eyes, raises her arms and places one hand over each ear. She, then hears a man's voice. The voice is all too familiar to Stacie. The voice of Mr. Elmwood aka Sam… *Principle! Is everything alright? Principle! Was something wrong with the food you just ate? Principle!* Sam places his hand on Stacie's' shoulder the touch causes Stacie's body to jerk. She, then sluggishly removes her hands from over her ears, lifts her head up, opens her eyes and turns slightly to her right. She looks and there's Mr. Elmwood standing on the right side of Stacie holding a bottle of water and a pack of aspirin. As she looks at Sam, Stacie shakes her head side to side with a no so happy grin on her face. She looks at the water bottle and the pack of aspirin he has in his hand.

Mr. Elmwood, I mean Sam. That wasn't very nice mister! That right there was your third strike sir! I'm going to remember that! As a matter of fact, when I meet the wife, I'm going to tell her exactly what you did! And how you almost gave me a heart attack! Stacie, then closes her eyes and takes in a deep stress relieving breath. She opens her eyes and when she does, she can't believe what she is seeing. Mr. Butler is now standing to the right side of her holding in his hand a water bottle and a pack of aspirins. Without hesitation Stacie quickly snatches the water bottle and the aspirins out of Mr. Butlers hand. She then rips the pack of aspirin and dumps both aspirins into her hand, before opening the water bottle. She then pops the two aspirins into her mouth and then takes a sip of water...

Principle Largen! I thought you might need this! I got your phone message, so I decided to come down here personally and keep you company! I also wanted to tell you that, I just ran into Mr. Elmwood and he.... Stacie sarcastically lifts her arm up in the air with all five fingers extended out a few feet away from Mr. Butlers face. Signaling that she wants him to stop talking right now. Stacie, turns around in her seat, looks at the cafeteria's exit and then back at Mr. Butler who is still standing there on her right side with an embarrassing and confused look upon his face. Stacie, balls up a fist, pulls her hand back away from Mr. Butlers face and then lowers her arm... *Mr. Butler, did you just say Mr. Elmwood? Yes, Principle he was here about a half an hour ago! And where is Sam, now?*

Excuse me Principle, Sam! I mean Mr. Elmwood! Oh, he been left the building! He said to tell you that he'll be contacting you later in the week and that he wishes he could of took you up on your offer! What offer, Mr. Butler? Lunch! Principle Largen, Mr. Elmwood said you offered to buy him lunch, but he had another appointment instead! So, therefore he couldn't sit with you this afternoon and have lunch! Stacie, looks across the table from where she's sitting and notices an empty plate, with a corner of a bun from an eaten burger, a few half-eaten French fries, a glass filled with ice, with a little bit of soda left at the bottom and one used napkin... *Mr. Butler, please tell me this was your meal and that you were sitting in that chair across from me, having lunch with me this afternoon here in this cafeteria*? Mr. Butler, looks at Stacie like she's crazy while in the back of his mind he's hoping not to offend her with what he's about to say... *Principle Largen, I'm sorry to disappoint you but I ate my lunch around twelve thirty today, maybe twelve forty-five, no! or was it twelve o'clock on the dot? Anyway! come to think about it, I don't think we ever had lunch together Principle Largen!* Stacie listens to Mr. Butler while deep in thought, she sits there just staring at the empty plate, the ice filled glass and the used napkin in front of her across the table.

I know Principle Largen, I was thinking the same thing! No need to be ashamed, Principle Largen! Sometimes I get so hungry, I order two or even three meals just to satisfy my hunger! Now getting bothered by the sound of Mr. Butlers voice and aggravated that he's not saying what she really wants to hear.

Jumping up from out of her seat Stacie stands in Mr. Butler's face. She now gets the attention of everybody in the cafeteria from the loudness of her yell… *Mr. Butler, I didn't order that meal you idiot*! Mr. Butler looks at the empty seat, the napkin and the plate left on the table. He then slowly turns his head around and looks at the vexed ad irritated expression Stacie now has on her face... *So, you mean to tell me… That's right Mr. It doesn't take a rocket scientist to figure this one out!* Mr. Butler raises his arm and starts scratching the top of his head while looking back and forth at the table and around the cafeteria. Mr. Butler, then shakes his head side to side in awe... *Well I don't mean to be rude Principle, but I'm confused!* Stacie raises both arms up in the air and then quickly lowers them before slapping both of her hands on each side of her hips... *Lord please help this man… You know what Mr. Butler just forget I even mentioned anything about this! Because I will be here all day trying to get you to understand. And you know what else Mr. Butler? Don't knock on my office door when I have a phone call! Please, just call me next time ok?* Stacie, forcefully pushes the chair in at the table, turns around and walks away leaving Mr. Butler standing there humiliated by Stacie's hostile remark and the aggressive reaction. Mr. Butler watches as Stacie walks out of the cafeteria. He then reaches into his pants pocket and takes out his cellphone. Mr. Butler looks at the recent text message left on his cellphones screen…

(Text Message) Mr. Butler! I 'm leaving my office for lunch, I'll be in the school's cafeteria and if you're not doing anything your welcome to join me. Lunch is on me and yes that's an offer. Principle Largen!

OUT OF CONTROL

"When Blinded By The Night, Look Out For Danger In The Light"

THE NO CONTROL

Pulling up into the gas station Stacie, stops at a pump and rolls her driver's side window down halfway, she turns her head to the left and watches as the gas attendant walks up to her driver's side door... *Hello, and what will it be miss? Fifteen dollars premium please! Oh, and sir would you mind checking the oil? Sure thing! And would you like me to clean the windshield as well?* Stacie nods her head up and down agreeing with a humbling smile on her face. She sits patiently in the driver's seat with both of her hands gripped to the steering wheel, as she watches the gas station attendant clean off the left side of her windshield after removing the gas pump and placing it in her car. Stacie, then reaches for the knob on the radio in the car… *Where is the freaking weather station*? Now mumbling to herself while changing the radio station Stacie, gets startled by the gas station attendant who is now knocking on the driver's side window. Stacie, looks at the gas station attendant, reaches for her pocketbook and pulls out her wallet while rolling down the window. She hands the gas station attendant a twenty-dollar bill... *Keep the change!* The gas station attendant looks Stacie directly in the eyes before walking around the front of her car to continue cleaning the other side of her windshield...

Mam! Your all done! With a toothpick sticking out from the corner of his mouth and a baseball cap turned backwards on his head, the gas station attendant yells out loud he removes the gas pump from her car and places it back in the pump. He then taps on the hood of Stacie's car while walking towards the front entrance of the gas station dressed in an oil stained navy-blue overall jump suit that has his name stitched on the front, with a dirty rag hanging out the right side of his back pocket. And just as Stacie, is about to pull off and out of the gas station a pale face teenage boy with a dark and creepy presence about him dressed in all black rides his bike directly in front of Stacie's car.

The boy drops the bike and stands there with troubled interest written all over his face Stacie, quickly steps on the breaks the car stops immediately, causing her body to jerk back and forth in the driver's seat. Her face is showing anxiety and discomfort, her jaws drop, and both of her hands tightly grip the steering wheel. The teenage boy stops the bike and drops one leg to the ground, he then stands there and stares at her with a messenger bag over his shoulder. His eyes the color of night and his demeanor is frightening with a look that can kill. Stacie is speechless as she looks around the gas station hoping to see the gas station attendant who just helped her or anyone who might be willing to come to her rescue but there's nowhere in sight. Stacie takes a swallow of air afraid as her grip on the steering wheel tightens.

Now silently praying to herself that she makes it out of the gas station alive and in one-piece Stacie, puts the vehicle in drive, the boy reaches into his messenger and pulls out a newspaper. Stacie eases her foot off the gas pedal and slowly lowers down in the driver's seat she closes her eyes real tight, she opens her eyes after a few seconds and starts repeatedly beeping the horn hoping the loud sound of the cars horn scares the boy away, but it doesn't. The unafraid boy who is dressed in all black just stands there, looking at Stacie with everything but good intentions. Stacie starts panicking the boy drops his bike to the ground in front of Stacie's car, he walks over to the driver's side window. The boy reaches inside the messenger bag and takes out a newspaper, he extends his arm out and taps the newspaper on the window. Stacie looks at the boy before checking again to see if all her car doors are locked. She looks at the newspaper, turns around in her seat and looks around the gas station, she turns back around and rolls down the driver's side window inches from the top just enough for the newspaper to fit through. The boy standing there pushes the newspaper inside the window, the newspaper drops down into Stacie's lap, she looks at the newspaper and then at the boy one more time before quickly rolling the driver's side window back up. The boy walks back around to the front of the car, picks up his bike, adjust his messenger bag over his shoulder, looks at Stacie one more time before riding off. Stacie quickly steps down on the pedal causing the vehicle to speed off like a bat out of hell.

The cars back tires are burning rubber, leaving a thick cloud of smoke in the air behind. She then makes a right turn, then another right, then a left she drives until she is far away from the gas station as possible. Stacie, pulls over to the curb breathing heavy, thinking about what just happened, she then places her right hand over her heart while pounding her left fist several times on the steering wheel. Now with her head down in her lap and both of her hands interlocked across the top of her head Stacie, lifts her head up and starts tapping her foot on the gas pedal. Then out of fear and panic she aggressively and violently steps on the gas pedal again this time as hard as she could. Thick heavy black smoke starts rising from the back tires up in the air covering the back window, with her eyes locked in on the road ahead Stacie, tries turning the cars steering wheel to the right but the tires goes left, the car is now out of her control she freaks out.

And out of nowhere, she gets hits from behind by a 16-wheeler truck the trucks impact pushes the entire car right over the divider and into the oncoming traffic. Her forehead hits the windshield, snapping her head and neck back, she lets go of the steering wheel her arms drops down by her side. The car starts spinning around doing a 360, the car stops spinning now facing oncoming traffic Stacie, lifts her head up and looks in the rear-view mirror. She's frightened by the sight of all the blood running down her face from the cut on her forehead from her head hitting the windshield. Then suddenly Smash!

Glass flies everywhere Stacie, collides head on with several cars driving towards her. The side of her head hits the driver's side window, her legs gets pinned by the driver's side door being pushed in, the front of Stacie's car gets demolished Stacie is knocked unconscious. With smoke and fire bursting into the air from vehicles involved in the accident a domino effect of accidents is triggered on the road. Gas and flames from different vehicles involved begin setting fire to other vehicles within its reach leaving passengers and drivers, men woman and children to bail out of their cars and run for cover. Stacie was in a terrible condition she was not only unconscious she had third degree burns all over her body, it was nothing less than a miracle she had survived.

Mr. and Mrs. Largen finally receive the phone call about their daughters devastating and injurious accident on the phone, the doctors told them that there had been an emergency and they needed to get to the hospital as soon as possible. So, Mr. and Mrs. Largen informed the rest of the family, the family rushes to the hospital where Stacie was being kept.

IT'S AN EMERGENCY

"Grief Can Be Deceiving, But The Pain Is Extremely For Real"

THE EMERGENCY

At the hospital the nurses, doctors and police all share information to the Largen family about the accident, the police that was on the scene of the accident informed the family that there were no personal items recovered from the accident, everything was destroyed from the car's flames. Stacie was not recognizable her eyes were closed, and she was breathing through a machine and needed brain surgery, So, the family stands by the hospital bed, she was lying in quiet shedding tears, holding hands and praying silently. Very depression and sad Stacie's brother Mark leaves the hospital and walks towards the parking lot where the family has parked their cars. Mark, then notice something on the windshield underneath the windshield wipers so he lifts the windshield wiper and picks up what seems to be an old newspaper wrapped in a black rubber band. Mark pops the rubber band off and unfolds the newspaper, he stares at the front page and what he is now seeing is not only shocking, but it surprised him as well. Mark had heard about this strange and mysterious newspaper but never had the opportunity to see it himself, now with THE JOURNAL in his possession Mark, without hesitation starts reading what's on the front page. He, then focuses his attention on the picture in full detail, the picture is devastating to the eye there's a picture of a several car accidents.

Not believing what he is seeing Mark sits down on the curb because the accident in the picture is the one his sister Stacie, was just in and the proof the family was looking for was right there. The picture that was taken was showing Stacie's body getting pulled out from her car's wreckage, her clothes were burned, and her body seemed lifeless. Blood was everywhere but what really was interesting to Mark, was that standing on the side behind Stacie's car in the middle of the street was his brother Edward. And standing right next to Edward was the teenage boy dressed in all black on a bicycle. Both was staring directly at whoever took the picture which made the picture even creepier because to Mark, it looked like his brother Edward and the teenage boy was starring right back at him.

And underneath the picture it says . . .

"On this day, a terrible accident happened in which a schoolteacher was killed, Ms. Stacie Largen. While on her way home from work, she was driving onto incoming traffic and unfortunately, she had a head on collision with several unknown vehicles driving in her direction. With the loss of Ms. Largen was the lives taken of Mr. and Mrs. Elmwood included was also a few others whose lives has been cheated by death!"

Mark outraged by the news especially after he just saw his sister and knows for a fact that she's still alive, she's badly injured but alive. Mark walks over to the trash can and stuffs the newspaper in as far as it will go. He then turns around in disbelief, and right before his eyes not even a couple feet away Mark, finds himself staring right into the eyes of the teenage boy who's dressed in all black. The boy's bike is in shambles, the tires are all flat, the rims are all twisted, the bikes chain is broken up and the boy is dragging the bike on the ground. His eyes are red, his face is scrapped with multiple scratches and bruises, he's bleeding from his head and there's a burnt rubber tire smell lingering from his body. The boy lifts his arm up in the air and holds up a THE€ JOURNAL the sight of the newspaper causes Mark to stumble back a few feet away from the boy after making eye contact and realizing what the boy is holding up in the air. Mark is petrified, fear takes control off balance Mark trips and falls to the ground the boy stands over him as Mark, looks up at the boy from the ground. The boy looks down at Mark and as the parking lot gets quiet the boy mumbles out TH€ JOURNAL! While lying on the ground Mark looks at the boys mangled up bike and then at the fire in the boy's eyes. The boy reaches his arm out towards Mark and hands him a newspaper. Mark extends out his arm and grabs TH€ JOURNAL his hand is shaking, his eyes widen with fear, then a voice can be heard calling out Marks name. Mark leans up and looks in the direction where the voice is coming from!... *Mark! Where are you? I have some good news, to tell you about Stacie! …*

After identifying the voice Mark, closes his eyes for a few seconds, but it's really been several hours that Mark has been in the hospitals parking lot. He finally opens both of his eyes and notices that the teenage boy, with the mangled-up bicycle has vanished. The burnt rubber tire smell is gone so Mark, slowly gets up off the ground with the newspaper still in his hand. He looks around and sees his sister Tara, who's crying, with her head in the arms of her brother Edward, Mrs. Largen is also crying while Mr. Largen slowly walks behind them a few get away. Shaking his head side to side Mr. Largen looks at Tara, Edward and his wife and can see nothing but worry all in their faces. They hold on to each other as they walk towards Tara's car Tara, has a look on her face like someone just died. Edwards wife hugs Tara before she walks over to her husband Edward, they both get inside the back seat of Mr. Largen s car. Once Mr. and Mrs. Largen, Edward and his wife are inside Tara, looks at Marks who is now standing up holding on to TH€ JOURNAL. He has a ridiculous expression on his face signaling that he has no idea what has happened but in the ack of his mind he's imagining that whatever it is it has something to do with his sister Stacie. Tara, opens the driver's side car door to her car and gets in Mark, walks around to the passenger side of the car, opens the door and gets in. Not saying a word Tara, watches her Father Mr. Largen pull off and drives towards the exit of the hospitals parking lot. Tara puts her car in drive, steps on the gas and follows Mr. Largen out the hospitals parking lot...

Mark! Why are you acting so strange? You look like you've seen a ghost! Mark looks at his sister Tara through the corner of his eye... *A ghost you say. You wouldn't believe me if I told you Sis! Try me! I might be your little sister but believe me I've experienced some big things in my life! And after tonight I don't think nothing will surprise me! Especially after this loss in the family*! Mark turns all the way around to his left in the passenger seat disturbed and troubled by what his sister Tara just said... *Hold up! What a minute! Tara, did you just say loss in the family?* Tara quickly looks at Mark with a frown on her face, she then wipes a tear from her eye before looking at the back of Mr. Largens car ahead of her. Tara, then bangs her fist on the steering wheel out of anger and rage... *Mark! Are you serious? You mean to tell all this time you didn't know? Oh, that's right you were too busy in the parking lot reading that stupid looking newspaper to be concerned about what has happened to you, I mean our sister! You disgust me right now Mark! That's just pitiful! And to think you were her favorite!* Puzzled Mark looks in the rear mirror and then through the passenger side window at the cars driving pass. *So! Tara, is Stacie going to be Ok?* Tara closes both her eyes and shakes her head side to side ashamed and furious at the same time. She opens her eyes looks back at Mark and screams… *Mark! Stacie isn't going to make it! Our big sister is going to die!* Getting closer to Edward and his wife's home Mr. Largen, slows down as they come to a red traffic light. Edward leans in from the back seat and puts his hand on Mr. Largens shoulder…

You can drop us off home! The kids should be asleep by now and the babysitter! I know she must be ready to leave. Edward, leans back and grabs his wife hand while his wife embraces, the sincere comfort from her husband as she places her arm around his waist, showing him affection as well. Mr. Largen makes a left turn and pulls up in the driveway of Edward and his wife's home, while Tara who is not too far behind them double parks her car in front of Edward and his wife's driveway. The lights in one of the rooms downstairs turns on inside their home... *Baby! Look, the lights in the living room are on! I see, either the kids are up, or the babysitter is downstairs watching television!* Mrs. Largen turns around in the passenger seat and frowns at Edward and his wife... *Those kids better not still be up this time of night! You tell that babysitter...Mother! Mother! It's certainly alright! Ann is a great babysitter she's been babysitting our kids since they were in diapers! No need to worry! Yes! Mrs. Largen your grand kids are in good hands, trust us! We know how you feel about those kids*! Mrs. Largen starts smiling at the remarks from her son and his wife... *Well then, no need to worry, I guess! You two get inside and give my grandchildren a big hug and kiss for me and their grandpa! Ok! Take care now and call me first thing in the mourning!* Mr. Largen shakes his head up and down while looking at Edward through the rear-view mirror. Edward, kisses his Mother on the cheek, taps his Father on the shoulder, opens the back-seat passenger side door behind Mr. Largen, closes the door walks around the back of the car.

He opens the back-seat passenger side door behind Mrs. Largen and helps his wife get out the car. Edward closes the door behind her, Edwards takes a few steps back and then waves goodbye to Mr. and Mrs. Largen while Edward walks down the driveway to his sister Tara's car whose double parked in front of his house. Mark sees his Brother Edwards walking towards then so, he opens the car door, gets out and leans on the car with the passenger door wide open. Edward walks up to Mark and grabs him by the neck, Edward pulls Mark closer to him and whispers in his ear… *Keep an eye out on your Sister, because something bizarre and weird has been happening lately! I can't explain it right now but be careful! You hear me little Bro? I love you!* Mark head slightly jerks back, shocked and speechless at what he his Brother just whispered in his ear, alarmed his eyes widen with concern. Edward, let's go of Marks neck, leans down inside Tara's car and kisses her on the cheek... *Love you Sis!* Tara looks at Edward and smiles. *I love you more, big Bro.!* Edward leans back up out the car and stands up, he looks at Mark one last time before walking back up the driveway towards his front door. He leans his head down and waves goodbye to his parents as Mr. Largen slowly backs out the driveway. Mark gets back inside Tara's car and closes the passenger side door shut. Tara, then puts the car in reverse. She backs the car up just enough to let Mr. Largen out the driveway once Mr. Largen has the car back on the street him and Tara drive off headed home...

I know you're not going to tell me, but what exactly did Edward say to you back there Mark? I mean it's none of my business but whatever he said to you, really had you speechless! Mark, scratches his head, looks out the passenger side window before turning to his left and looking at his Sister Tara... *Don't tell me then! I know it's a Brothers thing, right? Yea! That's right! Just like you females and your little secrets! Come on Tara! I know how you and Stacie…*Tara, punches Mark in the shoulder before he could continue what he was about to say... *Mark! Don't talk about my Sister Stacie! Your Sister! She my Sister too! Well, you sure wasn't too concerned about your Sister at the hospital, were you? Remember our sister just died Mark! And, where were you? Too busy in the parking lot reading some stupid newspaper! Was that newspaper more important than Stacie? Huh Mark! Tell me what was so important about the newspaper that made you leave your Sister Stacie right before her death?* Tara starts crying she looks at Mark he looks back at her, then Mark starts feeling embarrassment and ashamed so, he takes in a deep breath and exhales before shedding a tear and breaking down... *Ok! Ok! Edward was taking about you Tara Ok!* Tara looks at the road ahead and then back at Mark... *About me! What could he possibly be whispering to you about me? Well! What did he say? He told me to look out for you! What! Are you serious? For What? It's kind of hard to explain, being that I think it has something to do with the newspaper I was reading in the hospitals parking lot!*

Mark looks at Tara, she's not saying a word the quietness in the car spells trouble Tara, hands tighten on the steering wheel, she tries not to look at Mark who is now wiping a tear from his eye... *Did you say it might have something to do with a newspaper? Yea Tara! That's exactly what I said! And what kind of newspaper are we talking about here? I don't understand what you mean Tara! What I am trying to say Mark is, what is the name of this newspaper?*

Mark waits a few seconds before leaning forward and reaching down under the passenger seat. He, then picks up the newspaper from off the floor, holds it up in front of him and points to the top of the front page... *It's called THE JOURNAL!* Tara quickly losses control of the car after hearing the name of the newspaper. The car serves to the right and then to the left, Mark drops THE JOURNAL in his lap, grabs the steering wheel with one hand trying to help Tara gain back control of the car. While other vehicles driving alongside and behind Tara's car start blowing their car horns at the sight of Tara out of control car. Tara gets back control of her car as she pulls up behind her parents Mr. and Mrs. Largen as they drive up into their driveway at home. Tara puts the car in park and looks at her Brother Mark who is already opening up the passenger side door. Mark, slams the passenger side door shut, walks over to the front of the house and lets himself in leaving the front door wide open. Mr. Largen who is standing there holding the passenger door open to his car, waiting for Mrs. Largen to step out.

Mr. Largen looks at Tara who is now closing the driver's side door. Darling! Is everything alright? Everything's fine dad! Mr. Largen grabs his wife's hand and helps her safely out the car. Mrs. Largen looks at Tara as she walks towards the front of the house... *Honey! What do you think could be wrong with the kids? It's probably Stacie! Remember darling this is just the beginning of our family's problems! This process is going to take some time! For heaven's sake were talking about our daughter here! She needs brain surgery! And we don't have that kind of money or insurance to cover the operation! God dam it!...*

Mrs. Largen starts crying, as she walks towards the front of the house, while Mr. Largen slams the passenger side door shut. And stands there for a moment, with his head down and his car keys jingling in his hand, before walking inside the house.

DRINKS ON THE HOUSE

"When Lies Sober You Up, And The Truth Gets You Intoxicated"

THE BAR

In the kitchen Mr. Largen opens the refrigerator door and takes out a cold beer. He, then closes the refrigerator door, open the beer, walks into the living room sits down and relaxes himself comfortably in his recliner in front of the television. Mrs. Largen has a broom in her hand sweeping the floor, she puts the broom down and walks over to where Mr. Largen is sitting taking sips of his beer. Mrs. Largen removes the beer out of Mr. Largens hand and places it on the coffee table, she then sits herself down on her husband's lap. While their son Mark, is in his bedroom looking out the window thinking about his sister Stacie and what his Brother Edward said to him earlier. And how the surgery his Sister badly needs, is affecting the whole family so, Mark, questions himself about everything that has happened, trying his best to put the pieces together, about what his big brother Edward, was really trying to say. But he couldn't, the thought alone was clouding his judgement and his way of thinking was becoming irrational. Mark drops his head in guilt, like it was his fault his Sister was in the hospital, breathing from a machine, he walks over to the dresser in is room and grabs his book of poems. He, opens the book, turns the pages and finds a poem that's suitable and appropriate to the situation at hand, Mark starts reading …

Life

What if we could experience all tragedies, without a single lost, would we all be just signatures signing each other's fate, would the world be filled with less love, and more and more hate. Think we can rub shoulders together in harmony, with all of mankind, while searching for the truth within ourselves, even though our ways and action, are blind. This choice of survival, has a bitter and untasteful sacrifice so, in order to live in peace, sometimes our tongue we need to bite, because the powerful words you speak, can multiply and give, or subtract from one's Life...

Mrs. Largen kisses her husband on the cheek before getting up off his lap and headed to the bathroom to freshen up before going into the kitchen to start preparing tonight's dinner. Mr. Largen leans forward and grabs the remote control from off the coffee table, he then turns the television on and changes channels as he sits there thinking about his daughter Stacie and how the family, will never be the same again, if she didn't return in their life. Mr. Largen takes another sip of the beer he has in his hand and continues turning the channels on the television.

Then suddenly, a breaking news flash interrupts all the aired programs so, Mr. Largen turns the television volume up, drops the remote control in his lap, leans forward in the recliner and pays close attention to the news reporter after the words breaking news flashes across the television screen…

(Breaking News! Breaking News) …

Good afternoon, I am Charles Peterson filling in for Debra Jenkins with K12 News and this just in, across the state of New Jersey there has been a trace of unexplained incidents involving people everywhere. There are no leads as to what is causing these unexplained incidents, but sources say it is what people are calling "Mysterious!" No one has been apprehended in the involvement, but the police say they are not going to stop until they find out who or what is behind this! Stay tuned for more updates at Ten on K12 News the channel that gives you Views on News! Now Back To The Previous Scheduled Program!

Now picking up the remote-control Mr. Largen, turns the television volume down... *What's Next? If it isn't one thing it's another, am I right pops?* Mr. Largen turns around in his recliner and sees his son Mark walking into the living room. With a book in his hand... *Son! Pops! You finish with that beer? Need me to throw it away for you?* Mr. Largen takes another sip of his beer, before handing the empty beer bottle to Mark... *Thank-you son!* Mark grabs the empty beer bottle from his Father and tosses it in the trash before sitting back down on the couch...

And your right Son! If it isn't one thing, it's another! What are we going to do about it? That's life! We have no other choice but to live with the worlds self-destruction! Just don't become part of helping it son, or you might self-destruct as well! You hear me? Mark, looks at his Father and shakes his head up and down, signaling that he fully understands what his Father is trying to say. In the kitchen and opening the refrigerator door Mark, looks around inside the refrigerator for something to snack on before dinner. He then closes the refrigerator door, opens the cabinet and grabs an unopen bag of potato chips from off the shelf. Mark, hops on top of the kitchen counter, opens the bag of potato chips and starts eating them. He then notices a strange, unfamiliar magnet that's stuck to the side of the refrigerator, Mark leans forward and squints his eyes to try and get a better look. He hops down off the kitchen counter with the open bag of potato chips still in his hand and walks over closer to the side of the refrigerator and looks at the unfamiliar magnet. Mark reaches out with his right hand and removes the magnet from off the side of the refrigerator. He holds the magnet up in front of him, his eyes widen, he then reads the phone number quietly to himself that's written on the front of the refrigerator magnet…

"1- 800-THE JOURNAL"!

With a frown now on his face Mark, seems confused by what he's seeing. So, he turns around and leans his back against the side of the refrigerator, while still holding the magnet up in the air in front of him… *Now why do I get the feeling, that I heard about this place before?*

Mark, puts the magnet in his pants pocket, leans up off the refrigerator, closes the open bag of potato chips, puts the potato chips back in the above cabinet, closes the cabinet door and walks out of the kitchen. Now back in the living room where Marks Father Mr. Largen is still watching the television Mark, sits down on the couch and leans his head back on the couch while closing both of his eyes. Mark, starts thinking to himself about his family's behavior lately he, lifts his head up, opens his eyes, looks at his Father one more time before deciding that maybe he should leave the house and go to the bar to have a few drinks. Mark hops up off the couch and heads for the front door Mr. Largen looks at his son and shakes his head side to side signaling disapproval of what Mark is now doing… *Son! You know dinner will be ready in about another two hours!* Mark, grabs the door handle, opens the door, turns around and looks back at his Father... *Pops! I'm good, I'll probably grab something while I'm out! Tell Ma, I will be back soon love you!* The front door slams shut; the sound causes Mrs. Largen to walk out of the bathroom... *Honey! Who just left out of the house? You know! That crazy son of yours Mark! Don't say that! Well! Did he say where he was going? And does he know, that dinner will be ready soon?*

Mr. largen turns around in his recliner and looks at Mrs. Largen who is now standing by the kitchen holding two oven mittens in her hand… *Who knows! He's probably headed over to some girl's house! Well! I hope he's back in time for dinner*! Mr. Largen turns back around and mumbles to himself… *Miss. Largen! Your son is crazy!* Mrs. Largen then turns around and walks into the kitchen to start preparing dinner, while Mr. Largen leans back in the recliner and continues watching the television. At the bar Mark finds a table in the corner, the light is dimmed down low above him, the atmosphere is gloomy and there's a lady and a man at the bars counter having rounds of shots back to back. The song "A Broken Heart" by Gladys Knight can be heard playing throughout the bar from an old fifties juke box posted up against the wall by the bars entrance. The bars waitress sees' Mark so, she walks over to him with a pen and pad in her hand, chewing on a piece of gum... *Hello handsome! What can I get you drink? I'll have two double shots of vodka, no ice and a Heineken! Ok! That's two shots of vodka, no ice and one Heineken coming right up! Smile baby! You look like you just lost your best friend!* Mark looks at the waitress and smiles, the waitress smiles back at Mark before turning around and walking back to bars counter. A few minutes later the gun chewing waitress returns with Marks drinks, the waitress sits down the two double shots of vodka and two bottles Heinekens beers on the table in front of him...

Excuse me waitress! Oh! Please call me Lauren! Well! Lauren, I only ordered one beer! The waitress then leans over the table... *Baby! Don't worry about it, this one on me!* The waitress reaches her arm out and touches Mark on the chin with her hand Mark, looks at the waitress like he knows exactly what's going on, the waitress turns around and walks away. After about a half an hour Mark, finishes the drinks he has in front of him on the table. Mark flags the waitress down and orders another round and then another. He lifts his right arm up and looks at his watch he has on his wrist, Mark see's that it's getting late and time is flying by. It's been three hours Mark has been sitting in the bar, Mark looks at the bartender, the bartender looks back at Mark while wiping down the bars countertop with an old dirty, ripped up dish rag he has in his hand. Lauren, the waitress is cleaning off empty and half full beer bottles and shot glasses from off the tables in the bar. The song then changes on the jukebox and the song "Just My Imagination" by The Temptations starts playing...

(Jukebox) "Just my imagination / Running away with me"

The woman who was sitting at the bar gets up and stumbles while putting on her jacket… *Good night everybody!*

She then turns to her left and looks at the gentleman that's with her. The man gets up from the bar stool and starts singing over the music playing from the juke box, while trying to help the woman he's with put on her jacket...

(Man Singing) "Running away with me! It was just my imagination, running away with me"!

The sound of the man's voice is off key and very annoying to Mark, the waitress and the bartender. Mark, then takes a sip of his beer, looks at the man who's still singing and shakes his head side to side signaling that the singing that the man is doing is terrible. The woman puts on her jacket and starts dancing to the music, she looks at the man that's with her and then at the bartender, the bartender continues wiping down the bar counter while looking back at the drunk man and woman... *Mam! Are you Ok? We are about to close in about 15 minutes!* The woman tries to take a step forward and stumbles into the stools at the bar, the man she's with grabs her by the waist and stands her back up before slowly walking himself and her to the exit of the bar. The woman stops and turns around at the doors exit, her mouth opens and for a few seconds, but she says nothing, she then places her hand on the shoulder of the man she's with... *I am just fine how about a drink on the house Mr. Bartender?*

Standing by where Mark is sitting at the table, the waitress laughs at the remark and picks up the half-full drinks Mark has left unfinished. She turns around and start walking towards the bar. She looks at the man and woman and then at the bartender who is now walking around the bar and towards the man and woman… *Ok! You two are done here! I'll see the both of you tomorrow! I think you had enough Miss!*

The bartender stands there at the doors exit and watches as the drunk man and the woman stumble together out the bar and walk on down the street. The waitress then walks over to the bartender and stands by his side... *Do you think they will be ok tonight?* The bartender turns to his left and looks the waitress dead in the face. *Of course! She only lives a few blocks from here and where do you think he's going tonight? And plus, neither one of them has a car so, they will be just fine!* The waitress looks at the bartender and inhales a deep breath. She, exhales and wipes her forehead with her hand. *Oh, Thank God! I just didn't want to imagine that picture in my head! What picture is that? The picture of the two of them on the front page of tomorrows newspaper!* The bartender shakes his head up and down signaling that he agrees with what the waitress just said. Then both turns away from the doors exit and walks back over to the bar. Sitting at the table feeling the shots of vodka and beers he's been drinking half the night; Mark slides the beer bottle he has in his hand away from him to the middle of the table. He rubs his face with both of his hands before lifting his head up and sliding back in the seat. Mark looks around the bar and notices two dark and gloomy looking people sitting way over on the other side of the bar, directly across from his table in a shadowy and blurred corner. So, he rubs his eyes before flattening out both of his hands and placing them in front of him on the table. With both of his hands on the table Mark leans forward and looks over at the two-people sitting there.

Mark looks for the bartender and the waitress, but they are nowhere in sight, Mark see's that there's no one else in the bar either, except the two dark and gloomy looking people and himself. The temperature in the bar drops rapidly, it gets cold, the lights in the bar start flickering, Mark can now see his breath lingering in the air every time he breathes, the music in the jukebox playing stops. Mark grabs the half full beer bottle from the middle of the table and out of fear and concern, he lifts the beer bottle and drinks the rest of the beer. Mark gets ready to sit the beer bottle back on the table but with his worrying attention focusing on the faces of the two-unfamiliar people sitting in the shadowy and blurred corner across from him. Mark misses the table and drops the beer bottle; the beer bottle smashes on the floor causing the two-people sitting at the table across from him in the corner to stand up. With fear pounding in his heart and concern flowing through his veins Mark, swallows some distressed air as a knot forms in his throat, he slowly gets up and stands there next to the table. Mark looks at the jukebox and then at the lights on the ceiling and then back at the two people who is now walking over towards him. Still not being able to make out the two-people faces Mark, just stands there rocking back and forth not realizing that he's had a little too much to drink. So, he puts his head down and closes both of his eyes while both of his hands again are placed flat on the table. Mark, lifts his head, opens both of his eyes and sees a man and an old lady who are both dressed in all black standing in front of him on the other side of the table where he's standing.

Out of shock Mark, takes a step back knocking over the seat behind him and then something catches his attention again as he looks down at what the old lady is holding in her hand. It's something that Mark has seen before, something that caused him to not be there by his sister's side when she died at the hospital, something that was kind of too familiar to Mark.

This was something that Mark thought was wicked and corrupt the first time he laid eyes on it, but even with that in mind Mark knew, that he couldn't reveal what and how he was thinking. Because not only would his family think that something was wrong with him, but the rest of the world would consider it as well and the last thing Mark wanted was for the rest of the world, to consider him to be crazy, insane and deranged. Mark. Just knew his sister Tara would haunt him with that for the rest of his and her life. So, to play it safe Mark, decided that it was best that he just kept his beyond belief secret feelings and emotions to himself. And before he thought about anything else Mark, realized that he had to deal with the mysterious looking man and the old lady who was still standing there in front of him dressed in all black, looking like something straight out of a Jordan Peele movie. And right now, Mark was thinking silently to himself about, how it must feel, to be that one person in the movie who always gets injured or killed first.

Before the storyline and narrative of the movie even begins and the thought alone was scary, the old lady then looks at the man standing next to her, he looks back at her, then they both look back at Mark. The old lady raises her arm up in the air with a newspaper clinched to her fingers in her hand. The old lady extends out the newspaper and touches Mark in the chest with it. Mark is speechless he eyes widen and his hands starts trembling, his toes curl up in in his shoes and a trickle of sweat starts running down the side of his face. Mark, stumbles off balance from the sight of what's going on, he's confused and in doubt about what to do so, he lifts his right hand up off the table and raises his arm. With no judgement or self-conscious Mark, grabs the newspaper from out of the old lady's hand and without looking at the newspaper Mark, looks directly into the eyes of the old lady. Her eyes the color of brimstone, her face pale and wrinkled, her finger nails the color of night. You can hear a pin drop in the bar, the jukebox continues playing, the temperature drops even more and the lights in the bar are still flickering as Mark stands there speechless with a look of fear and concern all over his face. Then suddenly, the bar goes pitch black. Mark, stumbles backwards reaching around trying to find his seat. He, drops the newspaper onto the table, bends down and reaches around for the chair. Mark, finds the chair, picks it up, pulls the chair closer behind him and sits down. Not being able to see anything in the bar Mark, closes both of his eyes and for about two to three minutes the bar goes completely and totally silent.

Mark rubs his hands together before raising them up to his mouth and blowing inside his palms to try and warm both of his hands. Then after a few seconds immediately the lights in the bar turns back on, the temperature goes back up to normal, the jukebox turns on and starts playing the song again from earlier by The Temptations…

(Music) "Just my imagination / Running, away with me" …

Mark opens his eyes and standing there in front of him is the bars waitress. She's holding a tray with both of her hands; she lays the tray down on the table where Mark is sitting and removes two double shots of vodka with no ice and two Heineken beers. Mark frowns his face up in confusion at the waitress he then leans his head to the side and looks around the waitress at the bar and there he sees a woman who appears to be drunk standing up dancing to the music playing on the jukebox. While the man she's with is singing the words out loud to the song while taking sips of his drink, the bartender is wiping down the bars countertop with an old ripped up dirty looking rag. So, Mark leans back in the chair at the table… *I'm sorry Miss but did I…*The waitress reaches her arm out, grabs one of the beers and pushes the beer closer to Mark before he could finish what he was saying. The waitress looks Mark in the face and smiles…

Baby! Don't worry about it, this one on me!

The waitress then touches Mark on the chin with her hand Mark, smiles while looking at the waitress surprised but at the same time, he's enjoying the direct and honest approach of how the waitress is flirting with him. Mark is acting like he's not excited but deep down inside he's enjoying every minute and knows exactly she's doing. Mark takes a sip of the beer as the waitress picks up the tray and gets ready to turn around and walk away.... *Thank-you Lauren! I really appreciate it*! The waitress stops in her tracks before quickly turning back around. She, stares Mark dead in the face before looking back at the bartender she turns back around and looks back at Mark who's sitting there confused while taking back to back light sips of his beer. The expression on waitress face is destroying Marks mood, the waitress then places the tray back down on the table where Mark is sitting. She, leans forward over the table, raises her arm and puts one finger up signaling Mark not to say another word. Mark respectfully puts the beer bottle down on the table and looks the waitress in her eyes...

I'm sorry Lauren! But did I do or say something wrong? No! You didn't do anything Mister! Then why the harmful looks and all of the sudden negative attitude?

The waitress puts her finger down and balls both of her hands up into a fist and places them on the table... *Mister! I just want to know one thing! Sure! What is it? How in the world, do you know that my name is Lauren?*

Marks, head slightly jerks back, one side of his mouth twist up, he grabs the beer bottle in front of him on the table and slides it back and forth, side to side while it's tightly grasped in his hand. Then a voice can be heard yelling over the jukebox music… *Enough already with the flirting over there! Let's get back to work! We got customers to serve! You hear me?* The waitress turns around and looks at her boss who so happens to be the bartender, who's standing behind the bars counter with both arms in the air holding in one hand a dirty old, ripped up dish rag… *Ok! Ok! Hold your horses! Who didn't sleep with you last night? Dam! Whatever! Just get back to work alright.* The waitress turns back around and looks at Mark, who is now tossing back one of the double shots of vodka he has in front of him...

We'll finish this later Mister! Mark shakes his head up and down signaling to the waitress that he understands clearly, the waitress picks the tray back up off the table… *Oh! And Mister! You dropped something!* Mark looks down by his side and sees a newspaper lying there on the floor wrapped in a black rubber band by his foot. Mark looks back up at the waitress, the waitress winks her eye at Mark, before she turns all the way around and walks towards the bar, while holding the tray with one hand down by her side. Mark bends down and picks up the newspaper, he places the newspaper on the table in front of him and stares at the black rubber band that's wrapped around the newspaper.

Grabbing the other double shot of vodka Mark tosses it back, slams the shot glass on the table and picks up the newspaper. Mark, pops the rubber band off, unfolds the newspaper and reads the headline and then the paragraph printed underneath the headline on the front page… *TH€ JOURNAL! …*

Today we're featuring a Poem entitled Drinks! By world renown Poet Sam. Elmwood!

(Mark Reading) …

House

When lies and the truth becomes part of the plan, make sure you're not getting intoxicated, by some creepy sober hand. And be aware of your surroundings, when in dark places that has a lot of sound, because some don't make it home, when receiving drinks, round after round.

Not everyone is polite, and well-mannered in front of your eyes, especially if their pupils are dark as midnight, and they keep sneaking up on you by surprise. And never take for granted, whatever the situation appears to be, because your imagination can be sober, at the same time your mind, was getting intoxicated for free.

It's not going to take a much, for you to fall down, once you've stepped inside that eerie room. And it' goings to take a lot, for you to get you back up, once you've fallen from a cursed life so soon.

So, don't get become speechless and walk around with an open mouth, just remember nothing in life will be, especially when strangers dressed in black, are all up in your house.

By Sam Elmwood

<u>THE FALSE BELIEVER</u>

"When The Truth, And The Lies Are The Same"

THE INFORMATION

Hold on for just a moment while I transfer you to a representative that can help you... *"To inquire what most people won't, just subscribe here to THE JOURNAL!"* An automated machine on the other end of Mark's cellphone repeats itself while elevator music plays in the background. Patiently Mark, sits on the edge of his bed watching a black screen on the television in his room. Mark gets up walks over to the window and moves the blinds covering the window to the side. He looks at the traffic in the street and the people who are up and about early this morning commuting back and forth to work...*"To inquire what most people won't, just subscribe here to THE JOURNAL!" ... Oh, my goodness! For the hundredth time, already!* Becoming entirely impatient Mark, picks up the remote control and turns the television on, he puts his cellphone on speaker before lying the cellphone down on the bed. The television comes on and there's a news reporter standing by a bar... *No! This can't be! I don't believe this!* Angry and in disbelief at what he's seeing on the television screen Mark, turns the volume up. He, then hears the voice of a woman who's shouting at the top of her lungs at the news reporter who's just standing there with a microphone in his hand. The woman's behavior is hysterical, she has her hand in the news reporters face right on the television, the news reporter tries to back away, but the woman follows his every move.

The police suddenly walk up on the scene and grab the woman by her arms as she tries fighting them back. The police lift the woman up a few inches off her feet into the air, they then carry the woman over to a parked police vehicle, that's parked a few feet away from where the news reporter was originally standing. Mark stands up and turns the volume up on the television more…

(News)

"This just in!... This is the second tragedy this week and it seems to be connected to the schoolteacher who is still in the hospital, breathing from a machine needing brain surgery! A few days ago, she was in a car accident, her name is Stacie Largen, and the young man possible in his early twenties, who was recently found dead outside of a bar last night, is her brother Mark Largen! Hold on! I'm hearing that there are no witnesses! But what was found in his possession was a book, that's right ladies and gentlemen a book.

The news reporter raises his arm that he's holding the microphone with and adjust the small speaker he has pinned in his ear...

Hold on! I'm getting word!... Ok! Their telling me that this is the picture of the young man, who was found dead this morning lying on the ground, in front of the bar, I am standing in front the bar right now!... Ok! Yes!... Mark Largen was found lying in the street, right here at approximately five am this Morning.

With what police describe as an unknown tragedy, there saying the cause of death is unknown and there are no witnesses!... Mark's face appears on the television screen in the top right corner... *I don't believe this! What is this, some kind of joke or prank? I'm not dead you idiots! I'm right here! I'm right here!* Angry and confused at what he's seeing Mark, changes channels on the television and on every other channel, the news reports are about him with a picture of him in the top right corner. Behind his picture on every channel their showing the bar, the bar Mark was in the past night. Mark, is furious his temper turns violent causing him to slam the remote control down on the floor he, picks up his cellphone that's lying on the bed and runs out the bedroom towards the stairs. Mark, rushes down the stairs, jumping oversteps headed towards the front door. Then suddenly, Marks cellphone rings!... *(Ringing)* With one hand on the doorknob and his other hand holding his cellphone Mark, stops by the front door and pauses for a moment. He looks down at his cellphone he has in his hand. The cellphone rings again... *(Ringing)* Mark, closes the front door and makes his way back up the stairs to his room, the cellphone rings again... *(Ringing)* Mark, takes a deep breath balls his fist up and walks inside his bedroom.

He closes the bedroom door shut, throws the cellphone on the bed and stands there looking back and forth at the television and his cellphone that continues to ring… *(Ringing)* While Mark was in his bedroom, his cellphone started ringing louder and louder so, Mark picks up the cellphone and takes the battery out, the cellphone stops ringing. He tosses the cellphone on the bed and that's when the volume on the television turns up so loud, it startles Mark. His, whole body jumps back from the unexpected scare, and immediately he raises both of his arms and places both hands over his ears trying to avoid annoying and irritating sound coming from the television. With his head down Mark, frowns his face up, his eyes start tearing and there's a drop of blood gently running down the left side, of one of Marks nostrils from his nose. With the televisions remote control in his hand Mark, tries turning the volume down but it's useless after several attempts so, out of aggravation and confusion Mark, smacks the side of the remote control before dropping it onto the floor. The batteries pop out, Mark walks over to the television, reaches out and tries turning the volume down manually, but it's also useless so, he leans over the top of the television, grabs the power cord that's plugged into the wall outlet, unplugs the power cord from the wall and the television shuts off immediately.

The screen on the television turns pitch black, the bedroom gets quiet and the only thing that can be heard in the bedroom is the heavy breathing Mark is doing, from the fear of being scared. Mark's, fear was caused from not understanding the phenomenon that was transpiring. Furious with anger inside Mark, punches the wall in his bedroom out of violence. He, punches the wall so hard it leaves a visible hole, bruising his knuckles in the process, leaving blood on the wall and his knuckles throbbing in pain. Mark, walks over to his dresser, opens the top drawer and takes out a towel, he wraps the towel around his fist, sits down on the bed while thinking about Stacie and the brain surgery she needs to survive, that hopefully will be taking place soon. Mark, just knew everything that was happening, had to be happening for a real reason so, he closes his eyes with his head down in his lap. He sits on the edge of his bed and after a few minutes, his eyes open, he lifts his head up and looks down on the floor and right there in plain sight, on the floor by his feet Mark, sees the magnet he removed from off the refrigerator in the kitchen. Without hesitation Mark, bends down and with his good hand he reaches out and picks the magnet up from off the floor.

He leans back up and holds the magnet out in front of him, Mark turns the magnet over and tries to read what's printed on the back but with the writing on the magnet being so small, it was hard for him to make out what it says. So, he gets up off the bed, walks over to his computer desk drawer, opens the desk drawer and finds a pocket size magnifying glass. After rolling out the chair from underneath the computer desk, in his bedroom Mark, sits down in the chair, opens the computers desk drawer, takes out the refrigerator magnet and his book of poems. He, places them both on top of the desk Mark, holds the magnifying glass directly over the refrigerators magnet and starts reading the small engraved print, that's written on the back....

(Engraved Print) To inquire about information others don't, subscribe here to: THE€ JOURNAL! Or call: 1-800- THE€ JOURNAL Were open 7 days a week, 24 hours a day, 365 days a year. "A Paper A Day, Keeps The Good News Away"

After putting the magnifying glass down on top of the computers desk next to the refrigerator magnet, Mark leans back in the chair and contemplates...

TH€ JOURNAL! Now why does that name sound so familiar? TH€ JOURNAL! TH€ JOURNAL! Repeatedly Mark, says the name over and over again, he just couldn't get the name TH€ JOURNAL out of his head for some apparent reason. Mark looks at his bruised hand and starts wiping the dried-up blood with the blood-stained towel. He then balls the towel up and tosses it into a small garbage pail in the corner of his bedroom, Mark gets up from the computer desk chair, walks over to the bed, reaches down and picks up his cellphone and cellphone battery from off the floor. Mark puts the cellphone battery in his left pocket and the cellphone in his right as he stands there staring at the television. With the bedroom door wide open Mark, then looks out into the hallway outside of his bedroom immediately after hearing the front door downstairs slam shut... *Hello! Anybody home? Ma! Dad! I'm starving I could eat a horse!* Tara takes off the jacket she has on and the pocketbook she has over her shoulder, she throws the jacket on the couch and lays the pocketbook down on the dining room table, before walking straight towards the kitchen. Then instantly she stops in her tracks, after hearing some sudden movement upstairs... *Mark! Is that you? Are you in your room? I can hear you breathing!*

Walking into the kitchen Tara looks back at the front door and up the stairs where Mark is unfortunately going through a phenomenal breakdown caused by panic. Standing in the doorway of his bedroom door Mark, puts the refrigerator magnet back into his pocket, then the front door to the house opens Mark, can hear his Mother and Father talking. He hears his Brother Edward and his wife's voice. Mark, walks over to the banister in the hallway outside his bedroom, leans his head over the railing and sees his big Brother Edward, and his wife walking inside the house behind Mrs. Largen. With several bags of groceries in Edwards hand Mark, watches as Edwards wife takes off her coat, Mr. Largen takes a seat in his recliner and Mrs. Largen walks straight to the bathroom. Edward, looks upstairs while carrying the groceries towards the kitchen and sees Mark standing there, leaned over the banister with a disconnected and bothered look on his face… *Well! Don't just stand there looking down at me, get your poetic ass down here and help me with these bags!* Mark leans back off the banister, and slowly takes his time as he walks over towards the top of the stairwell, once downstairs where Mr. Largen, Edward and his wife are Mark, walks over to Edward and extends out his arm with nothing but good intentions on his mind…

Here, Bro! Let me help you with that! Never mind now! This is it! You can go back upstairs! Oh! Stop it Edward! Mark was just trying to be helpful! Well it's to dam late! Listen to your wife Bro! Edward, bumps Mark in the shoulder as he walks pass him towards the kitchen Edwards, wife and Mr. Largen both watch as Edward walks into the kitchen with bags of groceries in each hand. Mark turns around and smiles at his sister in law Edwards wife… *What's with him Mary? Who Edward? Mark don't pay Edward no mind, he's been acting strange all day, for some apparent reason. How are you doing anyway dear? I'm fine! Thanks for asking! And where's my niece and nephew! Oh! They're in school today Mark! Where have you been hiding, under a rock? Today they went on a field trip! They were so happy to go!* Mary, then notices the bruises on Mark's hand and before she could say another word, she's interrupted by the horrific and alarming expression Mark has on his face, once he realizes what she's looking at. *My God! Mark, your hand! And is that blood? What in heavens name happened to you?* Mr. Largen promptly leans up in the recliner, after hearing how Mary addressed Mark. Mr. Largen, turns and looks at his son with concern…

Here! I think I have some alcohol wipes in my purse! No! I'm good! Are you sure? Yes! I'm good sis, it's nothing really, it's nothing! Well! I think you need to at least put something on it, so it doesn't get infected! Your knuckles are bleeding for Christ sake! Mrs. Largen walks out of the bathroom… *Boy! Get over here and let me look at that hand! Don't you know me and your Father, have been trying to reach you all day! Where, have you been and why haven't you picked up the phone? And have you seen your sister Tara?* Mark walks over to his Mother and holds his hand up near her face. Mrs. Largen, grabs Marks wrist, looks at his hand and then shakes her head up and down signaling disappointment, before letting his wrist go and walking towards the kitchen. Mark stands there speechless with a dumbfounded look on his face like he just caught amnesia, both his eyebrows are raised as he turns around at looks Mary in the face. Walking back into the living room from the kitchen while holding and eating out of an open bag of potato chips Edward, passes his Mother before she walks into the kitchen. Mrs. Largen snatches the bag of potato chips out of Edwards hand she, then reaches inside the bag, takes out a few potato chips and hands them to Edward before closing the bag of potato chips and walking inside the kitchen. Mrs. Largen stops at the kitchen entrance and turns around…

Since, you and the wife will be staying for dinner Edward, I don't want you to ruin your appetite! That's right Mrs. Largen! Get on him, because I have to almost every night! Mary, punches her husband in the shoulder Edward, eats the potato chips he has in his hand, looks back at his Mother and then back at his wife. He, then places his hand on his shoulder and frowns at what his wife just did. Mark walks over by Edward and gently smacks him in the back of his head… *Ok! Enough already! Did anybody hear what I just said? No! Pops, what happened! Yea! Pops what did you say again? Well, if you all were paying attention! No! Disrespect intended Mary! None taking Mr. Largen! I mean these two knuckle heads! I'll ask again, have anyone seen or happen to know where your sister Tara is?* Edward grabs Mark in the headlock, they both jokingly starts to play wrestle. Edward lifts his head up and looks at his Father Mr. Largen, while his wife Mary calmly walks over by Mr. Largen and takes a seat on the couch… *You want to know where your daughter Tara is? Dad! She's, in the kitchen! Edward! Did you just say that Tara was is in the kitchen?* Edward looks at his wife and shakes his head up and down signaling yes. Mary gets off from off the couch and stands there for a few seconds before headed in the direction towards the kitchen…

Well! Excuse me fellas but I must go and see my girl! She, kisses her husband on the check, rubs Marks on the shoulder before walking pass him headed towards the kitchen, where Tara and Mrs. Largen are… *And Mark! Would you please put something on that hand! You're getting blood on Edwards shirt!* Immediately letting go of Marks neck, Edward pushes his brother up off him and looks down at his shirt for blood stains but there aren't any. So, he looks up at Mr. Largen and then at Mark who is standing there smiling enjoying the paranoid look on his brother's face… *Nice one Mary! I bet that will stop them two from rough house playing around in here!* Mr. Largen stares at his two sons, turns around in the recliner, shakes his head side to side while looking for the televisions remote control. Edward looks at Mark making fun of him so, on impulse Edward grabs Mark by the neck again. He puts him in the headlock then they both start rough house playing in the living room. In the kitchen Mrs. Largen, Mary and Tara are helping Mrs. Largen put up the groceries so, she can prep tonight's dinner. After all the groceries are put up Mrs. Largen opens a cabinet above the sink and starts handing dinner plates to Mary while Tara just stands there with her arms folded watching…

And you my dear! Where have you been? And how long have you been hiding here in the kitchen? That's right Tara! Is everything Ok? Once, Edward said that you were in here, I just had to come and see my girl! You good Tara? Come here give your sister in law a hug! Tara, and Mary embrace each other with a devoted and compassionate hug, Tara leans back while still in Mary's arms, Tara looks Mary in the face with an expression on her face that's not so convincing. Slowly removing her arms from arounds Tara's shoulders Mary, takes a step back and leans on the kitchen's countertop she, then stares into Tara's eyes and then on instinct she, realizes that something isn't right... *Well, Tara! I'm fine sis! School is fine, believe me! Everything is just fine! Ma! You know me, if something was wrong, I would let you know! I don't know Tara! Lately, you've been distancing yourself from the whole family! Your starting to remind me of how your sister Stacie used to act before the accident!* The kitchen gets silent, the quietness is making the atmosphere feel like the rest of the house is empty and there's no one else left in the world but Mrs. Largen, Tara and Mary. With her head down Tara, walks over by the kitchen table and places both hands on top of one the chairs underneath she, stands there for a few seconds before looking up at her Mother.

She, then looks at Mary and without saying another word Tara, walks out of the kitchen into the living room where Mr. Largen is watching television and Edward, still has Mark in the headlock, rough house playing around. Edward sees his sister walking out from the kitchen… *Dad! There's Tara right there! Little sis what's going on?* Then suddenly Marks cellphone starts ringing in his pocket… *(Ringing)* The ringing surprises Mark, he's in disbelief right now especially after remembering that he, took the cellphones battery out and it was in his other pocket. So, Mark pushes Edward in the chest and slips out of the headlock while Edward is also paying attention to the ringing of his cellphone…. *Well! Aren't you going to answer your phone Mark? Don't you see daddy is over there trying to watch T.V.? Edward, I never known you to be disrespectful but Mark, on the other hand! Oh, never mind! It's, a waste of breath*! Mr. Largen and Edward start laughing at what Tara just said as Mark, walks over by the table in the living room, reaches out his arm and places his hand flat on the table, trying to catch his breath while his cellphone continues to ring… *(Ringing)* Mark, turns his back to Mr. Largen, Edward and Tara and takes out the ringing cellphone and the cellphones battery out of his pockets. He holds them both in each hand while the cellphone continues to ring…

(Ringing) For the last time Mark! Please, answer your phone! She's right Mark! If you're not going to answer it, at least turn the dam cellphone thing off! Or, better yet little Bro! Take the battery out instead!

The statement Edward just made catches Mark off guard, it gets his undivided attention so, he turns around looks at his brother Edward and puts the cellphone that's still ringing back in his pocket, while holding the cellphones battery in his other hand. Passing his sister Tara, while walking towards the stairs headed towards his bedroom, Tara looks at Mark and shakes her head side to side. Halfway up the stairs the television in Marks bedroom comes on, the volume is so loud it's drowning out the television that's playing downstairs in the living room. Once Mark, reaches the top of the stairs he, looks down and sees his sister Tara looking right back at him… *Do I have too? I mean really my Brother!* Mark, kindly walks over to his bedroom door and steps inside the room, then immediately the bedroom door slams shut and locks by itself. Mark jumps startled by the reaction and the force of how the door just closed, he then turns around, grabs the doorknob with one hand and tries to open the door but it's useless.

Mark, shakes the door, pulls it and even thinks about kicking it down before the lights start blinking off and on and the T.V. starts rapidly changing stations. Mark's, body gets cold from the temperature in the bedroom dropping. In the kitchen Mary walks over to the kitchen table and starts placing the plates down one by one in front of the chairs underneath the table, while trying to avoid any conversation about what just happened and how Tara reacted when Mrs. Largen spoke about Stacie. So, Mary kindly and considerately goes over to where Mrs. Largen is by the sink and starts helping her take out some more dinner wear from out of the cabinet… *Mrs. Largen, did you hear about what happened last night? Are you referring to the bar incident? Yes! Mrs. Largen, wasn't that crazy? I didn't get the whole story Mary, but the people down at the grocery store, was saying something about some man found lying in the street, outside the bar! Well, was he drunk? I don't know Mrs. Largen, but whatever happened they say its connected to Stacie!... Stacie, my Stacie? You have to be kidding me?... No! Mrs. largen I'm serious, it was just on the news! Does my husband know about this? We'll whatever happened, it must have happened, once he left the bar? I mean, was he found dead? Your And its connected to my Daughter Stacie?*

Yes!... Only God knows what happened to that man! Only God knows! Downstairs in the living room Mr. Largen, turns around and looks at Tara as she is walking over by him, she, leans over and kisses her Father on the cheek before moving a pillow over on the couch and sitting down. Tara, grabs the pillow, puts it behind her head, lays sideways on the couch with her arm in-between her head and the pillow. Mr. Largen, looks at his daughter Tara and can sense that something is wrong so, instead of striking up what might be aggravating conversation instead Mr. Largen, picks up the remote control and hands it to her. Tara, leans up off the pillow, reaches out her arm, grabs the remote control and starts changing channels until she finds something she wants to watch. Edward, looks at his Father his Father looks back at him before Edward, walks over where Tara is lying on the couch. He, grabs her leg, moves it to the side from off the couch, hops down on the couch next to her and starts watching the television. With the door to his bedroom locked Mark, has no way to get out of his room. He's, freezing it's so cold in the room Mark, can see his breath lingering in the air, from his nostrils and mouth every time breathes.

Shaken in fear and frightened by the dreadful antics that's taken place in front of him. Mark, just stands there trembling afraid to death, being that all that's taken place is horrifying and unexplainable to the human eye which is also out of his control. With his back pressed up on the bedroom door, his arms are folded, and his hands are trembling Mark, stares at the unplugged television that's is mysteriously on, with the volume blasting attacking his ear drums. Reaching into his pocket Mark, takes out his cellphone that's constantly ringing, he tosses the cellphone and the cellphones battery on the bed he, walks over to the television, leans over the top of the T.V. and looks at the televisions power cord that's unplugged from the wall's outlet. Mark is stunned and shaken up terribly by what he's seeing right now. So, he cautiously takes a few steps back from the television while rubbing his arms he, then raises his hands to his mouth and blows inside both of his hands, that are now balled-up into a fist. Trying to keep himself warm, Mark starts mumbling softly to himself, his speech is stuttering from the below temperature freezing air, that's blistering his lips every time he tries to speak… *What isss… going onnn… here? Thissss… is immmm…possible! This cannot beee… happening!*

Then out of nowhere the window in Mark's bedroom rapidly opens, the curtains covering the window rips down from the silent strong and powerful wind, that's whistling through the bedroom from the outside wind, that's is now causing a small artic storm in Mark's room. The strong and powerful wind cuts through the room like a knife, blowing items all around the bedroom. Mark forces himself off the door, he tries and walks towards the window to close it, but the wind is so strong and powerful, it pushes him back two steps every time he takes one. Mark looks to his left and can see the computers desk on the other side of the room, his dresser draws are all open and his bed has moved closer to the wall. Mark looks to his left and can see the poem book that's lying on his desk, the book is open but it's not moving, all the pages in the book are flapping recklessly back and forth like if someone was looking for a specific chapter. Mark suddenly gets pushed and pinned back up against the bedroom's door, the force of the wind intense. Then, unexpectedly Mark's whole-body jerks to one side, from the loud and alarming sound of somebody banging on the door, from outside of his bedroom. Mark struggles with himself trying to move away from the door and with all his strength, Mark forcefully takes two steps forward.

He carelessly steps on the televisions remote control that's on the floor, it causes him to trip and stumble over by the bed and then onto the floor. He gets up quickly and sits on the edge of the bed, he raises both of his arms and covers both of his ears, with each hand Mark then closes both of his eyes. Then out of nowhere, simultaneously the lights stop flickering, the T.V. shuts off, the cellphone stops ringing and the strong and powerful cold artic wind temperature, gradually returns to normal. Mark opens his eyes and watches as the thrilling, breathtaking insane behavior throughout the bedroom comes to an end. The banging on the other side of bedroom door immediately stops, the room gets quiet for a few seconds, silence cuts through the room like a sharp knife. Then a female's voice can be heard, from out in the hallway behind the door, the familiar voice gets Mark's undivided attention....

Mark! What are you doing in there? It's about time, you turned that television off and answered that constantly irritating ringing cellphone! Anyway! Mommy said dinners ready crazy! Now getting up off the couch Edward, walks over by the bottom of the stairs, he places one hand on the banister and looks upstairs at Tara who is now walking away from Mark's bedroom door...

Is everything alright up there Tara? Yea! Crazy here finally decided to turn the T.V. down and answer his stupid cellphone! I think the boy needs some psychiatric help! Or better yet! He needs to stop reading all the poems in that book, he carries around! I'm telling you; it's messing with his head! Not paying Tara or Edward any mind Mr. Largen, leans forward and calmly picks up the remote control he, turns the volume up a few notches on the T.V. and leans back. On the other hand, Mary and Mrs. Largens hears all the commotion that's going on in the Livingroom so, they both decide to walk out of the kitchen. Mary has in her hands two oven mittens while Mrs. Largen is wearing a kitchen apron that has flour patted all over it.... *What's going on out here? Tara! Did you tell your Mark that dinners ready? And would you would stop yelling! Your Father is watching T.V.* Mrs. Largen, turns back around and heads back into the kitchen while Edward removes his hand from off the banister and walks over to his wife Mary. They stand there in front of each other, Mary raises one hand holding an oven mitten and softly smacks Edward on the side of his face Edward grabs Mary by the waist and carefully forces her back into the kitchen. At the top of the stairs Tara is now making her way back downstairs she, looks back up at Mark's bedroom door and then back downstairs.

Tara walks back over to the couch and stretches out she grabs a pillow and places it back behind her head and starts watches the T.V. with her Father. Mr. Largen, turns his head to the left, looks at Tara and then looks back at the television, before shaking his head side to side signaling disapproval. In the bedroom Mark, is now finally recovering from the bizarre, unusual and unexplainable happenings that just transpired a few minutes ago. And with his self- confidence humbling down Mark, kindly gets up off the edge of the bed. He stands up and looks around the room at the disastrous and unexplainable wreckage leftover by the mysterious happenings. Mark, walks over by the bedroom door, leans in and places his right ear on the door, trying to hear what's going on outside of his bedroom and in the rest of the house. The house seems quiet, except for the sound of the television, that's playing downstairs in the living room. Now, pressing his ear firmly and closer on the door Mark, hears a news reporters voice, one that he recognizes from watching the news earlier so, with no hesitation Mark, backs away from the door. He reaches in and grabs the doorknob and gently turns it to the right, the bedroom door opens Mark, stands in the doorway with one leg out in the hallway and his back leaned up against the door frame.

While quietly listening to the woman's voice, who is standing there reporting some news on the television....

(News) Debra Jenkins here and this is the second tragedy this week! It seems to be connected to the schoolteacher; whose name is Stacie Largen! The woman who needs brain surgery, due to a car accident on the highway, driving home from work! A few days ago.

After hearing the woman news reporter say the name of his daughter on the television Mr. Largen quickly leans up is the recliner, reaches out and taps Tara on the leg, while paying close attention to what the news reporter has to say about Stacie... *Tara! Tara! Go in the kitchen and tell your Mother, that their talking about Stacie on the news!* With her eyes widening Tara, looks at the television and then at her Father Tara, jumps up from off the couch and runs into the kitchen. Tara's running so fast, once she's in the kitchen she, bumps right into her Brother Edward he, turns around and holds her up by her arms, before the both of them falls onto the floor...

Girl! Slow down before you hurt yourself! Or someone else!... Tara! Now why are you running through the house like that? What's the matter with you child? And take a deep breath before you pass out! Mary! Look in the refrigerator, take out a bottle of water and give it to Tara please!... No, Ma! I'm good! But Hurry up! There're talking about Stacie on the news! Hurry up it's on right now!

Standing by the refrigerator door, Mary looks at Edward while Tara, runs back out the kitchen. Edward, follows her while his wife Mary, promptly takes off the two kitchen mittens she has on her hands. She throws the two mittens on top of the kitchen counter, by the sink before walking out of the kitchen behind her husband. Wasting no time thereafter Mrs. Largen, quickly removes the kitchen apron from around her neck she, lays the apron over the back of one of the chairs in the kitchen, that's empty seated underneath the kitchen table. Mrs. Largen, swiftly walks out of the kitchen and into the living room she, walks over by Edward who is seated on the couch with Tara and Mary, Edward gets up and lets his Mother sit down on the couch. Edward, then stands in front of his wife, turns around, bends down and sits in between her legs on the floor. Upstairs still leaning on the door frame, thinking about the paranormal activity Mark, eventually moves away from the bedroom door. He walks over to the banister and leans over it; he then folds both arms and places them on top of the railing. Feeling awkward and uncomfortable, Mark sluggishly rest his chin on top of his hands and like everyone else in the house, his eyes are now glued to the television downstairs as well. As he watches and listens to what the news reporter has to say about his sister, their daughter and friend Stacie Largen and what they know about the unidentified man, who they say was found drunk lying in the street, in front of the bar this Morning…

(News) But before we get into that story, concerning Stacie Largen and how these two stories are connected! First! Let's cover the story about the young man, possibly in his early twenties! Who was found drunk lying in the street, outside of a bar this Morning! Hold on!... I'm being told! … We still don't know the name of the young man! I'm hearing!... That they are not releasing any footage either! Sorry folks, but we seem to have some technical issues occurring again! Please bear with us! As we try and resolve the matter!... I'm Debra Jenkins, channel 12 Views on News! Back to you Charles!... Camera man! Do we have any sound at all?... No! Not yet Debra!... That Figures!

While the woman news reporter for K12 News and the cameraman filming her are waiting to get word back, that the technical issues with their equipment has been resolved. In the background on the television screen, there's a police officer in uniform in front of the bar, just standing there. And on the other side of the street there's a few bystanders standing around, with cellphones to their ears talking to friends and taking pictures. Then a short time later, other news camera vans can be seen driving up near the scene and hoping out while newspaper reporters walk up and starts taking pictures, for their local newspaper. Back at the Largens home, everyone sitting in the living room has their eyes glued to the television, waiting for the woman news reporter to return and continue covering the mysterious story of the man. The front doorbell to the Largens home rings twice…

(Ringing) Well! Is anyone going to answer the door? Son! You heard your Mother! See, who's at the door please! Edward turns his head to the right and looks at his Father, before placing both hands on his wife's knees while pushing himself up off the floor. Edward, then walks over to the front door, turns the doorknob and opens the door… *Daddy! Daddy! Where's Mommy? I'm hungry! Me too Daddy! Well Dam! Don't I get a hug anymore?*

Edwards, two kids' steps inside the house and walk right pass their Father and head straight to the refrigerator, while taking off their bookbags before dropping them onto the floor. The school bus driver waits outside by the door and then waves bye, once they're secure inside the house, the children look at their Mother and walk over to where she's sitting on the couch. Leaving the refrigerator door in the kitchen wide open. Mr. and Mrs. Largen, smiles at the sight of their two grandchildren while Tara, quickly sits up on the couch, smiles and extends out both of her arms. Hoping to get a hug from either, Star her niece or Suny her nephew…

Come here you two! Now get over here and give your Grandmother and Grandfather a hug and kiss! Star, Suny! Get over here!... Hi! Grandma and Grandpa!... How, are you kids doing? And how was school? Here! Give me some sugar!... So, the both of you are just going to walk pass me and over to them?...

Tara! You know the Grandparents have to get the love first! You should see how they act when Grandma and Grandpa Largen, call our house! Those kids love their Grandparent's! Right kids?... Mary! You know I know that! I was just playing around! But I better get my hugs from Star and Suny too! Who's your favorite aunt? After getting their kisses from their Grandparents and hugs from their favorite aunt Tara, the kids stand there in front of the couch blocking the television, while unzipping their coats. While their Father, is standing by the open door, with his hand on the doorknob, nodding his head at the woman school bus driver. Who's smiling back at him, before she turns around and walks away back toward the school bus, that's doubled park in the street, in front of the Largens home. Now, standing in front of her two children, Mary is also smiling at the sight of her two children, she then looks over by the front door where her husband is and sees two bookbags, lying there on the floor. Mary, looks down at her two children and the welcoming smile she has on her face, is now turned into an unpleasant frown. So, she raises her arm appalled and points with her index finger over by the door, at the two bookbags that's lying there. Star and Suny, both get the impression that something is wrong so, they simultaneously turn around to look at what their Mother is pointing at. Edward, closes the front door, removes his hand off the doorknob, turns around and clearly sees his wife pointing down at the floor. Edward looks down and attempts to pick up the two bookbags…

Oh, no! Edward don't even think about it! Don't you even think about, picking up those bookbags off the floor! These, two! They know better! Now! The both of you, get over there and pick those bookbags up! And put them on the table! Before you even think about taking off those coats…! But!... Don't but me boy! Now get! And after you pick up those bookbags! Hang you coats up!... But, Ma! I can't reach the hangers!... Well find a ladder! Star and Suny look at Mr. and Mrs. Largen, then at their aunt Tara who has both shoulders shrugged up in the air, while shaking her head side to side, signaling to her niece and nephew, that she can't help them with this one. Star who's the oldest, pulls her younger brother Suny by the coat and they both sluggishly walk over together by the front door, where their Father is letting go of the two bookbags. Edward, leans up, looks at his two children who's walking towards him.

While walking pass Star and Suny Edward, rubs both of his kids on top of their heads as he heads back over to the couch, he sits down next to Tara in the spot, where his wife Mary has just gotten up from. While Mary, stands there with both of her arms folded frowning, making sure both of her children do exactly, as they were told. Tara looks up at her sister in law Mary and then at her brother Edward, before getting up off the couch and walking over to where her niece and nephew Star and Suny, are picking up their bookbags from off the floor.

Tara bends down in front of Suny and unzips his coat, before getting up reaching in the halls closet and taking out two hangers. Mary stands by the couch now with her arms down by her side and looks at Tara, she then shakes her head side to side, signaling that she's disagrees with how Tara is treating them, after she specifically informed her two children what to do. Tara puts her arm around both Star and Suny and escorts them towards the kitchen for a snack… Alright, now Tara! Don't be ruining those kid's appetite! Remember they still have to eat dinner! Oh, sit down and watch television sis! Aunty got this! Right kids?... Ok! Whatever you say Tara! Mary turns around and looks at her husband Edward!... *Well! Aren't you going to say something? Move over!* Now, bothered at how Edward is ignoring her, out of anger Mary leans over, reaches out her arm and pushes her husband to the side. Edward slides over and lets his wife sit down, Mary hops down in Tara's spot next to her husband on the couch. Mr. and Mrs. Largen look at each other with their eyebrows turned up, before looking back at the television screen. And there on the screen, a male news reporter is standing there, adjusting his earpiece with her left hand, while holding a K12 imprinted microphone in front of him with his right hand….

News Reporter) Are we back on?... How's my microphone working?... Ok! I'm ready! Your Live in …4, 3, 2, 1 … (News Reporter) K12 News! And I want to apologize to our viewers out there!

That was our news coverage reporter Debra Jenkins! Who's covering these two stories! I guess she'll have more information when she returns! And again, I want to apologize for the technical difficulties!... How about we cut to a commercial, until Debra returns… (T.V. Commercial)

Downstairs in the living room Mr. and Mrs. Largen, Edward and his wife Mary are all sitting quietly and calm, as they watch the commercial that's airing on the television screen. Mark, who's upstairs in the hallway in front of his bedroom door, still shaken up about the mysterious and bizarre occurrences, that happened to him a little while ago in his bedroom.

Looks at his niece and nephew, walking towards the kitchen with his sister Tara, Marks who's leaning on the banister, with his arms folded and his chin rested on top of his hands. Back and forth with his eyes Mark, looks at the commercial on the television and at everyone downstairs sitting in the living room, while feeling alienated and confused. The commercial goes off and the woman K12 news coverage reporter Debra Jenkins, is standing there holding in front of her an imprinted microphone, in her right hand and with the other hand, she's fixing the earpiece that's plugged in her left ear…. *Finally! Were back? Ok! How do I look?... Like a million bucks!... Great! And sound…Perfect! Debra You're live in 4, 3, 2, 1… (News Reporter) Debra Jenkins, here with K12 News on Views! I'm standing here in front of the bar, where the unknown named man, was found lying here dead last night! The police are telling us that the man was… Is that right?...*

In his early twenties and in his possession, they found a wallet, house keys and a book! That's right people! A poem book!... (News Reporter) I'm sorry! They say the book had a several pages ripped out of it and the police on scene have recovered, a few of the pages not too far from where the man was lying! And yes! I'm also being told that K12 News exclusively have a few of those pages!... Just give me a minute! Here!... Let, me find one of the poems from the book to read!... Should we go to a commercial? While I get these pages together?... No! Alright then!

With the wrinkled page in her hand, from out of the poem book, the woman news reporter holds the paper up in front of her and gets ready to read what's written on the page. Standing by the banister, Mark rubs the top of his head out of confusion and dismay, Mark then backs away from the banister and walks over to the top of the stairs. He sits down with his legs close together, his arms folded over his knees and his chin rested on top of his hands, that's placed flat over each other. Sitting, there in deep thought Mark, watches as his parents Mr. and Mrs. Largen, his Brother Edward, and his sister in law Mary, all wait patiently and listen for the woman news reporter, to read the verse from the page, that was recovered from the dead man's book of poems…

Ok! Here we go! Can you find out who the author is for me? (Laughing)… What's so funny? I'm serious, I really want to know!... Ok! Ok! Are we on the air? Your Live in 4, 3, 2, 1… (News Reporter) Debra Jenkins here!

And in my possession, I have a page from the poem book, recovered from the unidentified man, who was found dead lying in front of this bar, that you see behind me last night! Ok! This poem is called Pictures! So, let me go ahead and read a verse from the page! …

(Debra Reading) …

Pictures

***H**ere's a man in disbelief, who drunk away his pain, but still couldn't salvage no relief. He only asked for help, when his heart was on fire, never realizing too much of anything, would cause what he loves too eventually expire.*

He never listened to his self-conscious, which corrupted the pictures and thoughts in his mind. He even thought about, putting a gun to his head or committing suicide in due time.

And when his feelings and emotions, suddenly got shot down. It left mood swings of bullet shells lying on the ground. Not realizing It would be family, who gets wounded by the lost, which will inflict self-mental injuries and executed pain to everybody around him, at any given cost…

(News Reporter) Wow! I must say that was interesting and attention-grabbing! You think? Let me see if I can find out who the author of this book is!... Ok! I'm being told now, that the author of the book! That I just read a verse from, name is Sam. Elmwood! …Did you say Sam Elmwood Debra? …That's right Sam Elmwood! I (Mumbling) I have to get myself a copy...Me To!... Again, I'm Debra Jenkins, on K12 News on Views!

(Confused) As Mark sat there on top of the stairs in dismay and in disbelief, he tries to make out the best of how, the news reporter can cover this story of him being found lying in street drunk on one television and dead on another, This was mindboggling but explained through …

<u>EYES ON THE ROAD</u>

"When The Objects In Mirrors

Are Closer Then They Appear To Be"

THE LICENSE PLATE

Where's your boyfriend at Tara? Boyfriend! No, not me! I don't have the time right now, for a boyfriend Daddy! Why not Tara? You're a beautiful young lady! And I know there's hundreds of intelligent, good home training young men out there, who would love for the opportunity! To take you out on a date! Plus! I do want some more grands and the chance to walk his daughter down the aisle! Tara! That's a dream come true! Well, Daddy! I hate to put you back to sleep! But your dreams might get shattered! Laughing under his breath Mr. Largen, shakes his head side to side at how his daughter is driving Tara, looks in her rear-view mirror and makes a sharp left turn at the light, that has just turned green. Paying close attention to the road Tara, has both hands tightly gripped on the steering wheel and her eyes on the road ahead of her. *Well, why not? Tara!* Now reaching her arm out and turning the station on the radio Tara, ignores her Father by not answering his question. Tara, then looks out the passenger side window at the cars driving by, while tapping her foot to the song that is now playing on the radio... *(Song Playing) Everybody knows these Boys, who live around here are trouble Dad! And seriously, I don't have time for trouble!* Avoiding eye contact with her Father, Mr. Largen starts smiling, he turns his head to the left and looks at his Daughter Tara, who's in the driver's seat, behind the steering wheel blushing and a little embarrassed, by the thought.

Of this brand-new conversation concerning relationships, marriage and kids with her Father. Her cheeks on her face are slowly turning pink and Mr. Largen can tell that Tara, is starting to feel very uncomfortable with this conversation with him. Tara turns her head slightly to the right and looks at her Father, who is sitting in the passenger seat now looking out the passenger side window…

Why are you smiling Daddy? Please Tara! Don't mind me at all! You just pay attention to the road! And get us where we both need to be safely! OK? Believe me dear! I'm not trying to make you feel at all uncomfortable! I love you dearly! I just want you, to be more than happy in life! That's all! You're my baby girl, for Christ sake! Smiling, at what her Father just said Tara, was again feeling like Daddy's little girl, the little girl who always got picked up into her Father's arms, every time he seen her, no matter where they were. The little girl, that got away with anything and even if she was caught red handed, doing something she wasn't supposed to. She never got chastised, Tara was feeling emotional and the feeling was making her sensitive, which briefly caused Tara, to start tearing up in both of her eyes.

Wiping her eyes Tara, looks in the rearview mirror, before sitting up in the driver's seat, and turning her signal on to make a right turn. Tara, drives one block down she, makes another right and then a sharp, left turn before driving through the yellow caution traffic light, at the next corner…

Tara Watch Out! Mr. Largen reaches over and grabs the steering wheel he, turns the steering wheel to the right, causing the car to serve slightly out of control. But at the same time the quick reaction of Mr. Largen, helped him and Tara dodge hitting another vehicle in the process. Yelling, at the other vehicle from inside the car Mr. Largen is highly upset, to the mere sight of the accident that could've just happened while Tara, is shaken up a bit and surprised by the quick response from her Father. And at that moment, it still didn't dawn on Tara, that because she drove through the yellow caution traffic light, the accident almost happened. Cautiously Tara, pulls the vehicle over to the shoulder of the road and sits there in the driver's seat, with both hands on the steering wheel she, rolls the driver's side window down half way, just enough so she can see the all black tinted limousine, that she almost had the accident with. The limousine intentionally does a U-turn in the middle of the street and terrifyingly drives pass Tara and her Father real slow… *Oh, my God! Did you just see that? Daddy! We were almost in an accident! Can you believe that? Calm down Tara! Were, safe! God was watching over you and me just now! Are you Ok? Take a deep breath and get yourself back together! Do you want me to drive? No! I got this! But Daddy! Was that a… I mean that was a limousine, right?*

Immediately Tara, unbuckles her seatbelt she turns to her left and stares at the all black tinted limousine, that is now terrifyingly driving slowly pass on her side of the car.

Tara, then lifts her right arm up and with her index finger she starts pointing at the limousine… *What are you doing? Tara! Stop pointing please! And roll that window back up! You don't know who's inside that limousine! And remember Tara! It was your fault, the accident almost happened anyway! Oh really, Daddy! Blame your daughter! How do you know, the limousine was making a legal turn anyway? Tara, seriously! They had the right away Tara! Well, how do you know Daddy? Tara! The light was red, when you made that sharp left turn, back there! Ok! Ok! It probably was my fault! But you're supposed to be my extra eyes Father!* Sitting, in the passenger seat with his nerves being wrecked Mr. Largen, unbuckles his seatbelt hoping to feel a little bit more comfortable and since Tara, has finally stopped pointing at the limousine Mr. Largen, felt safe enough to roll down the passenger side window, to breathe and get some fresh air.

While looking out of the driver's side window, immediately something abnormal comes over Tara, which causes her eyes to shift down and she stares diligently at the strange and unfamiliar looking license plate, that's on the back of the limousine. One look was all it took and Tara, knew right away that something about this license plate, was very weird and very unusual and the language it was written in, was nothing Tara, had ever seen before….
(License Plate) qoqX rXA rQIIrQ The text on the license plate, was written in some type of calligraphy inscription and it had a dark and eerie nature about it, that just seemed dangerous and threatening.

This license plate was making Tara, feel very uncomfortable every time she looked at it so, out of concern for her and her Father Tara, quickly rolls up the driver's side window, turns back around in the driver's seat and places both of her hands tightly on the steering wheel, as she stares out the windshield at the road ahead of her…. *Daddy! Did you happen to see the license plate, on the back of that limousine? No Tara! Why?... I'm not sure!... What I mean is! Never in my life, have I seen a license plate like that one before! Tara! I'm not sure I follow you! Was the license plate from another state? No, Daddy! The license plate…*

Then out of nowhere, before she could even finish what she was saying, an extremely loud horn catches Mr. Largen and Tara's attention while they sit in the car, parked by the shoulder of the road. The sound of the horn is so extremely loud, it causes Tara's whole body to jump while in the driver's seat, out of instant both of her hands, let's go of the steering wheel. She, then grabs her Father's arm aggressively, out of fear and pure shock. Mr. Largen looks at Tara before leaning forward and looking in the side-view mirror. There, to his surprise Mr. Largen, sees bright headlights coming from a sixteen-wheeler truck doing way over the speed limit, Mr. Largen was thinking the truck driving up behind them, had to be doing at least seventy-five to eighty miles per hour. And with his experience Mr. Largen, knew very well that objects in these mirrors, are closer than what they really appear to be.

So, he reaches his arm out and over towards Tara and quickly turns the key that's in the ignition, the cars start up. Tara, is now honestly confused by what her Father has just done so, out of concern she looks in the rear-view mirror and can also see the truck, closing in behind them on the road as they are parked, to the shoulder of the road. Without hesitation or question Tara, puts the car in drive and moves the car over closer to the shoulder of the road. Making sure she and her Father are not in harm's way, from the sixteen-wheeler truck driving up behind them nonstop, doing seventy-five to eighty miles per hour full speed. As the sixteen-wheeler truck and its driver, gets closer to Tara's car that's parked on the shoulder of the road, immediately Tara grabs the driver's side seatbelt and fastens it back around her waist, Mr. Largen looks at what his daughter is doing he, then looks in the rear-view mirror and sees the bright head lighted truck speeding, in route towards them. So, without any hesitation or doubt Mr. Largen, grabs the passenger side seatbelt and fastens it around his waist as well. The sound of the truck's engine is threatening, and Tara and her Father's integrity is being intimidating by not knowing what's to come. The, headlights on the sixteen-wheeler truck becomes brighter, the closer the truck gets. The ground underneath the car is shaking, from the power of the trucks force, as it continues speeding becoming the bully of the road. Tara, and her Father turn and look each other in the eyes, the expression on their faces are showing panic.

And their body language is telling frightening and terrifying stories, summed up into one word, Scared. With his left-hand Mr. Largen, grabs Tara by her right arm and with his right hand, he firmly and securely holds the passenger side handle, above his head on the ceiling…. *Daddy I guess now would be a good time to tell you! Tell me what Tara? Daddy! Don't be mad at me, I lied!... You lied! About what Tara? Daddy! I have …* The bright headlights from the sixteen-wheeler truck is now reflecting, off all the mirrors on the car and shining onto everything else in and out the vehicle. These lights are now making it impossible, for Tara or Mr. Largen to see anything, behind them or in front of them. Which becomes a major distraction, the piercing glare from the bright headlights, has forced Tara and her Father to close both of their eyes shut. their eyelids are now protecting their pupils, that are dilated from the emotional adrenaline rush they both have from being afraid. Not being able to see a thing, all Tara and Mr. Largen can do right now is pray, as they continue being tortured mentally, while feeling the ground rumbling underneath their feet and the trembling of the car, both caused by the force of the speeding sixteen-wheeler truck. Tara, and Mr. Largen has no other choice, except to sit there in silence and use their own imagination about what might happen, if the sixteen-wheeler truck did smack into the back of them, while driving at almost ninety miles per hour.

To Tara, the thought alone was more than devastating it was critical so, Tara covers her nose, hoping to avoid smelling her own unstable and impulsive fear, that has already left her and Mr. Largen terrified, sitting on the edge of their seats inside the parked car. Now as the sixteen-wheeler truck gets closer Tara, can distinctively hear something different now in the air, something not so spine chilling and intimidating and more so, not life threatening. Sitting there stiff as a board in the driver's seat, with one hand tightly gripped to the steering wheel and both of her eyes closed. Tara, can distinctively hear the sixteen-wheelers truck, driving up behind them on the driver's side of her car.
Then suddenly, out of nowhere the piercing reflecting glare, caused by the trucks bright headlights dim down, the ground rumbling underneath their feet and the trembling of the car, caused by the powerful force of speed surprisingly ends. But through all, that has already happened, the sixteen-wheeler truck still drives pass Tara's car like a bat out of hell, while doing almost ninety miles per hour, nonstop. The truck driver leans over near the passenger side window and quickly eyeballs Tara, from the chest up he, then leans back up, raises his left arm and grabs a string that's hanging from the ceiling, attached to a bull horn that's securely bolted down, outside the front of the truck near the roof. The driver of the truck looks to his left and then back at the road ahead, while shaking his head up and down signaling frustration while smiling to himself.

The truck driver pulls the string that's attached to the bull horn, the bull horn sounds off twice, Tara and Mr. Largen open their eyes. Laughing under his breath Mr. Largen, shakes his head side to side signaling that how he can't believe how his daughter is driving, Tara, looks in the rear-view mirror and makes a sharp left turn at the light, that has just turned green. Paying close attention to the road Tara, has both hands tightly gripped on the steering wheel Tara, reaches her arm out and turns the station on the radio. She looks out the window at the road ahead, while tapping her foot to the song that is now playing on the radio…
(Song Playing) While Tara, sings along to the song playing on the radio she, looks in the rearview mirror before sitting up straight in the driver's seat and turning her signal on to make a right turn. Tara, drives one block down she, makes another right and then a sharp, left turn, before driving through the yellow caution traffic light, at the next corner… *Tara Watch Out!* Mr. Largen reaches over and grabs the steering wheel he, turns the steering wheel to the right, causing the car to serve slightly out of control. But at the same time the quick reaction of Mr. Largen, helped him and Tara dodge hitting another vehicle in the process. Yelling, at the other vehicle from inside the car Mr. Largen is highly upset, to the mere sight of the accident that could've just happened while Tara, is shaken up a bit and surprised by the quick response from her Father.

And at that moment, it still didn't dawn on Tara, that because she drove through the yellow caution traffic light, the accident almost happened. Cautiously Tara, pulls the vehicle over to the shoulder of the road and sits there in the driver's seat, with both hands on the steering wheel she, rolls the driver's side window down halfway just enough so she can see the all black tinted limousine, that she almost had the accident with. The limousine intentionally does a U-turn in the middle of the street and terrifyingly drives pass Tara and her Father real slow... *Oh, my God! Did you just see that? Daddy! We were almost in an accident! Can you believe that? Calm down Tara! Were, safe! God was watching over you and me just now! Are you Ok? Take a deep breath and get yourself back together! Do you want me to drive? No! I got this! But Daddy! Was that a... I mean that was a limousine, right?* Immediately unbuckling her seatbelt Tara, turns to her left and stares at the all black tinted limousine, that has just made a U-turn in the middle of the road and is now slowly driving pass, on the driver's side of the car. Tara, quickly rolls down the passenger side window, lifts her right arm up and starts pointing at the limousine... *What are you doing? Tara! Stop pointing please! And roll that window back up! You don't know who's inside that limousine! And remember Tara! It was your fault, the accident almost happened anyway! Oh really, Daddy! Blame your daughter! How do you know, the limousine was making a legal turn anyway? Tara, seriously! They had the right of way Tara! Well, how do you know Daddy? Tara!*

The light was red, when you made that sharp left turn, back there! Ok! Ok! It probably was my fault! But you're supposed to be my extra eyes Father! While sitting in the passenger seat with his nerves being wrecked, by his daughter's behavior Mr. Largen, unbuckles his seatbelt hoping to feel at ease and a little bit more comfortable. And with Tara, not pointing at the limousine Mr. Largen, felt safe enough to roll down the passenger side window, to get some fresh air and breathe. Feeling embarrassed, at how her Father verbally chastised her unintentionally, about the accident that almost happened Tara, turns her head to the right and looks at Mr. Largen, as he's making sure that all the doors in the car are locked. He, then turns all the way around in the passenger seat, to look out the back windshield and there lying on the backseat Mr. Largen, sees a newspaper wrapped in a black rubber band. His, eyes widen, and his heart skips a beat at the mere sight of the newspaper. So, he turns to his right and looks at Tara, who has her head turned to the left looking out the driver's side window Tara, turns around and looks at her Father who's turning back around in the passenger seat, holding a newspaper in his hand. Tara and her Father look at the newspaper Mr. Largen has in his hand, they both simultaneously look up at each other attentively, with a point of interest and concern all over their face. Traumatized with both of their mouths wide open and both of their eyes widen to the sight of what they are both seeing in front of them.

Tara and Mr. Largen stare out the front windshield and observe attentively, the limousine that just made a U-turn in the middle of the street. The limousine has now slowly pulled up a few feet in front of Tara's car and stopped at the red traffic light so, she raises her right arm and points at the license plate, that's on the back of the limousine in front of them. Frightened and afraid Tara looks back and forth at the license plate and at her Father, who is sitting there still and speechless in the passenger seat, holding on tightly to the newspaper he has in his possession. He, then nervously looks at the strange and unfamiliar text written on the license plate and tries to make out what the dark and eerie calligraphy inscription says…

(License Plate) qoqX rXA rQIIrQ Snatching the newspaper out of her Fathers hand Tara, pops the black rubber band off and for some apparent reason Mr. Largen, tries to snatch the newspaper back from Tara but she quickly turns to her left and holds the newspaper down by the driver's side door. She, unfolds the newspaper and right there, written at the top in bold letters Tara sees the word THE€ JOURNAL! And underneath the bold letters, there's a picture of the same all-black tinted limousine, that's in front of Tara's car in the street right now, stopped at a red traffic light. And underneath the picture of the limousine there's a written paragraph entitled laws…

(Paragraph) "For every action, there is a cause. And the cause, sometimes brings disappointment to all, who don't practice its laws. Pain and Agony, tormented words damaging the heart. And when the light shifts in the wrong direction, be sure not to be there when the night turns dark. Because in the end, who's going to take the blame, when the suffering is caused, by those with the same name. So, for every action there is a cause, and the cause sometimes brings disappointment, to all who don't practice its laws." Tara quickly lifts her head up and looks at her Father she, then looks out the front windshield at the limousine that's stopped a few feet ahead of her car, at the red traffic light. The traffic light turns caution yellow so, Tara looks back down at the newspaper she's holding down by the driver's side door, in her hand by her left side. Tara, suspiciously and carefully stares at the strange and unfamiliar license plate that's on the limousine, in the picture on the front page of the newspaper… *(Mumbling) THE€ JOURNAL?* Now realizing that the strange and unfamiliar language, written on the limousines license plate, spelled out THE€ JOURNAL! Tara wasted no time handing the newspaper back to her Father Mr. Largen, who grabs the newspaper surprised, more than Tara was at her own reaction to THE€ JOURNAL! With THE€ JOURNAL now in Mr. Largens hand, the silence inside the car accelerates and the swollen friction of tension sparks leaving the mood uncomfortable for Tara and Mr. Largen.

Alongside the already unanswered questions that Tara, had for her Father and Mr. Largen had for his Daughter it left her, feeling a little awkward and him feeling more disconnected. So, while in the passenger seat Mr. Largen, turns his head slowly to his right, while at the same time in the driver's seat Tara, slowly turns her head to the left. They both look at each other with hidden concern, while the smell of lies and deception prolong in the air. Then suddenly, black thick smoke can be seen coming from the back tires of the limousine again, the smoke rises in the air covering all Tara's windows, causing it hard for her or Mr. Largen too see. And with the passenger side window rolled down, it gets worse Mr. Largen starts coughing from the thick black tire smoke, the smoke rapidly enters the inside of the car, through the rolled down passenger side window. So, Mr. Largen grabs the top of his shirt with his left hand and uses it to cover his nose and mouth, trying to avoid inhaling any more of the limousine smoke. And with the top of his shirt covering his nose and mouth Mr. Largen, turns his head to his left and looks at his daughter Tara, who is also covering her nose and mouth with the top of her shirt as well. Mr. Largen, coughs again after inhaling some smoke while opening his mouth under his shirt trying to breathe, quickly Mr. Largen reaches out his right arm and rolls up the passenger side window…

(Mr. Largen Coughing) Try not to inhale, … (Coughing) too much smoke Tara! The smoke continues to linger inside the car but progressively, it starts to slowly disappear. After a few minutes and with the passenger side window now rolled all the way up, the smoke disappears completely, which helps Mr. Largen to stop coughing and Tara to safely breathe again. The windows in the car clear up from the black smoke then Tara and Mr. Largen, both remove their shirts from covering their nose and mouth, Tara and her Father both look out the front windshield at the traffic light, that has just turned green. And with urgency and full speed, the all black tinted limousine stopped in front of Tara's vehicle a few feet ahead, drives off like a bat out of hell. Tara turns to her right and looks at her Father before looking back down at the newspaper she, now has placed in her lap… *Daddy look!...* Mr. Largen turns his head to the left and looks at his daughter while the cellphone, that's in her pocketbook starts ringing…

(Cellphone Ringing) …(Ringing) … Yes, Tara! What's the matter dear? Daddy! I have something to tell you! …Well, aren't you going to answer your phone first? I guess not! Well go ahead I'm listening! … Daddy! … What is it Tara? … Daddy! Don't be mad at me for lying! But I do have a boyfriend! And his name is Paul!

SOME READING ISN'T FUNDAMENTAL

"When Books Are Doing The Judging

Take Cover"

TH€ LIBRARY

With a book in his hand Mark, stands between two bookshelves in the library he, reaches forward and puts the book he has in his hand back on the shelf, before reaching for another book. Mark leaves the room he's in and walks into a reading room in the library. As soon as he steps foot inside the second room, Mark notices that there ae several school kids huddled in a circle and each one has a book a book in their hand. Standing in the middle of the room, the kids are surrounded two schoolteachers, the teachers are looking down at the kids giving a small speech, after a few minutes the kids separate and find places at the tables in the library. While the two teachers both walk over to a corner in the room, stand there and chaperone the kids by watching over them all. While Mark, humbly walks over to the opposite corner in the room with a book also in his hand and finds a place to read. He, puts the book down on top of the table, pulls out a chair from underneath, takes his jacket off and places it on the back of the chair before sitting down. Mark looks at the school kids and then at the two teachers who are standing directly across from him, on the other side of the room. Then a man walks in the room and takes a seat a few chairs down from Mark, the man looks at Mark, he looks back at the man and they both give a friendly and greeting nod at each other, before opening the books they have in front of them.

After a few hours goes by, the reading room in the library where Mark is sitting down reading slowly starts to become empty, the school's kids and the two teachers are gone. And the man sitting at the table a few chairs down from Mark, closes his book and gets up from the table, he pushes the chair back away from the table, stands up looks at Mark reading, picks up the book he has and without pushing the chair back underneath the table, the man leaves the room headed towards the library's front desk were a librarian is standing there chewing on a piece of gum, typing on the laptop she has in front of her… *Mam! Excuse me!... Oh! I'm sorry! Would you like to check that book out? Yes! If you don't mind! Sure, no problem!* The librarian behind the desk, looks at the man oddly who's is standing with the book in his hand, the man has his head turned to his left and for some apparent reason he's staring at Mark, in an unusual way. Mark, who has no idea the man is staring at him, turns the page in the book and continues reading while sitting at the table. The man then takes two steps forward, towards the room where Mark is.

The librarian leans forward over the desk, looks in the direction where the man is looking, before leaning back in her chair she, blows a bubble with the gum she has in her mouth and then she, quietly pops the gum while staring at the man… *Sir! Excuse me, sir! Are you going to be checking that book out today?* The man hears the librarian talking to him, so he stops, turns back around and walks back over in front of the librarian's desk.

He, then places the book he has in his hand on top of the desk, while looking back and forth at Mark and the librarian, the librarian picks up the book from off the desk and holds it up a few feet away from her face. The librarian turns the book over and looks at the back while peeking at the man from the side of the book, the librarian's face turns into a slight frown as she's trying to find the books check out information in the computer. The librarian blows another bubble and again quietly pops the gum before lying the book flat down, on top of the desk.... *Sir! Would you excuse me for a minute?... Sure, take your time! ...I'll only be a minute!* The librarian hops up from out the chair she's sitting in behind the desk, she then gets ready to walk off before she quickly turns around and grabs the book that's lying on top of the desk. She, then walks towards the back of the library to a small office, she reaches out her arm and grabs the doorknob, turns the doorknob and walks in before closing the door back shut. After a few minutes goes by, the door to the room opens and two women walk out, one of the women closes the door back shut, before following the other librarian back over towards the library's checkout desk. Once behind the library's desk, one of the librarians looks for the man who was standing there about to check out the book, while the other librarian site down in the chair and starts typing something on the computer in front of her.

The librarian, standing up looks and sees the man standing in the doorway of the room where Mark, is still sitting at the table reading, she taps the other librarian on the shoulder and points in the direction where the man is standing, the librarian sitting down leans to her side and looks at the man then both librarians, whisper amongst themselves about what's going on…

(Ann & Dana Whispering) Is that him Ann?... Yes, that's him!... Well, he doesn't look at all strange to me! He's just standing there!... No Dana! You had to see how he, was looking at the man in that room! I mean he was looking at him, like he wanted to kill him!... Dana, I told you about reading all those thriller and suspense novels!... Well, then explain to me why he's standing over there looking so creepy? And not over here, checking out this book?... I don't know Ann, let's ask him! Sir! Excuse me sir! Would you mind coming over here please?...

I'm telling you Dana! If he looks at that man, in the room one more time like that! I'm calling the Police!... Would, you please stop it?... Alright! I'll stop for now, but I'm watching Mr. creepy!... Be quiet Ann, here he comes! And would you please, get rid of that gum? All that bubble blowing and popping, is getting on my nerves!... Whatever! You worried about this gum! When you need to be worried about the Library killer, over there! While handing Ann, a piece of napkin to put her gum in Dana, takes the gum out of her mouth and places in the napkin Dana, is holding out in her hand she, balls the gum up in the tissue and tosses in to a garbage pail underneath the desk….

Excuse me sir!... (Ann Whispering) Don't you mean creep? Dana, shoves Ann in the side before calling out to the man one more time, the man hears the librarian calling out to him so, he quickly turns around and sees the librarian who's sitting down waving one of her arms in the air, signaling for him to come over by the checkout desk. Mark hears the librarian calling the man as well so, he looks up from the table and sees the man turning around from the doorway, the man gradually walks back over to the library's check out desk, where the two women librarians Dana and Ann are waiting. The man walks up to the desk with both of his hands in his pockets and stands there looking at Dana, who's sitting down and has his book in her hand. The man shifts his eyes on the other librarian Ann, who's standing up and was assisting him earlier when he first wanted to check out the book.... *Hello, sir? I'm Dana the library's manager! And I see, you've met Ann already!... HI, Dana, Ann! Is there something wrong?... No! Well not exactly! You see sir! The book you have here, cannot be found in our library's data base!... You don't say!... Yes! And I'm not sure, if the book is from here at all! Where, exactly did you find the book?... Well! Actually, I got the book from some kid!... Did you say a kid?... (Ann Whispering) I told you! ...Yes! I guess the kid was with the students, who was here earlier!... Oh! The six grade students from St. Mary's!... I guess so! Anyway! One of the young boys... (Ann Whispering) Perverted and creepy! ... had the book and as he was getting ready to put it back on the shelf! He turns to me and just hands me the book!... Well, did he say anything Mister? ...*

That was the strange part! Because, seconds after I received the book from him! I looked at the cover, looked up and the boy was gone! But you know what! Strange enough, there was something, that caught my attention! … And what was that sir?... The young boy, the student didn't have on the school uniform, like the other children! … You don't say! Well, what was he wearing?... Dana, you said your name was right?... Yes, I'm Dana! Well, Dana! The boy who I got the book from, was dressed in all black! About four feet tall and another thing that surprised me! Was how he got a bike in here in the first place? …

(Whispering) Oh, hell no! I'm calling the police!

Sitting there smiling at what Ann just whispered to her Dana, looks at the man standing there and then at the book she has in her hand she, kindly lays the book down on top of the desk before adjusting her glasses on her face. Ann then reaches over, extends out her arm and picks up the book Dana then grabs the book from out of Ann' s hand and hands the book back to the man who's been standing there waiting impatiently. Ann, then sucks her teeth and frowns at how her manager Dana, just snatched the book from out of her hand, the man looks at Ann as she stands there quietly behind the desk next to the computer. With a disturbing look on her face Ann, looks up at the man who is looking back at her Ann, shakes her head side to side before looking away and focusing what's on the screen of the computer.

The man standing there in front of the library's checkout desk holds the book in his left hand he, then places his right hand on the edge of the desk… *So! I'm assuming the book is not from here! Am I right? …Yes! You're absolutely correct mister! And I'm so sorry sir! Usually, when things like this happen, someone checked the book out at another library! Or the book isn't even from a library at all! … Oh, no! … What I'm trying to say is! That sometimes people bring books from home and leave them here by mistake! And that could be what happened with this book! Especially, that I'm noticing that this book, doesn't even have a library checkout slot in the back! … Well, I'll be dam! And to think, I really wanted to read this book! … You still can! … I can? Are you sure? …. Definitely! All you have to do is show me some identification! And I will check the book out in your name! So, just in case someone comes looking for the book! We can contact you unless you have already finished reading it and returned it back to the library! … That's great! … Now all I need is some I.D. sir and you're all set! … Wow! I still get to take the book home and read it!*

(Ann Whispering) He's still creepy!

The man digs in his back pocket and takes out his wallet he, opens the wallet and removes his identification he, then hands the I.D. to Dana she, takes the I.D. and looks at it before turning around in the chair and handing the I.D. to Ann who is standing there in front of the computer, ignoring Dana and the man like she's so busy with what's she's doing on the computer.

Dana, gets up from the desk chair, stands there and looks at Ann who's typing on the computer trying to ignore them both Dana, shakes her head side to side signaling to Ann, not cause any problems while putting the man's information, in the computer and checking out the book....

Ok, sir! Well, I guess I'm all done here! Ann, here on the other hand, will take very good care of you! Right Ann? ... Right Ann? ... Oh, for sure! You have nothing to worry about! (Ann Whispering) Especially now that I have your address! ... Excuse me! Did you say something? ... Oh, no! She was just saying, we have your address now we can contact you! ... Oh! Well, that's good, I guess! ... Ann, take care of the man, will you? ... (Dana Whispering) Don't embarrass me! ... And you enjoy that book sir! ... Trust me I will! ... (Dana Whispering) Ann! ... Ok, Ann! I heard you the first time!

Walking away from the library's checkout desk Dana, the library's manager smiles at the man she, then looks at Ann one more time and frowns her face up at her before walking back towards the office. Dana, stops by the room Edward is in she, peeks her head inside and sees Mark, sitting at the table reading and standing up a few chairs down from him at the table, is an old lady and a tall man. The old lady and the tall man are both dressed in all black, the tall man is helping the old lady take off her coat he, then folds the coat over in his arm before walking over to the door.

The tall man stands there militantly and attentively in silence with the old lady's coat folded over his arm Dana, then peeks her head back out of the room she, walks over to the door of the library's office. She, reaches her arm out, turns the doorknob, opens the door and steps inside before closing the door shut Dana, walks over to her desk in the library's office, pulls out the chair from underneath the desk and sits down. She, then places her right hand on the computers mouse and navigates to the search bar on the computers screen. Dana let's go of the mouse and places both of her hands on the computers keyboard she, then begins typing… *(Typing)* while Ann is at the library's front desk checking out the book…

Mr. Butler!... Yes! Is Everything Ok Ann? … Oh! Everything is just fine Mr. Butler! I was just reading the name off of your I.D. … Well, that's me alright! … John Butler! It's Just, sometimes I wish my name was different! You know what I mean? … No! I'm afraid I don't know what you mean Mr. Butler! Are you telling me you have another name? Well, do you? … Oh, no! That is my real name alright! I mean the last name! With me working at a school and all! Sometimes the kids, start clowning around! And make jokes about my last name! … So, you are a schoolteacher? … No! I wish, I am a school secretary Ann! … (Ann Whispering) Creeping through the school! … Excuse me Ann! Oh, nothing! But what did you say, the name of the school was Mr. Butler? … Please! Call me John! And the name, St. Mary's! … Yea! I know that school! That's the school for the blind kids, right?...

I'm afraid your right Ann! ... Wow! That has to be amazing! And an honor as well! I really did underestimate you John! You're a real hero, in my book! That's very kind of you to say Ann! ... And I mean that John! ... But I'll tell you what Ann! Just because those kids are blind! Doesn't mean they act any different, then any other kids! They have as much fun, as anybody else! And like I said before, they love making jokes about my last name! All in fun I might ask! And to tell you the truth Ann, I enjoy it sometimes! ... Well, God bless you man! And if there is nothing else, can do for you! I guess your all done! Here's your I.D.! ...Can't forget that! ... And If someone stops by, looking for the book! Before you return it, we'll contact you! So, I guess that's it Mr. Butler! I mean John! It was nice meeting you!

Mr. Butler smiles at the librarian Ann before turning around and walking away from the checkout desk towards the library's exit. As Mr. Butler, gets closer to the exit he extends out both arms and pushes into the revolving doors, Mr. Butler then takes a step inside the revolving doors... *Sir! Mister! John! You forgot your book!* Mr. Butler hears Ann yelling out to him so, he quickly turns around and puts his foot in-between one the revolving doors to stop it from spinning. He, then pushes the door backwards so he can step out he, walks back over to the library's checkout desk he, stands there shaking his head where Ann, is holding the book in the air...

I don't believe this! After all of that, I forgot the book! Thanks so, much Ann! I would have hated to get all the home and had to turn back around! ... I know what you mean! ...I hope this book is worth it! ...It's looks like a great thriller, suspense to me! And if I don't find another copy in the system! I'll definitely be reading that one next once you're done! ... Sounds like a plan, to me Ann! Oh, and Ann! One more thing before I forget! ... Sure! What is It? ... The man in the room to your left, sitting at the table reading! ... (Ann Whispering) I knew this was, too good to be true! ... Yes! Mr. Butler, what about him? ... Do you happen to know his name? ... His name? Why, I sure don't Mr. Butler! I mean John! I'm pretty sure he's never been here in this library before! I would know! And if you don't mind me asking! What's it to you? ... He just looks so familiar! Like I seen him somewhere before! Or know someone in his family! ... Well, they say we all have a twin in the world John! ... No! It's not that! Dam it! I hate it, when I can't remember something! Anyway! If you are here when he leaves, find out if he's related to the Largen family! Would you? I would appreciate it! Because If he is, then I know his sister, we worked together! ... She was killed! ... Oh, I'm so sorry to hear that! How did she die? ... A car accident! Her name was Stacie Largen! And she had a beautiful soul! Rest in peace Stacie! ... That's a shame! But I will find out John! ... Thanks for stopping by! And you enjoy the rest of your day Ann! ... And you enjoy the book John!

Once Mr. Butler left the library and the coast was clear Ann, leans forward in the chair and looks in the room where Mark is still sitting at the table, she, then leans back in the chair and opens a drawer underneath the desk. Ann, searches through the files of people's names, who are registered to check out books from the library. Ann flips through pages and looks for Mark Largen, she finds the file, removes it and looks at the photo copied picture of his I.D. in the file. Nervously Ann, looks back and forth at the library's exit, the office and the room Mark is in she, then types the name Stacie Largen in the search bar on the computer and surprisingly shocking, a beautiful family picture pops up on the screen of Mark Largen, his parents Mr. and Mrs. Largen, his older brother Edward, his younger sister Tara and Stacie Largen.

They are all at some sort of family gathering dressed in all white, to Ann the picture looks as if it was taken at some sort of expensive banquet hall, being that there are marble tables all around decorated with candles and flowers, glass chandeliers hanging from the ceiling and everybody in the picture who can be seen, are sitting down dressed up in their finest attire... *(Whispering) Mark Largen! That's his name, Mr. Butler was right! Now I feel stupid, for thinking negative about him! Edward Largen! I wonder which one is his sister Stacie.* Quickly putting Mark's file back in the drawer Ann, closes the drawer back and sits there staring at the beautiful picture of the Largen Family on the computer.

Ann examines the picture then she sees two things in the photo that really catches her attention so, she clicks the mouse and navigates the curser to where the computers screen zoom is located. Ann zooms the picture larger and there, she sees something in Marks hand, that looks like it doesn't suppose to be there. Ann, then zooms the photo larger and sees that Mark is holding a newspaper in his hand, at first it kind of bothered Ann, being that she kept on thinking why, would any be carrying better yet, holding on to a newspaper and while taking a picture, at an elegant establishment like that. Then, Ann realized where Mark was now, and she thought too herself that he was a reader, or he wouldn't be here at the library so, that thought was erased from her conscious. She, then moves the curser of the mouse over by Stacie Largen and there seated behind Stacie Largen, was a man that looked all too familiar. So, familiar Ann had too zoom in one last time and when she did, she saw in the picture, seated behind Stacie Largen, also dressed in elegant attire with his face shaved. Not only was Mr. Butler in the picture but lying on the table in front of him, was the book he just checked out the library, the book, that the young boy dressed in all black, handed to him. Ann was blown away at what she was seeing. So, she prints out a copy of the picture while looking back and forth at the library's exit, the office and the room Mark is in, just to make sure no one catches her playing Sherlock Holmes while at work.

Ann, removes the copied picture from the printer she, look back at the computer screen and searches for a date and time the picture was taken. She, finds the date and time so she, picks up a pen from off the desk and writes down the date and time on the back of the photo copied picture she, then folds the picture up, opens the drawer underneath the desk and puts the picture inside along with the pen.

Ann, then types in the word The Journal, in the search bar hoping to find and locate some credible and reliable information about the book or its author that Mr. Butler has claimed to have been given by some young boy, who was dressed in all black here in the library. Ann, started searching web sites she, even contacted libraries and bookstores that were local and well known around the world, but still Ann, had no luck. Ann was unable to find any information on anything concerning a book entitled THE JOURNAL. Even through all the calling and searching, Ann's purpose still wasn't fulfilled, there was something missing, something that kept her wanting to get to the bottom of the suspense. Just because there was proof, that the book had existed, it just wasn't confirmed yet, where the book had come from and author who wrote it. Ann went even further lengths to find some reliable answers, by picking up the phone on the desk next to the computer and dials the number too, St. Mary's school for the blind where Mr. Butler, said he had worked…

(Phone Ringing) Good afternoon! This is St. Mary's, school for the blind! How can I help you? ... Hello! My name is Ann! And I'm calling from the library, located on west 8th street downtown! ... Well hello, Ann! I'm Mr. Gean and how can I assist you today! ... Well! I was wondering if you could help me, with something? ... Sure! What is it? ... By any chance does anyone work there, by the name of Mr. Butler. First name John! ... John Butler! I'm sorry, but that name doesn't ring a bell! And I've been working here, for seven years straight! So, I would know if there were someone, who worked here by that name! Trust me, I know everybody! But just to make sure Ann! Let me pull the name up, on the school's database! Because here, there are a lot of substitute teachers who come and go! But every one of them, has to be screened and registered before they can work here! So, just give me a minute! ...(Typing) ... (Mumbling) John Butler! John Butler! John Butler! ... Ann! You still there? ... Yes, I'm here! ... Ok! I've did a database name search for the school! Going back far as three years and still no Mr. Butler, can be found! Are you sure that's the person's name? ... Well! To tell you the truth Mr. Gean! I'm not sure, reason being today a man checked out a book!

That was not from this library and said a young boy here, handed it to him! He, then said his name was John Butler and that he worked at St. Mary's school for the blind! He even gave me his I.D. so I could check out the book! ...Wow! Sounds to me like somebody's playing games, or this guy is just plain old crazy, if you ask me! I think you should check with authorities! Like find out if the I.D is stolen! You can't be too careful these day's Ann! ...

I know Mr. Gean! The first time I saw him, I thought he was creepy! …Well! Good luck with that! And if you need anything else, call me! … I will Mr. Gean! …Oh, one more thing Mr. Gean! … Go ahead shoot! … Mr. Butler! Or whoever he really was, asked about somebody name Mark Largen! Does that name, ring a bell? … Mark Largen! Wow! If isn't one thing, it's another! …You know what Ann! I thought that name would come up! And just so you know, Mark Largen, is the brother of the woman who was killed, in the car accident a few days ago! You probably saw it on the news! Ann, she also was the principle here at the school before she died! …Are you serious! What a tragedy! I feel bad now, and he's here! …Did you say he's there? Are you talking about Mark Largen, Ann? …

Yes! He's in one of the library rooms right now, reading a book! … Well! At least something got accomplished by you calling Ann! …I don't understand! …Oh, nothing to worry yourself with! I just have a book here, left by his sister Stacie! The book was signed to her from him! And I was thinking, when would a good time to get it to him? And Wala! I get a call from you! … So, I guess you want me to go and get him? …No! Don't bother! I'll bring it myself, with no traffic I'll be there in five minutes! Just tell him Mr. Gean, has something for him, he knows me! And I'm on my way there now! Ok, Ann? … Sure! Anything I can do to help, a grieving family I'm all in! … Settled then! Is there anything else I can help you with Ann? …Why unfortunately, there's one last thing! …Ok! …Mr. Gean! The book that you have for Mark! Would it so happen to be called TH€ JOURNAL? … No! I'm afraid not Ann! This book is entitled War!

Hanging up the phone Ann, grabs the computers mouse and closes the search bar she, logs out of the internet leaving the computer on Ann, pulls the desk drawer back open and takes out the Largens Family photo copied picture. She, puts the picture in her back pocket, reaches back in the desk drawer and takes out an office desk sign that says… *Out to lunch* Ann, sits the sign on the desk before getting up out the chair and headed over to the library's office, where her manager Dana is. On her way to the Library's office Ann, stops by the reading room where Mark is and peeks her head inside and there, she sees the old lady and the tall man.

The old lady quickly turns her head and surprises Ann, by the frightening look upon her face, the look on the old lady's face is a poltergeist pale, her eyes the color of the sky before the storm. And her hair was disguised, by a black hat that shadowed her face from the large round rim, that circled around the whole hat like an umbrella. The old lady and Ann, eyes connect while Mark is closing the book, he has in front of him Mark, pushes the chair back he's sitting in away from the table and attempts to get up. Promptly the old lady, takes her eyes off Ann and turns back around in her seat at the table Ann, quickly moves and walks over to the library's office door. Ann digs in her back pocket and takes out the printer copied photo of the Largen Family…

My God! I don't believe this! Mr. Butler, well, John! Mark and Stacie Largen all in one picture! Wait, until I tell Dana! Or should I? … I must tell her, what I just found out! This is crazier than I thought! By the door Ann, reaches out her arm and grabs the doorknob she, then out of excitement Ann, opens the door. She, steps inside the office and turns around she, then closes the door shut and locking it behind her before walking over to Dana, who's sitting down at the managers desk inside. Ann unfolds the photocopied picture and holds it up in the air she, then drops the picture in front of Dana, onto her desk. Dana looks at Ann before picking up the picture, she looks at the picture and immediately she jumps up from desk excited as well. Dana's, behavior is overwhelming she's, not only thrilled to see who or what is in the picture she's, also on edge of great disappointment as she stands there holding the printer copied picture in her hand. Dana, gets up so fast she knocks over the chair behind her and a few ornaments and pictures she, has on top of her desk. Dana, eyes widen, and her mouth is wide open by what's she is seeing, the look on her face is devastating Dana, is looking and acting like she just saw a ghost literally… *You must be kidding me! Ann! Tell me this is picture photo shopped? Please, tell me this is a photo shopped picture? … Photo shop! … Yea! You know, those pictures where people cut and paste! To make the picture, look different from the original! … I know what phot shop is Dana! But this picture, was copied from the internet! … We'll! It still can be Photo shopped Ann! … Dana! Your confusing me here! …*

Ann, use your brain! You work in a library, for Christ sake! At least, act like you do some reading! ... To shay, Dana! To shay! ...Anyway, look at what's on the table! In front of this guy! Who's sitting all by himself, behind Stacie! That was the first thing I noticed, besides this guy here! And isn't that the same person, who's here in the library right now? ... Yep! Dana, that's him alright! And what about him? ...I don't know too much about him! Except that he's, been here a several times before! But Ann, what I'm concerned with, is that book! The book Ann! The Book! ...

Now you're on my page Dana! Because, that's one of the main reasons, why I printed the picture, in the first place! Besides, the newspaper! And Stacie Largen! ... What? Who? ...Oh, never mind! Now what about this here book Dana?... Oh, Yea! The book! Listen, this man who checked out the book um, Mr.! What's his name again... Mr. Butler! ... Yes, him! Remember he was telling us, that a young boy handed him the book? ... Ok, and so what! ... Ann, think about it! How could the boy give him the book, if he already had it! And when was this picture taken! ... Wow! Look on the back Dana! ... Is this the date! Ann, please tell me this is the date when the picture was taken? ... That's right! That's the date and the time! ...So, you really are getting your Sherlock Holmes on! That's good Ann! Now if this date, is from three years ago! You tell me Ann! How in the hell, can your boy John, have that same book in his possession then! If the boy, just handed it to him today, here in the library? ...Dana, that is true! ... And what's his connection to Stacie Largen and THE JOURNAL? Need I say more! ... I knew it! I knew it! Mr. Butler, more like Mr. Creep again! ...

Ann, you might be right this time! ...Dana! I'm calling the police and don't try and stop me either! ... I don't think that will be necessary Ann! ... I knew you was going to say that! ... No! It's not that at all! There's no need, we already have all his information on file Ann! ... We sure do, don't we? ... Ann, we even know he works! And now we know he, has connections too Mark Largen! So, if he doesn't return the book, we go to his job and show him the picture! Or we can just go out there and talk to Mark Largen right now! ... Dana, I don't think that will be a good idea! ...Whatever Ann! But whatever we choose, you can get your unsolved mystery on, Mrs. Holmes!

At the table in one of the reading rooms in the library Mark Largen, places a book marker in between the pages of the book he's reading, he closes the book and gets up from the table, out of courtesy for the old lady who, is now preparing to sit down. The old lady, digs inside the bag she has in her lap and takes out a newspaper that's wrapped up in a black rubber band and a book she, places the newspaper and the book on the table in front of her. Mark looks at the newspaper and the book before sitting back down and watching as the old lady opens the book and start reading. Mark, then lifts his head up from off the book and awakes from someone shaking him and tapping him on the shoulder he, squints both of his eyes, raises his right arm and wipes the corner of both of his eyes with his fingertips.

While yawning and stretching at the sight of the librarian senior citizen woman, who's standing on the other side of the table, in front of Mark wearing bifocal glasses, button up shirt, oversized plaid dress down to her ankles and a shawl wrapped over her shoulders…

Excuse me Mister! I'm so sorry to ruin your beauty rest! But the library, will be closing soon! … Where am I? … Sir! Your, at the library on west 8th street downtown! … Did, you just say Library? … Why, yes! And we are closing soon so, I suggest you finish reading your book! Or, check it out up front, by the desk! … Ok, thankyou I will! The librarian, elderly woman looks at Mark strangely as she continues collecting the books, left on the table in the reading room where Mark, is recovering from being fast asleep. The elderly woman holds the books securely in her arm as she gently walks out the reading room, back towards the front desk. Mark, wakes up, leans forward, stretches and watches the elderly woman walk out the room, a few feet outside the room the elderly woman stops and turns around … *Don't forget your newspaper too dear! I'm an old lady and I don't want to be making several trips! Back and forth collecting left books and newspapers! By strong young men, such as yourself! Ok, dear? (Mark Laughing)* Raising his right hand in the air while shaking his head up and down, signaling that he understands exactly what the elderly woman has said. The elderly woman, smiles back at Mark before slowly turning around with several books, secured in her arms.

Staring at the newspaper and the poem book, that's lying there on the table in front of him Mark, reaches out his arm and places his right hand on top of the newspaper. He pulls the newspaper closer towards him, while thinking twice before popping off the black rubber band and unfolding the newspaper. Mark had a bad feeling about this newspaper and he just knew that he would regret it something terrible, if he opened it and reading the stories printed inside. Mark didn't even want to look at the front page because this wasn't Marks, first time being introduced to TH€ JOURNAL! He had saw a picture of his sister Stacie, at the scene of her own accident in TH€ JOURNAL. And this was before his sister's accident had even occurred so, Mark was thinking that if he didn't show any interest or indulge in the newspaper's actions and events, then maybe just maybe, he'd be somewhat in control of his own fate and someone else's destiny. But still none of this was making sense Mark, was thinking and he still didn't know where this newspaper was coming from. The librarian Ann gets Marks attention as she rapidly walks by the reading room, Mark gets up from the table and snatches up the poem book and the newspaper, that's still has the black rubber band wrapped around it. Mark, rushes over to the open door of the reading room he, looks to his left and then to his right, he then sees Ann opening the door to the library's office, a few feet away down the hall. With the printed copy of the picture in her left-hand Ann, reaches her right arm out, turns the doorknob handle and calmly steps inside the office, before closing the door and locking it behind her.

Mark cuffs the newspaper up under his right arm and stuffs the book in his back pocket, as he walks over by the front door to the library's office, he then stands there by the office door a few seconds go by. Mark removes the newspaper from up under his arm, with his left hand before delicately, knocking on the library's office door, with his right hand balled up into a fist … *(Mark Knocking) Ann! Did you hear that? …. Hear what? … (Mark Knocking) …That! … I heard that! Who, could that be? … We'll! We know it's not Mrs. Harris! She never comes in here! And there's nobody else working tonight! Besides us! … (Mark Knocking) …Well, Ann! Aren't you going to answer it? …Dana! You answer it! This is your office! And you are the manger, right? …Ok! Ok! I'll answer it!* Dana, the library's night manger walks around from behind the desk, she pushes Ann on the shoulder, as she walks pass her towards the office door. Ann, slowly walks a few feet behind Dana as she's now standing behind the office door, looking back and forth at Ann, who is now standing inches behind Dana, smiling leaning her chin on Dana's right shoulder …

Who is it? … I'm sorry to bother you! My name is Mark Largen! And I just want to ask you a question! I know its closing time, but if you could just help me out! It would be more than thankful! … Dana and Ann are silenced by the guest appearance by Edward, and they both are looking at each other, face to face in total shock speechless Ann, has her mouth wide open out of surprise while Dana, has her left arm raised covering Ann's mouth with her whole hand …

(Dana Whispering) Don't, say nothing about the picture, the book or the newspaper! I'm warning you! ...Hello! Are, you still there? ...Please! Just a minute I promise! Beside! I don't want grandma hitting me with a ruler! For still being here! ... (Dana Laughing) Ok! One, minute Mr. Largen! It is closing time! And, only because Grandma Harris, does have a ruler! ... (Dana Whispering) Not a word! Not one word!
Dana removes her hand from over Ann's mouth and reaches out her arm and unlocks the lock she, then grabs the doorknob and opens the door. There, standing in the doorway of the library's office door directly in front of Dana and Ann is Mark Largen, who has a newspaper with a black rubber band wrapped around it, cuffed up underneath his left arm. Mark, looks at Dana's face and can see some powerful lies, concealed secretly hidden in her eyes and on Ann's face Mark, he can see some investigating in her eyes caused by pure honest and genuine integrity. After a few seconds standing there in front of Mark, Dana and Ann gently move to the side and the both of them closely watches as Mark, grabs the newspaper that he has cuffed, underneath his left arm and holds it in his hand. Before stepping inside the office and nodding his head up and down, greeting them both as he, humbly walks pass them Mark, takes two steps to the side stands there and then him and Dana, watches as Ann closes the door and locks it shut. Ann, looks at the newspaper Mark is now holding in his hand and can see the black rubber band wrapped around it she, stands by the door and looks at Dana, who has her undivided attention on Mark and not paying her any mind.

Ann, walks away from the office door, stands next to Dana and leans her head into Dana's left ear ... *(Ann Whispering) I think that's the same newspaper, from the picture!* Gently Dana, pushes Ann in the side while stepping over by where Edward is standing Dana, looks back at Ann and frowns, turns back around and smiles at Mark as he stands there not sure what to think ... *Ladies! Is everything alright? ...Hello Mr. Largen! And yes, everything here is just fine! Right Ann? ...Why of course! Nothing to see here Mr. Largen! ... Anyway, I'm Dana, the library's night manager! And I'm sure you know, if haven't been already introduced! ...I can speak for myself! Hello! I'm Ann! ...Yes! I saw you speeding pass the reading room earlier! ... It's a library thing Mr. Largen! Books, books, books ...Please! Call me Mark! ...Ok, Mark! ...We'll Mark! Like I said I'm Ann! How, can I be of service to you this evening! ...Glad you asked! May I have a seat? ...Sure, help yourself! ...Thankyou! We'll as you know ...Excuse! I'm sorry for interrupting you! But can I see your newspaper? ...Ann! Don't you see us talking? ...It's totally fine, I was just about...* Mark, gets disrupted by the knocking on the office door so, he quickly pushes the newspaper back up underneath his left arm and looks at Ann and Dana, who's been acting really strange, ever since he stepped foot inside the office. Edward gets up from the chair he's sitting in, he stands there in front of Dana, as she leisurely walks over to Ann ... *(Mark Knocking) Ann! ...Yes, Dana! ... (Mark Knocking) ...We'll aren't you going to see who's at the door? ...Oh, the door! Silly me, what was I thinking Ann! Let me get the door Ann!* ...

(Mark Knocking) Smiling at the amusing behavior Ann and Dana, are showing him Mark turns his head to the left and looks at Dana's office desk he, notices that the chair behind the desk is lying on its side on the floor, the picture frames and ornaments on top of the desk all knocked down. Mark, eyes widen, and his eyebrows lift from seeing the untidiness and clutter left by the library's manager, who he knew for a fact was hiding something but at the same time, was so well dressed and spoke polite with good manners.

Opening the door Ann, sees Grandma Harris standing there at the door wiping her nose with a handkerchief she, blows her nose, balls the handkerchief up and places it back inside her button up shirt pocket, that tucked in the oversized plaid ankle length skirt, that she's wearing. Looking back and forth at the library's checkout desk and at Ann Grandma Harris, leans her head to the side and up over Ann's left shoulder, trying to see who else is inside the office, along with Ann and Dana …

Hello! Grandma Harris! Do, you want Ann? ...Oh, no child! It's you I came to see! Me! Grandma Harris? Ann! Is everything Ok? Who's at the door Ann? …It's Grandma Harris Dana! Hello Grandma Harris! …Hello Dana! …Grandma Harris! You said you came to see me? Why, yes dear! There's a man here to see you Ann! … Ann! Tell Grandma Harris we are busy at the moment! Grandma Harris where is this man? …Oh, he's in the reading room, sitting at the table reading a book! I told him this was closing time! But he insisted that he spoke with you!

(Grandma Harris Whispering) He, said it was of urgent emergency! ...I'm sorry Dana! But it seems like a bad time, for me to be here! Oh, please Mr. Largen! She'll be only a minute! ...No! I think I'd better go! ...I'll return tomorrow! And then we can finish, where we left off! Will that be alright Dana? ...That will be just fine Mr. Largen! I mean Mark! Turning around at the door Ann, looks at Mark who is now walking towards her Mark, nods his head at her and looks at Grandma Harris, who's raising her right arm and tilting her bifocal glasses, on her nose below her eyes. Grandma Harris, is looking Mark up and down Mark, smiles before squeezing in between Grandma Harris and Ann, who's standing there blocking the library's office door *...Good day ladies! Grandma Harris!* Now, stepping smoothly out of the office into the hallway of the library Mark, walks pass the checkout desk and down towards the exit of the building, while Grandma Harris, Ann and Dana all stand there and watch *...Ok, Grandma Harris! Where is this man that's here to see me? ...He's in the library's reading room! ...The reading room Grandma Harris? He's in there right now? ...Yes! .... Ann! Someone's here to see you! And you didn't tell me! Well! Let's, not keep him waiting! Come on! ...Dana! I think he's here to see me! ...Oh, don't be silly! In the reading room Grandma Harris?* Walking out the office pulling Ann by her arm Dana, let's go of Ann's arm and walks down the hallway of the library she, looks inside each room trying to find the man, who's there to see Ann.

After shaking her side to side disagreeing with what Dana is doing Ann, looks at Grandma Harris before following Dana, down the library's hallway in search for the man, who showed up at the library to see Ann. Grandma Harris, stands there and watches as the two- walk side by side, peeking their heads inside the open doors to each reading room in the library, looking for the man who's there to see Ann. Grandma Harris, turns around outside of the office door she, looks inside the office and notices that the chair behind the desk, is lying on the floor and the picture frames and ornaments are all knocked down on top of the desk, the office is cluttered. … *(Grandma Whispering) My God! This office is a mess! Doesn't anyone do any cleaning, around here!* Now, stepping gently inside the office Grandma Harris, looks to her left and sees a chair up against the wall, with a newspaper laying on the seat, with a black rubber band wrapped around it. She walks over by the chair and picks the newspaper up she, then looks back at the open office door before walking over, towards Dana's managers desk, with the newspaper held tightly in her hand. Grandma Harris, bends down and picks the chair up from off the floor she, drops the newspaper on top of the desk, before cleaning and sweeping up the office she, sits up the fallen picture frames, ornaments and everything else that has been disorganized on top of the desk. Now with the library's office clean, the chair picked up and the desk back organized Grandma Harris, sits down in the chair seated behind the desk she, picks up the newspaper and pops the rubber band off, before unfolding it and looking at the front page …

(Grandma Whispering) TH€ JOURNAL! She panics her eyes widen out of fear and concern, by what she's seeing on the front page of TH€ JOURNAL so, she quickly drops the newspaper back on top of the desk and leans back in the chair, offended confused and upset. She, then raises both of her arms and uses both of her hands, to adjust the bifocal glasses that's sliding down her nose on her face, then the temperature in the office slowly starts dropping. Grandma Harris, blood pressure starts rising through the cold chill, that is making the office feel like one big refrigerator, the cold chill is deliberately biting her body. And as the temperature drops, it starts cutting through her clothes like a pair of paper scissors Grandma Harris, starts feeling lightheaded as she rubs her arms and legs, trying warm herself up while sitting in the chair, behind the desk ... *My God! Who turned off the heat? It's freezing in here! And, what blasphemy is this? What is this some sick joke? Dana and Ann! These girls will do anything, for a laugh! But this right here is not funny!* Smacking the newspaper with the back of her hand out of resentment Grandma Harris, sees the printer copied picture of the Largen family on the desk, that Ann printed off the computer. She also notices that Mr. Butler, who she got of glimpse of earlier leaving the library after checking out a book, is also in the picture with the Largen family. Mr. Butler is seated at a table all by himself behind Stacie Largen. Grandma Harris remembers Stacie's face and name from being reported, on almost every channel on the news regarding the unfortunate accident of Stacie Largen.

The Accident she had while driving her car home from work on the highway. Now, holding the printer copied picture up next to the newspaper on top of the desk Grandma Harris, stares intensively at Mr. Butler, who also has his picture on the front page of THE JOURNAL. Mr. Butler, is in the library's office with a book in his hand, standing over Grandma Harris as she's laying lifeless on the floor, behind the office desk with both of her eyes closed. And on the floor, there's blood around her head and in her possession tightly gripped, Grandma Harris is holding on for dear life to THE JOURNAL. Knocked over a few feet away on its side from the desk and Grandma Harris, is the chair she's sitting in right now, and sadly enough she's observing her own self, lying down on the floor in a pool of blood, looking lifeless in the library's office behind the office desk. And even though how uncomfortable and awkward it seemed to Grandma Harris, she will forever as long as she lives, remember this newspaper ... *(Grandma Whispering) What! In the world is going on here. How! ... But I'm! Where's Dana and Ann? ...I don't feel so good! I have a serious migraine, right now!* Grandma Harris, reaches her arm out and picks up the office phone from off the desk she, places the phones receiver to her ear and can hear a loud, solid dial tone. She looks up at the ceiling and sees the lights uncontrollably flickering off and on, the library's office door then immediately slams shut, causing some of the small items on top of the desk to fall off.

Grandma Harris jumps in the desk chair startled by the loud sound of the office door slamming shut and the ceiling lights flickering off and on. So, she looks back at her picture on the front page of TH€ JOURNAL before hanging the phones receiver back up with her hand shaking nervously and uneasy. While placing both of her hands firmly, on the edge of the desk Grandma Harris, attempts to try and stand but with the migraine and the lightheaded feeling she's and weak. The cold temperatures drop in the office, it's now become so cold that Grandma Harris, breath can be seen by her lingering in the air, every time she breathes. Her hands are freezing and the bones in her body are stiffening, to the point where she's moving around the office and behind the desk very slow. As the lenses on her bifocal glasses start fogging up Grandma Harris, reaches for the newspaper on top of the desk she, picks the newspaper up and holds it in her hand while stumbling, to the side after taking a step forward.

She stands there behind the desk looking back and forth at the printer copied picture of the Largen family, the office door and TH€ JOURNAL, then out of nowhere a strong thrust and powerful cold wind, moves silently but violently throughout the office and the force shoving things around off the floor and on top of the desk, up in the air. The violently, strong and powerful freezing cold temperature wind, throws Grandma Harris into the wall she, trips over the chair behind her trying to regain her composer, while holding on tightly to the newspaper.

But the cold front wind is so powerful and strong, it knocks Grandma Harris, over and onto the floor. While falling over Grandma Harris, gets knocked out unconscious, from hitting her head on the corner of the office desk, the desk injury to her head, puts a small but severe and brutal gash above her eyebrow. The gash opens and quickly and starts immediately bleeding, leaving a puddle of blood underneath her head as she, lays on the floor lifeless behind the office desk, with both of her eyes closed. Her fall knocks the desk chair over, she was sitting at the time of the fall and not too far away from where she's laying, are her bifocal glasses that have flew off her face on the floor, from the hard impact of Grandma Harris, head hitting the floor. With the bifocal glasses laying rim side up with one cracked lens Grandma Harris, lays there lifeless with blood spilling from her head, unconscious on the office floor. And in her possession tightly gripped Grandma Harris, is holding on for dear life to the newspaper now known to her and other unfortunate individuals around her as TH€ JOURNAL. With the office door now completely shut, the lights on the ceiling are still flickering off and on and the strong thrust of the powerful cold wind, continuing to move silently and violently throughout the library's office. The force of the freezing cold temperature is still uncontrollably picking up and throwing things around, from off the floor and on top of the desk, up in the air. Until someone knocks on the office door, from outside in the library's hallway *(Mr. Butler Knocking) …*

(Mr. Butler Knocking) Then, immediately the lights stop flickering on the ceiling, the strong thrush and powerful cold freezing temperature, gradually returns to normal. And the uncontrollable wind, that was picking up and throwing things around in the office, from off the floor and on top of the desk up in the air, unexpectedly comes to a halt. There's stillness and a paranormal silence, coming from inside the office and besides Mr. Butlers, tapping from the hard-bottom shoes he's wearing on his feet, you can hear a pin drop.

Along with the sound of the light scratching that can be heard from the constant rubbing in-between his legs when he walks, due to the cheap discounted polyester two-piece suit he's wearing, alongside the wrinkled-up button up shirt and uncoordinated color bowtie … *Hello! Anyone in there? Ann! Dana! …Librarians! (Mr. Butler Knocking) It's Mr. Butler, again! …Hello! (Mr. Butler Knocking)* After several attempts of trying to get someone to open the library's office door Mr. Butler, turns his head to the right to see if anybody is looking before he reaches out his left arm and gets ready to grab the doorknob. And as soon as he's about to turn the doorknob, the door to the office slowly and thrillingly opens. Mr. Butler is in shock as he looks to his right one more time, before pushing the library office door, all the way open and suspiciously creeps inside leaving the office door open…

(Mr. Butler Mumbling) Dam it! Why is it so cold and dark in here? (Mr. Butler Exhaling) I can see my own breath in here, it's so cold! And maybe therefore, they keep the door closed! Dam it! This place is a total disaster! ...Looks like it's been hit, by sandy in here!

The office is dark and dim from the ceiling lights almost blowing out when the paranormal happenings occurred inside. But Mr. Butler, can see just enough due to the hallway light in the library, shining through the office open door, the light from the hallway is flashing on one side of the office. Now extending out his left arm Mr. Butler, reaches around the office as he walks through, trying to secure himself from bumping into anything that might be in the way. He, then gradually and cautiously walks pass the chair that's surprisingly still leaned up against the wall, through all that has happened in the office in the last couple of hours. Mr. Butler, steps on a picture frame and cracks the glass, from the pressure of his foot he, notices the office desk ahead of him so, he rushes over and stands in front of the desk, with both of his hand place flat on top while looking down at the clutter and mess. Then a woman's voice can be heard, the woman is whispering which is making it hard for Mr. Butler, to hear or understand what the woman is saying or where the voice of the woman is coming from. And because of the stillness and paranormal silence all throughout the office Mr. Butler, was able to pinpoint exactly where the whispering of the woman's voice was coming from ...

(Grandma Whispering) Help, me! Please! Help, me! I'm down here! The voice catches Mr. Butler's attention again as Grandma Harris, lays on the floor and calls out for help and with both of his hands placed flat on the desk Mr. Butler, uses his hands and the edge of the desk, to maneuver around and over to the left side of the room.

Being that the further away he's from the open door, the lower the library's hallway shines inside the office. Mr. Butler takes a small step to his left and hears more glass cracking from underneath his feet so, he looks down and realizes that he has stepped on a pair of glasses Mr. Butler, carefully bends down, reaches his hand out and picks up the glasses. While bending down near the floor Mr. Butler, looks at the glasses in his hand and sees that there's blood all over the frames of the glasses and on his hand. He hears the woman's voice again along with some light breathing that's not his own. Carefully Mr. Butler, extends out his arms and reaches blindly around the office while still bending down and after a few seconds of reaching his hand touches something, something that caused him to jump back out of fear and for a quick second it scared the life out of him , but Mr. Largen knew that this something was not just anything, he, knew for a fact that this was where the voice of the whispering was coming from and that something was a person and that person was Grandma Harris, the elderly librarian …

Mam! Are, you alright? What happened? Your bleeding for Christ sake! (Grandma Whispering) Help, me please! …Ok! But where are you hurt? I need to know so; I can tell the paramedics! Mr. Butler is now freaking out at the sight of the woman lifeless body lying there on the floor, behind the office desk. With blood on his hand and on the bifocal glasses he, picked up off the floor Mr. Butler, tosses the bloody glasses on top of the desk, digs inside his polyester suit blazer pocket and takes out his cellphone. Trembling nervous as hell Mr. Butler, is shaking with his cellphone in his hand he, pressing the numbers on his cellphone to dial 911 … *(Cellphone Ringing)* Then suddenly, the lights on the ceiling in the office comes back on and Mr. Butler, is in a state of shock after realizing that he's the first one to find Grandma Harris. Mr. Butler drops the cellphone he has in his hand on to the floor, once he hears the loud voices of the two women, yelling and screaming at the top of their lungs. The screen on the cellphone shatters from the hard-hitting impact to the floor, while the two-woman continue yelling and screaming as they stand by the library's office door looking at Mr. Butler. Whose standing over Grandma Harris, the elderly librarian woman whose body is lying on the office floor, behind the office desk, with a pool of blood leaking from her head …

Oh, my God! Somebody call the police! What, happened? …. He killed Grandma Harris! You, murderer! This mans a murderer! What have you done? …Ann! Now, call the police! And the ambulance! Hurry!

Mr. Butler turns his head to his left and can see Dana the library's manager and the other librarian Ann, who helped him out earlier when he was checking out a book. Ann and Dana are both in disbelief at what they are witnessing. Ann raises her left arm up by her face and covers her mouth that is wide open with her hand she, then reaches in her back pocket with her right hand and takes out her cellphone. Ann dials 911 … *(Cellphone Ringing) … (Cellphone Ringing)* Taking a step back from office door Ann, holds the cellphone up to her ear and waits for the 911 emergency operator to answer the phone while Dana, now has her left arm extended out across the entrance of the office doorway. And with her right arm extended out straight forward Dana, is pointing at Mr. Butler with a look of overwhelming, devastating all over her face. As Mr. Butler, stands over the lifeless body of Grandma Harris looking at Dana and Ann he, slowly bends down by Grandma Harris side and can hear her breathing as he, leans his head in closer by her face … *(Mr. Butler Whispering) Grandma Harris! The ambulance is on its way! I think one of the Librarians has called! You're going to be ok! Just lay still, help is coming!* Mr. Butler, lifts his head up turns around and looks at Dana who is now stepping inside the office Mr. Butler, quickly turns back around after hearing Grandma Harris say something and that's when Grandma Harris, gently raises her arm which gets Dana's attention. Mr. Butler, looks and sees a newspaper in Grandma Harris hand he, then jumps by the slight startle of the feeling of an unexpected touch on the shoulder.

Mr. Butler quickly looks up to his left and sees' Dana standing there with her right hand on his shoulder she, then reaches her left arm out and snatches the newspaper out of Grandma Harris hand. While holding the newspaper Dana, looks Mr. Butler directly in the face as he's looking back at her, the office gets quiet and only the sound of Grandma Harris breathing can be heard. Dana, looks at the newspaper and then back at Mr. Butler while grabbing his arm and helping him up of the floor Mr. Butler, stands there in front of Dana and they both look down at the newspaper Dana is holding in her left hand …

(Dana and Mr. Butler Whispering) The Journal!

STOP THAT BUS

"When The Ride, Cost More Than The Fare"

TH€ RIDE

With the newspaper in his hand Mark, lifts his arm up and pushes the rotating doors forward to the library, he steps inside and walks through to the other side of the rotating doors. Once outside he, then stands at the top of the library's stairs for a few minutes, before walking down the stairs near the curb on the sidewalk by the street. Mark, then looks to his left and then to is right before stepping off the curb and crossing the street, while on the other side of the street Mark, steps inside an overhead sheltered, fiber glass roof and siding bus stop that has a bench attached to the sides inside. With the newspaper still in his hand and the only one there at the bus stop Mark, sits down and places the newspaper down on the bench on his left side, as he waits patiently starring at the library across the street and the vehicles riding pass, until the next bus arrives. After a few minutes, a bus suddenly pulls up and the side door opens Mark, steps onto the bus before quickly turning around, taking a few steps back over to the bench and picking up the newspaper. Mark, turns back around and walk up the few steps on the bus, the side doors to the bus closes while the bus driver looks Mark in the eyes and shakes his head side to side strangely. Not understanding and totally confused to why the bus driver was shaking his head and looking at him like that .

Mark, ignores the bus driver's behavior, cuffs the newspaper up underneath his left armpit, digs into his pocket and takes out some change to pay the fare for riding the bus. He, then walks to the back of the bus and finds a seat in the corner of the bus and sits down, the buses open doors close and then the bus pulls off. Sitting in the back of the bus Mark, looks up and glancing at the rearview mirror to the right, above the bus drivers head and there Mark can see the bus driver looking right back at him, through the rear-view mirror shaking his head again side to side. So, Mark grabs the newspaper from underneath his armpit, holds it in his hand, pops the black rubber band off, unfolds the newspaper and reads what's on the front page. While trying his best to ignore the bus driver and not look back up at the buses rearview mirror to the right, above the bus drivers head …

(Mark Reading) … Today there are still no leads to the missing person's case, about the two New Jersey people who have been missing for five days now. Police, are asking if anyone has seen them or might have some credible information to their whereabouts, please contact the New Jersey police department at area code 723-000-5555 or the missing person hotline at 1-888-MIS-SING all calls will be kept confidential! … THE€ JOURNAL!

Mark looks at the bottom of the page underneath what he wat just reading and sees his name and right above his name was his picture sitting at a table reading a book and to his left at the table was an old woman dressed in all black reading a newspaper.

Shocked and shaken by the picture and out of paranoia Mark, kindly lifts his head up and looks around on the bus, to see if anyone is paying him any mind he, then looks at the buses rearview mirror to the right, above the bus drivers head and notices that the bus driver is no longer looking at him shaking his head so, Mark looks back at the newspaper he has in his hand, turns the page over and there he sees another picture of him, but this time much larger and placed directly in the center of the page. A picture of him at a bus stop, sitting on a bench attached to an overhead shelter, with fiber glass roof and siding and lying next to him on his left on the bench is THE JOURNAL! And parked on the corner of the bus stop, with only one passenger on the bus there's a lady, sitting by the window looking at Mark, sitting down on the bus stop bench, reading a newspaper. Mark leans his head in closer to the newspaper and starts to remember the face of the woman who's sitting on the bus by the window looking at him. He, looks up and around the bus again before closes the newspaper, folding it and pushing back up underneath his left arm pit Mark, takes a deep breath, leans his head back in the seat and mumbles …

(Mark Mumbling) … Grandma Harris! … Next Stop! Martin Blvd! The bus driver announces over the loudspeaker, as the bus makes a sudden stop and the side doors open Mark, then turns his head to the right and looks out the window to see where they are, while leaning to the side and watching as people get on and off the bus.

He, then removes his book of poems from out of his back pocket, leans back up straight and looks at the book he now has in his hand. Mark, opens the book flips through the pages until he finds a poem in the book he wants to read He, starts reading silently to himself as the side doors to the bus close and the bus driver slowly drives off while looking back at Mark, through buses rearview mirror to the right, above his head …

WATCH THE COMPANY YOU KEEP

"When There's A Change Of Plans
But You Didn't Make Them"

THE€ COMPANY

After washing the few dishes left in the sink Mrs. Largen, wipes her hands with a towel and tends to the food on the stove she, then picks up a large spoon from off the counter and starts stirring the gravy simmering in a pot on the stove. She, then tastes it to see if it needs any more seasoning before laying the spoon down and grabbing two oven mittens she, puts the oven mittens on and opens the oven door to the stove. Mrs. Largen, then pulls the pot of turkey out halfway and checks to see how much longer the turkey must cook before being well done. She, then pushes the pot of turkey back inside the stove, closes the oven door, takes off the oven mittens, places them both back on the kitchen counter and looks at the house phone that has been ringing a few times now … *(Phone Ringing)* … Mrs. Largen, walks over to the phone in the kitchen hanging on the wall and picks the phones receiver up …

Hello, the Largens residence! … Well Hello! Mrs. Largen, I assume? … Yes, that's correct! I'm Mrs. Largen who is that? … And a good Morning to you Mrs. Largen! My name is Mr. Johnson! And I'm calling from the car and insurance company of Feildstead and associates and with all due respect! I need to come by and discuss with you the results of the claim! …Did you say claim? …Yes! That's right the claim Mrs. Largen! … Well! My husband is not here right now! Do you think you can call back another time?...

Well Mrs. Largen to be honest! This is an emergency! And since you are the Mother and beneficiary of Stacie Largen! I don't think you will be needing your husband! ...Like I said my husband is not here right now! So, could you please call back later? .... Mrs. Largen! I really don't think that would be a good idea! You see I have in my possession the accident insurance money and only you are eligible to sign the release forms so that the money can be released! ... Insurance Money! Are you sure you have the right information Mr. Johnson? I'm sorry sir but I really don't understand! You're going to have to call back when my husband arrives! I'm sorry goodbye! ... Wait! Wait! Mrs. Largen! I truly apologize for not explaining myself more clearly! You see Mrs. Largen you are your daughters The Last Beneficiary! ... Sir could you hold on for just a minute! ... Sure!

Putting the phones receiver down on the kitchen table Mrs. Largen walk over to the stove, picks up the two oven mittens and gets ready to open the ovens door until she hears her husband's voice ...She, quickly takes off the two oven mittens, picks up the phone from off the kitchen table and walks over by the kitchens entrance as the front door slams shut ... *Honey I'm home!* Mr. Largen walks in the house and smell the aroma of the food cooking in the kitchen ... *The food smells delicious! What is it?* Mr. Largen, takes off his coat and picks up the mail off the coffee table next to the coat rack while Mrs. Largen, rushes out from the kitchen with the phone in her hand she looks at her husband and frowns while shrugging both of her shoulders up in the air.

Mr. Largen looks at the phone and then at his wife his, eyes widen out of confusion as he walks towards Mrs. Largen and whispers …

(Mr. Largen Whispering) …Who is it? Is everything ok?

Mrs. Largen walks up to her husband and pushes the phone receiver into his chest, while covering up the mouthpiece on the phone …

(Mrs. Largen Whispering) … Here! Please talk to this man! I don't know!

With a genuine look of confusion on his face Mr. Largen, hands his wife the mail he has in his hand and kindly grabs the phone receiver from out of his wife's hand … *(Mrs. Largen Whispering) … He said he's from the Johnson's Insurance Company! … The insurance companies! What insurance company? And for what? … Here just talk to the man dear! …* Mr. Largen lifts his arm up to his ear with the phone's receiver in his hand, while shaking his head side to side signaling that he's not in the mood for any of this as he stares Mrs. Largen directly in her eyes.

Hello! … Hello! Baby! There is no one on this phone! … Well are you sure? Then he must have hung up, here let me see! Mrs. Largen quickly grabs the phone receiver from out of Mr. Largens hand and places it to her ear *…Hello! Mr. Johnson are you still there? Hello!* Mrs. Largen, looks at her husband who is still standing there in front of her, shaking his head side to side. Mr. Largen, then reaches out his arm and takes back the mail Mrs. Largen is holding.

Leaning forward Mr. Largen kisses his wife on the cheek before walking pass her towards the kitchen ... *I'm starving! What's for dinner?* Mrs. Largen, feeling a little embarrassed stand's there with the phone's receiver to her ear, listening to an irritating dial tone sound, that signals either the man on the other end of the phone has hung up or they both just got temporarily disconnected. But after thinking about it for a few seconds Mrs. Largen, came to the realization that the call from the insurance company, might have just been an insurance fraud scheme.

Now turning around Mrs. Largen, watches her husband walk pass before she, calmly walks back toward the kitchen behind him, with the phone's receiver in her hand down by her side ... *Dinner will be ready in a little while!* In the kitchen Mr. Largen, who is over by the stove with a spoon in his right hand and the top off the pot in his left hand, tasting the green beans that's simmering on the stove his wife has made. Mr. Largen, then turns his head to the left as Mrs. Largen, walks into the kitchen, over by the wall and hangs up the phone ...

I really don't know what could have had happened! I'm telling you there was some man on the phone! And he said he was with some accident insurance company! ... Well, honey! Is that all that he said? ... No! He also said something about some money! I had to claim for being the beneficiary of Stacie! ... What! Wait a minute! You mean somebody called here and said you were the beneficiary of our daughter Stacie? And there was money involved? ...

Yes! That's what I've been trying to tell you! But you were acting like you didn't believe me and didn't care! ...No! No! I never said I didn't believe you! And of course, I care! I was just waiting for you to realize that phone calls like that are most likely a fraud shame! Somebody who heard about Stacie's accident and thought they could get some personal information that would lead to them emptying out your bank account! ... My bank accounts! Don't you mean our bank account? ...Well! You know exactly what I mean! ...Anyway dear, your absolutely right! I thought about that too! ... You see! So, don't even worry about it! And if he calls back, give me the phone next time! ... (Mr. Largen Laughing) ... I'll love to talk to him!

Putting the top back on the pot of green beans Mr. Largen tosses the spoon in the sink and opens the refrigerator he, takes out a carton of orange juice and starts drinking it straight from the container ... *Get a glass, would you!? My god! Your worse than the kids!* Mr. Largen ignores the smart comment from his wife as he continues drinking the orange juice from straight from the container ... *Oh well! If it wasn't a scheme and it was that important, he'll call back or someone else from the company, especially if money is involved! ... I guess your right dear!* Mrs. Largen, opens a cabinet above the sink, walks over to Mr. Largen and hands him a clean empty glass Mr. Largen, looks at that clean glass and continues drinking from the container ... *Seriously! You see me standing here with a glass! And you're going to keep drinking from the container?* Then unexpectedly the phone starts to ring ...

(Phone Ringing) Mr. and Mrs. Largen both stop what they're doing and look at each other for a minute Mr. Largen, quickly closes the juice container, puts it back in the refrigerator and slams the refrigerator door shut.

While Mrs. Largen, looks at the phone that's ringing … *(Phone Ringing)* and then back at her husband before picking up the phone's receiver, covering the mouthpiece of the phone with her hand and then handing the phone to her husband Mr. Largen … *(Mrs. Largen Whispering) Honey! That must be him calling back! …Well! I sure do hope so! Give me that phone! Hello! … Hello! Is this Mr. Johnson? … What! Dad, it's me Edward! Oh! We thought you were somebody calling here about some insurance money! Dad! Did you say insurance money? … That's right why? The wife said she got a call earlier from some man name Mr. Johnson! About some insurance money too! … Well, I'll be dam! … Well! Do you know if it was concerning your sister Stacie? I'm not sure we didn't talk long! I told her we would talk more when I returned home! Right now, I'm picking the kids up from school! Dad! Is everything alright? … I'm not sure Son! We'll talk about this later! And Where have you been? Your Mother has been trying to reach you all day! … Who is it Dear? …It's your son Edward! … Edward! Well tell him I said to bring the kids around today or tomorrow! … Did you hear your mother?... Yes! I heard her! … And ask Edward, how's his wife doing! … He said her, and the kids are all doing just fine! … Well! That's always good to hear!*

Lifting a lid from off one of the pots on the stove Mrs. Largen, smiles from hearing the good news about how her daughter in law and grand kids are all doing ... *Edward! You know how your mother feels about her grand kids! She's just being a concerned Grandmother! …Well! Tell grandma, I love her and that everything is fine! … Honey! Ask him did he eat? …Your mother wants to know did you eat? … (Edward and Mr. Largen Laughing) You knew that was coming, right? …Yes pops! But tell her, I'm fine! Plus, me the wife and kids, plan on going out and getting something to eat later! … Honey! He said he's fine and that he's taking the family out later!* Mrs. Largen, places the lid back on the pot on the stove, picks up a dry towel, wipes her hands while walking towards her husband she, quickly grabs the phones receiver from out of Mr. Largens hand and places it to her ear… *Son! Now, you know you are always welcome! To bring the family over and get something to eat! Those kids need more home cooked meals Son! And not so much fast food all the time! You hear me Edward?* Mom! Relax we are all fine! I make sure the wife cooks at home! Even when she doesn't want to! … Well! If you change your mind, dinner will be on the stove! Just hop right in the car and bring the family over here and get something to eat! … *Honey! Let that boy take care of his family! He's a grown ass man! … (Edward Laughing) Ok! I love you son! … Love you more Ma! Goodbye!* Hanging up the phone in the kitchen Mrs. Largen, watches as her husband leaves the kitchen and heads back into the living room while Mrs. Largen, turns around and continues preparing tonight's dinner.

Once in the living room Mr. Largen walks over to his leather recliner and sits down, then unexpectedly the front door to the house slams shut and Mr. Largen looks quickly looks up and sees his son Mark, standing there by the front door with a book in his hand. Mrs. Largen hears Mark's voice so; she walks to the entrance of the kitchen with all intentions of seeing his face …

You won't believe the day I had today! I've seen it all, I just can't get over what happened! I really didn't think I was going to make it home tonight! … Boy! What in god's name are you rumbling on about? Honey! Do you hear your son? …Yea! I hear him alright! What's the matter Mark? Did you get into a fight? Is somebody bothering you?... No, pops! I told you I'm good! … Get over here boy and let me look at you! …Ma, I wasn't fighting! I'm good! Trust, me! … Well! What's all the commotion about? And Mark, do you know where Tara is? … No! I haven't seen her! But what I do know! Is that there's some strange and bizarre things happening! Here, and around this city!

Mr. and Mrs. Largen both look at each other with a weird and odd expression on their faces from what Mark, just said so Mr. and Mrs. Largen, both quiet down for a few seconds. Before turning their heads and looking back at their son Mark, who is still standing by the front door now speechless and numb at how the atmosphere in the room, quickly went from a concerned conversation of importance, to a moment of hair-raising behavior of silence … *I'm telling you! I was at the library right! And, this…*

Mark gets interrupted by the sound of the front door opening and closing shut so, he turns around and sees his sister Tara standing behind him with her hand on her hip shaking her head side to side with a mocking grin on her face … *Ma, I'm starved! Is dinner ready? … Boy, move!* Tara pushes Mark to the side as she walks over to her Father, who's sitting down in the recliner chair Tara, leans over and kisses Mr. largen on the cheek, leans back up and looks at her Mother, who is standing by the kitchen frowning, shaking her head side to side at the sight of her daughter Tara … *And where have you been Ms. Lady? … Out with friends! … Friends! Who crazy Keisha and stupid Janice? …I know you're not talking Mark. You don't even have friends! At school they call you a nerd! And the bad thing about it, the nerds don't even want to hang with you!*

Tara and Mark start laughing while Mrs. Largen stands by the stove shaking her head side to side signaling that she can't believe how her two children are acting right now …

And please don't talk about Ronnie! Because the whole city knows! That, one friend you got! Might as well propose to his hobbies! And get married to his career! Both of you are Nerds! … Oh, really Sis! But when you first met him, you were all in his face! Like Hi, Ron! Hay, Ronnie! Acting like a high school groupie! You even wanted too …Ok! Ok! Enough already please! We all get the point Mark! And I'm sure your Father, has heard enough! Because I know I did! Right dear? …

Mr. Largen shakes his head up and down signaling that he agrees with his wife, as he leans up in the recliner he's sitting in, looking around for the televisions remote control …*You kids! Anyway, Tara! …Yes, Mother! …Once you and Mark finish the back and forth bickering! Wash your hands and help me here in the kitchen! … Sure, Ok!* Mrs. Largen, gently turns around and walks into the kitchen while Tara, sticks her tongue out at Mark while adjusting the pocketbook strap that's over her shoulder she, walks pass her Brother, up the stairs towards her bedroom …

(Tara Mumbling) At least I am helpful! Not like some people I know! Who go around reading poems all day! … Yea, whatever! Just get yourself in there and help with dinner! I'm hungry! While walking up the stairs Tara, looks at her Brother Mark, smiles and bats her hand at him, before removing the strap of the pocketbook from over her shoulder she, then holds pocketbook in one hand down by her side and walks into her bedroom. Mark walks over by Mr. Largen and hops down on the couch he, then reaches down in between the couches cushion and pulls out the televisions remote control. He hands the T.V.'s remote control to his Father and sits there in silence as Mr. Largen turns the television on …

*Son! You were saying something about the library? … Oh, The library! Yea pops! I'm telling you it was crazy…*While trying to explain to his Father about what happened Mark, finds himself talking over the television being that Mr. Largen, has just turned the volume up so loud that Mark could hardly hear himself think.

Now leaning up on the couch Mark looks at his Father who's not paying him any attention or showing any signs of concern about what he's saying so, Mark leans back on the couch and continues watching the television …

Son! Would you mind going in the kitchen and getting me something to drink? ... Sure, pops! What do you want a beer? …A beer sounds good! And thanks! Oh, and a bag of those pistachios to son!

Mark gets up off the couch and walks towards the kitchen he, then stops and stands by the kitchens doorway before turning around and looking back at his Father, who is leaning forward in the recliner with his arm extended out. And with the remote control in his hand Mr. Largen, changes channels on the television Mark, turns back around and walks into the kitchen where his Mother Mrs. Largen, is preparing tonight's dinner. In the kitchen Mark, kisses his Mother on the cheek, walks pass her and over to where the refrigerator is, he opens the refrigerator reaches inside and takes out a beer. Mark looks at his Mother as she stands over the stove adjusting the fire that's underneath one of the pots, she then gently turns the knob attached to the front of the stove. The phone in the kitchen rings and gets Mark and Mrs. Largens attention … *(Phone Ringing)* Mrs. Largen and Mark, both turn their heads and look at the phone in the kitchen, as it continues to ring.

Mark closes the refrigerator door and walks over to an overhead cabinet above the sink he, opens the door to the cabinet and grabs a pocket size bag of pistachios before closing the overhead cabinets door back …*Ma! Aren't you going to answer the phone?* Mrs. Largen turns around and looks at Mark, who's standing a few feet behind her with a beer in one hand and a pocket size bag of pistachios in the other, with both arms raised in the air. … *Look! My hands are full! … Move out of my way boy! And let me get the phone! … (Phone Ringing) And bring your Father that beer, before it gets warm! … (Phone Ringing)* Mrs. Largen, watches as Mark leaves the kitchen with two beers and a pocket size bag of pistachios, once Mark is out of the kitchen Mrs. Largen, walks over by the phone, picks it up and places the phones receiver to her ear while looking at the fire she just lowered on the stove, underneath one of the pots that is now simmering on low heat …

Hello! The Largens residence! …Hello! Ms. Largen! This is Janice, Tara's friend! … Oh, Janice! How have you been? … I've been just great Mrs. Largen! Is Tara, home? I tried calling her cellphone, but she didn't answer! …Tara! Yes, she's here! Hold on for just one-minute darling! I'm downstairs and Tara, I guess she's still upstairs in her bedroom! … Mrs. Largen covers the phones mouthpiece with her hand while pressing the phones receiver up against her chest Mrs. Largen, walks to the entrance of the kitchen, sticks her head out and yells throughout the house …

(Mrs. Largen Yelling) Tara! The phone, its Janice! Tara! Mrs. Largen, steps back inside the kitchen, raises her hand and puts the phones receiver back to her ear while looking at the pots on the stove *Janice, dear! …Ma! I got it! You can hang up now! …Ok! Janice, you take care! …You to Mrs. Largen and tell Mark I said hello! I sure will darling!*

While hanging up the phone Mrs. Largen starts smiling at her daughter's best friend Janice and how she asked about Mark. Knowing that Tara can't stand the fact that Mark already has a secret crush on her best friend. So, instead of hanging the phone up right away Mrs. Largen, decides to ease drop for a few minutes, just to see what these girls were up to … *Really Janice! Really! …What! I was just being polite! …We all know the kind of polite you like! …Whatever! … Just stop asking about my Brother already! Would you! … Anyway, Tara! It's movie night at my house! Tell me you didn't forget? Because, Keisha and Pat are on their way! And you can pick up Dana on your way here! She said she got something to smoke! Hold up! What! …. Be quiet, don't say another word! …What do you mean? Be quiet! …Janice! Shut up, for a minute! …Well! Since you put it like that Tara!* Janice, then immediately stops talking and without a clue she, couldn't understand why Tara, her best friend had suddenly become so, emotional and with authority was demanding there be silence over the phone. Then after a few seconds of being muted Janice, started feeling uncomfortable especially being that she has no idea why Tara, just silenced her …

Are you crazy! Don't be talking like that over this phone! My Mother could be listening! Wow! My, bad Tara! You really think she's listening? ...Who knows! Maybe she is! Maybe she isn't! But just in case she was! Don't talk reckless! ...I got you! So, what time are you leaving? ... Right now! Call my cellphone, Bye! ...Tara! Turn your cell Before Janice, could get another word in she, gets cut off by Tara, who quickly hangs up the phone up Tara, then gets undressed, grabs a bath towel and wraps it around her body. She leaves the bedroom and walks into the bathroom too take a shower, after she finish showering Tara, dries herself off, wraps the bath towel back around her body and walks back into her bedroom to get dressed. Tara, grabs her pocketbook, keys and cellphone off the charger before leaving her bedroom, closing the bedroom door and heading for the stairs. Tara, softly walks down the stairs, trying not to draw too much attention to herself, or make too much noise Tara, looks at her Brother and Father and notices that the movie has their undivided attention and their eyes are glued to the television. Mark, who is laying out across on the couch while Mr. Largen is taking sips off his beer and snapping pistachios open one by one... *The name of this movie is The Pseud Masterminds! Right Mark? ...I think that's the name of it! ... I heard that was a good movie! How long has it been on? ... Not even five minutes! You haven't missed anything!* Tara, sneezes unexpectedly causing Mark to turn his head around from where he's sitting on the couch, he looks at his sister as she walks down the stairs.

Mark, then notices that Tara, has changed clothes and is looking like she's about to leave. Mark, shakes his head side to side, turns back around on the couch, looks at his Father and then continues watching the movie on the television. Mr. Largen looks at Mark before turning his head around in his recliner he, then looks at his daughter Tara, who's walking towards the front door jingling car keys in her hand … *Somebody either got a date! Or going to a party! …Mind your business nerd! And for your information! I'm going to my girlfriend Janice house! As a matter of fact, It's really none of your business! … Tara! …Yes, Father! …I thought your Mother, needed your help in the kitchen? Well! At least see what your Mother wants before you leave! … Alright! Alright! …And tell Janice, I said hello! …Whatever!*

Removing the strap of her pocketbook from off her shoulder Tara, throws the pocketbook on the coffee table by the front door before walking over by Mark, and smacking him in the back of the head. Tara looks at the television before and then back at her Brother … *Mark! You said this movie is called The Pseud Masterminds, right? … What are you deaf? For the last time Tara, yes! …Well! The housekeeper fakes her death, the billionaire of the estate gets framed for killing her, then the billionaire's son and the housekeeper move to Costa Rica and spend the billionaires fortune! … Are you serious Tara? You just had to tell us the whole story? …No! Just you! Me and Dad, watched this movie last week nerd! …Wow! Tara! It's like that? … Yup! It's like that nerd! Love you too bro! …Yea, Whatever!*

Raising her hand up to her lips Tara, blows a sarcastic kiss at her Brother Mark with all intentions of insulting his personality while Mr. Largen, takes another sip of his beer while looking at his son Mark. Mr. Largen smirks a grin while shrugging both shoulders up in the air and shaking his head side to side signaling that unfortunately, what his daughter Tara has just said is true. So, out of aggravation and humiliation Mark, grabs a pillow from off the couch and throws it at Tara, the pillow hits Tara in the arm Tara, catches the pillow and throws it back at Mark, who dodges the pillow as it flies over his head and lands on the floor, a few inches away from the television. Then the loud sound of his Mrs. Largens voice can be heard coming from the kitchen, her voice gets Mark, Tara and Mr. Largens attention. Tara, then turns and face the direction of the kitchen while Mark, leans forward and picks up the couch pillow from up off the floor *...Pops! ...What is it son? ... If you just watched this movie last week! Why are you watching it again? ...What can I say! It's a good movie!*

Mr. Largen continues watching the movie The Pseud Masterminds, while sipping on his beer, eating his pistachios and ignoring the playful behavior from his two children Mark and Tara ...

(Mrs. Largen Yelling) Tara, darling! You still in there? Come here in the kitchen, for a minute dear! I need your help with something! ... Without hesitation Tara, walks into the kitchen where Mrs. Largen is finishing up preparing tonight's dinner once inside the kitchen.

Tara, looks at her Mother who's bending down by the ovens open door of the stove, with oven mittens on each hand. Mrs. Largen, reaches inside the oven and grabs the large pot inside she, takes the large pot out and places it on top of the stove then she, removes the top from off the large pot and with the top in her hand she looks at her Daughter Tara, who's now standing beside her. Mrs. Largen, puts the top down on the kitchen counter, removes both oven mitten off her hands and pokes the rotisserie chicken that's inside the large pot with her finger, before picking up an empty bowl and sitting it on top of the kitchen counter … *And where are you going young lady? …To Janice house Ma! You know on Wednesday me, Janice, Pat, April and Dana all get together and have a girl's night out! … Well! Aren't you going to eat something before you go? …No! I'm fine! We usually eat pizza and fries and often too much ice cream! … We'll! That explains a lot! …I know Ma! I'm gaining some weight right! …You think Tara? …Anyway! That sure does look and smell delicious! We'll! Don't be out too late! With all these strange happenings going on! You hear me? Yes, Of course Mother I hear you! …. We'll before you go! Help your Mother drain this rotisserie juice from this pot! I want to make your Father some gravy! …Ma! Can't Mark, help you? I don't want to get gravy on my shirt! And I don't want to be smelling like rotisserie chicken! … Child! Look over there and grab that apron and those mittens! Now, just hold that side of the pot for me! Be careful now Tara! That pot it's hot! … What else did you make? …Tara! Hold that steady now! I made rice, cornbread, corn on the cob, scallop potatoes and asparagus! And I might bake a pie! We'll! I hope it's apple!*

And you can keep the asparagus! Yuk! …I already know Tara! After Tara, and her Mother drain the rotisserie juice from the large pot Tara, takes off both oven mittens and places them on the kitchen table she, then removes the apron from around her neck and lays it over the back of one of the kitchen chairs, that's pushed underneath the kitchen table … *(Cellphone Vibrating)* Reaching into her pants back-pocket Tara, takes out her cellphone and looks at the recent text message left on the screen by her best friend Janice ... *(Text Message) … Change of plans girlfriend! Me and April are pulling up in front of your house right now*! *Pat and Dana said they will be there in an about an hour!*

After reading the text message left by Janice Tara, puts the cellphone back in her pocket she, then takes a few steps forward, leans in by her Mothers shoulder and kisses her Mrs. Largen on the cheek. Mrs. Largen looks at her Daughter and smiles as Tara, kindly turns around and start walking towards the exit of the kitchen before walking right into her Brother. Mark looks at his Mother while sticking out his leg and foot causing Tara, too trip and slightly stumble. Tara catches her balance and regains her composure before standing back up straight she, then raises her arm, balls up her fist and punches her Brother in the chest. Mark swallows some air from the sudden punch which caused him to tuck his stomach in, while raising both of his arms and covering up his chest.

The sudden punch put an expression on Mark's face, that showing surprise and pain so, with his guard now up Tara, pushes him out of the way and walks back into the living room where her Father, Mr. Largen is still sitting in the recliner looking heavy-eyed and drowsy. Nodding off with his head jerking back and forth every couple of minutes Mr. Largen, hears the doorbell ring the sound of the doorbell causes Mr. Largen to quickly lift his head up and open his eyes as he looks around the room. He looks at the television and then at Tara, who's standing by the front door, looking through the peek hole with her one hand on the doorknob and her other hand placed flat up against the door…

(Doorbell Ringing) … What are you waiting for Christmas Tara? Open the door! It might be that insurance man; your Mother was talking too on the phone earlier! While looking at her Father Tara, frowns at the commit as she gently opens the front door Tara, looks at Janice and April who are both standing side by side outside the front door. April is holding up with both hands a pizza box while Janice, has a grocery bag tightly gripped in her fingers down by her side … *So! This is the change of plans? … Look! Were here now Tara! …Yea! And this pizza won't say hot forever girl! …Move, Tara! Let's us in! …Here, Tara! Take this ice cream and put it in the freezer! Before it starts melting! …And what's that smell? Tara! Let me find out Mrs. Largen, is in the kitchen getting her Rachel Ray on! …Give me that ice cream Janice! And come on in you two!*

After reaching out her arm and taking the grocery bag with the ice cream from Janice Tara, takes a few steps back away from the front door, turns around and walks pass her Father, who's still looking heavy-eyed and drowsy, nodding off with his head jerking back and forth every couple of minutes as he sits comfortably in the recliner. Janice, then moves to the side outside by the door and lets April walk in first Janice, then walks inside behind April before closing the front door shut. Janice and April, both look at Mr. Largen, who's looking heavy-eyed and drowsy, as they both walk over by the stairs and wait for Tara, who is now in the kitchen with Mark and Mrs. Largen ...

Tara! Your back? I thought you were going to your girlfriend Janice house. ...Ma! Janice and April are in the living room! What! Why? ...Change of plans! And they brought pizza and look here ice cream! Ma! Could you put this in the freezer for me please? Well! Tell the girls I said hello! And if they want something else to eat, they are more than welcome! I cooked more than enough food! ...Sure, ma! ... Tara! You said Janice, is here? Here! In the living room? ... What's it to you? Hold, up! And where do you think you're going Mark? ...To say hi to Janice! ... No! I don't think so!

Tara, then quickly grabs her Brother, Mark by the arm as he tries to rush pass her with excitement and go into the living room where Janice and April are. So, with emotion Tara pulls Mark, back towards her and steps in front of him, blocking the entrance to the kitchen ...

No! Not today bro! Janice is not here to see you! And you're not going to bother her either! Nope! Not today!... Wow! A Ma! Do you believe this? Tara, hating! ...Call it what you want! But you won't be calling her! While Mrs. Largen, is putting the ice cream in the freezer Mark and Tara, start laughing at what she just said Tara then slowly and cautiously let's go of Marks arm before she, decides to push him lightly in the chest, causing him to stumble to the side a few feet away from where Tara, is standing. Tara, then lifts her arm up by her face, sticks out her index finger and wags it side to side at Mark, signaling that today is not the day. Tara looks at her Mother Mrs. Largen and sees her now standing there by the sink with the overhead cabinet open and with her arm extended Mrs. Largen is holding some paper cups and paper plates ... *Here, Tara! Don't forget these! And boy! Leave Tara, friends alone please! Can't you see Tara, doesn't want you bothering her friends? ...But, ma! ...Don't, ma me! Just let it go! Thank-you, Mother!*

With the paper cups and plates in her hand Tara, looks at Mark and sticks out her lounge at him, before walking out of the kitchen and back into the living room where April and Janice, are now sitting down on the stairs in the house both holding and taking bites off their slice of pizza ... Dam! Tara, what took you so long? ...And how is Mrs. Largen doing? Besides in there cooking up a storm! ...Tara? Is that Marks voice I hear in the kitchen? ...Who, Mark? Yea! That's but face! The nerd! ...Janice! He must not know you are in here! Because if he did! Girl! ...

Should we go in and say hi to Mrs. Largen? Please, No! Your good! She said hello! Let's just go upstairs! And pass me one of those slices April! …

(Janice and April Mumbling) Is it me! Or is Tara, acting kind of strange? …No! It's not you April! But she, is acting different! …Anyway! This pizza is slamming, right? … Oh, hell yea! But, wait a minute! ...What now Janice! What happened? Did, you forget something? …Sure, did! …What? …. I forgot the soda! It's in the car! Who's going to go and get it? …Don't look at me! My, hands are full! Tara! Do you mind? …I'll go and get it! Unlock your car door Janice! …I did already! … Just meet me in the bedroom! … (Tara Mumbling) And don't let my Brother in my room! Under no circumstances! I just brought a brand new T.V.! And I don't want him, in there watching it! You hear me? …Yea! We heard you alright! You heard her April? … Loud and clear Tara!

April and Janice move to the side as Tara, walks back down the stairs towards the front door once Tara, is at the bottom of the stairs April hands Janice, who is standing two steps behind her the pizza box. Janice opens the lid to the box and puts her half-eaten slice of pizza inside before following April, up the stairs in the direction where Tara's bedroom is. Opening the door to Tara's bedroom April, walks inside and holds the door open for Janice, who's a few feet behind her. Once Janice, is inside the bedroom April, closes the bedroom door shut while Janice, walks over to a dresser pushed up against the wall by a window.

Janice, sits the pizza box down on top of the dresser, opens the lid to the box reaches inside and takes out the half-eaten slice she just had. Janice, stands there by the window looking out at the traffic and pedestrians commuting back and forth outside while taking small bites off the slice of pizza she, has in her hand. April, looks at Janice before walking over to the bed and picking up the televisions remote control April, presses the power button on the remote control the television comes on, the volume is on high. Janice, then turns around with a mouth full of food by the window and looks at April, who is looking right back at her. Janice, points at the television with the pizza in her hand hoping April, also realizes and gets the impression that the television is up to loud. Janice, turns back around with the pizza in her hand as April, looks for the volume button on the remote control.

April presses the volume button but it's useless April, notices that the volume on the television is not lowering so, with the remote control in her hand April, walks over by the television. She reaches out her arm grabs the knob on the television and tries turning the volume down manually, but that doesn't work either. So, after a few minutes Janice and April, start getting upset at the irritating loud surrounding sound coming from the brand-new television. Janice looks at April who's fiddling back and forth, with the volume knob on the television turning it right to left.

Janice, opens the lid to the pizza box and drops inside the crust to the slice of pizza she, has just finished eating Janice, wipes her mouth with the napkin she has in her hand, before walking over by where April, is standing and having trouble turning down the irritating loud sounding television …

(Janice and April Yelling) Are, *you serious? What seems to be the problem April? Is the television broke? I don't know! I tried turning it down with the remote control! And with the volume button on the T.V! But nothings working! …The hell with that television! Just unplug it for now! Tara should know what's wrong with it! Yea, right! Stupid T.V.! And didn't she, mention that this was a brand new T.V.! … Maybe she did! Maybe she didn't! Who cares! New, old just unplug the freaking thing! I'm getting a headache overhear! Plus, I can't hear myself think!*

April, then leans over the T.V. to see where the televisions power cord is and there behind the television April, gets the shock of her life at what she's seeing, to April this was unexplainable and unbelievable to any human eye. April quickly leans back up and looks at the picture on the screen on the television she, then looks at Janice who is now laying on her back on Tara's bed with a pillow behind her head, pressed up against her ears trying to block out the loud sound coming from the T.V. April, takes a step back with all intentions of trying to believe what she has just seen isn't true.

So, she steps back up to the television and looks behind it again, this time April, picks up the power cord from off the floor and holds it up in the air over the television. With the power cord tightly gripped in her hand April, turns and looks at Janice, who is laying down on the bed starring at the power cord April, is holding in her hand. Both of Janice, eyes are wide open, and her eyebrows are raised with concern, her mouth is wide open and she's speechless. While April, stands there frightened also lost for words she watches as Janice, gets up off the bed, runs over to the bedroom door and turns the doorknob. Janice tries to open the door but it's useless and with all of her might she tries repeatedly but it's useless the door won't open.

So, she runs back over to the bed, sits down and takes a deep breath. April, then let's go of the televisions power cord she has in her hand and runs over to Janice, who's now sitting up on the edge of Tara's bed. Janice is tightly and firmly embracing the pillow; she has pressed against her chest with both of her arms interlocked. April and Janice, both jump up a few inches from off the bed out of fear, from the unexpected and sudden loud ringing sound of the phone in the bedroom, that catches them both off guard …

(Loud Phone Ringing) … (Loud Phone Ringing) While sitting back on the edge of the bed April and Janice, both look at each other before simultaneously turning around.

Then with concern on their faces they both look at the loud ringing phone behind them … *(Loud Phone Ringing)* Janice, removes the pillow from the tight embrace in her arms close to her chest she, lifts the pillow up and places it behind her head, covering both of their ears, with all intentions of trying to tone down the loud sound of the ringing phone and the T. V's volume that's surrounding the bedroom. April raises both of her arms and places her hands over each ear, with all the same intentions as her friend Janice. April, turns their head to the right Janice, turns her head to the left they look at each other for a moment, then suddenly, the television shuts off completely and the phone immediately stops ringing. The doorknob to the bedroom, slowly and surprisingly starts turning, causing the bedroom door to squeak, as it calmly and peacefully opens, leaving thoughts of unanswered questions marks and wondering ideas roaming around inside both April and Janice's head, as they both sit there on the edge of Tara's bed starring at the bedroom door. Janice, drops the pillow from behind her head while April, removes her hands from over her ears, they both get up and together walk over by the bedroom door and outside the bedroom door in the hallway, they see Pat and Tara's Brother Mark, standing there with frowns of concern on both of their faces. Pat, has a grocery bag tightly gripped in her fingers down by her side while Mark has a box of pizza up near her chest, holding it from the bottom with both hands while looking Janice directly in her eyes and smiling …

Where should I put this pizza sexy? ...You can put it over there, on top of the other box! Oh, I see! ...April, Janice didn't either one of you hear us knocking? I could understand if there was loud music playing! But it's quiet as a cat in here! Right Mark? ... For, real! And look, the television isn't even on! ... Pat, where's Dana? ...Yea, Pat I thought Dana was with you? ...Dana had other plans! She said she'll call if something changes! That's all I know! Anyway, Mark your welcome to some pizza! .... I think I will have a slice! Thank-you Pat! ... And the soda is in the bag with the snacks! Just to let you all know! Who want some potato chips? The soda is still cold too! So, ladies! What's the movie for tonight? ...Did anybody see The Pseud Masterminds?

Entering the bedroom Mark, walks over to the dresser and sits the box of pizza he's holding on top of the dresser, next to the first box of pizza. While Pat, walks over by the computer desk and puts the grocery bag with the soda, snacks and potato chips on top of the desk. Pat turns around and looks at Mark, who is now opening the lid to the pizza box he, takes out two slices and hands one of the slices to Pat, before pulling out the chair from underneath the computer desk and sitting down. Folding the pizza, he has in his hand Mark, takes a large bite while looking at Janice, who is looking at Pat, take small back to back bites of the slice of pizza she, has in her hand. Pat, then walks over near the brand-new television she, then analyzes the T.V. from front to back she, looks up at Janice and April who both are looking at Mark,

Sitting down finishing up the slice of pizza he has in his hand Mark starts feeling out of place and uncomfortable Mark, watches as Janice, hops up off the bed and kindly walks over by the bedroom door. Janice stands there behind the bedroom door, with one hand on the doorknob and her other hand on her hip starring at Mark, with her head slightly tilted to the side in the direction of the hallway. April looks at Janice turns around and looks at Mark, with both of her eyebrows turned up and her shoulders shrugged hoping Mark, clearly gets the impression, that his company and welcome amongst them has just run out. So, without any questions asked Mark, takes another bite of the pizza he has in his hand, before getting up out the chair and kindly walking over by the bedroom door where Janice, is standing there with good intentions and patients by the bedroom with her hand on the doorknob that she is now opening …

So, it's like that sexy? … Boy, please! This is girl's night! You want another slice of pizza, before you go? …Oh, you got jokes too! You, funny! …No! Just trying to get you to leave! …Ok, ladies! I know when I'm not wanted! So, I'm gone! And thanks for the slice Pat! … (Mark Whispering) Janice! Call me when you get time! You got the number! …Goodbye Mark! Janice gently closes the bedroom door while watching Mark, as he takes short steps backwards away from the bedroom door, with his hand up by his ear and his index finger and thumb sticking out from his fist, making a phone sign with his hand …

(Mark Whispering) Call, me! Janice, then slams the bedroom door shut, turns around with her back leaned up against the door and looks at April and Pat, as they both are looking back at Janice. April, still sitting on the bed is shaking her head and Pat, whose over by the television picking cheese from off her slice of pizza *...What! I don't even have his number! And besides the point! That's Tara's brother you guys! ... To be honest! I don't remember Brothers, ever stopped you before! I know that's right April! ... (Janice and April Laughing) Now you two got jokes? Real comedy central! Anyway! Did either of you know, that this television over here is unplugged? ...What! You don't say! Pat, is it really unplugged? I didn't know that!*

Nope! Didn't have a clue! Maybe Tara, unplugged it! ...Yea, Pat! You ever thought about that? ... We'll, even if she did! I still can't figure out, how nether one of you heard me and Mark, knocking on the door! Why, would you say that Pat? ... And what's that supposed to mean? ... What I mean is! With it being so quiet in here! From no music playing, nether of you talking on the phone and no volume from television! Since, me and Mark first walked up to the door! And now! How, could you two not hear us knocking? And honestly speaking! Please, don't say you didn't hear us knocking! Because clearly, we heard you two cats fighting about the televisions volume! That's right! We, was standing there by the door listening to you April, call the T.V. stupid! And you Janice, complain about the T.V. giving you a headache!

And to be honest! That seems really, strange! Being, that I'm standing here right now! Looking at this television power cord! And yes, April and Janice, the television is unplugged!

It's quiet now in the bedroom so, Janice looks at April and then April, looks back at Janice, then they both look at Pat, who's standing there picking cheese from off the slice of pizza she has in her hand. Pat takes a large bite off the crust while looking back and forth at the television, April and Janice, who's facial expression proves that what pat has just said was true ...

We'll! Don't all talk at once! ... I'm thirsty! Anybody else what something to drink? I'm going downstairs, to get some paper cups! ...Hold, up Janice! I'll go with you! ...No! I'll be right back April! ...It's no problem, I have to use the bathroom anyway!

Without saying another word Janice, walks over to the bedroom door, opens it and eases her way out the bedroom without looking at April or Pat, Janice then heads to the top of the stairs. While April, slowly staggers behind on her way to the bathroom leaving Pat, in the bedroom with the pizza, soda and no cups all by herself. Pat, walks over by the dresser near the bedroom window and lifts the lid up on the pizza box she, tosses the left-over crust she has in her hand inside and rips off another slice of pizza. Pat takes a bite while turning around and looking at the computer desk. She, then walk over by the chair near the desk and sits down Pat, picks up a paper plate and places her slice of pizza on it before opening the computers desk draw.

Inside the desk drawer Pat, sees a refrigerator magnet She picks up the magnet and reads the text on the front before turning the magnet over and whispering to herself while reading what's written on the back ... *(Pat Whispering) ...*

To inquire about information others don't, subscribe here to: THE€ JOURNAL! Or call: 1-800- THE€ JOURNAL Were open 7 days a week, 24 hours a day, 365 days a year. "A Paper A Day Keeps The Good News Away" 1- 800-THE€ JOURNAL!

THE COLD BODY

"When Visitors Are Unexpected, And You Still Opened The Door"

TH€ BODY

Tara, walks pass her Father and over to the front door she, opens the door and there unexpectedly, shocked and to her surprise Tara, notices what appears to be four people standing behind Janice car in the front yard dressed in all black. In disbelief it confuses Tara, so she slowly closes the front door while starring at the old woman, the tall man, the boy and the young girl. The old lady eyes were black as the night her, face pale as stormy clouds with wrinkles all over showing off her age, with the black scarf wrapped around her head. Tara turns her head away for a second and looks at her Father who is now getting up from out of the recliner and headed into the kitchen where Mrs. Largen is. She then turns back around and just before Tara can get the door fully shut, she, notices that the old woman and the tall man are now standing a few inches outside in front of the door. The old woman and the man are looking Tara directly in her face, the old woman then lifts her arm and points at Tara while the boy and the young girl just stand there behind them like. Out of confusion and fear Tara, slams the door she then jumps back with one hand on the doorknob and the other hand on the chain lock. She, then drops her head and stares at the floor trying to understand what she was seeing but Tara, couldn't believe it she then pinches herself just to see if she was dreaming or if this was just a figment of her imagination.

Her, grip on the doorknob gets tighter and tighter as she locks the front door, she, then turns all the way around with her back now pressed up against the door. Tara looks around the living room, but no one is there she, then looks upstairs and still there is no one in sight the house starts to feel creepy and the silence throughout the house is disturbing and nerve wrecking. All Tara could think about was if these strange looking people were still standing outside of her house dressed in all black looking like they were either going or just leaving a funeral. Tara, turns back around and with caution she, leans forward and looks into the peek hole Tara, then jumps back from the sight of her seeing the old lady standing there with her face up to the door looking directly into the peek hole. Her, heart skips a beat and her blood level drops causing a cold chill running throughout her entire body as she wraps her arms around her shoulders while rubbing her arms. Tara, turns back around and runs towards the stairs headed to her bedroom where her company is. On her way up the stairs Tara, sees her best friend Janice, who is about to walk down the stairs from the top step Janice, suddenly stops and watches as Tara, rushes up the flight of stairs. Janice, then reaches out her arm and grabs Tara as she tries to walk pass her … *Tara! Tara! What is wrong with you? Girl! You look like you just seen a ghost, or something are you ok?* Trying not make eye contact with Janice or respond to any of the questions she keeps asking Tara, stops and stands there in front of Janice, with both of eyes widen while doing some heavy not normal breathing.

Tara! Your acting very strange! Well! are you going to tell me what happened or what? Come on! Let's go back downstairs, sit on the couch and watch a movie and talk about it! Ok? You good with that? Tara! Do you hear me talking to you? ...I hear you Janice! But, where my Brother? ...I thought he was downstairs! Maybe he's in his bedroom! You want me to go and get him? .... No! No! I'm good, leave him alone! A movie you said.

Tara, and Janice both walk back down the stairs while holding on to each other's arm once downstairs Tara, hops down on the couch while Janice, walks over by the television and looks for a movie to pop in the VCR

Here! I found one! Let's watch THE€ JOURNAL! Tara, maybe this movie will calm you down! Because I swear your face is pale and your hands are freezing! Plus, I have not seen the ending!

Janice pops the movie TH€ JOURNAL! Inside the VCR she then picks up the remote control, turns around and walks over to the couch she, sits down next to Tara while pressing play on the VCR remote control. Tara, and Janice now has their eyes glued to the television while Tara, repeatedly looks back and forth at the television and the front door. Janice, looks at Tara as the movie starts and catches Tara, looking at the front door so, Janice looks at the front door as well she, then looks back at Tara, before raising her hand and getting Tara's attention by shaking her on the shoulder. Tara! What are you looking at? ...Oh, Nothing! I thought I heard the doorbell! ...The doorbell? Girl!

The movie hasn't even started and you're already hearing and seeing things! Maybe this movie isn't a good choice right now! ...No! I'm just fine with watching THE JOURNAL! Plus, it gets me every time when the family finds out who the old lady and the tall man really came to get ... *(Tara Mumbling) Who they came to get? The old lady! The tall man! ...Tara! Did you say something? I didn't quite hear you!* Tara, then grabs a pillow from the couch and presses it up against her chest with both of her arms she, then looks at the front door again and then back at her best friend Janice, who has all her attention on the television and at the movie THE JOURNAL!

After turning the volume up on the television with the remote-control Janice lays the remote control in the corner of the couch, she then gets comfortable by leaning back on the couch with her legs bent and her feet up underneath her. Tara, then gets up with the couch pillow in her hand while looking back and forth at the front door and the television ... *I'm going in the kitchen Janice! You want something?* Janice shakes her head side to side signaling that she's good so, Tara throws the couch pillow back on the couch and starts walking towards the kitchen ... *(Tara Mumbling) That old lady!* Tara just couldn't seem to get the image of the old lady out of her head, then all of sudden the television shuts off and the T. V's screen turns pitch black. The VHS tape inside the VCR pops out by itself and lands on the floor.

There is no sound in the living room except for the heavy breathing Tara is doing so, out of confusion and curiosity Janice, gets up from of the couch, stands up and looks at Tara, who is now walking back towards the couch. Janice, bends down and picks up the VCR tape that's on the floor she, tries to put the VCR tape back in but every time she pushes it in, but the VCR forcefully pushes it back out. So, Janice lays the VCR tape on top of the T.V she, then goes over by the couch and picks up the remote control she, opens the back and looks at the batteries before smacking the side of the remote control. Janice aims the remote control at the television while pressing the on button, but nothing happens the television and the VCR is not working. Janice looks back at Tara, as she walks over to the back of the T.V Tara, and Janice both stand there now leaning over the television checking to see if the power cord is plugged in. Tara, and Janice look at each other simultaneously … *Something is wrong Tara! …You think Janice?* Then out of nowhere the bell rings and the sound alone catches Tara and Janice off guard, frightening Tara, so much she, goes into a state of shock causing her to pass out onto the floor, from the frightful thought and terrifying surprise of who she, thought might be standing there behind the door dressed in all black. Janice starts screaming and calling out Tara's name her eyes are rolled back up in her head and she's not moving her breathing stops, as Janice falls to her knee's … *Tara! Tara! What happened are you Ok?*

Janice grabs Tara's arm her and lifts it up in the air she then let's her arm go and watches as tar's arm quickly and lifeless drop back down by her side. Janice, then places her hand on Tara's chest hoping to feel a heartbeat but there is none she then puts hear finger behind Tara's ear hoping to fell a pulse but there was none so, Janice sits up and yells for help.

Oh my God what's wrong with my friend! Help! Mark! Mr. Largen something is wrong with Tara! Somebody please help me! Still on her knees by Tara cold and lifeless body that's lying there on the floor, Janice then jumps up and runs over to the house phone sitting on top of the coffee tables. Janice picks up the phones receiver she places the phone to her ear but there is no dial tone so, she clicks on the receiver again and again while crying her heart out. Janice, then remembers that the doorbell had recently rung so, she jumps up with the phone's receiver in her hand and heads towards the front door. She, removes the chain locks, open the door and looks around outside before she starts screaming for help at the top of her lungs … *Help! Help! Somebody Help me please!* Janice, then runs over to Tara's neighbor house and rings there doorbell again and again but no one answers so, she walks over to a window and starts knocking on the window while yelling and screaming *Please! Somebody help my friend!* Janice, then runs back inside the house she, slams the door behind shut without locking it she, looks at Tara, who is still lying there she, then puts the phone receiver back up to her ear and checks for a dial tone.

Now with her nerves uneasy and in panic Janice, dials 911 ... *911, what seems to be the problem? Hello, 911?*

It's my friend I think she's dead! She just fell out and she's not moving! Her body is cold too! ... Ok! First who am I speaking with? You said your name is Tara? No, it's my friend her name is Tara! My name is Janice! ... Now listen! You are going to half to calm down! So, I can find out what exactly happen! You want to help your friend, right? ...Yes! ...Ok! Now tell me what happened? ...Like I said before! I don't know why she fell out! She is just lying here! I really don't know Ok! ...Alright! What is your address? ... We are at 18 Hammer Hill Terrace! Please hurry please! ...You just stay calm and don't hang up until the paramedics arrive! Are you still there? ... Yes! I'm here! ...They should be there shortly Ok! .... But please hurry up! With Tara's lifeless body lying there and Janice, on the phone with 911 crying her heart out Janice, decides to walk towards the kitchen ... *Janice! Are you still there? Yes! I am still here!* Then the bell rings followed by a knock on the door which catches Janice off guard, frightening her into a state of shock from the frightful thought and terrifying surprise of who she, thought might be standing there behind the door ... *911! ...Yes! I'm here Janice! ...Someone is at the front door! ... Well, Janice! See who's at the door it could be the paramedics!* ...Janice holds the phones receiver down by her side as she slowly walks over by the door ...

Hello! Anybody home?

Janice can hear a woman's voice from outside behind the door … *Hello! Is there anyone home? Someone called 911?* Janice, looks in the peek hole and then immediately she, drops the phones receiver on the floor she, then looks back at Tara before opening the front door …*Here! We are in Here!* Janice, opens the door and to her surprise the voice, was not who she expected it to be Janice, thought the Paramedics was here outside the front door coming to take Tara, to the hospital. But instead when Janice, looked it was an old lady, the tall man, the boy and a young girl all dressed in black standing there. In the front was the old lady, while the tall man, the boy and girl were all standing behind her. And Janice knew for a fact that these people standing in front of her, was not the paramedics but instead they reminded Janice, of characters out of a movie that for the life of her she couldn't remember. And before Janice could say another word the old lady and the tall man who both ae dressed in all black enter Tara's house leaving the boy and the young girl outside standing by the open door. Once inside the old lady and the tall man directs their attention on Tara, who is still lying on the floor the old lady walks over to where Tara's body she stands over Tara, raises her arm and points her finger down at Tara's body while raising her other arm up to her face and covering her mouth with her hand. The old lady stands there for a minute before stepping to the side and letting the tall man walk over to Tara kneels down, places both of his arms around Tara's body and picks her up before taking two steps backwards, turning around and facing the open door.

The boy and the young girl are now making a path for the old lady and the tall man to walk out the house and through them …

(Janice Screaming) Wait! What ae you doing? Where are you taking her? Who are you Stop?! Stop! I'm calling the police! You can't do that, your kidnapping my friend! Janice looks to her left and then to her right she, then sees the house phone on the coffee table she rushes over by the table and picks up the phone receiver and dials 911… *(Janice Dialing 911) …Hello! Operator are you there? Hello! Anyone there? Operator!* But there is no dial tone, no answer and no operator the house phone is completely quiet Janice, then quickly turns her head and stares at the television that's playing but without sound then the old lady, walks out the house followed by the tall man who has Tara's body laid securely in his arms by his chest. Once outside the boy and the young girl looks inside the house one more time before turning around and following the old lady and the tall man to the all-black tinted limousine. After realizing that her call to 911 is useless Janice, quickly drops the phones receiver to the floor after watching Tara's body get carried out the house by some strange tall man dressed in all black. Now feeling paralyzed by the scene Janice just stands there and watches with an expression on her face showing that she's not only scared but frightened and terrified by the unexplained nerve wrecking dramatic scene she has just witnessed.

Not moving Janice, stands there looking outside through the open door and watches as the boy opens the passenger back door to the limousine. The boy, then closes the passenger back door after the old lady and the young girl gets in the boy, then walks around to the driver's side of the limousine where the tall man is standing there holding Tara in his arms. The boy opens the driver's side back door and watches as the tall man bends down and lays Tara's body down inside on the back seat the boy, hops inside the backseat of the limousine as the tall man, closes the door behind him. The tall man, then walks to the front of the limousine, opens the driver's side door, gets in slams the door shut and slowly pulls off leaving a dark cloud of limousine tire smoke lingering in the air. After hearing the driver's side door slam shut something came over Janice, as she then rushes over to the open door, and runs outside into the street she, watches as the limousine slowly drives down the street. While waving both of her hands across her face, trying to clear the smoke from her eyes Janice, gets a good look at the limousines license plate she, memorizes what written on the license plate before running back inside the house finding and pen and paper and writing down what she's seen …

(Janice Writing) … Limousines License Plate # qoqX rXA rQIIrQ …

After writing down the limousines license plate number on the paper Janice, folds the paper up and places it inside her pocket she, then tosses the pen on the coffee table before slamming the front door shut, she then locks the door and picks back up the house phones receiver and places it up to her ear while crying and screaming out names … *(Janice Screaming) Mr. Largen! Mrs. Largen! Mark! Where is everybody?*

Then strange enough Janice finally comes to the realization that she's the only one in the house with no dial tone, broken glass shattered on the floor and the television playing with no sound. All of this caused Janice, to panic even more so, she slowly walks over to the couch with tears rolling down her face and, in her eyes, there was soul wrenching fear as she sat down with both of her arms folding across her chest. With the house phones receiver tightly held in her hand Janice, stares at the television and in bold text flashing across the screen it reads THЄ JOURNAL!

INSULTED DRIVERS

"When Road Rage, Leads To More Road Rage"

TH€ ACCIDENT

(Reading to himself from his book of poems Mark, starts feeling tired as his head tilts back and his eyes slowly closes, he, then falls fast asleep dropping his book of poems onto the floor)!...

News flash this just in a disturbing but unusual death occurred yesterday evening turn from the news Mrs. Largen screams at her husband I am tired of hearing about someone dying all the time Wait dear! No if you don't turn I will Ok! I guess your right you know I'm right it seems like everyday something like this happens and if not here somewhere else in the world. As Mr. Largen gets up to turn the TV, where is the dog on remote when you need it you can find it and When you're not looking for It's right there in your face boy wake up Mrs. Largen yells at Edward and pushes him. Get up! Boy go and help your father find the remote oh! Never mind here it is here make yourself useful Edward run to the store and get some milk, cheese and eggs and pick up the news Paper Mrs. Largen tells Edward. Go on now boy get! Edward wipes his face and then yarns he then picks up his book and heads for the front door.

Hello! Edward the neighbor yells from across the street how's the family? There are doing just fine Edward waves off heading dorm the street taking his focus off for a minute he looks at his book Oh!

Excuse me Edwards says being that he just bumped into the Girl in front of him lie then looks up and It's his sister Tara friend she is crying acting like someone just died, she's real pale in the face is that you? Edward asked she looks at him in sorrow not saying a word are you Ok? Edward asks again she then screams out I'm Sorry! It wasn't my fault then she pushes Edward out of her way tripping as she runs down the street taking one look back, she then dashes into the street *Watch Out!*

Edward yells when out of nowhere a Black limousine doing about 60 mph comes from nowhere and in the blink of eye Tara's friend smacks dead into the limousine flying several feet into the air *Oh my God!* No Edward screams the limousine stops a few feet ahead, no one gets out Edward just can't believe what he just seen so he drops his book of poems runs to the street.

While Tara's friend is still lying there motionless, Edward places two fingers on her wrist and then on her neck too check or a pulse but it's hopeless what Edward just witnessed was not what he expected on his way to the store. He then looks at the limousine the engine still running, he then turns his head and looks at the girl before jumping up out of excitement and running towards the limousine yelling at the top of his lungs. Open the Door! Edward yells at the tinted window of the limousine, *Do You Know What You've Done! Stop! Stop!*

Walking to the driver side of the limousine Edward raises his left arm and with his fist balled up he bangs on the driver side window, he then stands there with both fists balled in rage while thinking about what he's going to tell his sister Tara about what happened to her friend. But the more he thinks about it the more upset and in rage he becomes. Edward then kicks the limousine door and bangs on the driver's side window again, he leans over with both of his hands pressed up against the window, peering into the glass trying to see who's sitting in the driver's seat. Then suddenly the limousines back window behind the driver side slowly rolls down, Edward lifts his head up, turns his body around and stare at the back window. The window rolls down just enough so that Edward can see the top of the persons head seated in the back seat of the limousine. He then screams at the person in the back seat before rushing over to the window, *Who Are You! Who Is Driving This Car? Get Out You Murderers!* Edward looks around the area before he yells out.

Somebody Call The Police! They Just Killed A Teenage Girl! Edward reaches for the limousine's back door handle, he shakes the handle hoping the door will open but it doesn't, he then tries sticking his arm inside the window but there's not enough room.

Get Out You Murderers!!! I Knew Her! I Knew That Girl You Killed!

Edward removes his forearm, wrist and hand from inside the window and grabs the limousines back door handle again, while still in rage and out of anger, he pulls and pulls the handle hoping to open the limousines back door. Then out of nowhere the person in the back seat, who's been quiet since the accident and throughout Edwards furious rampage, the person who rolled the window down just enough so that Edward could only see the top of their head slowly sticks out the window what looks like a newspaper.

Edward looks at the newspaper the person in the backseat of the limousine is steadily holding out the window, he then smacks the newspaper to the ground and bangs his fist on the roof of the limousine. The back window quickly rolls up, the limousines engine revs up, Edward starts coughing from the thick black smoke that's building up from the back tires of the limousine. Edward takes several steps back away from the limousine and the tire smoke, he raises his right arm and covers his mouth with his hand. His eyes start burning while water fills his pupils, so he closes both eyes and holds his head down to avoid any further severe, excruciating pain. The limousine slowly drives off on down the street.

While silence controls the environment, the thick black tire smoke is slowly vanishing but besides Edward there's not a person, vehicle, or house in sight. So out of frustration and anger Edward removes his hand from over his mouth and shouts out into the quiet but nerve-racking atmosphere.

Can Anybody Hear Me? Please Is There Anyone Out There?

With the tire smoke now gone Edward's vision is back, his eyes stop burning he looks up and see's the back of the limousine as it drives down the street. Edward runs behind the limousine shouting and screaming, not for once thinking to get the license plate number after chasing behind the limousine halfway down the block. His wind finally gives out, he becomes fatigued, so he stops and falls to the ground on one knee, while holding his head down with his right hand on top of his head breathing rapidly. After a few minutes Edward catches his breath, he gets up and makes his way back to the scene of the accident where the teenage girl was hit, but the girl was gone there wasn't a trace of her or any of her belongings in sight. Edward was alarmed with disbelief; he couldn't believe it he closed both of his eyes hoping that maybe just maybe when he opened them, he would see the girl. But he didn't and every time he thought about it the thought of the girl being gone frightened him. Because he knew for sure that the girl was dead, no one could withstand or survive a hit like that, Edward kept thinking. This girl was thrown almost six feet into the air and not only that she hit the ground headfirst, Oh! Hell, no there isn't any way she just got up and walked away, or did she? Edward scratches the top of his head again in wonder. Edward jumps startled as a car quickly drives pass him on his left side and honks its car horn several times.

Get Out The Street You Ass Hole! A guy yells at Edward with his head sticking out the passenger side window. Causing Edward to step back even closer to the curb side of the road, while dodging another vehicle who misses him by inches as he jumps back startled again. Standing curb side Edward stares at scene where he knows for sure something just happened, he then looks both ways up and down the street before walking back into the street. When out of nowhere a young girl on roller skates catches his attention, she stops in front of where Edward is standing. *Excuse me mister! Is this yours?* The young girl reaches out her left arm and, in her hand, she is holding a book, Edward looks at the book and realizes that the book she is holding is his little brother's poem book. Lost for words and speechless Edward looks back at the young girl, he shakes his head side to side in reason of not being able to comprehend or understand what or why this young girl on roller skates was doing out here this time of night, by herself. But what made the situation more mind boggling was the fact that she had Marks poem book and was trying to give it to him. *Well Aren't You Going To Take It?* While in front of Edward and not moving the young girl rolls on her skates, her legs move back and forth one after another as she holds out her arm and tries handing Edward the book. Edward then forces himself to smile, but deep inside he's really scared to death not at the sight of the young girl but the shock and thought of what's happening.

While not being able to respond Edward digs deep inside to muster the courage and strength just too raise his arm and take the book from out the young girl's hand. Once the book is in Edwards hand the young girl on skates rolls off down the street, and once she's halfway down the street Edward walks out into the middle of the street and calls out to the young girl. *Wait! Wait!... I need to Know Where Did You Get This Book?*

The young girl on skates stops in the middle of the street for a few seconds with her back-facing Edward, she then slowly but creepy and disturbingly turns only her head and shoulders around and looks back at Edward. Silence controls the environment again, but this time Edward can hear the ball barring's inside the wheels of her skates, as she stands there staring at Edward while rolling on her skates in one place, with both of her legs moving back and forth one after another.

Edward hears a loud engine; the sound is so loud and so close Edward knows that this could only mean danger, not for him but for the young girl who honestly is acting like she doesn't have any idea what's headed her way, or even care for that matter. So, he yells as loud as he can at the young girl, who is still in the middle of the street, rolling on her skates in one place, with her head and shoulder turned staring back at him.

Get Out Of The Street! I Think A Car Or Truck Is Coming! Edward puts the book in his back pocket while standing in the middle of the street and with both of his arms raised in the air, he waves them both side to side. Edward can now see bright lights coming from the direction in front of the young girl, so out of nervousness, fear and concern for the young girl's safety Edward silently preys that the young girl gets out the street and out of harm's way, of whatever is headed towards her. The sound of the engine gets louder and louder, Edward can now see large bright headlights meaning that its either a van or truck that is driving their way. The headlights are so bright it's now blinding him from seeing the young girl clearly, and Edward knew from being a driver for many years and seeing so many different vehicles on the road. That the only vehicle that could have headlights that bright and an engine sounding that loud had to be a van or a truck. Edward yells at the girl again hoping this time she realizes that something is wrong. *You're Going To Get Killed! Get Out Of The Street! Please Get Out Of The Street!* Even though Edward didn't know this young girl he still had all the concern in the world for her. And every time Edward thought about her his mind would flashback to the scene earlier, when his little sister Tara's friend was struck and killed, by the limousine. And that thought just made him delusional in a sense being that there was no evidence of any accident or body.

So, with no hesitation Edward quickly walks back over and onto the sidewalk, he then starts to slowly walk down to where the young girl is in the street while making sure he stays on the sidewalk and out the street. The young girls head and shoulders follows Edwards every move, and as creepy and disturbing as everything seemed, Edward was in panic by the thought of what might and could happen to this young girl, if she didn't acknowledge this vehicle headed towards her and get out of the street in time. On the sidewalk Edward stops a few feet away from the young, who is still staring at him and following his every move, with her head and shoulders. And as Edward stands there motionless on the sidewalk, looking up and down the street the bright headlights and loud sounding engine approaches. With the vehicle being only a few feet away from the young girl Edward thinks twice about running in the middle of the street towards the young girl, grabbing her and throwing himself and her out the way of the oncoming vehicle. But this was just a thought and even if Edward wanted to make that life-threatening move, that might just save the young girls life he couldn't being that once he made eye contact and looked the young girl directly in the face. Edwards whole body froze, he couldn't move an inch, his heart was looking out for the young girl, while eyes was staring right into fear. Edward found himself not being able to speak as hard as he tried, his mouth was open but the words he wanted to say was closed.

This was not a figment of his imagination being that the truth was a nightmare, and if he was dreaming the thought of what was about to happen woke him right on up. Edward couldn't feel his heart pounding in his chest, the blood in his veins was making his skin cold, his head felt like it wasn't attached to his body anymore and he could now hear and see the sixteen-wheeler truck speeding down the street, getting closer and closer towards the young girl.

Not being able to move, yell or inform the young girl of what was about to happen, Edward couldn't do nothing but watch as the tragic event right in front of him unfolds. As water accumulates in his eyes, a tear discharges from his pupil and trickles down his face, the tear drop makes it way to his chin and slowly, like a still shot in a movie the tear drop separates itself from Edwards's face. And as the tear drop makes it way to the ground, silence control the atmosphere again and nothing can be heard, not the sixteen-wheelers horn, engine, or the ball barring's inside the wheels of the young girl's skates. Edward's heart is silently pounding faster and faster, as the sixteen-wheeler truck and blinding bright headlights is only few feet away from the young girl, who is still in the middle of the street, rolling on her skates in place with both of her legs moving back and forth one after another.

Then finally the tear drop hits the ground and simultaneously, the tear drop splashes, the young girl's head turns around towards the sixteen-wheeler truck, the young girl stops skating in place, her legs stand still, Edward is released from the out of body experience, he could feel his heart beating in his chest, the blood in his veins was warming up his body, he was able to move his head and neck, Edward could speak again.

Without second guessing himself or thinking twice about what to do, Edward steps into the street with all intentions of trying to save the young girl's life, even though he knew it was too late, his heart wouldn't let him stand there and be a witness to another tragic accident, without doing something even if it meant his life would be taken as well. And just as Edward rushes to take another step in the street, the sixteen-wheeler's, loud horn, engine, and blinding headlights did the impossible. Edward couldn't believe what he was seeing, so he stood there by the curb of the sidewalk in the street, with his mouth wide open and his heart pounding through his chest. The young girl still standing there in the middle of the street facing the sixteen-wheeler, not moving an inch or showing any signs of fear. It was like the bright headlights from the truck, the loud horn and the loud engine didn't even budge the young girl, not only did it not move her, she even had the nerve to look back at Edward one more time before life, counting down the last minutes and seconds of what was about to be her last days on earth.

To Edward this was more than shocking, it was so shocking that he was numb to how he was feeling, but this time it was different, this time the odds was in his favor. And all he could think about is that this young girl, who was standing in front of him in the middle of the street on roller skates, had to be blessed with a righteous spirit or cursed with a wicked soul, to have escaped what was looking and turning out to be a no escaping incident that was going to turn out no other way but fatal.

With the sixteen-wheeler bright headlights blinding Edward as he looked at the truck and how its direction quickly changed, as the truck approached closer to the young girl who was still in the middle of the street.

What Edward was seeing changed his beliefs, faith and religion per say, Edward had seen a lot in his life on this earth and what happened earlier, had nothing on what he was witnessing right now. The sixteen-wheeler truck somehow with no explanation rapidly turned to its left as it approached closer and closer the young girl. The truck was only inches away from her, and this was very hard to understand how a 30 to 40 pound sixteen-wheeler truck, moving at over 60 miles per hour can on instinct and inches away miss this young girl. And with its left side wheels up on the sidewalk, the truck passes on by, leaving a hard pushing wind that thrust so powerful it pushes Edward back a few steps, causing him to fall to the ground.

Edward looks on as the sixteen-wheeler truck speeds on pass, he then looks at the young girl who has her head turned towards him, starring him in directly in the face. Without a single reaction or change of facial expression or body language, the young girl standing in the middle of the street on roller skates, slowly turns back around while the sixteen-wheeler truck rapidly passes by. Once the truck is out of sight and the loud horn and engine has silenced, and the full thrust of wind has ceased, the young girl gracefully skates off down the street, with a cheerful attitude and a joyful state of mind. Edward raises his right arm and rubs the side of his face, he then inhales and exhales out a deep sigh of relief, while thinking that maybe what he thought happened earlier involving the limousine and his sister Tara's friend never did, and maybe all of this was just a figment of his crazy imagination. Then Edward remembers the book the young girl gave him so, he stands up and reaches in his back pocket but there's nothing there, Edward then taps both back pockets before looking down at his front pockets. But still there's no book, and with no book Edward now has to question himself and his own truth, about the realism of what really happened. And did he really witness all the things he thought he did, or was this all just a pure figment of his crazy imagination playing tricks on him?

Edward closes his eyes hoping that when he opens them, he would have a different perspective about all of this, and the negative thoughts running wild throughout his head. And with every second he has his eyes closed, Edward get flashes of tragic and horrifying scenes of his sister's friend getting hit by the limousine. The scene is in all red and there's blood all in the street, Edward can even hear the Tara's friend whispering to him THE JOURNAL...THE JOURNAL...

THE JOURNAL...

Scared to death by the flashes and bloody, horrific scene Edward quickly opens his eyes as wide as he could and takes a deep breath, he then exhales out a tremendous sigh of relief. Edward walks into the middle of the street and looks in the direction where the young girl went, he then turns all the way around and faces where the sixteen-wheeler truck has gone. Edward then notices something lying in the street up ahead, so he calmly walks in the direction where the unknown thing is and as he gets closer, he can identify that the thing lying in the street is a newspaper. He walks up to the newspaper, bends down and picks it up, he then pops the rubber band off, before unfolds the newspaper and holding it up to his face. While looking at the front page, Edward walks back over on to the side.

And as he takes a second look, Edward sees his sister Tara laying lifeless in the middle of the street and parked in front of her body is an all-black limousine with tinted out windows.

The same limousine exactly like the one he remembers seeing all throughout those horrific flashes, Edward takes a closer look and notices that the young girl on roller skates from earlier is also in the picture. And she's standing inside the open back door to the limousine, with her arm extending out with a book in her hand. And her eyes seem like they are looking directly back at Edward as he stares back at the young girl in the picture, and like if seeing his little sister lying lifeless in the middle of the street wasn't creepy enough. But besides his sister and the young girl in the picture another strange thing that caught Edward's attention was that Tara and the young girl was dressed in all black, plus the limousine's window was rolled down just enough, so Edward could see the top of the persons head sitting in the back seat of the limousine. And sticking out the back window behind the driver was the newspaper

THE JOURNAL...

Edward then reads out loud the fine print below the pictures on the front page of the newspaper...

THE JOURNAL

Confused and in disbelief, trying to hold on to your past,

Not knowing it's the main reason, your future won't last.

And if you don't accept, what's already been witnessed

You will never have any peace

When quoting poetic verses and self-made scriptures.

Living this way, will be a life changing mistake

It will cause your behavior, to act out vengeance

Whenever dangerous situations are faced.

Read in between the lines, it's secrets that the family will keep

And to end, mirror mimicking occurrences

Remove THE JOURNAL *from your dreams*

Then you'll wake up from your sleep.

MISTAKES AND IDENTITIES

"The Inaccuracy Of Confusion

Causes People To Straight Suffer"

TH€ ARREST

Dinners ready! Edward's wife yells out from the kitchen, she then raises her arm pointing and directing their children, to go and wash their hands before they eat. The children start pushing and shoving one another in a playful manner, while on their way to the bathroom. The phone rings, *Edward could you get that my hands are full*, the phone rings again and again, *I got it Hello! Hello! There's no one on this phone!* And just as Edward is about to hang up the phone, he hears his little brother's voice on the other end. *Mark! It's me your brother* Mark's voice catches Edward's attention just before he passes his wife back the phone, *Little Bro! What's going on?... I'm good and you?... Oh, me I'm about to have dinner with the wife and kids! Little Bro!... We'll you don't say! And enough already with the little bro! We'll look at my little Brother getting all grown on me!... Funny Edward!... Anyway, your more than welcome to come over for dinner! Just don't be bringing one of your one night stands over like you usually do ... Not even Kim...And who is Kim? And when did she come over for dinner?* Edward holds the house phone receiver down by his side and covers the mouthpiece with his hand. He then looks at his wife and frowns his face, while shrugging both shoulders. *(Whispering) Babe! And when did Mark have a girl name Kim over for dinner?* Edward's wife then shrugs her shoulder with a look of confusion, as if she doesn't remember. *(Whispering) You said Kim? Honey I have no idea, we are talking about Mark, right?*

Edward shakes his head up and down, signaling that his wife does a point. Edward then raises the phone receiver back up to his ear, removes his hand from over the mouthpiece and start laughing. *And what's so hilarious Bro?... Oh! It's nothing, I was just thinking about something. I Bet! And I could just imagine what you were thinking about, you don't remember Kim do you?... Too tell you the God honest truth, No! And that is what was so funny little Bro…Ha! Ha! Edward but I know I be playing tennis with these females! And maybe I shouldn't be bringing so many different ones over to the house, it could confuse my nephew, hopefully in a good way! But you must understand Edward! I'm a king, and kings need their queens!*

Edward starts laughing again. *Ok! Miss me with the king speech already! …Edward I'm serious!... You serious Mark! You're the same person who be calling females, by other female's names! Oh! And don't forget that one chick you brought here, or should I say lady! She as a real cougar...You are talking about Mrs. Hellen! She was only like thirty something!... Thirty something! Mark you were still in high school! And she was married!...*

Mark and his brother Edward both start laughing after what Edward just said, then the doorbell rings, and rings again. *Listen little bro! I mean Mark someone is at the door so, let me call you back or if not, I'll see you at dinner Ok?... Sure, thing Bro! Later...Alright later!* Edward hangs up the house phone and watches as his wife, makes her way to the front door to see who it is. Edwards wife wipes both of her hands off with a kitchen towel, while standing a few feet inches away from the front door.

*Who is it? …It's me Sis...*Edward's wife turns and looks at her husband Edward in the face, while pointing at the front door. She then places her right hand up to her face and signals a phone gesture with her hand. Edward looks at her and smiles. *(Whispering) I think it's Mark!* Edward frowns and shakes his head side to side, signaling that it can't be and that his wife is wrong. She then leans forward and looks through the peek hole, she then turns back around, looks at Edward and shakes her head up and down signaling that she's right. (Whispering) Its Mark! She then addressing the person behind the door. *Just a minute, I'll be right there.* Edwards wife throws the kitchen towel over her left shoulder, unlocks the front door and opens it. *Sis, it's me...We'll what a surprise! What am I thinking come on in, you staying for dinner? Hold up wasn't you just on the…*Edward cuts his wife off. *So, you were outside the whole time, while we were on the phone?...Not the whole time, I was waiting for my friend...Did you say friend?...*Mark turns around and extends his arm out, he grabs hold of the female's hand, who has just walked up behind him. *Everybody this is Joy...*Edward and his wife look at each other, before focusing their attention back on Marks new female friend Joy. *Well Joy, any friend of my brother in law is a friend of mine! Welcome...*

Edwards wife closes and locks the front door behind Mark and his female friend once they are in the house. Edwards wife walks over by her husband and nudges him on the arm, while trying to keep a smile on her face.

Edward! Don't you have something to say dear? Edward! ...Oh! Nice to meet you Joy! And please stay for dinner? Mark pulls Joy lightly by the arm in between Edward and his wife, and head straight towards the living room. *Why, I think we will big bro! How about you Queen, you hungry?... I'm famished!* Joy smiles and looks at Edward, and his wife while walking pass. *Nice meeting you! And you have a beautiful home*! Edwards wife smiles back at Joy. *Why thankyou Joy! Well, let me go in here and set two more plates! Edward, dear! You want to take the roast out the oven for me...Roast! I thought it was...*Edwards wife nudges him in the arm again, while trying to hold a straight face. *Oh! That's right the roast!* Edward and his wife both walk towards the kitchen.

A big bro you still have Netflix, right? Edwards wife looks at her husband and waits for him to answer, he looks back at her as she shakes her head side to side signaling Edward not to be rude. *Of course, Mark! The remote control is inside the cabinet, underneath the television! (Whispering) Enjoy King!* Edwards wife looks at him and frowns, she then stops by the kitchens entrance. *Joy! Is there anything I can get you?... No! I'm good thank-you...Ok, then don't hesitate to ask...Thank-you!*

In the kitchen Edwards reaches out his arm, grabs his wife by the wrist and pulls her into the kitchen with him. She looks at him and starts laughing! *And could you please tell me what's so funny...Its nothing...No its something...Well, evidently, it's something, because you keep laughing! I want to laugh too!*

Edwards wife walks over to the cabinet above the sink, she lays the kitchen towel down on the countertop before removing two plates, she places the plates on the kitchen table before reaching back inside the cabinet and taking out two glasses. She then sits the two glasses, next to the plates she just placed down. *Ok! Ok! We'll if you really want to know, what's so funny...Yes, I do! Because your hysterical right now!* Edwards wife walks over to him, and wraps her arms around her husband's waist, she looks up at him in the face and smiles.

Well...Ok! It was your facial expression, when you found out that it was Mark, at the front door! That's all...What, do you mean my facial expression...What I mean is, you had this look like you didn't know if you were happy to see him or not! I can't explain it, but your face said a lot! Edward shakes his head side to side signaling that what his wife just said doesn't make no sense. *We'll can you tell what my facial expression, is saying right now...Don't get offended baby!... No! tell me what my facial expression is saying right now?* Edwards wife places both of her hands on her husband's face and gives him a kiss, before letting his face go and walking back over to the cabinet, by the sink. She turns around and faces Edward, she stares at him for a quick minute before turning the faucet water on in the sink. *I give up! I don't know what your facial expression is saying right now baby!* Edward walks over by the kitchens entrance, and look's in the living room and around the house, before turning his head and looking at his wife.

We'll, if you really want to know what my facial expression is saying? It's saying once Joy and Pain eat, I'm going to let the doorknob hit them, where the good lord split them! Edward and his wife start laughing.

I don't mean to interrupt, this beautiful husband and wife moment! Edward and his wife are startled, as they both quickly turn and face Mark, who is standing by the kitchen entrance. *But do you think it would be a problem if Joy, uses the bathroom upstairs? Nephew got this one occupied!*

Edwards wife walks over by Mark. *Oh! No, that wouldn't be a problem at all let me show her where it is, that way we can get to know each other better...We'll sis! Whatever you do, please don't talk about her moles on her face! She has a complex about that! I told her they were passion marks!* Edwards wife lightly pushes Mark to the side, as she walks out the kitchen and into the living room. *Excuse me boy, Joy! You in there?* Edwards wife stops outside the kitchen. *And Edward, could you check up on the boy's, they seem to be having a little too much fun in there!... We'll, at least you know after a bath and dinner, they go straight to bed...Yea! I remember those days, you remember Ma, had us do the same thing...The only difference was you couldn't stop peeing in the tub...No! you peed in the tub...No! You kept peeing in the tub!*

Edward and Mark start laughing. Mark walks over to the refrigerator and opens the door, while Edward steps out the kitchen headed to the downstairs bathroom to check up on his two sons. Edward knocks on the bathroom door.

(Knocking) *Boy's alright time to get out the tub and get ready for dinner...Ok! day...Dad! I'm drying off now...Good to hear that boy's, now put some pep in your step, because dinner is ready Ok?... Yes...Yes dad. Plus, your uncle Mark is here!* Mark closes the refrigerator door and leaves the kitchen after taking out a water. He stands behind Edward by the bathroom door. *Nephews! ...Uncle Mark! Uncle Mark!* Edward turns and looks at Mark standing behind him, then the bathroom door opens and both of Edward sons, rushes over two their Uncle and simultaneously greets him with two hugs. *Well, who are these two fine and handsome gentlemen?* Edward, Mark and his two nephews look up and see Joy, standing there behind them. *Nephews! This is my friend Joy!... Hi...Hello!* Then Edwards wife walks in-between Joy and Edward, she then places her hands on her two sons' shoulder, and gently pulls them away from Mark. *Ok! There will be more than enough time to greet and meet, but first let's get these two ready for diner...Bye!* Joy waves as Edwards wife escorts her two sons to their room, Joy then stands by Mark and kisses him on the cheek before laying her head on his shoulder. Then Edward, Mark and Joy all walk towards the kitchen and wait for Edwards wife and their sons, so they all can start eating dinner. After the boys have finished eating their dinner, they get up from the kitchen table and get ready for bed, after saying goodnight to Joy and their uncle Mark. The boys leave the kitchen and head upstairs to their bedroom, while Edward, his wife, Joy and Mark are still seated at the kitchen table.

Either finishing what's left on their plate or drinking the last of their beverage in their glass. Once the boys are put to bed and everyone has finished their meals, Joy gets up from her seat at the kitchen table and starts collecting the empty plates and glasses. She then walks over to the sink and places the dirty dishes inside.

Joy! My dear you don't have to wash the dishes! I can take care of that...No! Problem, I wash the dishes at my house all the time! Edward and his wife quickly look at each other, from across the kitchen table. *Joy! ...Yes, mam! ...Did you say at your house...Yes, I did! I recently became a homeowner! ...We'll congratulation honey!* Edward takes his attention off his wife and looks at his brother Mark. *I didn't think Mark had any friends who owned their own home!* Mark looks at his brother Edward. *It's a lot you don't know about me Brother!... Ok! Boys let's not be rude, we have company...No, it's fine sis! We all know my brother doesn't think, I can be successful as him! Right Bro?* Before Edward could answer Joy, walks away from the sink and sits down on Mark's lap at the kitchen table. *My King is all the success I need...Speaking on success! No disrespect! But aren't you kind of young to be a home owner, Joy?... She is...*Joy steps in and cuts Mark off. *No! I understand your concern; I get that a lot lately! But to answer your question, I am 25 years old, and I became a homeowner when my parents divorced. My Father owns his own law firm and my mother! We'll let's just say she inherited from the courts and is happily involved!*

Edward and his wife have a confused look on their face concerning what Joy just said about her Mother. What's she's trying to say is, her Mother like Mothers...*Oh! ok, then that explains the happily involved...You got it Sis...I knew that!* Edward gets up from the kitchen table and stretches before walking over to the refrigerator and taking out a cold beer. *Mark, beer?... Sure, why not!... Joy, could you pass tis beer to Pain for me? I mean Mark! ... Anyway! It must feel good being a homeowner at your age...It sure does, and I enjoy it more and more every day with my King!... You tell them Queen!* Joy leans over and kisses Mark, while Edward closes the refrigerator door and his wife walks over to the sink to finish washing the left-over dishes. *So, what exactly do you do to pay the bills? Because I could just imagine you just graduating a few years ago, and owning a home isn't cheap. You have mortgages, water bills, light and gas bills right...Yes, your absolutely correct! But unfortunately, I was blessed to get a job right out of school...Sis, she works for her Father!... So, you're a secretary? Mark and Joy start laughing. No!... nothing like that, I'm a lawyer! I'll be graduating from Harvard Law School, next year and in the meantime, I practice law at my Father's firm, until I start my own Law Firm!*

Edward takes a long guzzle of the beer he has in his hand, before looking at his wife and then at his Brother Mark. Who has his head leaned behind Joy as she continues sitting on his lap, with a big smile on his face looking back at his Brother Edward.

Edward holds the beer down by his side, raises his left hand and sticks out his thumb, signaling to Mark that he appreciates what's he's hearing about Joy.

We'll I must say Joy! You are doing great things for yourself, and your future looks very bright, young lady...That's my Queen...And that's my King! Joy leans over again and gives Mark a kiss, before getting up off his lap. Mark get up, grabs his beer from off the table and takes a sip. *I guess we are all done here!... And I must say dinner was superb, I truly appreciate your hospitality...Please Joy, call me Tina and Anytime Joy! A friend of my Brother is a friend of mine!... Joy starts smiling. Why thank-you Edward! You have a wonderful family! ... I think she was talking to me dear!* Mark, Joy and Edwards wife Tina starts laughing. *How about we take this into the living room? I heard the movie The Journal is a great movie...I'm down Tina, a movie sounds great! I'm sorry I might not be able to stay throughout the whole movie. Being that I must get up during the early bird hour tomorrow! But while I'm here let's watch it...Sure, I'm up for a good movie...Yea, me too bro!*

Mark and Joy walk pass Edwards wife Tina and head towards the living room, while Edward and his wife follows behind them. *(Whispering) So, what do you think about your Brothers selection in woman now?... Game changer for him! But there's only one Queen in this house!* Edwards wife places her arm around her husband's waist, as they slowly walk a few feet behind Joy and Mark, headed into the living room. Edwards wife looks him in the face, and he look back at her and smiles.

Now in the middle of the movie Joy nudges Mark the side signaling to him that it's time for her to leave, Mark gets up off the couch first, and Joy follows. Edwards wife then leans up off her husband's shoulder and stands up to see her Brother in law and his new friend Joy properly out.

Don't just sit-down honey, go and get their coats!... No! relax bro, I got it sit down and enjoy the rest of the movie...Again thank-you for a great evening Tina. You are more than welcome, and please come back and visit sometime Joy. Maybe next time we can get through a whole movie together!... I would like that very much, goodnight Edward...Yes! Goodnight to you too, Joy, and drive home safely...Give my love to those two handsome gentlemen, will you?... Sure thing! Peace big Bro!

Edward gets up off the couch walks over to Mark and gives him a hug, while Tina and Joy are hugging goodbyes by the front door. Joy waves bye to Edward and steps outside, Edwards wife Tina gives Mark a hug right before he follows Joy outside to the car. *Oh! And Mark if you're going home, tell Ma I'll stop by tomorrow after work...Got it Bro! That's if I make it home!* Edward sits back down on the couch and continues watching the movie The Journal. While his wife stands in the doorway and watches as Mark and Joy drives off, out the driveway and down the street. Edwards wife waves goodbye as Mark and Joy disappear into the night.

Edwards wife turns around, walks back inside the house, closes and locks the front door before heading upstairs to check on their two sons, who's in the bed sleep getting ready for school tomorrow.

You could at least pause the movie for me...Oh! my bad baby, let me do that for you!... No need to now, I don't want you watch the same part all over again...Are you serious? (Mumbling) Some people have no kind of consideration!... Baby, I just said I would...Anyway, did you see the car Joy was driving...No, what kind was it, a Mercedes or a BMW or maybe a Jaguar? It was one of those right...Nope! Edwards wife stands at the top of the stairs and looks down at the television and then back at her husband, before slowly walking towards their son's bedroom.

She was driving a 2018 four door Telsa Coupe...A Telsa Coupe, you don't say! We'll I'm surprised and impressed!... Why dear?... Because for starters she has good taste, and on the other hand, she seems to care about the planet!... The planet? What does the planet have to do with the price of tea in china...There's a lot about cars besides the name Tina!... Like, what? ... None other than the most important aspect in cars today...And what's that Ford Motor Man.... Ha! Ha! Very funny, but it's that those Telsa cars, are electric efficient! Meaning no gas!... We'll if that's it, then big deal! Me personally, I would have preferred a Mercedes or a BMW! And honey!... Yea...Could you pause that movie? Edward looks up the stairs from the couch and sees his wife, walking towards their son's bedroom.

Edward turns back around on the couch and faces the television. *(Mumbling) You got to be kidding me! Dam it! Where's the remote control?*

Stopped at a red traffic light a few blocks from Marks Brother house, Joy patiently sits behind the steering wheel and starts yawning, her body language is showing signs of fatigue. While Mark sits there in the passenger seat leaned back. *Mark! You might want to put your seat belt on, you know how these people be driving this time of night...This time of night? It's not even ten o'clock!... Do you know what time it is?... About nine thirty!... Boy! It's a quarter after eleven, it's almost midnight*! Joy removes one hand from off the steering wheel and points to the clock highlighted in neon green, on the dashboard. *We'll that's why I didn't know, your clock is looking like a glow in the dark stick! Can you change the features of the color to neon normal?* Joy and Mark start laughing, as they wait for the traffic light to turn green. *Get a watch boy...I have a cellphone...My point exactly Mark! But baby did you hear?... Hear what...Speaking about people driving at night! A terrible thing happened to a young woman last night!... What?... She was killed in a hit and run Mark!... Dam! That's devastating to hear! How old was she...I don't know!... We'll did they at least get the driver, or the license plate number of the vehicle that hit her?... I'm not sure but they did say they have a witness! A young man saw the whole thing!... Well I hope they get the bastard who did it! ... I hope so too!* The traffic light turns yellow and then green. Joy then gases the vehicle and drives off down the street.

Mark! You are coming to my house right...You sound like you want me to move in, is that what you're asking...You would want me to answer that, but I'll pass!

Mark then sits up in the passenger seat, leans to his left and starts kissing Joy behind her ear. *Mark! Stop it, what are you trying to cause me to have an accident...Never that!... Then cut it out and behave yourself, while I'm driving! Didn't we just talk about a hit and run?* Smiling Mark leans back over in the passenger seat and leans back. *Oh! We talked about a hit and run, but once I get to hitting there won't be nowhere for you to run!* Joy turns her head to the right, and smirks at the remark. *And may I ask, what makes this time so different?* Then suddenly Mark quickly sits up in his seat, he reaches over and grabs the steering wheel turning it to the right. While at the same time Joy forces the breaks, just missing hitting the back of a car, waiting in traffic in front of them. *Oh! My God! You see what happens when you distract me Mark? I almost ruined the front of this eighty-thousand-dollar car, on a 2001 Honda Civic! So, for the rest of the way home keep your lips to yourself crazy! I don't believe this!... But you were on point! And you saved me from what could have been a serious insurance lawsuit...Yea, whatever! So, Joy maybe you should let me drive the rest of the way?* At the next corner Joy pulls over, Mark gets out, Joy slides over in the passenger seat. Mark gets in the driver's seat, closes the door, pulls off and drives the rest of the way, headed to Joys house.

Back at Marks Brother Edward's home the movie THE JOURNAL is over, and Edward and his wife Tina are in the kitchen, Tina is preparing her husband a late-night meal and her a late-night snack before they both go to bed. *Honey! About that accident we just saw on the news!... And what about it Baby...Do you know what was so strange about the accident?* Edward looks up at his wife as she is fixing his plate. *No, What...At the scene of the crime they mentioned they found a book!... A Book!... Yes! A book of poems, by Author Sam Elmwood! Just like the one your Brother Mark carries around!* Edward and his wife both get quiet, they stare at one another in in question. *Do you think he!... What! You're asking me to do I think my little Brother did that? We'll of-course not and don't be ridiculous! My little Brother may be a lot of thing, but a Murderer he's not!... We'll I'm just saying! Your saying what Tina...Maybe he was there, I don't know! Then why don't you call him, and ask him where Is his book of poems? Because me and you both know Mark, always carries that book of poems around with him...Your imagination is really running wild, with this here Tine! We'll why don't you just, call and ask?*

With the plate of food in front of him at the kitchen table, Edward picks up a fork and then drops it back down on the table, upset at what his wife might be insinuating Edward, with blunt force pushes the chair he's sitting in, away from the kitchen table and gets up. Edward leaves the plate of food untouched at the table.

Tina tries to grab Edward by his arm, but Edward snatches away from her and storms towards the entrance of the kitchen in silent rage. *Edward! Where are you going...I'll be back...We'll aren't you going to eat first?* Edward turns around by the kitchen door and looks back at the plate of food on the kitchen table, before leaving the kitchen. *Just put it up, I'll eat it later!... Edward! Your acting very childish right now! I didn't mean to upset you dear!... That's my little Brother were talking about Tina! I only have one! And I'll do any and everything to protect him! If anybody should know that, I expect you too!* Edward angrily walks over by the front door, grabs a jacket hanging on the coat rack, puts the jacket on, unlocks the front door, opens the door and walks out slamming the front door behind him. Tina rushes behind Edward, out the kitchen and over to the front door, with his wrapped-up plate of food in her hand. She then quickly unlocks and opens the front door; she then sticks her head outside. *(Yelling) Call me! I love you, be careful!* Tina, stands there and watches as her husband, pulls out the driveway and into the street. Once he is down the street and out of her sight, Tina looks up and down, and around the community before sticking her head back inside the house, she then closes and locks the front door, before walking back into the kitchen. In the car with no seat belt on, behind the steering wheel Edward turns the radio on, he starts tapping his fingers on the steering wheel to the music playing, Edward's nerves get the best of him, so he starts biting his bottom lip.

After driving a few blocks, Edward decides to pull the car over at the next corner and pulls into the parking lot of 7 eleven convenient store in the neighborhood.

Edward gets out of the car, leaving the keys in the ignition, and the car running. He walks up to the front of the store, and the automatic sensor doors opens up and as he walks in the store, the customer entrance alarm sounds off, the sound gets the 7 eleven cashier clerks attention, who is comfortably seated behind the counter. Edward starts wondering what yesterday's newspaper had to say about the hit and run, as he walks straight up to the 7 elevens cashier clerk.

Welcome to 7 eleven, how I can help you?... Would you happen to have yesterday's newspaper?... Why, I think we have a few left! I'm not sure, but you can check! The stores cashier clerk, points Edward in the direction to the back of the store, Edward follows the clerk's directions. While on his way to the back of the store, he grabs a loaf of bread, he then opens the refrigerator door, and takes out a gallon of milk plus a dozen of eggs. Edward places the eggs and bread in one hand, while carrying the gallon of milk in the other. While in the back of the store, Edward looks around for any available copies of yesterday's newspaper, as he searches around, Edward sees a small stack of newspapers, at the bottom of a rack. He checks the rack for yesterday's newspapers, but there are none, so instead of wasting any more precious time, in the store Edward secures the items he has in his possession and returns to the stores counter to pay for what he has.

Edward places the bread, eggs and milk on the counter, the cashier clerk rings the total up. *That will be eight dollars and thirty cent sir!* Edward takes out his wallet, digs in and removes a ten-dollar bill, he hands the ten-dollar bill to the 7 elevens cashier. The cashier bags the three items up, and hands Edward the grocery bag, Edward quickly turns and makes his way the exit of the store, and just as he's about to walk out, the stores cashier clerk gets Edwards attention.

Excuse Me Sir! Edward turns around. *You talking to me?* The cashier raises his arm, flashing a dollar bill and some change in the air. *Sir! You forgot your change...You keep It!* Edward replies as the automatic sensor door, opens up and the customer exit alarm sounds off. Once outside Edward waste no time walking towards his car, he then opens the driver's side door and places the items in the passenger's seat. He gets in and just as he's about to close the driver's side door.

A young girls voice can be heard yelling out...*Journals!* Her voice gets Edwards undivided attention, as he sits with one leg out and one leg inside the vehicle with his right hand gripped onto the steering wheel, behind the driver's seat in the parking lot of the 7 eleven. *Journals! Journals! Come and get your Journals!* Edward looks around, but he doesn't see anyone, but he can hear the young girls voice. Then a knock on the passenger side window, startles Edward causing him to jump in his seat, by the off-guard approach that scared him so much, he quickly sits up in the driver's seat and accidently pressed the horn.

(Knocking On Window) Edward turns to his left and sees a young girl on roller skates, carrying a cloth messenger bag with the strap of the bag around her neck, the bag is filled with newspapers. *Journal Mister! You want a Journal?* Barely understanding what the young girl is saying and trying to read her lips, Edward can clearly see that the young girl standing is selling something. Edward then closes his driver's side door and rolls down the passenger side window. *Journals sir! Would you like to buy a Journal? Why yes! Let me get one precious!*

The young girl standing there rolling on her skates in one place, with her legs moving one after another, digs in her messenger bag and takes out a newspaper, she then extends out her right arm and hands Edward the newspaper, through the passenger side open window. Edward leans forward, digs in his change area in the car beneath the radio next to the cup holders, and grabs a handful of change. Edward counts out two dollars in change, before handing the change to the young girl selling the newspapers. The young girl smiles grab the change from Edward and hands him the newspaper. Edward takes the newspaper and places it on his lap before waving goodbye to the young girl, as she is already turned around skating throughout the 7 eleven parking lot yelling out Journal's. Now driving out the 7 eleven parking lot in route to meet up with his little brother Mark, Edward stops at a red light a few blocks away from the store, he looks down at the newspaper in his lap, picks it up and stares at the bold title of the newspaper on the front page. *The Journal...*

While silently questioning himself about the title of the newspaper, Edward continues looking at the front page as a crossing guard who the middle of the street is, directing the oncoming and outgoing traffic. Edward leans back in the driver's seat and centers his undivided attention now on the headline of the newspaper.

The crossing guard blows her whistle, which catches Edward attention as she stands there with both arms raised in the air. *(Whistle Blows) Lets' move it along! You keep it moving (Whistle Blows) Wait...Ok! go ahead!* The crossing guard walks up to Edwards car and taps on the hood, the sound causes Edward to quickly drop the newspaper he has holding up in front of his face, which is blocking his sight through the windshield. *(Whistle Blows) You...*Edward looks at the crossing guard as she stands directly in front of his car, Edward and the crossing guard make direct eye contact, So Edward quickly leans back up and grabs the steering wheel with both hands. *Yea you! What are you waiting for Christmas? Move! Your holding up my traffic!* Edward presses on the gas lightly and beeps the horn as he passes the crossing guard in the street, he then slowly drives off. As traffic continues moving slowly, Edward looks in the rear-view mirror to make sure the crossing guard is away from his car, and busy with traffic as he picks the newspaper back up and reads the headline.

The headline alarms Edward by what it says, he notices that there is no picture of the accident that the headline is about, but instead there is a vivid, detailed article about what happened.

Edward reads the article out loud. *(Edward Reading) About the death of the young woman who was killed by a reckless driver, it is said that a family member was there when the accident occurred. But the family member couldn't get help in time, to save the woman's life and this caused her to become deceased.*

Edward peeks over the newspaper he has up to his face, to see if slow moving traffic is moving forward, he then looks back at the newspaper and continues reading...

"On this day of Friday May 8, 1969 at approximate 5:30 there was a terrible accident, which makes this the third hit and run this month, and who can ever live with the memories of this and what caused it, must be an evil person. The young woman's name or age is not being released for safety reasons, there are no witnesses at the scene of the crime. And the only one who has any credible information about this, is the person who committed this terrible and intentional act. So, here at "The Journal" we ask if anyone who has any information concerning tragic accident, to please come forward. The family is having a hard-enough time mourning, and knowing the perpetrator is still out there isn't helping, any leads it would be appreciative and would help with some closure" ...

After reading the article about the tragic accident, Edward places the newspaper on the passenger seat and opens the glove compartment, he takes out his cellphone leaving the glove compartment open. Edward glances at the newspaper on the passenger seat, before looking down at his cellphone and dialing his Parents home number. Edward waits a few seconds and then the house phone rings.

(Phone Ringing) Hello...Dad this is Edward...I know who this is! I might be getting old, but we do have caller ID! Edward giggles at the remark his Father just said. *Son, where are you?... Dad! I'm on my way there, have you seen Mark? Yes, he's here! As a matter of fact, the whole family is here except you. I'm on my way.* Edward hears his Mother in the background. *Honey! Is that Edward on the phone? If it is, tell him to bring the wife and kids by for dinner tonight...Son! You heard your Mother? …I heard her! Tell I love and her, and that the wife and kids are home right now...Here son, you tell her...Wait dad! Is that Edward on the phone...Yes, it is! And what's the problem now?... Let me speak to Edward! I have something important to tell him...* Mr. Largen is looking at his son Mark likes he's crazy, especially the way he's reaching for the house phone receiver, trying to take it out of his father's hand.

Ok! Ok! one-minute son...Edward your brother is losing his god dam mind! So, I'm going to give him this phone before he goes crazy! Edward starts laughing on the other end of the phone. *Love you Pops!... Love you too son...And tell Mother I love her too...I sure will Edward...(Yelling) Is That Edward dear?* Mrs. Largen yells from the other room, as Mark is reaching for the phone's receiver from Mr. Largens hand. Mr. Largen slowly and carefully hands it back to his son Mark, while having nothing but concern on his face Mr. Largen, then attentively looks at his wife Mrs. Largen and then back at Mark. Who now has the phones receiver up to his ear, with his head slightly turned looking behind him as he walks in another room, away from everyone in the house. *Big bro! What's going on and, where are you? I'm on my way there now, I'm about four blocks away! Is everything alright?* The phone gets quiet, while Mark quickly covers the phones receiver and peeks out the room, he's in looking to see if anyone is either listening or headed where he's at. *Mark! Are you still there? Mark...I'm here Edward! ...Dad was right, your acting kind of crazy! You know what*! *I'll see you when I get!... Ok, bro!* Mark replies in a low and not convincing voice, while Edward hangs up his cellphone, turns his head to the right and looks back down at THE JOURNAL, that's still laying in the passenger's seat.

Edward then puts his cellphone back in the glove compartment. With being only one block away from his Parents house, Edward decides to speed up and drive a little faster, to get to his parents' house sooner, Mark again peeks outside the room, before walking back in the other room and hanging the house phone up. Mark stands there looking at the phone, before turning his attention on his Mother, Father and sister who are all in the living room, having what sounds like a serious conversation about some important topics. As Edward turns the corner to where his parents live, Edward can now see red and blue flashing lights coming from several police cars, that are double parked in and out his Parents driveway. Edward eyes widen as he reacts to what's he's seeing, he then quickly pulls the car over, and puts the car in park. Edward reaches over to his right and picks up THE JOURNAL, he rolls the newspaper up and stuffs it into the glove compartment, before removing his cellphone. Edward slams the glove compartment door shut, leans back over behind the steering wheel and slumps down in the driver seat, Edward dials his parents' house phone, while staring at the red and blue police cars flashing lights. Back inside the house there are several police officers, Mr. and Mrs. Largen, Mark and his big sister Stacie.

Excuse me sir! Are you Mark Largen? Mark looks at the police officer with fear and concern on his face. *Yes! I'm Mark Largen!* Then out of nowhere a police officer leans forward and tries to grab Mark by the arm. *Mr. Largen! You are being charged with Vehicular homicide!* Mark then jumps at the mere sound of what the police officer just said, he then quickly pulls away from the police officer, as the officer tries to retain him. Then another police officer in the room, steps in and grabs Mark by his other arm. *Are you police officers crazy! You have me mistaken with someone else! Mom, Dad! What's going on?* Then Mrs. Largen tries to step in-between the two police officers and Mark, but Mr. Largen grabs her by the waist and pulls her back. *No! No! don't get involved right now dear! There must be an explanation, because we all know the truth that my son is innocent! But for now, let these police officers do their jobs...Their jobs! Are you kidding me! These police officers are arresting the wrong person! Who happens to be my son!...* Marks sister Stacie walks up behind her Mother and puts her hand on her Mothers shoulder, hoping to calm her down. *Ma! We all know mark is innocent! This is why they have lawyers! Just calm down and lets work on getting him out!...* Mrs. Largen turns around and looks at Stacie, who is tearing up in both of her eyes. *(Whispering) Ok, honey!...*

Mrs. Largen turns back around and watches as one police officer holds Mark tightly by his neck, and the other police officer handcuffs both of his wrist behind his back. The police officer who just handcuffed Mark, then grabs one of his arms tightly, while the other police officer tightly grabs his other arm, then together both police officers and Mark, all start walking towards the front door. Followed by the other police officers, who are all standing around with their hands on their guns, that's placed inside the gun holster clipped to the belt on their waist. *(Phone Ringing)* After a couple of rings no one answers the house phone so, Edward hangs his cellphone up, and immediately unlocks the car door, he gets out of the car leaving the keys in the ignition, the driver's side door open and the car still running. Edward walks towards his parents' house after noticing that the front door, to his parent's house had been left open. While walking towards his parent's house, Edward sees several police officers leaving the house, and in-between two of the police officers is his brother Mark, who has his head down and his hands handcuffed behind his back, being escorted to a police vehicle by the two police officers. Edward then sees his Mother, Father and Sister standing in the doorway, his mother is yelling at the police officers.

His sister is crying, and his Father is standing there shaking his head side to side, signaling that he's ashamed and embarrassed by what's happening to his son Mark right now. Mr. Largen has his arm tightly wrapped around his wife's waist, trying to prevent her from rushing off the porch and attacking the two police officers, who are now opening the door to the police vehicle, while pushing and shoving her son inside. *(Yelling) You police officers, don't have to treat him that way! My son's not a criminal! He hasn't done anything wrong!...* Once the police vehicle door, behind the front passenger seat is closed, Mark adjust himself in the back seat trying to avoid tightening the handcuffs placed on his wrist, he then turns his head to the right, and looks at his Mother, who is still crying. Mrs. Largen has both of her arms up in the air as she waves, points and addresses all the police officers. Then one of the police officers closes the back door, while the other police officer walks around to the driver's side of the police car. *Son! Don't worry, we are coming to get you! You haven't done anything wrong! You have nothing to worry about!* Mr. Largen hugs and then kisses his wife on the cheek before he raises his arm and wipes the falling tears from her face. Mr. Largen looks at his son Mark through the passenger side window, and then at the police officer's vehicle that Mark is handcuffed in.

As the police vehicle slowly drives away with the siren on, and the red and blue lights flashing Edward slowly walks up to the house, he makes eye contact with his Brother Mark as he is being driven away handcuffed in the back seat of the police car. Speechless Edward just stands there and watch as the police car drives off down the street, Edward then turns and looks at his Mother, Father and Sister who is now standing in front of their house. Mr. Largen is shaking his head side to side, with his arm still tightly cuffed around his wife's waist. While his sister Stacie is leaning up against the house, with both of her arms folded, looking at her Brother Edward as he approaches highly concerned, with disapproval written all over his face. As Edward reaches the house Mrs. Largen pulls away from her husband, opens her arms and starts walking toward Edward, she then embraces him with a loving, caring hug that shows nothing less than genuine support, that a Mother has for her son. Edward embraces his Mother back, while looking at his Sister and Father who is now slowly walking back inside the house. Mr. Largen stops in the doorway. *Son! You can park your car in the garage!* Mr. Largen then digs in his front pocket and takes out some keys, he presses a button on one of the keys, that ignites the garage door to slowly open.

Once the garage door is fully open Mr. Largen turns back around and walks inside the house. Edward lets go of his Mother before kissing her on the cheek, Mrs. Largen grabs Edward by the face, with her palms placed flat against his cheeks, she looks him in the eyes and smiles before letting go, she then turns back around and starts walking back towards the front door of the house. While Mrs. Largen is walking inside the house, Edward turns around and heads back towards where his car is parked, he gets in the driver's side, closes the driver's side door, puts the car in drive and pulls off driving towards the garage. Edward pulls into the garage and the garage door automatically closes; Edward then turns the key in the ignition off. He then opens the driver's side door, gets out, and just before he slams the driver's side door shut, Edward sees the newspaper laying on the passenger side seat. So, he leans back inside the car and picks the newspaper up off the passenger seat, before slamming the driver's side door shut and walking inside the house through a door located in the garage.

SEPERATION AND DEPARTURES

"When You Take Your Body

But Leave Your Heart At The Door"

TH€ PLANE TICKET

Star Suny Let's go! Let's get moving! We have to catch a flight at 10:34 tonight. (Yelling) Kids are you all ready?...Yes!...Were ready Mom! The kids reply as they walk out their bedroom, and towards the front door. *Alright! Alright! It's a quarter to ten right now!* Edwards wife Stacie walks out from the bathroom, she turns the light off and closes the bathroom door before looking inside the kid's bedroom...*We'll I'm almost ready! I have to make one more phone call! ...Phone call! You've been making calls all-day baby! Who could you possibly be calling?*

Edward yells out to his wife, while picking up two suitcases and a bag before walking them out the front door, outside to the truck of the car. With her cellphone in her right hand up to her ear, Stacie stands in the doorway with her legs crossed watching, as her husband places the two suitcases and the bag he has tucked underneath his armpit, inside the truck of the car. *Baby! I still don't know why me, and the kids must leave, I think at least I should stay? The kids will be fine at their grandmother's house alone! Mark needs both of our support!... Trust me, I know how you must feel! But everyone thinks it would be best, if you and the kids just stayed with your Mother, until all of this madness is resolved!* Edward walks pass his wife, she moves to the side and lets Edward through, Edward looks down at his two kids sitting on the floor, behind the front door playing games on their tablets.

Edward goes into the kid's bedroom and picks up two more suitcases off each of their beds, before walking back outside to the trunk of the car, Edward walks pass his wife again. Only this time she is gossiping to somebody about her and the kid's departure.

(Phone) You know that's exactly what I said! Separation is bad karma right now! (Yelling) But some people can't seem to figure that out! (Whispering) I swear girl, the day I'm able to change his mind, will be the day I have another child!... Edward walks up to the front door, from outside and sticks his head inside the house. *Enough on the phone already Stacie! Remember we have a flight to catch!... (Whispering) I don't know what he's talking about, but we got a flight to catch! Me and the kids! You hear me?* Stacie gets up out the seat, walks towards the bathroom, opens the bathroom door, steps in and closes the door behind her. *Listen girl it's time to go! So, I'll call you as soon as my flight lands! Ok! I'll give the boys your love! Yup! Yup! And I love you too, bye!*

Stacie hangs the cellphone up, opens the bathroom door, walks out and heads back towards the front door, where she stops and stands in the doorway, with her arms folded holding her cellphone in her hand. Stacie looks out to where the car is parked and sees her husband Edward, closing the truck to the car. She then looks through the back-seat passenger window and sees her two kids, sitting inside the back seat of the car. Stacie puts her cellphone in her front pocket, steps out from the doorway and walks towards the car, she opens the front passengers side door and gets in.

Stacie then slams the door shut which catches the attention of her husband Edward, as he's now walking back inside the house to make sure everything is turned off, the windows are closed and all the doors in the house are locked. Edward locks the front door, turns around and returns back to the car, he then walks around to the driver's side and gets in. While his wife Stacie, turns around in the front seat of the car and looks at her two boys, who's paying her no mind as they continue playing games on their tablets. Stacie turns back around, sitting quietly in the front seat as Edward starts the car and pulls out of the driveway headed to the airport, where his wife and kids will be catching their flight to Stacie's Mother house. At the airport Edward and Stacie are sitting in the airports waiting area, waiting for the flight to be called while their two boys are running around, back and forth playing musical chairs.

I'm really scared Edward! I have been having bad dreams ever since what has happened to Mark! And the kids keep asking me about their uncle Mark! I'm running out of excuses, what am I going to do? What am I going to tell them, when they see their uncle on the news? Or on the front page of some newspaper? I can't keep lying to them! Edward this is not only damaging our marriage, it might be damaging our kids' future!

Edward gets up out of his seat exploding with rage and fury, as he stands directly in front of his wife, with his both of his arms extended out pointing his index finger on his right hand, a few feet away from her face.

(Yelling) Damaging our Marriage! Are you serious? This is my Brother's life; we are talking about! My only Brother at that Stacie! And as far as I can see, you have your freedom!
(Whispering) Baby! Calm down your embarrassing me!
...Embarrassing you! Please! My Mother and Father are the ones, who should be embarrassed! And my Brother! He is being humiliated, violated and ridiculed! But your embarrassed right? Mark is being charged with Murder Stacie! Or have you forgot?

Stacie sits up in her chair and looks around the airport, where she notices that several people who are also in the airports waiting area, are looking in their direction with concern all over their faces, including the airports staff and labor workers. Then suddenly two of the airport security guards patrolling the facility, acknowledge the small commotion across the room coming from Edward so, they calmly and leisurely walk up behind him unannounced and unnoticed, while his attention was on his wife. Stacie turns back around in the chair she's sitting in, and the look on her face instantly became overwhelming, the look was so personal it immediately gave Edward the impression, that something was wrong. Causing his intuition too to kick in so, with caution Edward slowly turns around, and sees the two airport security guards standing right behind him.

Sir! Is there some sort of problem...Mam! is everything alright?

Stacie looks at the two security guards, and then back at her husband Edward before standing up in her chair, she then calls out to her two boys, they come running and just as Edward is about to address the two airport security guards, and answer their question by voicing his opinion, a female voice can be heard loud and clearly throughout the airports loud speakers.

Loudspeaker flight 235 to Atlanta Georgia ready for departure, leaving from gate 5! Again, flight 235 to Atlanta Georgia ready for departure, leaving from gate 5! Please have your tickets out when boarding the plane thank-you and enjoy your flight!

Stacie steps in-between the two security guards and her husband Edward, she then grabs her two boys by the collar of their jackets and pulls them away. *We'll that's our flight! Oh, and we truly appreciate your concern officers! But we are quite alright! No, problems here right baby?* Stacie looks her husband in the face, while escorting her two boys over by the airports boarding desk, where she starts digging into her pocketbook, looking for the three plane tickets. *I'm sorry I can't seem to find my tickets!* After a few minutes pass Stacie, looks over to where her husband is still talking to the two security guards. *(Yells) Honey!* ...Edward hears his wife's voice and looks in the direction, where Stacie and their two kids are standing by the airport boarding desk. *(Yelling) Baby! Do you have the plane tickets? ...I'm sorry miss, but you are going to have to move to the side! There are people behind you, also waiting to board the plane! ...Oh, I'm sorry! My husband has our tickets, and he is right over there...*

I understand that! But Mam! You are still going to have to stand to the side so, the people behind you can board the plane!

Edward reaches into his pocket and takes out three tickets, he raises his right arm and waves the three tickets in the air, while ignoring the two security guards, before walking away towards the airport boarding desk where his wife, and two boys are standing to the side waiting to board the plane.

Mommy I don't want to go...Me, nether! Can't we just stay here with Daddy?... Stacie places each of her hands on the side of the boy's face, she then pulls them closer to her waist, as she looks down at the top of their heads. Stacie begins rubbing their faces, and then back of their neck and head. *I'm so sorry boys, but this is what your Father wants! And your Father knows best! …(Mumbling) We'll at least your Father think he does...*Stacie inhales and then exhales a deep breath, that is followed by an unhappy and disappointing look upon her face, she looks up and sees her husband Edward standing at the boarding desk with three plane tickets in his hand. Edward hands the plane tickets to the airport boarding desk attendant, she takes the three tickets checks them, and smiles at Edward and Stacie's two little boys. Edward walks over to his family, he bends down, open his arms and gives his two sons a big heartwarming hug, that touched his heart so much, it caused both of his eye to start watering up. *Listen you two! Remember I will always be just a phone call away! You two are in charge now! So, make sure you look after your Mother!*

Ok? I love you both...Love you too Dad...Me Too Dad! Stacie hears the love and concern emerging from her husband's voice so, she bends down to eye level with him, and quickly extends out her right arm. She then wipes away the almost falling tear, from underneath Edwards left eye. They both stand upright and embrace one another, with an affectionate hug that escalated to a long overdue affectionate kiss, while their sons watch and giggle as their parents engage, in an activity that was embarrassing to them, which made it even harder for them to understand.

(Loudspeaker) Last call for flight 235 to Atlanta Georgia, leaving from gate 5! Again, last call for flight 235 to Atlanta Georgia, leaving from gate 5! Please have your tickets out, when boarding the plane thank-you and enjoy your flight!

With both of her elbows on top of the desk, and her palms faced up securely underneath her chin, the airport boarding desk attendant is touched by what she's seeing, she leans back up.

I'm so sorry to ruin this dear moment, but Mam! Sir! I think this is your last chance to board your flight! The planes doors are about to close!

Edward and his wife gently separate themselves, from the affectionate and warm embrace, that has them squeezing and hugging one another at the moment, Stacie quickly grabs hold of both of her son's hands, she turns towards the airports boarding entrance to the plane, as the airports boarding glass doors slowly open.

Once the doors are open Stacie, and her two boys promptly make their way down the airports boarding hall, while at the same time Edward stands there attentively, behind the airport boarding doors entrance. Edward then watches as the boarding glass doors slowly close, with his arms folded and a single tear racing down his face. The sight was wounding to Edwards heart, but the thought of his family leaving, was even more troubling too his mind so, Edward stood there by the doors entrance, until every visual, every image and every graphic memory of them leaving was completely gone. Boarding the plane Stacie, and her two sons are greeted at the planes entrance, by two female flight attendants dressed in uniform. With welcoming smiles on their faces, the two flight attendants standing by the planes entrance, are getting ready to close the doors to the plane securely shut, previous to the plane taking off.

Welcome to Pan Am flight 235 to Atlanta Georgia … May I have your tickets please? Stacie hands one of the female flight attendants at the door, three plane tickets. *Thank-you! Please follow me, I'll show you too your seats!*

Once Edward had confirmation that his Sister in-law and his niece and nephew had safely boarded the plane, he then turns around and walks over to a secluded spot, inside the airports waiting area and removes his cellphone from his front pocket. Edward dials a number on the cellphone, the phone on the other end rings.

(Ringing) With no one answering the phone on the other end, Edward hangs up and dials the number again. *(Ringing)* Again, no one is answering the phone on the other end so, Edward decides to walk back over to where the airport boarding attendant is, the attendant sees Edward and surprised by him visiting again. *Hello again sir! How can I help you?* …Edward walks up to the airports boarding desk, and places both of his hands flat on the desk. *I don't mean to be a pest!... No! problem! Here at Pan Am, we are here to help you! To the best of our ability! So, what can I help you with Sir?* …Edward turns his head slightly around, before acknowledging the airports boarding desk attendant, he looks up at the airports huge flight schedule billboard size monitor, hanging up on the wall behind the desk. Edward then looks back down and stares at the airports boarding desk attendant, directly in her eyes. *Is it too late to buy a plane ticket, too catch the last flight?... I'm sorry Sir! But if you turn around and look over there, out the west window! You will see that the plane, your family is on has already taken off! Again, I'm sorry! Is there anything else, I can do for you?*

Disappointed and hurt by what the airports boarding desk attendant just said, Edward immediately turns around ignoring her, while walking over towards the west window. Edward stands there looking out the west window, at flight 235 take off into the air, the flight that's headed to Atlanta, where his wife Stacie Mother lives.

With both of his hands placed flat up against the window, Edward stands there wounded and motionless as the plane, his wife, and his kids are on climbs higher and higher in the sky. Even though seeing his family leave was painful and unbearable to watch, Edward continued watching the plane sore, until he finally got over the mere thought, of not being able to board the flight, and his vivid visual of the plane in the air, was entirely gone.

QUESTIONS AND ANSWERS

"When You're Absolutely Sur,
But Really Don't Have A Clue"

(One Day Ago)

THE DOUBT

It's late and on the couch the kids have fallen asleep so Edward walks over to them, shakes them both hoping they will wake up or acknowledge his presence. *Get up you sleepy heads, it time to go to bed. Star, King! Get up now! I'm tired and me and your Mother needs to get some rest!* Edward then leans down and picks his daughter Star up from off the couch by her legs and waist, he leans back up and shoves his son King in the side, while rubbing the top of his head. King yarns, looks up and sees his Father standing over him with his sister laid out in his Father's arms. Star and King look at each other before King slowly and hastily gets up from off the couch. Now with his daughter in his arms Edward heads towards the stairs and up towards the kid's bedroom, King lazily follows behind them. Once at the top of the stairs King walks straight towards his bedroom, Edward walks inside his daughter's bedroom and carefully lays her on top of the bed. He then leans down and pulls the cover back from off the bed and tucks her in goodnight, before leaning over and kissing her on the cheek. He leans back up, turns around and walks towards the door after turning the lights in the room off. Now closing the door halfway shut, Edward hears his wife's voice. *Baby! Are the kids alright? Do you need my help?... No Darling I'm good! Star is in the bed and I'm about to check on King!*

Edward walks a few feet down the hall towards Kings bedroom, he walks inside and sees his son King lying on the floor, fully clothed and fast asleep. Edward turns the lights on in the bedroom. *King! King! Wake up son and go to bed! You can't be sleeping on the floor Son!* King turns over on the floor with one eye open and sees his Father standing by the bedroom door, King slowly gets up while rubbing his eyes. He starts taking off his clothes before throwing them down piece by piece on the floor, King hops onto the bed and tucks himself in before falling back fast asleep. Edward smiles at his son, turns off the bedroom lights, closes the door halfway and heads towards the stairs. In their bedroom Edward and his wife are stretched out on the bed, watching television while sipping on some coffee Edward has two sugars and creamer in his coffee while his wife has hers straight black.

I don't know how or why you continue drinking your coffee like that! How do you still manage to sleep at night, or do you even get any sleep?... Mr. Largen has jokes tonight I see, ok! Well for your information Mr. cream and sugar, I sleep very well thank you!

Edward and his wife start laughing while taking sips of their coffee he, has both of his legs extending out across the bed. His wife reaches her arm out, places her cup of coffee on the nightstand, turns around and cuddles up underneath her husband's arm in the fetish position.

She looks him directly in the face while waiting for her husband to finish his coffee, she then grabs the cup from out of his hand and places it on the nightstand next to hers. *Baby! Can I ask you a question?...* Edward looks at his wife in surprise, hoping she doesn't ask him anything that has to do with what has been going on concerning all the insanity, that has been surrounding their family. Or anything that might bring back up what happened to his sister, little brother, Mr. and Mrs. Elmwood and their son. So, Edward takes a deep breath and looks at his wife, he then raises his hand and wraps his arm around his wife's shoulder, with all intentions of making him and the atmosphere as comfortable as possible, before she asks her question. *Sure Honey! What seems to be the problem? You know you can ask me anything!...* Silence surrounds the bedroom and for some reason to Edward, the television's volume has been turned down so, Edward leans his head up over his wife, looking for his cup of coffee as his wife stares directly at him. Not remembering that he has already finished his coffee and with concern on his face Edward, looks back at his wife. *So, what is it? ... What is what dear? ...The question you had to ask me, or did you forget already?...* Edward's wife slowly sits up in the bed and grabs her husband by the hand, she tightens her grip as she continues staring him directly in the face. With emotion in both of her eyes and plenty of nail-biting tension in the bedroom, a disturbing look appears on her face and tears starts forming in both of her eyes.

Baby what is it, what's the problem? You are starting to scare me with that look, you know I hate when you start looking like that!... Edwards wife sits all the way up in the bed, she then releases her tight grip on Edwards hand. *Do You Think He Did It?* She screams out with heavy emotion and alarm. *Well Did He?* Edward takes a deep breath before extending out his arms and wrapping them both around his wife's shoulder. He pulls her closer to him and lightly kisses her on the forehead., while holding her close to him hoping to make her feel better and maybe not think so much about him answering her question. A few minutes goes by and all of a sudden, she burst out and starts crying, *Baby! Baby! It's alright, everything is going to be alright!...* Now whispering in his wife's ear, while gently kissing her on the neck and cheek Edward, focuses back on the volume that's down on the television.

<u>Past Whispers</u>

"When You Know And They Know You Know"

Good afternoon passengers! This is the pre boarding announcement for flight 235 to Atlanta Georgia! We are now inviting those passengers with small children and any passengers requiring special assistance, to begin boarding at this time! Please have your boarding pass and identification ready! Regular boarding will begin in approximately ten minutes time! Thankyou!

After Edward and his wife and kids spend several hours in the airport's gatehouse, a female gatehouse information worker finally taps Edward on the shoulder from behind and interrupts the quiet rest the they all seemed to be having. And in a low, concerning voice the female airport desk information worker taps Edward on the shoulder again. *Excuse me! Excuse me! Mam, Sir! Your flight is now boarding…* Slowly opening his eyes and turning around in his seat, Edward looks at the female and nods his head up and down, before moving his head to the right of the gatehouse worker and looking at the people, by the information desk, in the gatehouse board the plane. *Thankyou!... Your quite welcome sir! You and your family enjoy your flight! By the way you have a beautiful family…* Obliged by the polite remark, Edward looks at his son and daughter and then back at the female gatehouse worker who's still standing behind him smiling. *Thankyou! And they are wonderful children! I couldn't ask for a better two!... Oh! I understand clearly! Playing Daddy? …*

Edward starts laughing. No! These are… Listen Sir! You don't have to explain! I see this all the time, believe me! The kids Biological Father is not around and your replacing him! I get it!... Miss! You really don't get it! Shocked by hearing the second voice, the female gatehouse worker takes a shaky step back and looks to her left and there getting up out of her seat, was Edward's wife Mary. She stands there staring the female directly in the face, with a frown on her face and a look in her eyes that could kill. All the time while rubbing her son and daughter's head one at time, while trying to wake them both up.

Listen, Mam!... No! You Listen to me now! I don't know what world you live in, but not all black kids don't have their Father in their lives!... Edward gets up out of his seat and walk over to his niece and nephew, shaking his head side to side suggesting that this gatehouse worker should have never opened her mouth.
He then helps his kids fix their clothes, while not once looking at the female who's getting a lesson in black history by his kids Mother and the love of his life.
Mam! Sir! Please I didn't…Hush! Don't say another word! (Silence) …Didn't you learn at home, not to interrupt, an adult when their talking, well did you?... Yes!... Yes what!... Yes Mam! Ok then, as I was saying! For your information this is my Husband and these two beautiful children are his kids! And if you, and I mean this with all good intentions! If you live…

{This is the final boarding call for passengers Mary, Star and King Largen booked on flight 235 to Atlanta Georgia! Please proceed to gate 5 immediately! The final checks are being completed and the captain will order for the doors of the aircraft to close, in approximately five minutes time! I repeat! This is the final boarding call for Sara, Star and Suny Largen! Thankyou!} The airports gatehouse intercom interrupts Mary's black history speech, just before she was about to tell the truth, to the female about where her husband Edwards brother and kids Father really was. *I'm so sorry! But I have to get to my gates! Bye, you all!* The female gatehouse worker, without hesitation quickly turns around and stumbles into a few seats in front of her, she then rushes towards her gate. She raises her arm in the air and waves back at Mary, Edward and the kids with her back turned, while speed walking away. Mary and Edward look at each other and start laughing hysterically, at how the female had almost tripped. Mary then looks at her two children, leans down and kisses them both on the cheeks before grabbing each of their hands and start walking with them both and Edward towards gate 5. With luggage in his hands, Edward follows behind Mary and the kids to the boarding platform. *Say goodbye to uncle Edward kids!* Edward leans down and kisses both of the children on the cheek and waves goodbye as Star, King and Mary walks down gate 5's boarding platform, onto the plane. *Taxi! Taxi! What am I invisible? God dam it, I know these taxi's see me out here!*

Outside the airport angry and frustrated, Edward yells at the yellow taxi driving pass, with both of his arms raised and swinging in the air, he's hoping to flag one down to stop. Now feeling a little depressed after seeing his sister Mary, and the kids board the plane, Edward puts both of his arms down and stands there by the curb and waits for a taxi to drive up in front of him. After several minutes goes by, a yellow taxi slowly pulls up. Edward steps off the curb, opens the back-passenger door and slams it shut. The taxi driver looks at Edward though the rear-view mirror, before slowly pulling off and driving away from the airport, heading towards the highway.

Where to my friend? Bad day my friend? ...More like a bad year! And If you don't mind, just drive! ... Are you from Jersey my friend, or just visiting? The taxi driver looks in the rear-view mirror and notices that his passenger, in the back seat has fallen fast asleep.

<u>Silent Prayer</u>

"When Your Faith Gets Discouraged"

THE SUNDAY MORNING

9:30 am Sunday Morning and at home Mr. and Mrs. Largen are getting themselves ready for church, the main thing on both of their minds is how their son Mark is doing, being that they both haven't heard from Mark since the arrest. *Dear! You think we can go and visit Mark one day this week?* ...Without a respond while ignoring his wife Mr. Largen, instead turns the television off, gets up out of his seat and heads towards the front door without saying a word. Mr. Largen stops by the front door and turns around making sure all of the lights are off in the house. Mr. Largen then moves to the side as Mrs. Largen slowly walks pass him, looking him directly in the face while mumbling. *That's my son as well! He shouldn't be in there!* Mrs. Largen grabs her husband's hand for a minute, before letting go as she steps out the house. Mr. Largen looks at his wife as she's walking towards the passenger seat of the car, He closes and locks the front door, before walking towards the driver's side of the car and gets in. He unlocks the passenger side door for his wife and once they are both secure in the vehicle they drive off. Neither one saying a word or paying attention to the other, Mrs. Largen looks at Mr. Largen and wipes some lent off of his shoulder before turning back around in her seat and staring out the passenger side window. The sky starts to darken, as the clouds move gracefully across the sky burying what's left of the sun's evening daylight.

The winds heavy thrust start to pick up and toss leaves, dirt and debris around in a whirlwind from off the ground, the sky now suddenly shows signs of a rain. Mr. Largen stops at the red-light, he turns on the windshield wipers as drops of rain fall and within seconds, the rain starts pouring down heavenly. *I don't recall the weatherman speaking on rain! Did you?...* Mr. Largen shakes his head side to side. *No!...* The car pulls into the churches parking lot, Mrs. Largen turns around in the passenger seat and looks around in the back seat for an umbrella. She then notices a newspaper rolled up with a black rubber band wrapped around it, as she frowns at the mere sight of it Mrs. Largen, reaches down and picks the newspaper up from off of the back seat. She pops the rubber band off and takes a couple of pages out and places it on her head while waiting for her husband to open the passenger side door. While opening the passenger side door, Mr. Largen extends out his arm to help his wife get out of the car.

With one arm above her head, she holds the newspaper in place to prevent her head and wig from getting wet. Mrs. Largen carefully grabs her husband's hand and steps out of the car. After closing the passenger side door Mr. Largen walks his wife inside the church, once inside Mrs. Largen puts the newspaper in a plastic bag and places it inside her pocketbook. Once inside Mr. Largen and his wife sees a church usher, dressed in all white ready to greet them at the entrance to the congregation inside the church.

With white gloves on both hands and wearing white shoes and matching skirt. The usher escorts them both to available seats. *God bless you!... Thankyou! And God bless you too! … Sister Largen, Brother Largen! It's nice to see you and your husband at service this Morning!* …The usher smiles at the couple, before turning around and quietly walking back to the back of the entrance of the church. Mrs. Largen sits down followed by her husband, someone then taps her on her shoulder, she turns around and sees two of her bingo friends seated behind her. So, she reaches out her arm and holds both of their hands. Mrs. Largen smiles and whispers…

How have you two been Gina? Haven't seen you and Claire since Bingo! And look at Ms. director in here! That's right, I heard about the promotion, congratulations! ...Thankyou! And you look exceptional this Morning Barbara! I just love the dress...We'll talk later… Yes!

The choir starts singing a selection so, Mrs. Largen lightly slaps the back of Claire and Gina's hand… *After the service we'll catch up!... Definitely…Love you!... Love you two!* …She slowly turns around in her seat, looks at her husband in the face, grabs his left hand and starts singing along with the choir. Coming to the end of his sermon, the preacher steps down from the pulpit and start asking offering prayer. Mr. Largen looks down at his watch, rubs his finger in-between his eyes while his head is held down. The preacher walks back up onto the pulpit and sits down, before the choir sings another selection, two deacons then gets up and stands in front of the church.

One of the deacons addresses the congregation… *Praise the Lord! I said praise the Lord!...* In sync the whole church responds… *Praise the Lord!...* Mr. Largen looks at his watch on his wrist again, he finally stands up and grabs Mrs. largens coat before, leaning down and whispering in her ear…*Dear! I'm ready to go!* Mrs. Largen looks at her husband with confusion all over her face, being that this was the first time her husband wanted to leave Sunday's church service before the service had ended.

Mr. largen steps into the aisle and takes a step forward, he looks back at his wife as she's waving her goodbyes to her Bingo friends and everyone else, she started to notice throughout the church. Finally, she catches up to her husband and watches as he walks pass the usher, towards the exit of the church. Once Mr. and Mrs. Largen are back inside their car Mr. Largen pulls off and drives home, it's quiet inside the car and to Mrs. Largen felt like her husband was acting awkward and strange. But instead of addressing the issue, she decided to keep quiet and hope that when he felt he wanted to talk, about why he decided to leave church early, he'll let her know. Now pulling into the driveway of their home Mrs. largen sees their son Mark, who's just standing there in the doorway, with his hands in his pocket. The car comes to a complete stop so, Mark starts walking towards the passenger side of the car, he opens the door and helps his Mother out the car…

Son! Why didn't you come to service? I thought I'd be seeing you and the family there this Morning! And where's my grand babies at?

Mark grabs his Mother by the arm and walks her into the house, he removes her jacket before escorting her over by the couch, as he's hanging her jacket up Mrs. Largen takes a seat onto the couch and stares at Mark. Mr. Largen walks in and closes the door before locking it, he greets his son Mark with a head nod. Mark returns the acknowledgement with a nod of his head back, with a depressing look on his face Edward starts wondering if what he is about to tell his parents will add more flame to the fire. Mr. Largen then takes his coat off and sits in his recliner, he turns around looks at his wife and then at Mark.

Boy! What is the problem! What have you done now?... Nothing, happened pops!... Well something must be wrong, because the look on your face says a lot!... Your Father is right Edward! You look like how I feel! And believe me, I feel terrible right now! So, come over here and sit next to your Mother! And tell your Mother what's wrong dear...Is it about your Brother or Sister? Mark raises his arm and starts scratching the top of his head, before walking over by the front door... *No! It's not about Them!... We'll you know God will make a way somehow son! Oh my God!* ... Mrs. Largen jumps up off the coach with her mouth wide open ...*Don't tell me! Something happened to those kids! Please don't tell me something happened to my grandchildren!...*

(Loud Voice) No! Star and Suny are alright! Mark looks at his mother, as he starts walking over to her by the couch. He then hops down on the couch next to her, while inhaling and exhaling a deep breath. Mark looks at his Father and then back at his Mother as a tear swells in bot of his eyes. Mark hops back up, from off the couch and stands directly in the middle of the room looking back and forth at his Mother and Father… *Well what is the problem Mark? Mr. Largen, please talk to your son! He is really starting to scare me!... Boy! Do you want your Mother to catch a heart attack? …No, pops! … Then for the love of God! Would you please at least, tell your Mother what's the problem?* Mark walks over to the room window, with his hands behind his back and his back facing both of his parents. He reaches into his jacket pocket and takes out his book. Mark opens it up to a page, he has been wanting to share with the entire family for a while. *Ma, Dad! I have been going through and seeing some strange things lately!...* After the remark from Mark, Mr. and Mrs. Largen look at each other with concern. *What I'm trying to say is, that I have been witnessing some things that I cannot explain, it might sound a little farfetched, but I assure the both of you, that I am not going crazy. And believe me, it is the Gods honest truth!* Mr. Largen rubs his chin, while looking at his son Mark. He then looks at his wife as she's now looking at Mark, before turning her head and looking back at her husband. Mrs. Largen gets up from off the couch… *Child are you Ok? You have not been taken any drugs, have you?... Yea son! This story sounds like, it's about to sound crazier than I expected!...*

Now raising his arm in the air and stomping his foot on the ground in a compulsive and angry manner, Marks Mother starts pleading for her son to stop acting like that.... *Mark! Mark! Calm yourself down boy, your scarring your Mother!...* Now highly upset at how his son is acting, Mr. Largen leaves the room and walks into the kitchen...*We'll whatever it is! Just don't end up like your Brother!... (Loud Voice) That's not what I am talking about! I'm talking about The News Paper!...* Surprised by what their son just said, Mr. Largen quickly stops by the kitchen entrance and immediately turns around, while Mrs. Largen looks at Mark with her eyes the size of quarters. She raises her arm and places her hand over her mouth in pure astonishment. With her hand still covering her mouth, she walks over to her son Mark, Mrs. Largen raises her other arm and places that hand over Marks mouth. She looks her son directly in his eyes, before removing her hand from covering her mouth, she then grabs the back of Marks neck and pulls him in closer to her face... *(Whispering) Hush Son! Now you just let those newspapers, rest in peace! You hear me! You just do it! You hear! ...* Now standing behind Mrs. Largen, Mr. Largen raises his arm and removes his wife hand from around Marks mouth.... *Hold up, wait a minute here! I think we should let the boy finish! Go ahead Mark! You were saying something about a News Paper?... Now, honey! You know your son has been through a lot! He's not thinking rational right now! Right Mark?...*
No! The boy is just fine, Mrs. Largen! Plus, I want to know what he knows, about this newspaper that got my Son, all in an uproar!...

Mark takes a deep breath, before taking a few steps back away, from his Mother and Father, while thinking about what his Mother said in his ear. Mark storms his way out the room, heading towards the basement of the house, Mrs. Largen looks at Mr. Largen with a life-threating and violent look. After Mark is out the room, Mr. and Mrs. Largen both heads over by the couch and sits down… *(Whispering) Do you think he knows about the News Paper! Don't just sit there, with that stupid look on your face! I asked you a question! Well do you?...* Before Mr. Largen could answer his wife's question, they hear their son Mark entering the room so, simultaneously Mr. and Mrs. Largen both turn around on the couch. With a stomach full of bad nerves Mark, is carrying in his arms a bundle of dusty old newspapers, Mark walks pass his parents and drops the bundle of newspapers on the table. He waves his hand across his face, to help clear the air and to keep himself, from breathing the basement dust and debris flying in the air, from off the bundle of old newspapers. Mark takes his jacket off and throws it on the back of the chair underneath the table, he turns around and looks at both of his parents, before reaching into his jacket pocket and taking out his book of poems. Mark places the book on the table, next to the newspapers…. *Mom, Dad What is this? Tell me! Please tell me! Why the hell are you collecting newspapers, dating back to 1605? I mean there are hundreds, maybe thousands of dusty, bundled old newspapers in our basement!*

After getting no response yet from his parents, Mark decides to remove one of the newspapers from the bundle, he holds the newspaper in the air and tries to blow the rest of the basements dust and debris off of it. He walks over to his parents who's still seated on the couch, with the newspaper in his hand, Mark wavs the newspaper in front of them both, before handing it to his Mother...

Here! Look for yourself, if you think I'm crazy! Here look!...

As Mrs. Largen leans up off the couch and reaches her arm out, for the newspaper Mr. Largen reaches over and snatches, the newspaper from out of Marks hand. Surprised by the antics, Mark takes a few steps Back and watches as his Mother and Father looks at the newspaper turning page, after page, after page. Mr. and Mrs. Largen look up at each other, they both still not saying a word so, Mr. Largen rolls the old newspaper up and places it on his lap... *(Yelling) Mom, Dad now you see, I wasn't lying! Just like I said, everything is inside! This is what I was talking about! This is what caused all the accidents and deaths! Mom, Dad! This newspaper is a curse of some kind I tell you! We have to get rid of them! Do any one of you hear me? Read it, look at the pictures and the articles inside! We are all in some serious danger, listen to me!*

Trying to calm down Mark, does some immediate soul searching hoping to figure out why, his parents are not responding, the way he thought they would after he clearly made an accurate and straightforward point. Still Mr. and Mrs. Largen showed no concern, and this made Mark furious.

How this strange, unknown newspaper can be right in front of his parent's face and under their nose and they can still ignore, all the honest facts right in front of them. This raised some deceiving questions about his parents to Mark, which had him thinking if his own parents were involved, or even knew this whole time about this newspaper called THE€ JOURNAL...
Besides having hundreds maybe thousands of newspapers in bundles, hidden in their basement was the ultimate mystery so, Mark pulls a chair out from the under the table and sits down. Out of anger and frustration, he pushes the bundle of old newspapers onto the floor, before banging his fist on the table Mrs. Largen now troubled by her son's behavior, she gets up off the couch walks over to Mark by the table and starts rubbing his back. Mrs. Largen bends down and starts picking up the loose newspapers from off the floor, Mark decides to help while Mr. Largen sits on the couch, shaking his head side to side. After all the loose newspapers are picked up, Mrs. Largen stands back up and pulls a chair from underneath the table and sits down next to her son Mark... *Son! I don't know, what you have been doing! But whatever it is, you need to get some help fast! Am I right honey?... Your absolutely correct dear...You see Mark! Me and your Father agree, that you might need some counseling! Especially after this little fiasco and I would hate to see you, end up in some kind of mental institution! Or some jail, for that reason!... (Loud Voice) You both are insane! You both are crazy! Mom, don't you see the pictures? Pop, did you even read the articles inside?*

There are some things, you just can't explain! These newspapers are dated back to the year 1605! And they have articles about today's tragedies, politics and events!... Mark pushes the chair back from underneath him, stands up, grabs a few loose newspapers on the table and starts turning the pages furiously from right to left, while pointing at the different pictures, articles and dates within the newspapers. To his surprise and after having already confirming the dates, articles and pictures he thought he had seen, had disappeared. The dates, articles and pictures were no longer there, Mark was dumfounded by what he was seeing, right in front of him. Then out of embarrassment, he slowly turns his head to the side and looks at his Mother, before turning all the way around, now with his back against the table Mark looks at his Father. Who is now standing up by the couch, shaking his head side to side in shame… *I don't understand! There were pictures on the front page and inside of everyone! Mr. Elmwood, Tara, Stacie! Ma, I really don't understand!... Son, we understand just take it easy!... No! Dad, you half to believe me!... Son, we understand! We understand!* Mrs. Largen steps in front of her son, as close as she could, she extends out both of her arms, wraps them around his shoulders and hugs him as tight as she can, before placing her head a few inches from his ear…. *(Whispering) Hush Son! Now you just let those newspapers, rest in peace! You hear me! You just do it! You hear!* … Mark heard this before, he remembers when his Mother whispered the same thing in his ear earlier.

But this time it was different, This time it hit a nerve, being that he had proof and she knew it so, Mark leans his head back at the comment, speechless and traumatized, his eyebrows raise, his eyes widen, and a water starts to form within both of his pupils. Mark is scared inside, but trying not to show any signs, being that his Father would not accept his weakness, this was unacceptable, and Mark knew better. Raising both of his shoulders, trying to remove himself from his Mothers phony hug, Mrs. Largen lets him go and walks over to where her husband is, by the couch. Mark takes a step back and stumbles over a loose bundle of newspapers, still on the floor he looks down at the newspaper, underneath his feet. Shocked again by what he is now seeing Mark, rubs his eyes with his fist and looks at the newspaper again and right there on the front page, is a picture of Mark in a 6x9 jail cell standing in front of a mirror and metal sink, he's looking in the mirror with a freshly wrapped bandage around his head and dried up blood on his shirt, his eye is slightly closed with a small bruise underneath his left eye. Mark kicks the newspaper and stumbles toward the front door, he opens the door and walks out without closing the door back shut.... *Mark! Where are you going? You need help dear! We can get you that help!...* Mrs. Largen takes a step forward to try and follow her son, but Mr. Largen grabs her by the arm and pulls her back...*Let him go dear! Let him go dear! Mark will be fine, that's our son! He's strong!...*

Mr. Largen walks over to the front door, looks at his son as he leaves and then closes the door behind him, Mr. Largen turns around, faces his wife and shakes his head side to side in shame. Mrs. Largen walks over to the table and picks up Marks book, she removes his jacket from around the chair and hangs it up, she stands there and stares, at the cover of the book, while rubbing her hand across the engraved words on the cover of the book of poems… *Honey! Do you think, we should have told him?... Of course, not dear!...* With the phone ringing, Mrs. Largen rushes over by the telephone and waits for another ring, before picking up the receiver… *(Phone Ringing)* She picks up the receiver and places it to her ear, while not taking her eyes off her husband, who is standing about face in the room, with his hands crossed in front of his chest… *Hello! Hello! Is somebody there? Mark! Is that you baby...Who is it dear?... Hello!...* Mrs. Largen slowly places the phone receiver down by her side, before she hangs the phone up. *Well, who was it?... There was no one there! I think they got the wrong number!... We'll, if it was of any importance! They're call right back!... I guess your right honey!* The night has fallen, and the wind is biting through the air, the streetlights are turning on outside, while the vehicles headlights are acting as a guide, to all the commuted drivers on the road. At home Mr. and Mrs. Largen watch television and sit patiently hoping someone calls, or better yet stop by with some good news.

Mrs. Largen decides to get up off of the couch, she walks over to the front door, unlocks it, opens it, looks around outside and prays silently to herself, that her family gets through these dreadful days of events. Mr. Largen stares out a window and watches as the cars drive down the street… *Close the door! There's nobody coming here tonight! You need to stop worrying! And Mark! That boy will be just fine, you did a fantastic job raising him! He knows the difference between right and wrong!... I know! I know, I'm his Mother! And I do believe, he will do the right thing! God will protect him!...* After closing the front door, Mrs. Largen walks into the kitchen… *Dear, Are you hungry?* Mr. Largen, lets down the window blind, turns around and heads towards the kitchen, where his wife is standing by the refrigerator, with both of the refrigerator doors wide open…. *Why, yes!... Well what do you have a taste for...Whatever you prepare, will be sufficient!...* The phone rings… *(Phone Rings)* Mrs. Largen waits a few seconds before answering the phone… *(Phone Rings)* She then walks over to where the kitchen phone is, picks it up while leaving the refrigerator doors open, she holds the receiver with both hands while looking at her husband, who is standing by the kitchens entrance, shaking his head side to side. Mrs. Largen lifts the receiver up to her ear and waits about two seconds, just to see if she can hear anyone on the other end but she doesn't so, she hangs the phone back up. She looks at her husband, while her hand is still on the receiver, Mr. Largen walks over to his wife and touches her hand.

He then pulls her away from the telephone and walks her back over to the refrigerator. Annoyed and afraid at the same time Mrs. Largen, closes the refrigerator and leaves the kitchen, she walks right pass her husband and heads upstairs to their bedroom. Mr. Largen just stands there and watches, without saying a word about the meal his wife was about to prepare for him, or anything about the unsolicited phone calls that keeps the phone in their home ringing. Once Mrs. Largen was secured in her bedroom, she slams the door shut, while Mr. Largen goes back into the living room and sits down on the couch, now thinking to himself how could he have let this get out of hand and how could him and his wife live with how things was turning out with their family, Mr. Largen was thinking maybe they should have said something, or maybe it was it too dam late. *(Phone Rings)* … On the couch Mr. Largen hears the phone ringing so, he turns around and stares at the phone placed on the table by the television… *Let It Ring! It's probably nobody again!... (Phone Rings)* …After not hearing his wife respond quick enough, Mr. Largen is now fully annoyed, by the continuation of the phone ringing throughout the house so, he gets up off the couch and picks up the phone and places the receiver to his ear… *Hello!... Dad is that you? It's me!... Who is it dear?...* Mrs. Largen yells, from the crack door of the bedroom… *Baby, It's one the kids!... OH, Thank God! Well is everything alright?... I don't know yet!... Yes! Tell Mrs. Largen that, everything is alright! Me and the kids are just fine...Oh, I'm sorry It's Edwards wife!... Did you say Edwards wife?...*

Mrs. Largen rushes back into the bedroom and picks up the phone… *Hello Dear! Well how are you and the kids? You know we miss you all dearly!... We are doing just fine Mrs. Largen! But we all really do, miss the family! Me, Star and Suny can't wait to come home! Well you just keep your head up! And as soon as things turn around, we will send for you all!* … Feeling like he's not getting acknowledged by his Daughter in-law or will even get the chance to speak to his grandkids, Mr. Largen decides to just hang up the phone, and let two of the women in his life, continue on with their daily conversation… *By the way Sara! How, and where are the kids?... They are sleeping right now Mrs. Largen! But really, I just wanted to call! Because I was worried about my husband! Has he called, or have you seen him since Marks arrest...Well, to be honest I have not spoken to him today! And I know Mr. Largen hasn't either! But were doing our best to make sure the family is alright! We'll that good news Mrs. Largen...We know he's doing just fine! He's a grown man, who can take care of himself! You should know that! So, don't you worry yourself at all! You just make sure my two grandchildren are in the best of spirit!... We'll I won't hold you up any longer Mrs. largen! Give Edward a kiss for me! And tell the Dad we love him!... Sara! That man is right downstairs, you tell him yourself...And don't forget to give my grands a big hug and kiss for me!...* Mrs. Largen yells downstairs for Mr. Largen to pick up the phone, but with no answer after two attempts, she leaves the bedroom and walks downstairs, to where Mr. largen is laid out across the couch…

I'm sorry dear, Mr. Largen is sound asleep on the coach! But don't worry yourself! I will make sure he gets your message! I Love you!... I Love you too Mrs. Largen! We'll if Mark calls, please let him know that we reached out! And the kids, miss him and love him dearly!... I will surely do! Now get some rest and call back tomorrow!

Or every day! Bye...Goodbye! Mrs. Largen hangs up the phone and looks at her husband, while wiping a tear from her eye, she hops down on the couch and lays her head, on her husband's shoulder. Mr. Largen looks at his wife and shakes his head side to side, before raises his arm and placing it around her waist, Mrs. Largen looks up at her husband and mumbles… *TH€ JOURNAL!*

<u>Incarcerated Or Incarceration</u>

"When Your Imagination, Turns You In"

THE JAIL

Lights Out!... The correction officer yells throughout the entire tier, as he gets ready to make his inmate head count rounds, before the night shift changes. Lying on his back on the top bunk, starring at the ceiling Mark wears a white t-shirt, green county pants and white tube socks. To Mark this was unreal and because of that, he started to feel animosity towards his Mother and Father, for not believing him when he was trying to prove, what he thought was the cause to all this madness in the city. With three weeks imprisonment and not a visit from anyone, Mark confines himself to his room and avoids all outside movement, except when it's time to eat. Mark hasn't even tried to call any of his family members, knowing that it would be a waste of time. He also couldn't understand why, he was framed for something he didn't do, or why he was alone in a two-man cell and choose to sleep on the top bunk, but it didn't matter because to Mark sleeping higher to the ceiling, kept him away from the smell of the toilet. With a flashlight shining through the cell door window, Mark leans up on his bunk and sees the correction officer...*How many in there...One! You said two, right?... Dam, I said One...Ok, Largen don't be getting smart! I'll make sure you miss breakfast! (Laughing)* The correction officer writes down his head count in Marks room, he then removes the flashlight from the cell door window and moves on to the next cell.

After the correction officer is away from Marks cell, he hops down off the top bunk, stands by the metal sink and toilet and washes his face with his hands. He then walks over by the door and looks out the cell small window, to see where the correction officer doing the count is located. Mark reaches underneath his mattress and takes out a deck of playing cards, he sits down on the metal stool in front of the metal table connected to the wall. And shuffles the deck of cards hoping if he plays a game of solitary, it will help put him to sleep. About an hour goes by and all the lights on the tier and in the cells goes out, Mark can't see his playing cards anymore so, he leaves the cards on the table, hops back up on the top bunk and falls asleep. Its Morning and the suns trying to shine, through Marks cell window located on the wall above his bunk, while outside his room the morning correction officer, is making his first-round inmate head count of the day. After the inmate head count, the cell doors start open up one at a time, the sound of the doors opening and the tier feeder...*(Yelling) Breakfast! Breakfast!...* wakes Mark right on up. Rubbing his eyes and yarning, Mark hops down from off the top bunk fully clothed, he stands in front of the metal sink and brushes his teeth, before standing by his cells open door. Marks looks around to see what guard, is working the tier and if breakfast is something worth eating this morning. Mark then steps out his room and walks to the banister railing, he leans over the rail with his arms folded and gets the attention of one of the feeders... *(Loud Voice) Big Bro! Feeding, what's for breakfast?... A, Yo Feeder!...*

The feeder looks around the tier, before realizing that the person trying to get his attention was upstairs leaning on the rail…*Oh, It's you! We got two boiled eggs and cold oatmeal!*

Mark frowns his face while shaking his head side to side, showing disgust and disappointment in the county jail nutrition system, he sees another inmate walking up the stairs, heading to their room with their breakfast. Marks walks over to him and looks at his breakfast. The inmate carrying the tray in his arms stops…*Pardon me!... Yea! What's going on...Listen! I'm not trying to eat that! So, I'll give you my whole tray, for that apple...Oh! Hell yea, go get it!... Ok! Wait right here!*

After exchanging his breakfast for an apple, Marks heads back to his cell, closes the door and tosses one of the apples in the sink, he sits down on the bench and takes a bite out of the apple. A half hour later an inmate worker, slides a letter underneath Marks cell door, Mark hears the worker as he's walking around announcing mail. So, he gets up and picks up the letter and being that Mark hasn't received any mail, or a visit since his three-week incarceration, he figured the letter was just another court notice. So, with the letter in his hand Mark hops back up onto his top bunk, but then all of a sudden, he starts feeling lightheaded and weak, Mark starts perspiring and sweating heavy. His breathing becomes hard to inhale and exhale, his eyes rolls inside the back of his head, he passes out.

Mark falls from off the top bunk and hits his head on the metal toilet, the sound of him hitting his head, sounded like a baseball bat hitting a baseball in a baseball game. Blood is all over the cell floor, the hit of the metal toilet knocks Mark out unconscious, causing a deep laceration to the side of his head blood starts to pour. Mark is knocked out with one leg bent under the table and his upper body twisted, his arm halfway underneath the bunk-bed frame and his head laid up against the side of the toilet. Mark is just lying there on the jail cells concrete floor, with not a single inmate or correction officer knowing what happened. As Mark body lie there on the floor, bleeding from his head the day goes on....

(Yelling) Lights Out!... The correction officer yells throughout the entire tier, as he gets ready to make his inmate head count rounds, before the next shift changes. The correction officer gets to Marks cell, he lifts the flashlight up to the cell door window and notices, that Mark is not in the top bunk. The correction officer puts the flashlight down, turns around and tries to get the correction officer in the control booths attention...

(Yelling) Open, up cell 18!

The door to Marks cell opens up, the correction officer walks in and immediately, he sees Mark lying on the concrete cell floor, bleeding from his head, out like a light unconscious.

The correction officer panics and drops his flashlight to the floor, trying to grab his walkie talkie, he drops to his knees inside the cell by Marks head and raises his walkie talkie up to his mouth…

(Nervous) I got a code red! I repeat code red! In cell 18, on tier A-pod! I'm going to need medical assistance and a stretcher! I got a head injury, looks self-inflicted!

The correction officer cleans out Mark cell, placing all of his personal belongings in a plastic bag, he then hands the bag over to medical, the correction officer walks back inside the cell and throws all the unimportant remaining items on the floor and closes the cell door… *(Yelling) Lock cell 18!*

Mirrors And Visits

"When You Know Where You Are
But Don't Recognize Who Your With"

THE INFIRMARY

Siting up on the edge of the bed, with a major headache that feels like, he was just hit in the head with a bat Mark, doesn't have any idea literally about where he is or why he's been moved there. And as the day moves on Mark, realizes that the room he is in, is not a regular jail cell so, he gets up weary almost losing his balance, grabs the rails on the side of the bed, to help him regain balance as he tries to walk over to the mirror and sink. Once Mark is close enough to the mirror and sink, he lets go of the bed rail and moves closer to the plastic mirror bolted on the wall. As he stands there weak and in pain, Mark sees his reflection in the mirror and notices that he has a freshly, white bandage wrapped around his head. With dried up blood all over his shirt and his left eye slightly closed with a black and blue bruise underneath, Mark carefully moves over in front of the room's door and peeks through the small window. He tries getting the attention of a nurse, who is going door to door pushing a cart filled with medication. He then tries knocking on the room's door, but he is too weak to make a sound louder enough, for the nurse or anybody else to hear him. Mark sees the correction officer and comes to the reality, that he's still locked up and have been injured some kind of way, which makes sense that he's recovering inside the infirmary.

While the correction officer clearly ignores him Mark, decides to move back over to the bed, as he turns around, he notices a letter on the table, Mark struggles to get close enough to the table, he uses all of his strength to reach out and pick it up. With the letter in his hand and no return address, Mark slowly rips open the envelope, takes the letter out, unfolds it and starts reading…

Dear Mark,

I hope this letter finds you...

Then all of sudden the correction officer bangs on the door…
(Loud Voice) Largen! You have a visit! Marks slowly gets up from off the bunk and drops the letter onto the floor and with him being incarcerated for almost a month, Mark is definitely surprised that he has a visit …

(Loud Voice) Largen! Be ready in five minutes!

Looking around the visiting area, Mark is seated in a wheelchair wondering who has come to visit him, he carefully rolls himself over to an empty space away from the kids, running around the visiting room playing. Mark looks at all the families visiting and all the children laughing and the babies crying, he then gathers some strength and lifts up a little in the wheelchair.

Hoping to see someone walk in he recognizes, but he doesn't so he holds his head down, with all intentions of trying to ignore the pain and the reality of the situation he's in. After about ten minutes something comes over Mark, he starts feeling strange like someone or some bodies was watching him. Mark rolls the wheelchair over next to an empty seat near the visitor's bench, he looks around the visiting room again. The room starts getting dark, the temperature starts dropping and all Mark can see is a group of people, way in the back of the room standing together in the corner. The group of people start slowly walking towards Mark, not able to see their faces clearly, due to the darkness in the room and his injury on his left eye, plus the headaches that's keeping him weary and weak. When the tallest one in the group, lifts their arm up and waves from the corner of the visitor's room, Mark waves back out of courtesy and that's when both of his eyes close overpoweringly, for about a millisecond. And when he opens his eyes back up, Mark can't believe what he is seeing, he is the only one in the visiting room besides the people walking over towards him. No correction officers, family, friends, kids, or inmates and this was eerie and creepy all at the same time to Mark. So, as the group of people started getting closer, Mark recognized and remembered seeing the little boy somewhere before. But could not remember where, there was also an old lady in the group, the tall man who waved and a younger female.

Mark was now thinking forget the darkness in the room, the temperature dropping and everybody disappearing, what was more eerie and creepy, was that all of them was dressed in all black, like it was somebody's funeral. The boy was in the front the girl next to him the old lady behind them and the tall man was behind her, they were just standing there not saying a word. So, Mark tries to get up or even move the wheelchair away from these people, but he can't his body became stuck and numb, his speech became speechless, he couldn't open his mouth. Both of his hands were pressed flat on his knees in a still position, Mark was frozen without the freezing temperature, the old lady places her hand on Marks shoulder, the tall man follows and so does the young girl. Then the boy stands in front of Mark, he's so close Mark can still smell the accident the boy was in, the boy pulls out a newspaper and holds in front of Marks face, Mark looks at the newspaper and on the front page he sees himself in a 6x9 cell lying on the floor, in a pool of blood with an open laceration to the side of his head. While still not being able to move, Mark has no other choice but to look at the boy, who's holding the newspaper pointing at the text so, Mark starts reading, the written what's written underneath the picture …

Confused and in disbelief, trying to hold on to your past, not knowing it's the main cause, your future won't last. And if you don't accept, what's already been witnessed there will never be any peace, when you quote from poetic books and self-made scriptures. Living this way, will only be your life changing mistake, it will cause peoples behaviors, to act out with vengeance whenever dangerous temptations, are up in your face. Read in between the lines, it's the secrets that family members keep, and to end all these mirror mimicking occurrences. Remove THE€ JOURNAL from your dreams, then you'll wake up from your sleep.

All of a sudden Mark is able to lift his arm up so, immediately he snatches the newspaper from the boy and that's when the lighting and the temperature in the room returns to normal. Mark looks around and finds himself in the visitor's room all alone, the man, the old lady, the young girl and boy are all gone and without question, Mark finds himself back in the wheelchair. Now headed towards the visitor's room exit, pass the correction officers, back to the infirmary room.... *(Loud Voice) Mark Largen! Mark Largen!...*

The correction officer shakes and calls out to him, trying to wake Mark up so, that he can take his medicine for the injuries, his has sustained. The nurse waits outside Marks door with a medicine cart in front of her, Mark finally gets up and waits for them to open his door...

Mr. Largen how are you feeling this Morning? Are you Ok! We'll here is your medication! Take two of these with some water, after your next meal!... Thankyou!... You are more than welcome Mr. Largen!... While the correction officer is standing there and Marks cell door is open, Mark decides to take advantage of the situation… *Officer!... Yea! What it is it Largen?... You think I can I ask you a question?... Sure! What seems to be the problem? Hurry, up! I haven't got all day!*
I had a visit earlier! And I wanted to know, the last name of the people who visited me?
The correction officer looks at the nurse and then back at Mark…
Hold, up! Hold, up! Largen did you just say visit?... That's right! I was visited today by a tall man, an old lady and a young girl and boy! I didn't know them! But I stayed for the visit anyway! They were strange people to! The boy had a cursed newspaper! But it won't curse nobody here, because I got it! The correction officer and the nurse look at each other awkwardly, with expressions of confusion on both of their faces, the nurse grabs the bottle of medication she was giving Mark, she holds it up and starts reading the side effects description.
Mr. Largen! Are you feeling ok? Have you been saving these pills and taking them all at once?... Of course, not Nurse! I know better than to do that! Where I'm from they call that an overdose!... We'll, your absolutely right there Mr. Largen! Mr. Largen! Are you sure, you had a visit today...Yes! Why am I feeling like you don't believe me? Go and check the visitors log, if you don't believe me!

The correction officer and the nurse step to the side and start whispering amongst themselves, not sure if they were talking about him, but it was making Mark feel very uncomfortable. Suddenly they stop talking and the nurse starts putting away, the open bottles of medication on top of her medicine cart.... *Largen! Could you step out of the room, for a minute! And stand outside the door!...* Not questioning the correction officer, Mark steps out the room and stand to the side, with his back pressed up against the wall, Mark looks at the nurse who is looking back at him.... *So, you said you were feeling ok Mr. Largen?... Yes! I'm feeling great!... Now would somebody explain to me, what is going on?...*
The correction officer steps out of Marks room and looks directly at the nurse, she looks back at him and watches as the correction officer, shakes his head side to side signaling to her that it's a no.... *We'll are you or aren't you! Going to check and find out the last names, of the people who visited me today! I really need to know because! The boy had a newspaper, with me on the front page!... So, Mr. Largen! You're telling us that at your visit today! Some, unknown boy had a newspaper! With your picture on the front page?... Yes! That is exactly, what I am saying!* The correction officer takes out his walkie talkie... *This is officer Roy! And I need to schedule an appointment, for inmate Mark Largen! To visit the shrink as soon as possible! Inmate number 567787! Injuries Head trauma and hallucinations!... Really! Officer Roy? So, you all don't believe me! And now you want to send me to the shrink!... Are you crazy or something Largen?*

The injury to your head, must really got you delusional! And gave you a stronger imagination! … Officer Roy! What do you mean?... Mr. Largen! What I think officer Roy, is trying to say is! You haven't been out this room since your injury! You were brought here unconscious! And just woke up today! So, you see Mr. Largen there's no way! You could have had a visit unless it was in your dreams.
Mark leans up off the wall and walks back into the infirmary cell, he stands in the open doorway of his cell and looks at officer Roy, and then at the nurse who has both of her hands on the medicine carts handle. Officer Roy tries closing the door to Marks cell, But Mark places his foot in-between the door and the wall…
Largen! Let's not act stupid! Move your foot Largen!...
Mark lifts his shirt up and starts reaching down into his pants, he then begins to slowly pull something out, not being able to see what it is, Officer Roy panics and starts reaching, for his walkie talkie… *Don't move! Largen! What are you reaching for? Stop reaching now!... Oh my God! He has a weapon! Mr. Largen what are you doing?...* With the walkie talkie up to his mouth officer Roy, calls for backup and within seconds the infirmary main doors open, and four to five correction officers bust in and rush towards Marks cell. The nurse takes cover and pushes the medicine cart, way over to the other side of the infirmary, she stands behind the cart and watches from afar. Before Mark could remove what was inside his pants, four correction officers bum rush Mark and tackles him to the ground.

They handcuff him inside the cell, the nurse pushes her medicine cart, back over by Marks cell and stands there next to officer Roy. They both stand there and wait as the four correction officers secure the weapon.... *Make sure you all get the weapon! Mr. Largen! You should know better than that!* After about fifteen to twenty minutes, three correction officers finally walk out of the room without Mark, leaving his cell door wide open, with Mark uncuffed inside. The four correction officers stand outside Marks cell, looking at officer Roy and the nurse...*(Laughing)*...Who seem confused that Mark is still in his cell and not in handcuffs...*We'll, Officers! Did you all get the weapon?...* The three correction officers standing there, start walking toward the infirmary's main exit door, while ignoring officer Roy and the nurse.... *I am a nurse here in this infirmary officer! And I refuse to have, any inmate carrying weapons! Especially when I have to get them, they're medication!...* The fourth correction officer walk out of Marks cell, he closes the cell door behind him and looks at officer Roy, he then tosses the newspaper, Mark had tucked inside his pants on top of the nurse's medicine cart.... *Here's your weapon, Officer Roy! Don't hurt no body with it! (Loud Voice) Hold up fella's! I heard an inmate in lockup, has a female in their room! (Laughing)*

After the four correction officers has left the infirmary, the nurse and officer Roy stand outside of Marks cell, staring at each other embarrassed and humiliated because of the uncertain and incorrect accusation, they said about Mark.

The nurse decides to pick up the newspaper and open it, she holds the newspaper up in the air so, her and officer Roy both can see what's on the front page at the same time. Quickly and simultaneously, the reaction on their faces are priceless, speechless and numb. They turn and face each other, without saying a word, then slowly they both focus their undivided attention on Marks cell window again. With the newspaper tightly gripped within her palm; the nurse and the officer Roy quietly walk in closer to the cell window. They peek inside the window and can see Mark, sitting on the edge of his bunk reading a letter…

Dear My Friend,

I hope this letter finds you in the best of health and also in good strength, before it does and If it has found you. Then I'm too late, but if you are reading this letter and you are in the best of health and strength, then may God be with and protect you and your family. Because my friend, I have been following you and your family for some time now. And I've come to the realization that you and your family, are in a world of danger. Please Let me explain! Have you ever read or seen a newspaper called The Journal? Well if not and once you do remember, this is not your ordinary newspaper! This newspaper possesses a cursed entity and once opened and read, it creates a domino effect of tragedies, to whoever and everybody who becomes fortunate enough, to get the opportunity to read the articles inside.

(Letter Cont'd)

And when they do, not only do they become prey, but everyone they surround themselves with, becomes prey to this un-aging newspaper that leaves a bitter and unfavorable taste, to everyone who connects with its stories, of the past, present, and future!

Anonymous

<u>Nobody Remembers</u>

"When Your Recollection, Never gets To Recollect"

Two Weeks Later…

THE NURSE

With her shift over the nurse, punches out and leaves the county jail, she walks to her car in the parking lot, gets in and drives home. She makes a stop at the grocery store, to pick up a few things to cook for dinner, the nurse pulls her car into the grocery stores parking lot, gets out and locks the doors before entering the grocery store. She makes her way over to the frozen food section, not in the mood to prepare a huge meal being that she's recently separated and lives alone with no children. The nurse opens the grocery stores refrigerator and grabs a few items, before walking back towards the cashier. While standing in checkout aisle she gets startle by a tap on her shoulder…*(Excited) Monica, is that you?...* The nurse turns around in the checkout aisle and looks at a familiar face, the face she recognizes is an old friend from medical school, who had a serious crush on her and every other female in their class…

(Surprised) Oh, My God! Is that you Michael? I don't believe this; I haven't seen you since medical school! How have you been? come here give me a hug!...

Trying to act as if, Monica really didn't want to give him the impression, she was happy to see him, being that during medical school, she remembered Michael as being broke, disliked, weird and unattractive…

(Confident)I've been doing quite well for myself and you?... (Bragging) Oh, I'm alright! Just the head nurse at the county jail, here in Hudson! With a $70,000 a year salary! I can't complain, I'm doing much better than most! ... Michael leans his head back, surprised with his face frowned up in the air, thrilled with joy and excitement, for his medical school classmate Monica… *You definitely are Monica, you definitely are!... And you Michael? What did the stars line up for you, after medical school? What did you end up doing? Let me guess, you got a job in a local high school, as a medical assistance! Am I right?... Well not quite Monica, I started a family!...*

And just before Monica could sarcastically respond, two beautiful twin girls with different cereal boxes in their hand, run up to Michael both hugging him on each side of his waist… *Honey! You have to have to control them, with their cereal craving! …*

Now smiling at Monica and trying to figure out who she is, with her arm tightly wrapped around Michaels waist… *Oh I'm sorry! Let me introduce you to my beautiful Model wife and our twin daughters! (Humble) Monica! This is my wife April and these two cereal monsters, are my twins Kay and Kayla!...*

Monica is speechless as she can't believe how beautiful Michaels wife was and if not that his twin girls who had to be A+ students in school, by the way they speak. Plus, that school uniform they were wearing, was affiliated to a very prestige school, you had to be financially stable, in order to pay that tuition and he had two children enrolled. Monica just stood there in a daze, starring back and forth at Michaels family, she couldn't believe that this broke, disliked, weird and unattractive guy. That every girl in medical school, even her had ignored had become this night and shining armor, who did pretty well for himself by creating the perfect family. *Monica! Monica! Are you alright?... Oh, don't mind me! I was thinking about something…What, if you don't mind me asking...Oh, just work! But believe me, it's nothing!... We'll Monica, it was nice seeing you again. Yes! Monica please stay in touch! And if your ever in Alpine New Jersey, look us up! I just bought a house there and there's more than enough room! As a matter of fact, bring your whole family!* Michael's twin daughters start pulling him, by his arms towards the 5 items or less checkout aisle… *(Loud Voice) So, you see Monica my hands are full! Oh, and I'll be in town for a few days! I'm doing a brain surgery on a female, tomorrow at the local hospital…* After hearing that Monica mouth is wide open, nervously she drops a few items from the cart… *(Loud Voice) So, you're a doctor?... (Yelling) No, I'm a Brain Surgeon!...*

With nothing to say after that, Monica watches as Michael and his family leaves, she finally understood that you can be an ugly moth in school, that went through metamorphosis and still soar in sky in life, as a beautiful butterfly…

Excuse me, Mam! Mam! Your holding up the line! Could you please pay for your items! Thankyou!...

Listening to the voice of the cashier, Monica turns around quickly in the checkout aisle, she reaches down in her pocketbook and then notices a newspaper, lying there at the bottom of the rack. Monica reaches all the way down and picks up the newspaper, while the cashier is ringing up her groceries. She places the newspaper flat on the conveyer belt and realizes its TH€ JOURNAL! And on the front page there's a picture of the her. Monica quickly tosses the newspaper back on the rack, looks around the grocery store, as she finish paying for the groceries, all of a sudden the lights on the ceiling in the store starts flickering, the conveyor belt starts running at a high speed, The temperature in the grocery store drops, the store starts feeling like a freezer. Its freezing cold, Monica blows in her fist, to try and keep her hands warm she's shaking. She looks around the grocery store and realizes that its empty, except for the cashier who's' standing there, dressed in all black. Monica looks towards the grocery stores window and notices that its actually nighttime.

She then quickly looks at the watch on her wrist, which tells the time of 1:00pm but outside it's looking like 12o'clock midnight, Monica runs out the store, leaving the grocery cart and all the items in it, by the cashier. Once outside the grocery store, Monica looks up into the sky, she sees nothing but a frightening old moon and a dimming star, all the streetlights are off and it feels like the middle of July. It's hot which is totally strange and uncomfortable, compared to the freezing cold temperatures, inside the grocery store that had Monica blowing steam, from her mouth every time she breathed. Monica also notices that there's not a person or vehicle in sight, the parking lot is dead empty, dark and ghost-like. Still shaken Monica is mystified, by the mysterious phenomenon, that not only made the day turn into night, but turned the month of October into July. Now profusely sweating, Monica stands near the curb and looks to see if any vehicles, are driving by in the dark, she then carefully and slowly crosses the street headed into the parking lot. While in the middle of the street, all of a sudden, the sound a car quickly slams on its brakes, the sound startles Monica so, on instinct she quickly jumps back and looks to her right. There she sees a 2019 four door black Telsa Model X, the car waits for Monica to cross the street, then slowly the car drives up beside her, the driver's side window gradually rolls down… *Didn't mean to scare you my friend! Still getting use to this electric car and its features! You understand! Where are you going, need a lift?* And Monica was thinking, could the incidents of the day, get any more interesting…

No! I'm good, my car is just over there! But I appreciate the offer!... The wife says, don't forget to look us up!... Of course! I wouldn't miss that for the world!... Great then! Enjoy your day Monica!... You too Michael! Bye!... Inside her car Monica lock the doors, she sits there pondering on if she was hallucinating, or was these occurrences just part of her imagination, or was everything that was happening for real. Monica looks at herself in the overhead mirror and comes to the final conclusion, that it was all in her imagination.... (Knock On Window) ... Monica jumps at the mere sound, she quickly turns to her left and sees Michael standing outside of her car, on the driver's side with his hands up to his mouth, blowing in each hand... (Loud Voice) *We'll aren't you going to roll the window down! It's kind of cold out here Monica! Its October sweetie!...* Monica hesitates for a moment before rolling the window down, she looks in her rear-view mirror and then out the passenger side window. She puts the key in the ignition, turns the car on and then rolls down the driver's side window...

Michael! You almost gave me a heart attack! What happened, how can I help you Doc... Please just call me Michael! But you dropped this newspaper so, I was returning it! Being that you were right here...Did you say newspaper?... Monica eyes widen, goose bumps torment her whole body, she forms a knot in her throat, after she swallows nervous air, Then Michael reaches on top of the roof and pulls down *THE JOURNAL!*

Pulling up in her driveway Monica parks the car and gets ready to get out, she turns the car off and takes the key out of the ignition, before looking to her right and seeing THE JOURNAL Lying on the passenger seat. Monica takes a deep breath, exhales and picks up the newspaper, with her nerves in her stomach and trickles of sweat developing across her forehead. Her blood pressure rises as she decides, to unfold the newspaper and without hesitation she stares at the front page and again there's a picture of her. The picture is located directly in the middle of a missing person flyer, with a message at the bottom, Monica turns the page and to her surprise, there's more information and more flyers about three more people missing…

Report

21-year-old Tara Largen, 12- year old Lee Halt and 16-year old Gina Halt are also missing! Anyone with information, please contact your local police department! All calls will be kept confidential.

Memo

With all three missing and not a trace about their whereabouts, we inform all New Jersey Residents to be on the lookout, for any persons resembling. The police department here in New Jersey, believe that the people missing whereabouts, will be obtained with the help of the city.

And at this time, we assure you with all the help of the police and our good citizens throughout New Jersey. We know that we will find them, and it will be only a matter of time before we do! Please anyone with any information! don't hesitate to call, The N.J. Missing Person Dept. The number to call is 1-800-NJMissingPersons

Monica puts THE JOURNAL down in her lap, she looks at herself in the overhead mirror, and silently questions the authenticity of THE JOURNAL! Or if she's been working so hard, she can't seem to think straight, let alone separate her own facts from fictions. She gets out the car, leaving the newspaper in the car, after locking and closing the doors Monica, checks her mailbox and inside there's a letter address to her, with no return address. Monica removes the letter from the mailbox, opens the house front door and enters, she closes the door, goes into her bedroom lays across the bed and starts reading ...

(Letter)

Monica

It's not important who I am, what's important is that you be properly informed of the dangers of the newspaper, entitled THE€ JOURNAL*! Believe me, I know the powers* THE€ JOURNAL *possess and how it targets its victims. So, if you have already come in contact with it, then you must warn your family, friends and protect yourself. Because now you and everyone, that has come in contact with it will be in danger! Not only will they be in danger, but for the rest of their life, strange things will be happening to them and the people they love and just to warn you, the outcome is sometimes ending in Death.*

P.S

This is not s joke so, takes this letter and THE€ JOURNAL *serious!*

Here are some things you and your family should avoid, from becoming a victim if you see or come in contact with The Journal!

1.) Leave it alone

2.) Don't ever pick it up

3.) Never read any of the articles

4.) Stay away from people who has it

5.) Repeat

Anonymous

Monica puts the letter down and lays across the bed, she stares up at the ceiling and contemplates on everything going through her twisted mind. She starts thinking about how the person who wrote this letter, choose her to send it to and why so, she sits up, looks at the letter and then at TH€ JOURNAL that's just lying there next to her on the bed. Monica picks up the newspaper, even though what the anonymous letter had warned her. Her eyes widen, her jaws tighten at the sight of what she's now seeing on the front page of TH€ JOURNAL! The news reporter on the television gets her attention, at the same time Monica in awe again about what she's witnessing, on the front page of TH€ JOURNAL that's in her lap. With crucial concern on her face, Monica lifts her head up, looks at the television and watches as the news reporter standing there, holds up a microphone to her face and gets herself ready, to start talking into the camera. As the news reporter stands there, her camera man is letting the viewers at home see different angles of the Largens home and how many people are gathered around and outside of the house. The camera man zooms in on local residents, ambulances, police, news camera vans and their reporters plus neighbors, family and friends.

(News Reporter) Views on news Kl2 news for you! And now we connect you to our news reporter, who's been covering the missing persons case of the Largen family, Diane Seeler! Hello Diane!... Hello, Charles!... Yes! I am told that you have some updated information, on the missing person's case?...

The news reporter stands there motionless and quiet for a few seconds, she looks at the camera man who shrugs his shoulder responding in question, that he has nothing either. So, the news reporter raises her free hand and starts messing with the ear plug that's in her ear. The camera man shuts down the camera, from viewing the live footage on television…

Diane! Are you ok? This is Charles Peterson, at the office!... No! I'm not alright Charles! I don't have any info, about the Largen family missing person case! I thought I was doing interviews...Oh, wow!... Wow! That's all you can say is wow! You fat son of…!

Diane rips the ear plug out of her ear and walks towards the back of the news camera van, with the microphone still in her hand, she sits down and shakes her head side to side in disappointment and frustration. Then out of nowhere Diane sees an old lady and an old man both dressed in all black, walking towards her and in the old ladies' hand is a newspaper. Diane jumps up from the back of the camera van and stands there smiling like she was seeing an angel for the first time, who just fell from out of heaven. But it was all the opposite, the old lady and tall man walks up to Diane the old lady looks at the tall man right before she extends out her arm and hands Diane the newspaper.

Diane grabs the newspaper quickly, nods her head up and down at the old lady in appreciation, puts the ear plug back in her ear, grabs the camera man by the arm and Diane and the camera man take their place and start delivering the news…

(News Reporter) Ready in 4! … 1, 2, 3, … This is Diane Seeler! Reporting to you live from Views on news Kl2 news for you! Here I am standing with an angel who just handed me the… Diane turns to her left looking for the old lady and tall man dressed in all black but they both are gone; she looks at the camera man who's shrugging his shoulders again responding in question. So, Diane turns back around with a frown on her face and opens the newspaper…

Well my angel must of went back to heaven! Anyway, I was told the Largens missing person case is all in this Sunday's newspaper, that I have in front of me! which is strange if you ask me! Yes, I said strange because first of all, I have never seen this newspaper in my life, am I the only one?... Second why not post a family tragedy and triumph in a newspaper, we all are familiar with, that gets printed every day? Not once a week if that! This newspaper is called THE JOURNAL! Again, I've never heard of it and this newspaper, is dated back to the year 1919? (Mumbling) Creepy I tell you! Really hair-raising weird! Anyway, it says…

The Largen family have been reunited and all is well, Tara Largen, Stacie Largen, and Mark Largen all are on the front page! Posing in a family portrait, with Mr. and Mrs. Largen, Edward and his wife Sara and two kids Star and Suny! Smiles and hugs are amongst them all, with plenty of love on all of their faces! It also says that Mark Largen, was released from the county jail last night, his release was due to wrong identity! As for Tara Largen, she was never missing, she was in Atlanta Georgia with her brother Edwards wife and kids. And Stacie Largen, was revived back to life two days ago! They are saying once the doctors and nurses realized, Stacie's condition was locked in syndrome! A type of coma, I think! This complicated the Doctors and nurse's procedure, being that the EMT confirmed she wasn't breathing, at the time of the accident and her diagnoses the time of her admittance, at the hospital was wrong. We'll I sure am ecstatic that this family is back together, I hope they stay that way! Again, I'm Diane Seeler and this was your Views on news Kl2 news for you!... The news reporter removes the earplug from out of her ear, while walking towards the news van, she puts the microphone down and looks at the camera man who is carefully, placing the news camera equipment in the back of the news van.... *Are you thinking what I'm thinking Karl?... Oh, I'm definitely thinking what you're thinking Diane!...*

(Simultaneously) We need to find out where this alarming and strange newspaper called THE JOURNAL, *is coming from Plus, camera man… What did I do now Diane?... Why'd you let the old lady, dressed in all black get away?... I didn't, she disappeared!... Another thing camera man! Please tell me what you see, when you look around here?... Um! A lot of people?... No, stupid look closer! They all have something in common! Something we should have been had, before we even pulled up!...*

Puzzled the news camera man steps up and stand right next to Diane, with the news camera still pressed up on his shoulder, he looks around at the Largens family home, the people standing around, the police, the ambulances and the other news camera vans. And with confusion on his face, while feeling awkward and dumb, he shrugs both of his shoulders up and down again, Diane raises her right hand with the microphone in it and points into the crowed area surrounded by faces that all look unfamiliar…

(Loud Voice) Look! They all have a copy of the newspaper called THE JOURNAL!

<u>Wonder Who's Wondering</u>

"When You Get Your Questions Answered"

TH€ ANSWERS

While sitting in the passenger seat of the news camera van, Diane the news reporter look's out the window, amazed at everyone who's standing there with the TH€ JOURNAL in their hand. She thinks to herself, that there had to be some type of reasonable explanation, to why this strange newspaper was creating such disorder in her city and how the circulation of TH€ JOURNAL, continued to exist with present and future news articles from 2015. Being that the newspaper publication was issued way back, in the year 1919.

To Diane who was a veteran news reporter, this just didn't make sense and she intended to get to the bottom of it and explain to her boss, co-workers and herself that, whatever was going on should be explained to the world and the city they all lived in. Diane grabs the vans passenger door handle, opens the door, hops down leaving TH€ JOURNAL on the van's dashboard, before getting the camera man's attention. The camera man wakes up, looks up and around and notices Diane, standing by the driver's side door geared up, with the microphone in her hand, the earplug in her ear and a look in her both of her eyes, that he only sees when she's on to some news that's big.

(News Reporter)

Ready in 4! … 1, 2, 3, … This is Diane Seeler! Reporting to you live from Views on news Kl2 news for you! This is your News on Views reporting on the latest update concerning, The Largen Family Reunion and the contagious orbit of this, un-aging newspaper that will leave a bitter and unfavorable taste, to everyone who connects with its stories of the past, present, and future. I've learned that these incidents will be shocking to the world, causing devastating, destruction and erupting chaos and mayhem in and out of the city. But what New Jersey and the world didn't know, was hidden from the world, the media and the people living in it. Was its contagious orbit, of what only some chosen few knew as THE JOURNAL …

The camera man quickly removes the news camera from off of his shoulder, he looks at Diane shocked as she's removing, the plug from her ear and wrapping up the microphone cord. Diane walks back over to the news van and that's when her and the camera man cell phone starts blowing up, Diane takes her cellphone out of her pocket and notices several calls from the office. There's text messages and voice mails nonstop, Diane and the camera man are getting call after call, after call. The camera man puts the camera down on the ground, takes out his cellphone and sees all the missed calla, text messages and voice mails. So, he walks over to Diane and puts his right hand on her shoulder, she turns around frowning and upset with the cellphone up to her ear…

Ok! Ok! I understand, but I thought… Yes, sir! I really was only trying to…. Yes, sir! I can do that! Sir! But you really need…Ok! Ok! … I'll tell him! Good day sir!... Diane hangs up the cellphone and looks at her camera man, as he's shaking his head side to side speechless… *Was that who I think it was...Yes...So! What did he say...He said he needs a major article!... So, when's the deadline?... Yesterday!*

Four Days Later…

Parked across the street sitting in the driver's seat of her car, in front of the Largens family house, news reporter Diane Seeler, is watching the home of the most recently publicized, televised missing and back to life family that has made the front page. Due to this mysterious newspaper in the city and being that she was a veteran news reporter, whose whole life was to report news, Diane couldn't and wouldn't let nothing stop her from finishing, what she had her heart set out to do. And that was get to the bottom of this newspaper called TH€ JOURNAL, which had a lot of people rerouting their lives, from a newspaper that painted terrible pictures, not on the walls but in the lives of families and friends! Causing a frightening epidemic to those who cannot seem to figure out, where this newspaper that's dated back to 1919 is coming from. So, Diane opens the driver's side door and with a small note pad, pen and a portable voice recorder in her hand, she starts walking towards the Largen family house.

Now standing on the porch, Diane turns around to her left and then to her right, she looks around the entire block, before gathering the heart to ring the Largen family doorbell... After years of reporting news and being considered a veteran news reporter with awards in American journalism and also a candidate with several considerations to be nominated for the Pulitzer. This was the first-time ever veteran news reporter Diane Seeler, was actually nervous with butterflies in her stomach. As she tried to have heart and control her nerves, to raise her arm and ring the Largens family doorbell, as hard as she tried, she couldn't, Diane was losing her first battle of being a veteran news reporter. And it felt weird but not weirder than her finding out what really was happening, with the Largen family and the newspaper the people in New Jersey now knew as THE JOURNAL. After standing there on the porch for about five minutes, just looking at the Largens family house with a pen, pad and voice recorder in her hand Diane decides to walk back towards her car. Once inside she places the pen, pad and voice recorder on the passenger seat, she takes a deep breath and slumps down in the driver's seat and falls asleep.

Six Hours Later...

As the temperature inside the news reporter car starts dropping and the day quickly turns to night, the stars and the moon in the sky gets shadowed out by ugly dark clouds.

The atmosphere outside looks paranormal and that's when the radio in Diane's car comes on by itself at a high volume. Diane wakes immediately, she lifts herself up in the driver's seat and wraps her arms around her chest. She slowly opens her mouth and can see the hot steam of her breath lingering in the air, the radio gets Diane's fully undivided attention, once she hears an all too familiar voice through the speaker, herself.

(Radio)

Views on news Kl2 news for you! And here to bring you the latest, on the THE JOURNAL *is our own Diane Seeler!... Thankyou Charles!*

Diane couldn't believe what she's hearing, she was thinking that this could not be her broadcasting the news, being that she hasn't even reported back, to the office since yesterday. And she definitely didn't have a major report as of yet so, this had to be a prank of some sort and if not, then something was mysterious and unexplainable about the whole thing. Diane leans forward to tries to turn the radio off, but it's useless she tries turning the volume down, but it's also useless she then turns the radio station, but every station she turns to she can hear her voice, over and over broadcasting the news, about this newspaper called THE JOURNAL...

(Radio)

Views on news Kl2 news for you! And here to bring you the latest, on the THE JOURNAL *is our own Diane Seeler!... Thankyou Charles!*

Diane is outraged at what she is hearing and to make matters worse, the battery on her cellphone is dead, she can't open any of the car doors, none of the windows will roll down and the car itself won't start. Diane is stuck inside of her own car, forced to listen to her voice over and over, as she broadcast the news about this newspaper, her city now knows as THE JOURNAL. With the temperature in the car freezing and no way to escape whatever supernatural happenings was happening, Diane tightly wrapped herself in her arms, as she leaned down in the driver's seat and listened...

(Radio)

Views on news Kl2 news for you! And here to bring you the latest, on the THE JOURNAL *is our own Diane Seeler!... Thankyou Charles! Diane Seeler here and I'd like to warn myself, about this newspaper entitled THE JOURNAL! Myself, if you are listening! And I know you are! Please be careful, when you encounter this unnatural newspaper! And while your locked in your car, freezing to death! With your arms tightly wrapped around your chest! Watching the Largen families house! Then as soon as this broadcast is over, look to your right! Grab THE JOURNAL from on top of the dashboard and give it back to who it belongs to!*

(Radio Cont'd)

Then your eyes will open, and your heart again will become fearless! I'm Diane Seeler! Reporting to you live from, Views on news Kl2 news for you!

Back to you Charles... All of a sudden, the temperature inside the vehicle returns to normal, the car doors unlock, the volume on the radio turns down and the night turns back today. Diane unfold her arms from around her chest, she sits back up in the driver's seat, turns to her right and can see, four people standing there a few feet away from her car. Diane quickly reaches for THE JOURNAL! And as she pulls THE JOURNAL down, from the dashboard she places it tightly in her hand, right before watching a young boy and girl through the window. Both dressed in all black walk towards the Largens family house, the boy steps up onto the porch and rings the bell, while the girl stands a few feet behind him. The front door opens and to the news reporters surprise, walks out Mr. and Mrs. Largen, the news reporter looks in her rear-view mirror and can see an all-black tinted limousine parked behind her. She looks to her right again and still standing a few feet away, was the same old woman who handed her the newspaper THE JOURNAL just the other day, Mr. and Mrs. Largen follow the young boy and girl back to the black tinted limousine. While the tall man opens the back passenger and drivers side doors, he lets Mr. and Mrs. Largen, the young boy and girl all get in the limousine, the tall man closes the back-passenger side limousines door behind them.

He then walks around the limousine and stands by the passenger side door, the tall man stands there, watching every move the old lady is making. The old lady walks up to the driver's side window of the news reporter's car and without hesitation Diane who's sitting in the driver's seat. Rolls down her driver's side window and hands the old lady THE JOURNAL, the old lady dressed in all black takes the newspaper and then opens the driver side door, to the news reporter's car. Once the car door was open, the old lady extends out her arm and waits for Diane to grab it, Diane looks at the old lady, grabs the inside door handle to the driver's side door and slowly starts closing the door. The old lady takes two steps back with THE JOURNAL in her hand, she turns and starts walking towards the limousine, where the tall man is holding the limousines passenger side door open for her. The tall man closes the passenger door, walks around to the driver's side, gets in, closes the door and the all black tinted limousine drives off. The news reporter starts her car and follows the limousine, while holding the voice recorder in her hand…

(Recording)

(Whispering) This is news reporter Diane Seeler! It is 3am, Thursday May 12, 2015 And I am leaving the Largens family home! Where Mr. and Mrs. Largen just got escorted into all black tinted limousine, followed by an old lady, young boy and girl and tall man all dressed in black! I will be tailgating the limousine, because I think they know about the newspaper called THE JOURNAL!

As she's driving behind the limousine Diane, tries to see if there are other people are inside the limousine, but the windows are so darkly tinted, she can't see a thing. With the radio off in her car, the news reporter quietly drives and just waits until the destination arrives, when the limousine stops. The look on the news reporter's face says nothing, she felt like she was under some kind of spell, the feeling was unexplainable. So, she was thinking if this wasn't a major story for her boss, then she didn't know what was. The limousine comes to a complete stop, all the doors open as everyone prepares to get out, Diane slowly and quietly pulls her car up a few vehicles away, from where the limousine is. She gets out and looks around and to her surprise there is only one house on the whole block, the news reporter was blown away, not only that this is the only house on the block, but that the size of the house, takes up the whole block, the house was a mansion. And with no street signs, stores or landmarks Diane couldn't write down any locations to help her find this place again so, she takes out her cellphone and tries to take a picture for the news, but her cellphones battery is still dead so, she pulls out the small note pad, pen and pad and starts writing down everything, she has seen and can remember, since she first pulled up, in front of the Largens family home. The tall man dressed in all black, closes all the limousines doors before walking ahead of the old lady, Mr. and Mrs. Largen, the young boy and girl up the stairs.

The tall man opens the mansions front door and stands there until everybody is inside, once they all are inside the tall man follows behind them, as they all walk to a very special room in the mansion. Outside hiding behind her car feet away, the news reporter is watching everything so, she decides to follow behind the tall man and go inside the mansion. To get an exclusive news story, about these strange people who obviously knows something, about this newspaper called TH€ JOURNAL. The news reporter crosses the street and walks up the stairs, she reaches her arm out and grabs the large door handles. She pulls as hard as she could, but the door won't open, she tries again and again but nothing so, she decides to sit down on the step, out of exhaustion and fatigued. A few seconds goes by and then all of a sudden, the doors open all by themselves, Diane's heart just dropped, her mouth is wide open, and her body has become covered with goose bumps. But she knew this was the only way, to get her major story and to also find out about TH€ JOURNAL and its origin. The news reporter tip toes inside the mansion, with her voice recorder in her hand…

(Recorder) (Whispering) It's now a quarter to 4 in the Morning! Thursday May 12, 2015 And I'm about to walk inside this huge mansion, who I'm thinking belongs to this creepy old lady! Who is escorted by a young boy and girl and a tall man! They all are dressed in black and they have Mr. and Mrs. Largen. With them! I will t and find them!

The news reporter hears the old ladies voice so, she quietly finds the room they are all in and waits in the hallway by the door, the news reporter peeks inside and can see the old lady standing there with a book in her arms covered in red velvet….

Go upstairs to your room, my children! And when I'm ready to send for you two I will!... (Simultaneously) Yes Mother!

The tall man dressed in all black, brings Mr. and Mrs. Largen two chairs so they can sit down, while getting comfortable in their seats Mr. and Mrs. Largen watches as the tall man closes all the blinds in the room. Then the old lady sits the book covered in red velvet on a table in front of her, she reaches over and turns on a dim lighted lamp next to the table. The tall man enters the room with a 20th century old chest, he sits it down in front of Mr. and Mrs. Largen before the old lady hands him the key, to the chest that's hanging around her neck on a chain. The tall man takes the key, placing the key in the lock and opens the chest in front of Mr. and Mrs. Largen, with the voice recorder in her hand, quietly the news reporter stands there outside the room, uncomfortable and confused by what's she's witnessing…

(Recorder) (Whispering) Its now 5:30 am in the Morning Thursday May 12, 2015 And what I am now seeing is something extraordinary! Something sinister, but informative at the same time! I don't see the young boy and girl anymore! Being that they were sent upstairs, by the old lady! Who appears to either be their Mother or Guardian!

And as for Mr. and Mrs. Largen, It looks like they've been here and around the block a few times!

Mr. Largen reaches inside the chest and takes out a large book, he places the book on his lap, while Mrs. Largen leans her head in and blows off some of the dust, that's covering the large book and some its pages. Mrs. Largen reaches inside the chest and takes out a bundle of old newspapers, she places them on the floor, closes the chest, and watches as her husband sits the large dusty book on top of the 20th century old treasure chest. The old lady gets up and walks over to where Mr. and Mrs. largen are sitting, she then looks upstairs…

(Yelling) Children! You two can come downstairs now, we are just about ready!

With the mansion quiet, you can hear a pin drop and also the footsteps of the young boy and girl as they both walk down the stairs from upstairs, as they reach where the old lady is, the young boy stands behind Mr. Largen, while the girl stands behind Mrs. Largen. The news reporter moves to the other side of the hallway's doorway to the room, she now can see the young boy, girl, Mr. and Mrs. Largen and the old lady. Who are all acting as if they are about to perform a sacrifice, but there's no animals involved and if not then whatever they are planning, has the news reporter, reporting the news…

(Recording) (Whispering) Its now 6:00 am in the Morning, Thursday May 12, 2015! And I am nearly going to the bathroom on myself! I can see everyone gathering around, what looks like an old chest! That seems to have the interest and undivided attention of Mr. and Mrs. Largen! And all this attention, is circulating because of some book! Mr. Largen removed from the old chest! Plus, there's a bundle of old newspapers on the ground! And I bet my job on it, those newspapers are entitled THE€ JOURNAL...

Mr. Largen opens the large book, that's placed in front of him, he turns a lot of pages until he finds the one he's looking for, Mr. Largen reaches his arm out, while looking up at the old lady, The old lady hands Mr. Largen a pen, once the pen is in his hand Mr. Largen starts writing inside the large book...

TH€ JOURNAL...

THE END

THE JOURNAL 1919

emergeprogroup@hotmail.com

THE JOURNAL 1918

Coming Soon…

www.ingramcontent.com/pod-product-compliance
Lightning Source LLC
Chambersburg PA
CBHW081138300726
48982CB00006B/995

* 9 7 8 1 0 8 7 8 5 6 6 9 8 *